W9-DIH-190

Not just for kids

What Lies Beneath The Bed

Parade of Lights

By

Gerald Sharpe

Illustrations By Patricia Moya

IJN Publishing, Inc.
Permissions Department
P.O. Box 630577
Miami, FL 33163

L.O.C. Control Number
2007933056

ISBN 978-1-933894-01-0

Printed in the U.S.A.

CONTENTS

CHAPTER ONE

SCARED STRAIGHT

From the outside, it looks like another typical Saturday morning at Tommy Smart's house. The next-door neighbor's dog is chasing a cat up onto the porch. Birds sing a perfect tune on the windowsills, hoping to get something to eat. Mr. Smart is out getting the morning newspaper with a cup of coffee in his hand. It's obvious by the frown on his face that his morning attitude hasn't left, watching the stray cat exit his porch. Mr. Smart is a cranky man with a bald head that could blind a person if the sun was bright enough.

Good thing Mrs. Smart isn't there to see her husband getting the paper. She'd be embarrassed by the untied, baby blue robe that he's wearing out in public. Mrs. Smart is a plump woman who loves to cook and take care of her family. As warmhearted as she is, she'd be mortified watching her husband walking toward the curb with his jiggling belly hanging out of his white tank-top.

"Good morning, Jack!" yells Mr. Smart, almost spilling his coffee.

Jack Turner is a tall, skinny man with thick glasses who has black hair, but only on the sides of his head. He's one of the nicest guys in the neighborhood and is an avid sports fan.

"Good morning, Ned. Have you seen Willy?" asks Jack, trying to hold back his laughter.

Mr. Smart's morning outfits amuse Jack and his friends.

"Yeah, he's chasing a stray cat around my house again," replies Mr. Smart.

"Oh. Sorry about that, Ned," says Jack, feeling somewhat guilty that his dog got out again.

Mr. Smart shakes his head because of his distaste for Willy. The only reason that he tolerates Willy's rambunctious behavior is that Jack has a big screen TV that they watch sports on together. No man can resist watching sports on a big screen television.

"Don't worry about it. Say, what time is the game on today?" asks Mr. Smart.

"Three o'clock," replies Jack, picking some weeds from his garden.

"Excellent! I'll see you at three," says Mr. Smart, smiling.

The payoff of free snacks and sports on a big screen TV are worth all the grief that Willy causes. As Mr. Smart reaches down to pick up the paper, Willy and the stray cat practically run over him, spilling his coffee.

"Ahhhhhh!" screams Mr. Smart as he pushes the cup of coffee away from his body.

Mr. Smart wipes the coffee off his tank-top and grumbles to himself, making sure that he doesn't allow Jack to see his true feelings about his obnoxious dog. Well, maybe it pays off sometimes.

SCARED STRAIGHT

As Mr. Smart regroups from the ambush, he looks up at Tommy's room wondering why the kids are still sleeping. Little does he know what the gang went through the night before. Inside Tommy's room, Bucky, Derek, Chuck and Tommy lie on the floor with their eyes wide open. Each one stares intently at the ceiling, waiting for something to happen. The boys have large bags under their eyes. None of them have been able to sleep since returning home from their adventure on the island of Maccabus. Tommy's *new found power* to reach the *nether world* under his bed is something that the boys aren't ready to talk about.

Tommy, a twelve-year-old boy with an incredible imagination, didn't wet his bed last night, which is his normal routine. Images of Omit the troll and Orin the wizard flash before his eyes, sending chills down his spine. As the leader of "the gang," Tommy sits up, making sure that his friends all made it back from their adventure.

Chuck, an eleven-year-old boy who is sarcastic and loves to eat, is breathing heavy under his sleeping bag; he remains still. Even though he can be brave at times, Chuck has his sleeping bag pulled all the way up to his nose, scared straight. The night has traumatized all the boys, to say the least.

Derek, a nine-year-old boy who acts tougher than he is and is always sick, is shaking under his sleeping bag quietly. Usually, Derek would be in the bathroom blowing his nose or coughing his lungs out. Instead, Derek has his hands straight down at his sides, not moving an inch. Each boy has no idea that the other boys are just as scared.

Poor Bucky, he's so preoccupied trying not to wet his pants that a large ant crawls over his arm and he doesn't even react. Normally, Bucky would scoop up the unsuspecting ant and make it a morning snack. This ten-year-old boy is scared of his shadow, loves to eat ants, and play in his tree fort. Bucky's tree fort is the coolest place in the world. It's there that Tommy and his friends have *Story Time* to plan their mischief and share their dreams, nightmares and fears of what seems to live under their beds at night. Their trip to Maccabus has proved that dreams and nightmares do come true.

Downstairs in the guest room, Mindy, Patricia and Tammy couldn't sleep either. Tammy, an eleven-year-old tomboy who loves to wrestle and instigate confrontations, is staring at the ceiling with her eyes practically popping out of her wrestling mask. Normally, Tammy would be asking one of the boys to wrestle, but instead she lies on the floor, shaking and having flashbacks of Maccabus.

Patricia, a nine-year-old girl that's extremely shy, gifted, and has a doll named Peggy that she talks to, holds Peggy close to her face as she shakes on the floor. Images of demons and Orin's wicked kids dance around her head.

Mindy, the last member of the gang, is a nine-year-old girl that thinks of others first and keeps the peace among her friends. She shakes her head back and forth, still amazed at what just happened to the gang. Mindy and Patricia are overwhelmed with fear as the two girls glance at each other. Just as Mindy is about to speak the first words of the morning, there's a knock on the door.

"Ahhhhh!" screams Patricia, throwing the covers over her head.

"It's Orin!" mutters Tammy as she jumps up, ready to wrestle. "You want a piece of this?!"

"Who is it?" asks Mindy, scared.

"It's Mr. Smart," he replies. "Breakfast will be ready soon."

"We'll be right out!" says Mindy. "You guys settle down! You're going to give us away!" whispers Mindy as Mr. Smart heads back to the kitchen.

The girls get up and look at each other, laughing at their close call. It's truly a miracle that they made it back from their escapades on Maccabus unscratched.

SCARED STRAIGHT

"What a night," states Tammy as she takes off her wrestling mask. "Frankie and Jimmy will never believe this one!"

"Did that really happen?" asks Patricia.

"I don't know. I don't think that we should talk about this with anyone. Let's pretend nothing happened," replies Mindy, getting to her feet.

The girls shake their heads in agreement and begin to get ready for breakfast. No one would ever look at them the same if they shared the story of their adventures on Maccabus. Staying the night at their friend Tommy's house was supposed to be a fun get-together. Instead, it turned into a nightmare that has matured the gang and given them a whole new outlook on life; *for now.*

Tommy's younger brother, Matt, is now awake and brushing his teeth. He's still trying to shake off his nightmare about Orin. Little does he know that it wasn't a nightmare. Chills pass through Matt's body as he visualizes Orin coming back through the wall to get him. His one visitation from wicked Orin doesn't compare to the many near-death experiences that Tommy and his friends had to endure on Maccabus.

It's too quiet. Something's up, thinks Matt.

Matt finishes in his bathroom and looks toward the wall where Orin had come out. Realizing that nothing is there, he searches for something that will scare the boys. Matt grabs the infamous pan and wooden ladle to wake up his brother and his brother's guests.

"This will teach them for leaving me out of their fun," says Matt as he exits his room. "The next time he locks his door, I'll break it down."

Matt can barely hold in the laughter at the thought of the boys' reaction to his homemade alarm.

Tommy is standing in front of his friends, still in shock about how Maccabus had turned from a fun, adventurous island into an island of terror. The feelings of guilt and anxiety race through his head for exposing his friends to an adventure that they wish they could forget. The room is full of tension as they boys try to act like nothing had happened.

"Guys, we can't tell anyone about what happened last night. First of all, no one will believe us. Second, we'll become the laughing stock of school," says Tommy.

"I don't want the same rumors going around school that you had to put up with when you went to Maccabus the first time," says Bucky as a vision of a gargoyle enters his head.

Derek sits up and shakes his head agreeing, still unable to speak. Chuck lowers his sleeping bag and pulls out a crunched up candy bar that he squeezed to pieces on his trip home. Still being terrified at what had happened on Maccabus, Chuck can't even eat the candy bar. Each kid checks himself, making sure that he's all there.

"I agree. No way can we tell anyone about Maccabus," says Chuck. "Just saying that name gives me the creeps!"

Bucky snaps out of his daze.

"That's right! They'll think we're crazy!" exclaims Bucky. "The teasing will be unbearable!"

"How do we tell the girls not to tell anyone?" asks Derek. "They're the ones with the big mouths."

"Yeah!" declares Chuck as he passes gas.

"CHUCK! What's wrong with you?!" asks Tommy, holding his nose.

"Sorry! ... Like you never fart!" replies Chuck defensively.

"That's enough, you two! What about the girls?" asks Derek, waving his hand in front of his nose. "You need to stop eating those burritos!"

Tommy scratches his head, knowing how the girls like to talk. Keeping the girls quiet will be the biggest challenge for the boys. Every time the gang makes a promise, it's the girls who usually break it first; Tammy in particular.

SCARED STRAIGHT

"Do you remember the time we set the woods on fire and Tammy told Frankie and Jimmy?" asks Bucky.

"Yeah! She was the one who got us in trouble!" answers Chuck.

"Let me handle it. Trust7 me," says Tommy as he heads to the door. "First things first, we need...."

Tommy opens the door and is greeted by Matt and his home-made alarm clock. "CLANG, CLANG, CLANG!" blasts from the pan as Matt hits it with the ladle.

"Ahhhhhh!" screams Tommy as he jumps high into the air.

"It's Orin! Run!" exclaims Chuck.

Derek and Bucky crash into each other as they look for a place to hide. Tommy slips and falls; his socks can't hold his feet on the slick floor. Matt laughs hysterically as he watches the boys run for cover. Chuck tries to hide under Tommy's desk. Unfortunately, his rump-roast behind prohibits him from squeezing under it.

Downstairs in the kitchen, Mr. Smart hears all the commotion coming from Tommy's room. This is the second major commotion of the night; the first was the kids returning home from Maccabus.

"Hey! You guys need to settle down!" yells Mr. Smart.

Mindy and her friends giggle as they walk into the kitchen. Mr. Smart becomes embarrassed that the girls saw him lose his cool. He suddenly realizes that they're probably laughing at his baby blue robe decorated with coffee stains. Mr. Smart quickly tries to act as though everything is copasetic.

"Sorry girls. Those boys need to learn to be quiet ... especially at this hour," mutters Mr. Smart, changing the tone of his voice.

"That's okay, Mr. Smart. We know how the boys get," says Mindy, holding back her laughter.

Mrs. Smart walks into the kitchen with her hair full of colorful curlers. She looks like a walking Christmas tree. By the look

7

on her face, the girls can tell that she's not fully awake. It's obvious that her morning coffee hasn't kicked in yet.

"Good morning, everyone," says Mrs. Smart as she kisses Mr. Smart on the cheek. "Good morning, dear."

"Good morning, Mrs. Smart," say Mindy, Patricia and Tammy.

"Did you girls sleep well?" asks Mrs. Smart, shaking her head at her husband's appearance.

The girls look at each other, confused. Each holds back their laughter, remembering their promise not to tell a soul about last night. Tammy steps up to address Mrs. Smart. She's the one that the girls turn to when there's trouble. Most people back away when Tammy's eyes twitch; a sign that she's serious.

"We slept very well, Mrs. Smart," replies Tammy, not flinching. "Thank you again for having us over your house. You guys are the best!"

Patricia grabs onto Peggy tight, anticipating a confrontation.

"Well, you girls still look tired to me," says Mr. Smart as he takes a sip of coffee, a little suspicious.

"Oh, Ned, leave the girls alone," insists Mrs. Smart, nudging her husband.

Mr. Smart backs down from his wife like a good husband should first thing in the morning. Before another word can be spoken, the smoke alarm goes off.

"The bagels!" screams Mr. Smart as he rushes over to the toaster oven.

"All I asked you to do for me was toast the bagels, and you couldn't even do that right!" says Mrs. Smart nervously.

Mindy and the others giggle at Mr. Smart's mistake and the fact that he's been trying to act cool.

Tommy and the boys finally realize that the noise came from Matt and not Orin. Derek has a little blood running from his nose because of his run-in with Bucky. Matt's laughter is silenced, realizing how bad he scared the boys.

SCARED STRAIGHT

"See what you made me do?" mutters Derek as he holds his nose.

Matt feels bad at the sight of Derek's bloody nose.

"I'm sorry," replies Matt. "I didn't mean for anyone to get hurt."

"What do you want?!" asks Tommy.

Matt notices how grouchy Tommy and his friends are this morning. He puts down the pan and ladle to find out the source of their attitudes.

"What's wrong with you guys today?" asks Matt. "Get up on the wrong side of the bed?"

Tommy, Derek, Bucky and Chuck look at each other as if Matt knows what had happened last night. They hesitate before answering him, for fear of giving their night away. If Matt were to find out, the whole world would find out about Maccabus.

"Nothing's 'wrong' with us! Maybe something's 'wrong' with you," replies Tommy, trying to turn the tables around with his mind games.

"Nothing's wrong with me! Each of you looks like a raccoon with the bags under your eyes, that's all. You guys are weird!" says Matt snobbishly.

Chuck and Bucky grab Tommy as he lunges to grab Matt. Tommy's lack of sleep and adrenaline rush from Matt's homemade alarm has Tommy ready to fight.

"Tommy, no!" says Chuck, fighting to keep a grip on his friend. "You're going to get us in trouble!"

"I'm telling, Dad!" screams Matt as he rushes back to his room.

Tommy regains his composure, realizing that he shouldn't draw more attention to the situation than necessary. Flashes of his last punishment for fighting in the hardware store straighten him out. He rubs his behind as the voice of his father yelling disappears.

SCARED STRAIGHT

"See what I have to go through everyday?" asks Tommy, adjusting his pajamas.

Chuck smells the bacon cooking from downstairs and remembers his appetite. His stomach sounds like a freight train heading into town.

"Sorry, guys, I have to eat!" says Chuck, smiling.

"Breakfast is ready!" yells Mr. Smart from downstairs.

Derek cleans off the last bit of blood from his face.

Tommy and his friends stare at the space under Tommy's bed, shaking their heads in disbelief. The gang has always been trouble makers and has always taken risks, but not as big as their decision to go to Maccabus from the nether world under Tommy's bed. *Tommy's incident at summer camp that gave him the power to reach the nether world under his bed will change the lives of his friends, forever.*

"Remember guys, not a word to anyone!" says Derek firmly.

The boys do their secret handshake that symbolizes their pact and head downstairs for breakfast.

Once again, Mrs. Smart has outdone herself with breakfast. There's one of everything on the table: eggs, waffles, fresh fruit, cold cereal and donuts. Oh yeah, and Mr. Smart's burnt bagels. Mindy and the girls sit at the side table, looking as if they see a ghost. Tommy notices their demeanors and realizes that they're in shock as well.

"Good morning, girls," says Tommy, careful not to make eye contact.

"Good morning Tommy," says Patricia, quickly looking at Mindy.

"No, 'good morning' to your mother and me?" asks Mr. Smart.

The gang chuckles at Mr. Smart.

"Sorry Dad. Good morning, Mom and Dad," replies Tommy, embarrassed.

SCARED STRAIGHT

"Good morning, dear," says Mrs. Smart as she tries to fix Tommy's hair.

Chuck's mouth is watering like a leaking dam as he canvasses the table with his eyes. The aroma of sizzling bacon and fresh strawberries travels under Chuck's nose, driving him crazy. All of a sudden, he's forgotten about the trip to Maccabus and those horrible cannibals that were trying to cook him and Derek. His focus is on the table and what food he'll dive into first. Mr. Smart notices the intense look on Chuck's face; he looks as if he's going to devour the entire table himself.

"Now, Chucky, settle down. There's plenty of food for everyone," says Mr. Smart, protecting the food.

Tommy and Tammy laugh at their friend.

"Sorry, Mr. Smart. I didn't eat before I went to bed," says Chuck, rubbing his belly.

"You'd still look this way even if you ate before, during, and after you went to bed," says Derek sarcastically.

The kids chuckle at Derek's comment. Chuck, however, doesn't find it so amusing.

"Wait until I get you outside!" whispers Chuck, eyeing Derek like he's dead meat.

"All right, kids, dig in," says Mr. Smart as he prepares to grab a waffle.

"Wait! Where's Matt?! Tommy, go and get your brother, please," says Mrs. Smart as she takes the waffle off her husband's plate.

"Do I have to, Mom?" asks Tommy, whining.

"Yes, Tommy. Listen to your mother," says Mr. Smart, frustrated that there's not a delicious waffle on his plate.

Tommy reluctantly gets up and heads back upstairs. He hates having to wait for his brother to do anything, especially with his hungry friends downstairs. Tommy knows that Matt sometimes does this on purpose to aggravate him. That thought makes Tommy mad as he stomps up the stairs.

SCARED STRAIGHT

Matt is in Tommy's room, snooping, noticing all the mud on the floor. The trail of mud leads from the center of the room to Tommy's bed.

"Where did this come from?" asks Matt, picking up the mud and smelling it.

He leans down to the floor and notices that the mud leads under Tommy's bed. There are pieces of plants unlike any that he's ever seen, lying on the floor as well.

Something's not right, thinks Matt.

He turns around to head downstairs for breakfast.

"Ahhhhh!" screams Matt as he throws up his hands. "You scared me!"

"What are you looking for?" asks Tommy nervously.

"I was looking at all the mud leading from under your bed. You'd better tell me where it came from or I'm going to tell Dad that you dragged mud into the house," replies Matt.

"Oh yeah, well I'll tell Dad that you took money out of Mom's purse last week!" states Tommy as he looks down at his brother. "What do you think about that?!"

Matt's eyes light up. The trouble that he would get into isn't worth finding out where the mud came from. One of Mr. Smart's pet peeves is STEALING.

"How did you know about that?!" asks Matt, rethinking his strategy.

"I saw you. Your mischievous ways don't always go unnoticed, you know," replies Tommy, peeking over toward his bed.

"Okay, I won't tell Dad ... but tell me what's going on with all this mud," demands Matt as he notices the change in Tommy's demeanor.

"It's none of your business! Now come down for breakfast before Dad starts yelling again!" mutters Tommy as he walks toward the door.

"Come on, please! Please tell me where all the mud came from," pleads Matt.

SCARED STRAIGHT

"No! ... And that's final!" mutters Tommy.

He quickly shuffles his brother toward his bedroom door.

"I'm going to find out whether you like it or not!" says Matt with an attitude.

"Whatever!" exclaims Tommy as he pushes Matt out of his room.

Everyone is now ready to dig into breakfast. Tommy's friends have been murmuring behind Mr. and Mrs. Smart's backs about last night. Chuck motions for everyone to settle down so that he can do what he loves best. Matt reaches for a muffin and is greeted by a smack on the hand. Once again, he's forgotten the morning ritual.

"Matty, you know better than that. We say grace, first," says Mrs. Smart, smiling at Tommy's friends.

All the kids know that this is a morning ritual in the Smart family. Tammy starts to get edgy and looks to Bucky for relief.

"What? Don't look at me," whispers Bucky, bowing his head.

"Sorry, Mom," says Matt.

Tommy and his friends fold their hands, waiting for Mr. Smart to say something funny. It's no secret that Mr. Smart struggles with his choice of words in front of all the kids, especially when it comes to blessing the food.

"Honey ... we're waiting," says Mrs. Smart.

Mr. Smart clears his throat nervously.

"Good food, do what you should, Amen," prays Mr. Smart.

The kids chuckle at Mr. Smart's prayer. Chuck is the first one out of the gate. He practically has a panic attack because it's been so long since he's eaten normal food. Actually, the panic attack comes because it's been so long since he ate anything. The last food that he ate was the Pula and apples given to him by Tuga's men on his way to be cooked with Derek. Chuck shakes off that vision from Maccabus and piles his plate with every food on the table.

13

"*What?*" asks Chuck, noticing that everyone's staring at him. "Haven't you seen anyone eat before?!"

"That's my boy!" exclaims Derek as he grabs a burnt bagel. "Ewww," he says, putting the bagel back on the plate. "Sorry."

"So, kids, what are your plans for today?" asks Mrs. Smart, comforting Mr. Smart for his attempt at making bagels. "It's okay, honey, I still love you."

Everyone hesitates answering the question because of what had happened during the night. No one wants to be the one to let the cat out of the bag. The kids' eyes pierce one another as they give each other the zip-it-or-else look.

"We'll probably go to Bucky's tree fort, Mom," replies Tommy, squeezing out a smile.

"You kids and that tree fort. I bet that you'd live there if you had your way," says Mr. Smart with a mouthful of food.

"Dear, don't talk with your mouth full," says Mrs. Smart, shaking her head.

"Yeah! Living in the tree fort would be the coolest!" says Tammy.

Patricia notices that Peggy is extremely quiet this morning. How can she blame her?

"Are you going to be okay?" asks Patricia.

"What did you say?" asks Derek as he smacks Chuck's hand for trying to steal his bacon.

Patricia didn't think that anyone heard her talking to Peggy.

"Ah ... I said, 'that would be great,'" replies Patricia, smiling.

The gang finishes breakfast in a hurry so that they can get to Bucky's tree fort and regroup. They know the importance of getting their stories straight to keep last night a secret. One comment about Orin the wizard or Omit the troll could devastate their reputations.

Mr. Hogwash is busy cleaning the dishes in the kitchen. It had been a quiet night for him with Bucky away. Bucky's dad is somewhat cranky, a hard worker, and looks like his last name. Mr. Hogwash has dark moles on his face and a nose that resembles a pig's. Even though he can be tough at times, Mr. Hogwash always looks out for his son. With his mother passed away, he does the best job that he can to give Bucky unconditional love. If Bucky could label it, he'd call it, "Tough love."

As usual, the pets acted strangely with Bucky not there to play with them. Fritz, their dog, wouldn't leave the front door, waiting for Bucky to walk in at any moment. Mr. Hogwash enjoyed the silence, but only for a short while.

"I wonder when Bucky will be home," mumbles Mr. Hogwash to himself.

As he finishes loading the dishes into the dishwasher, Mr. Hogwash sees his son coming down the sidewalk through the kitchen window. Bucky is walking like a zombie, still thinking about all his close calls on Maccabus. An image of the wicked praying mantis destroying Orin's backyard flashes before this eyes.

All right Bucky, keep your mouth shut, thinks Bucky, almost tripping over his own feet.

Bucky pauses in front of his house as he tries to regain his composure. He knows that his father will grill him like a police officer if he looks at all suspicious.

"Here it goes," mutters Bucky as he heads into his house. He walks right over a trail of ants crossing the sidewalk. *Not today,* thinks Bucky.

Mr. Hogwash notices that his son is in deep thought. The look on Bucky's face makes him feel strongly that something had happened at Tommy's sleepover. Mr. Hogwash knows his son too well, and can tell by Bucky's expression that the gang must have been up to their usual selves; ROTTEN.

"I wonder what they did this time?" mutters Mr. Hogwash, scratching his chin.

He wipes his hands clean and heads to the front door to meet Bucky.

15

SCARED STRAIGHT

Meanwhile, Chuck's mom is waiting on the front porch with some milk and cookies. Ms. Puddin is a naïve, skinny woman who loves her one and only son. Chuck loves her just the same. He crushes the neighborhood kids who make fun of her large, neon-colored hair with his patented *steamroller*. With her husband long gone, she can't stand to be away from her Chucky. One night at Tommy's had seemed like one week. Ms. Puddin paces back and forth, flinching at every kid that rides his bike down the street, hoping that it's her son on the bike.

Where is he? thinks Ms. Puddin, as she checks her watch.

Chuck appears from behind the bushes.

"There's my angel!" exclaims Ms. Puddin as she turns around. "Come to Mommy!"

Chuck was having a flashback of Maccabus. He was reliving the time Tuga, the head tribesman, made the gargoyles appear and one of them lunged at him like he was a sweet roll.

Get a grip, Chuck! thinks Chuck, as he struggles to smile at his mother.

"Did you have fun with your friends last night?" asks Ms. Puddin as she heads toward the steps.

That isn't quite the question that fits what had happened the night before. Chuck doesn't want to worry his mother, so he puts on his best fake grin and looks at her in the eye.

"Yes, Mommy, we had a blast," replies Chuck as he walks onto the porch.

Ms. Puddin is concerned by Chuck's somber demeanor and the manner by which he's walking. Usually, Chuck is jumping up and down like a panting dog, telling her stories about what the gang had done. In fact, he doesn't even go after her delicious cookies as he walks toward the front door.

"What's wrong, pumpkin?" asks Ms. Puddin worriedly. "Something's not right."

Chuck gets nervous. He feels as if what he had done the night before is written all over his face.

SCARED STRAIGHT

"Nothing's wrong, Mom," replies Chuck, trying to keep a blank face.

"Well then, come here and have some cookies," insists Ms. Puddin as she extends the tray toward Chuck.

"No thanks, Mommy. I'm not hungry," says Chuck.

To Chuck's mom, hearing that he's not hungry is like hearing that the world is about to end. Ms. Puddin feels as if he had just spoken in slow motion.

"Okay, now I know that something's definitely wrong. What happened last night?!" asks Ms. Puddin, setting the tray down.

Chuck's forehead begins to sweat like a garden hose. This lie is way beyond any that he's told his mother in the past. The fact that Chuck was almost cooked, eaten, and destroyed by Orin isn't something that's easy to hide.

"Mom, I swear. Nothing's wrong," insists Chuck.

Derek pops out from the opposite side of the porch.

"Hi, Ms. Puddin!" says Derek.

"Ahhhh! Derek, you scared me! What do you want?!" snarls Chuck.

"Sorry brother. Cookies! Can I have some?" asks Derek, licking his chops.

"Good morning, Derek. You and the kids must have had some night. Little Chucky doesn't want any of my fresh-baked cookies. Go ahead, take some," replies Ms. Puddin.

"Mom! Don't call me, 'Chucky,'" mutters Chuck, embarrassed.

"It's okay, 'Chucky,' I won't tell," says Derek, grinning as he helps himself to a cookie.

Chuck can't believe that Derek has an appetite after everything they had just eaten for breakfast, and because of their nightmare on Maccabus. The adventure weighed heavy on Chuck's mind on his trip back home from Tommy's house. That's why he passed on his mother's cookies. Chuck figured that the same

17

would've happened to Derek, but it looks like Derek's adventure on Maccabus toughened up his skin.

"Help yourself, there's plenty," says Ms. Puddin, smiling.

"Derek, I'm going to change first, and then we'll go," says Chuck as he races into the house.

"'Go' where?" asks Ms. Puddin.

"We're going to Bucky's tree fort … you know, for Story Time," replies Derek with a mouthful of cookies.

"I should've known. You kids and that 'Story Time.' Chuck never tells me about the tales that you kids tell up there," says Ms. Puddin, shaking her head.

"They're not tales, Ms. Puddin. We share our dreams, nightmares and fears at Bucky's tree fort. You'd be surprised how real Story Time can be," says Derek.

Derek quickly ends the conversation, realizing where it could go if he's not careful.

Over at the Tutu residence, Tammy is sitting in her room staring out the window. She's having a flashback about Omit when they first arrived on the island. Tammy recalls the time when Omit turned Derek into a frog and grew to the size of a giant. The flashback is soon broken up by the presence of her mother. Mrs. Tutu is an older mother who's worn out from raising eleven kids. Even with all the work, she loves each one of them as if they are her first.

"Sweetheart, you haven't taken off your wrestling mask since you got home," says Mrs. Tutu. "Is everything okay?"

Tammy has a vision of Gilford, the giant serpent, coming up from the murky waters, sending the gang on their first adventure.

"What did you say, Mom?" asks Tammy, snapping out of her trance.

"You're starting to worry your father and me. Is everything all right?" asks Mrs. Tutu.

Tammy finally turns around and takes off her wrestling

mask. She knows that her mother won't stop asking questions if she continues to behave strangely.

"I'm sorry, Mom. I'll be okay," replies Tammy quietly. Now Mrs. Tutu knows that something's definitely wrong. Tammy hasn't been this quiet since her favorite wrestler retired. The only explanation for this behavior is the gang. Mrs. Tutu recognizes the difference between Tammy's happiness before she went to Tommy's for the sleepover and her behavior since coming home.

"What happened to you last night at Tommy's?" asks Mrs. Tutu, concerned.

Tammy recalls Mindy's last words, "Remember, we can't tell a soul."

"Nothing special happened. Just the usual teasing and video games, that's all," replies Tammy, lying through her teeth. "I mean it, Mom, everything's okay."

Mrs. Tutu shrugs her shoulders and smiles at her angel. Tammy can do no wrong in her eyes. She figures that if it was something that bad, she would've pulled it out of her daughter by now.

"Okay sweetheart. There are fresh-baked muffins in the kitchen if you want some," says Mrs. Tutu, smiling. "I suggest you hurry before your sisters have at them."

"Thanks, Mom, I'll be there in a minute," says Tammy.

Mrs. Tutu turns and heads to the kitchen to check on the rest of the family.

Meanwhile, Mindy and Patricia are walking down the sidewalk toward Bucky's house. Both have been extra quiet, not knowing exactly how to accept their journey to Maccabus and the images that stain their minds. All they know is that it happened and they have to keep it a secret.

"Did your parents grill you on what happened last night?" asks Mindy.

"Yes ... it was a nightmare. My brother Fred wouldn't leave me alone either," replies Patricia as she squeezes Peggy.

Mindy gets nervous because she knows how weak Patricia can be. On several occasions in the past, Patricia had given the secret handshake that she wouldn't tell anyone about her friends' mischief and had broken her promise.

"You didn't tell them where we went, did you?!" asks Mindy nervously.

"No ... I promise," replies Patricia, noticing that Mindy's eyes are widening.

Mindy lets out a sigh of relief. She was sure that Patricia would blow it for the gang.

"Good ...," says Mindy.

"I can see that you thought I would give into the pressure. No way! My parents would think that I lost my mind if I started talking about demons and Orin," interrupts Patricia.

Mindy gets chills just thinking about Orin when he turned into a giant warlock.

"I'm glad that we don't have to worry about them anymore ...," says Mindy.

Before Mindy can say another word, Frankie and Jimmy jump out from behind a car. Frankie is a feisty boy, same age as Derek, who loves to instigate trouble. Jimmy, his sidekick, is a nine-year-old boy, somewhat nosy and walks with a limp. His mother calls him, "Special." These two boys have been dying to become members of the gang, but no luck. The fact that Tommy and his friends won't include Frankie and Jimmy in all their shenanigans has frustrated them forever.

"Booo!" screams Frankie.

"Ahhhhhhh!" scream Mindy and Patricia.

The boys laugh hysterically at the sight of Mindy and Patricia, who are thinking that Orin and his henchmen are back.

"It's about time we scared you guys!" says Jimmy.

"Yeah!" exclaims Frankie.

Mindy and Patricia regain their composure and become angry with the boys.

"That wasn't funny!" says Mindy as she steps in front of Patricia. "You could've hurt someone!"

"You're not the only ones that can scare people," says Jimmy. "Your friends never think about that when they scare us!"

"Yeah!" exclaims Frankie.

Frankie notices that something's wrong with the girls and backs off. Mindy and Patricia are shaking more than they should from their little prank.

"I'm sorry, we didn't mean any harm. What's with you two girls?" asks Frankie.

Mindy and Patricia have guilty written all over their faces. Neither one wants this conversation to happen. It's only a matter of time before Patricia cracks under pressure.

"Nothing's wrong with us. You just scared us, that's all," replies Mindy.

"Come on, I know that look anywhere," insists Frankie. "You're hiding something."

"Really, there's nothing wrong," says Mindy, starting to get frustrated.

"I wish they would leave us alone," says Patricia to Peggy.

"Okay, if you say so. Where are you girls going?" asks Frankie.

"Bucky's ...," replies Patricia.

Mindy throws her hand over Patricia's mouth.

"'Bucky's!' Can we go too?!" asks Jimmy excitedly.

"Not today," replies Mindy.

"I knew it! Something is wrong!" declares Frankie as he nudges Jimmy.

Frankie notices Tammy running down the street, heading their way. They don't realize that Tammy has no intentions of wrestling them, which is her normal routine. The boys' adrenaline skyrockets as they prepare for an attack.

SCARED STRAIGHT

"Look, there's Tammy! I don't want any part of her!" says Frankie.

"Let's get out of here!" declares Jimmy.

Frankie and Jimmy take off running in the opposite direction to escape Tammy's wrath.

"I didn't know that Tammy was so feared by the other kids. That's pretty cool," says Patricia.

"Hey, guys, where are they going?" asks Tammy as she catches her breath.

"They ran when they saw you," replies Mindy, chuckling.

"Really?!" asks Tammy.

"Yeah," replies Patricia as she tries to feel Tammy's muscles.

Tammy smiles to herself, knowing that she has the respect of Frankie and Jimmy. But the smile is quickly replaced with a look of terror as Tammy has a sudden flashback about Orin in the dungeon. An image of his hands raised with several demons crawling her way appears in her mind.

"What's wrong with you?" asks Mindy as she grabs Tammy's arm.

"I just remembered something from Maccabus," replies Tammy, trying to shake off the visual. "I hope that these visions will go away."

Patricia grabs hold of Peggy, looking around to see if anyone heard Tammy mentioning Maccabus. Mindy looks at her watch and realizes that they're going to be late for their secret meeting at Bucky's tree fort. Not wanting to keep the rest of the gang waiting, the three girls rush off to Bucky's.

The gang is finally alone at Bucky's tree fort to recap the life changing event that happened on the island of Maccabus. The night was so traumatic that no one thought to bring snacks to this meeting; a first in Story Time history. Each kid sits quietly, staring at

Tommy as he stands before his friends. Their eyes bulge out as they wait for him to speak. Tommy begins to pace back and forth, trying to gather his thoughts. As he begins to address his friends about the previous night, Chuck's stomach lets out a giant roar. The kids are startled by Chuck's grotesque stomach noises.

"Chuck! What's wrong with you?" asks Tammy as she nudges her pudgy friend.

"Sorry, guys, I'm hungry!" replies Chuck as he shrugs his shoulders. "What are you looking at Tammy?! Don't make…!"

"Hey, guys! … That's enough about Chuck. What happened last night isn't to be told to anyone! We don't need this town in an uproar over our discovery. This place won't be the same if we tell others," says Tommy.

"You hear that, Bucky?!" asks Derek.

"That goes for you, too, Derek!" says Tammy, motioning that she means business.

"All right, settle down. This is serious! What do you have to say about all of this?" asks Tommy.

Mindy stands up and walks to the front with Tommy. Tommy smiles as a sense of comfort washes over his body. Mindy has always had a way of bringing peace to the gang; something that her friends are still trying to figure out.

"Look, the other kids will think we're crazy if we tell them that we went to the nether world under Tommy's bed. Think about it!" replies Mindy.

"They already think that we're crazy," says Chuck as he tries to sneak a bite of a cookie.

Derek and Tammy chuckle to themselves about the stain on Chuck's shirt. The others, however, are still straight-faced about dealing with what had happened the previous night.

"I'm serious, Chuck! This isn't funny!" insists Tommy. "My house will be mobbed with every kid from school!"

"Yeah, Chuck! We can't tell this to anyone. Maccabus only

happened between us. If we want to talk about it, we do it here," insists Mindy.

The gang looks at each other and realizes that this is probably the best solution. Before you know it, every kid will want to go to Maccabus.

"I don't want to talk about it. Those islanders and Orin's wicked children and demons are going to give me nightmares forever," says Bucky as he moves closer to Tammy.

"Yeah. I'll have nightmares if we keep talking about it! Look, we're already talking about it!" mutters Derek.

"I agree! Let's drop the subject and act as if it never happened," says Tammy as she messes with her wrestling mask.

"I'm afraid to go to sleep tonight," says Patricia. "I've been having weird visions all morning."

Tommy realizes that he needs to change the subject and ease his friends' minds. After all, it was his bed that brought them to the island and he wasn't truthful about Orin's warning not to return to Maccabus.

"All right, guys, let's talk about the upcoming parade. We know how much fun the Hummel County Parade can be, don't we?!" asks Tommy, smiling.

His friends' eyes light up as images of the parade dance before their eyes. Every year the gang goes to the Hummel County Parade and causes havoc. There's no holiday or occasion that brings them this much pleasure. Tommy and his friends are known throughout town for starting trouble and disrupting the parade; this makes them popular among their peers. Fortunately, there had been no hard evidence supporting these so-called rumors that would have ended their reign of mischief. Tommy notices that his friends' zeal isn't quite what he would've liked for this year's parade.

"Okay, guys, what's up? We're talking about the Hummel County Parade!" states Tommy, trying to fire up his friends and take their minds off the island of Maccabus.

"I don't know about you guys, but I don't feel like planning trouble this year," says Chuck as he puts down a cookie. "Don't even think about it, Bucky!"

"I agree! Especially with the recent event in our life ... *hello!* We're lucky to be alive!" declares Derek as he stands up.

"I agree with Derek. We should count our blessings and behave this year ... before something worse happens to us," says Mindy convincingly.

"I think that we should 'behave' in school as well. I don't want Orin to come back somehow. We don't know what he's doing there and if he has the power to come here," says Bucky fearfully.

The gang becomes nervous at the thought of Orin paying them a visit. The kids look around the tree fort, making sure that Orin's face doesn't appear in thin air as it did in the jungle.

"Yeah. Maybe it's time to change. I don't want to see Orin or his giant praying mantis either," says Tommy.

Patricia smiles at Peggy at the thought that the gang might become nicer to each other and the other kids at school. Chuck looks around to see if the coast is clear for him to sneak a bite of a candy bar.

I'm so hungry, thinks Chuck, as he lifts the scrumptious candy bar to his mouth.

"Got you!" screams Tammy from behind.

"Ahhhh!" screams Chuck as the candy bar flies out of his hand. "What's your problem?!"

Derek catches the candy bar and holds it up as evidence. He wants the others to see what Chuck was about to do.

"You had food and you weren't going to share?!" asks Tommy as he grabs the candy bar. "We let you slide with the cookie! Now you have a candy bar?!"

"How could you do that, Chuck?!" asks Bucky, disappointed. "I'm sure that the girls would like to eat, too."

"Wait! I ...," says Chuck, embarrassed.

"I say we divide it up!" suggests Derek.

Chuck's eyes grow wide as he watches his snack being split

up among his friends. There's nothing worse than for Chuck to watch other people eat while he's hungry.

From the kitchen window, Mr. Hogwash notices that it's extra quiet in the tree fort. By now, the kids should be running around or screaming from someone's scary tale, but they're not. Bucky's behavior earlier in the day along with the aloofness of his friends when they arrived at his house, have Mr. Hogwash's curiosity level on alert.

"I bet those kids are up to no good. I'd better go and check on them before they get into trouble," mutters Mr. Hogwash to himself.

He finishes his glass of juice and heads to the tree fort to investigate. As Mr. Hogwash approaches the back door, the doorbell rings.

Who could this be? thinks Mr. Hogwash.

Mr. Hogwash opens the front door and sees Frankie and Jimmy smiling. They have come over to do a little investigating themselves. They peek around Mr. Hogwash, hoping to get a glimpse of Bucky.

"Hi, boys," says Mr. Hogwash.

"Hi, Mr. Hogwash," say Frankie and Jimmy, acting a little suspicious.

"Are you here for the others?" asks Mr. Hogwash.

"Yes, Sir," replies Frankie.

"We came over to see what's wrong with our friends," says Jimmy.

Mr. Hogwash raises his eyebrow. First, Bucky acted strangely when he came home from Tommy's sleepover. Now, his friends show up concerned for their well-being. Mr. Hogwash knows about the envy that Frankie and Jimmy have toward his son's friends. Things are definitely not adding up for Mr. Hogwash as he tries to smell trouble from the boys.

"Come on, boys, let's get to the bottom of this!" says Mr. Hogwash.

Frankie and Jimmy follow Mr. Hogwash to the backyard. They know that the gang is lying, but can't prove it yet. Nothing would be greater for Frankie and Jimmy than to outsmart Tommy and his friends, or uncover some kind of secret that they could use as blackmail.

The gang is once again settled down in front of Tommy. Each kid has pleaded his or her case about the importance of change and bad luck. Mindy has reminded her friends about what had happened to them after they put soap in the town's giant fountain. Chuck and Derek glance down at their arms, recalling the burns they had received from spilling hot coffee on their arms. Little does the gang know that Mr. Hogwash is on his way with the troops.

"Okay, guys, everyone must shake on our secret," insists Tommy, extending his hand out. "This is the last time that we're going to talk about this."

Tommy's friends get up and put their hands together, swearing to the secrecy of what happened on Maccabus. The gang finally realizes the seriousness of leaking information about this adventure. Tommy and Mindy make sure that they glare into their friends' eyes as they hold their hands. As the gang finishes their handshake, the tree fort door slams open.

"It's Orin and Tuga!" screams Derek with bulging eyes.

"RUN FOR YOUR LIVES!" shouts Chuck.

Chuck pushes Derek to save himself. Tammy grabs Bucky in a headlock to scare off Orin. Mindy falls to the ground and begins to pray. Patricia and Tommy hold onto each other, waiting for certain disaster. Mr. Hogwash begins to laugh as he watches the chaos created by this so-called Orin and Tuga.

"Kids, take it easy! It's only me!" declares Mr. Hogwash.

The gang settles down as they realize that it's only Bucky's dad. Bucky brushes himself off and becomes angry with his father.

"Dad, you know the rules of the tree fort! NO PARENTS ALLOWED!!" exclaims Bucky with his hands on his waist.

"I know, I know. Your friends, Frankie and Jimmy, are here to play," says Mr. Hogwash. "I think they're here for something else," mutters Mr. Hogwash as he examines the tree fort.

Tommy looks out the window and sees Frankie and Jimmy waiting to come up.

"Hey Frankie! Hey Jimmy! We'll be right down!" shouts Tommy.

They all look sternly at one another and then head down to meet Frankie and Jimmy.

Mr. Hogwash is standing in his backyard at a distance, snooping on the kids. He desperately wants to find out what's going on with the gang. His hunch that something's up haunts him like a tick; it won't go away. The last time that Mr. Hogwash had a premonition that something was wrong, Bucky and his friends started a fire that almost burned ten acres. Bucky, once again, becomes angry with his father for being so nosy.

"Dad! This is our time!" states Bucky. "Can you please give us some space?"

The gang looks at Mr. Hogwash like he has six heads.

"Okay, okay, I'll leave. But finish whatever it is you are going to do in time for dinner," says Mr. Hogwash as he heads back to the house.

"Yes, Dad," says Bucky.

Tommy and his friends are nervous with Frankie and Jimmy present. Usually, it's Frankie and Jimmy who are nervous. Tommy, Bucky and Patricia shuffle their feet in the dirt, waiting for someone to speak. Chuck and Derek murmur in the background, careful not to make eye contact. Frankie can sense the tension as he glares at Mindy.

"How's it going with you guys?" asks Tammy genuinely.

SCARED STRAIGHT

Frankie and Jimmy are taken back by Tammy's concern for their well-being. Now they know that something's up, considering this is the first time that Tammy has expressed interest in their lives. Frankie looks at Tammy with a weird expression, trying to figure out her motive.

"Do you guys want to hang out with us?" asks Bucky, panicking.

Tommy and Chuck glare at Bucky with looks that could kill as Jimmy and Frankie approach their rivals. The boys' whole childhood has been spent trying to discover ways to dismantle Tommy and his friends.

"Okay, what's up with you weirdos today?" asks Frankie.

"Nothing!" replies Chuck quickly.

The kids look at each other, hoping that Frankie and Jimmy will disappear. It's only a matter of time before someone cracks and spills the beans. Chuck pulls Patricia close to him, protecting her from any type of interrogation.

"Do you guys want to come with us and tease Mr. Lincoln's dog?" asks Jimmy.

"No thanks," replies Tommy, stepping forward.

Jimmy's mouth drops to the floor. Tommy and his friends have never turned down the opportunity to tease Mr. Lincoln's dog. It's been a long tradition in the neighborhood to tease his dog and watch it run back and forth along the fence, trying to get a hold of whoever is teasing him.

"We have decided to change the way we treat others. That's 'what's up,'" says Mindy, taking charge of the conversation.

Now Frankie's mouth drops. He can't believe his ears. The gang is going legit?! No way! No more food fights? No more toilet papering Old Man Jones' house? No more fire crackers in the mall?

"*What?* You're telling me that each one of you is going to

be nice? You guys must be sick!" says Frankie as he shakes his head.

Jimmy walks up to Tammy, cautiously, and looks at her like she's some kind of wax statue. This can't be happening.

"You mean, no more sleeper holds?" asks Jimmy, pulling quickly away from Tammy.

"That's right, things are going to be different ... watch!" replies Tammy, trying to keep her oath as Jimmy begins to push her buttons.

"You mean that I can tease you and not get attacked?" asks Jimmy, smiling.

"Don't push your luck!" replies Tammy as Tommy grabs her arm.

Frankie looks at his watch and realizes that he and Jimmy are going to be late. They want to be the first kids of the day to tease Mr. Lincoln's dog. Besides, Frankie needs to discuss this change of attitude in private.

"Jimmy, we have to go. If you guys change your minds, you know where we'll be," says Frankie, pulling on Jimmy to leave Tammy alone.

"Okay. Be careful!" shouts Tommy as Frankie and Jimmy take off running.

"Guys, I'm tired. I say we call it a day," suggests Derek.

"Yeah, I could take a nap," adds Patricia.

"All right, let's end the day. But remember, we can't tell anyone about Maccabus, understood?!" asks Tommy, somewhat worn out himself.

"Agreed!" says Chuck.

"Agreed!" says Bucky.

The gang hugs each other goodbye and heads home with an empty feeling in his or her stomach. Frankie and Jimmy have become a thorn in Tommy and his friends' sides. The gang knows that they'll be back for more badgering. This is only the beginning of their headaches, covering up their trip to Maccabus.

SCARED STRAIGHT

Tommy lies on his bed staring at the ceiling, feeling somewhat disoriented. Thoughts of Omit and Orin race through his head. Tommy cringes as a manifestation of his sword fight in the dueling arena appears in his imagination. The sight of blood quickly makes this vision disappear. The trauma for a boy this age dealing with the near-death experiences that he went through on Maccabus is starting to take its toll on Tommy. He should've listened to his parents' warnings about the realities of living life on the edge and pursuing what seems to be a good time.

Matt walks past Tommy's room and notices the blank look on his face. It's the same look that Tommy has when he's done something wrong or when he's trying to hide something. Matt's brotherly instinct causes him to change course.

"What's with you?" asks Matt, stepping into Tommy's room.

"Nothing," replies Tommy as he sits up.

"Something's wrong with you! You've been acting weird ever since you came home from Bucky's," says Matt.

"I don't want to talk about it," mutters Tommy.

"Well, you'd better change your attitude. Even Mom and Dad are talking about your unusual behavior. It's like you've turned into an angel overnight," says Matt with a smug look on his face.

"I'll be okay, really. Doesn't everyone deserve a chance to change without persecution?" asks Tommy.

Matt looks at Tommy as if he'd just spoken to him in Chinese.

Mr. Smart walks into the room and sees that his two sons are talking and not fighting. This is a first. He's relieved by this unusual sight, but still remains cautious, not letting his guard down. Mr. Smart knows when his sons are ready to pull a fast one.

"I can't believe it. Are you two sick or something?" asks Mr. Smart as he checks his underarm for body odor.

SCARED STRAIGHT

"Ewww, Dad! Don't do that in front of us!" mutters Tommy, turning away.

"What?" asks Mr. Smart.

"I'm not sick, but Tommy is," replies Matt, nudging his brother.

"No I'm not!" declares Tommy, ignoring his brother's weak attempt at starting a fight. "Dad, please tell Matt to leave me alone."

"Oh no, I'm late!" mutters Mr. Smart, looking at his watch.

Mr. Smart realizes that he's late for his three o'clock date to watch sports with Jack. He doesn't want to miss the free snacks and big screen action. Besides, Mr. Smart is very conscious that Benny Flastafo, the neighbor around the block, is eagerly waiting in the wings to take his place as Jack's sports buddy. That explains the tension at the neighborhood association meetings. Mrs. Smart thinks that it's childish. Mr. Smart disagrees.

"You're going to be 'late' for what?" asks Matt.

"I'm supposed to be next-door with Jack. I'll talk to you boys later!" replies Mr. Smart.

Tommy and Matt laugh as they watch their dad almost bang into the door as he hurries out of the room. They know why he befriends Jack and is always there at his beck and call. Matt turns his attention back to Tommy as he senses his brother's weakness.

"Do you want to wrestle?" asks Matt, throwing his hands up and assuming the position.

"No thanks. I'm pretty drained from Bucky's," replies Tommy as he peps up with his new attitude. "Besides, you're going to see a different Tommy from now on."

Matt's mouth opens as wide as a hippopotamus's. He can't believe that his brother is turning down a challenge to wrestle. Even when Tommy has been sick, he's never turned down an opportunity to wrestle. And a new Tommy? No way! Matt's dumbfounded, watching Tommy smile at him cheerfully.

"That's it! I can't take this Mr. Nice Guy! I know that something's definitely wrong with you! I bet it has to do with that mud under your bed!" states Matt as he looks toward the floor.

Tommy begins to get nervous, but is quickly relieved by his mother walking into the room. Mrs. Smart always has a way of changing the boys' mood with her overcompensating love and affection. Her gleaming smile penetrates Matt's troublesome heart.

"Look at my babies. Can I get my angels something to eat? How about some fudge? Or better yet, some ice cream," suggests Mrs. Smart with a smile that could brighten up the darkest cave.

Tommy and Matt are moved by their mother's good intentions. Her suggestion melts the tension between Tommy and his brother.

"Mom, we just ate. Remember?" asks Matt.

"Oh. Anyway, your father is doing his thing next-door. Would you two like to watch a movie with me downstairs?" asks Mrs. Smart, motioning for Tommy to get off his bed.

"Sure," reply the boys in unison.

Tommy and Matt follow their mother downstairs for a movie and some hot, buttered popcorn. There's no way that she'll let them watch a movie without having some food. It's too bad that the boys don't appreciate times like this like they should.

Over at Patricia's house, Fred, her older, obnoxious brother, is hanging up a painting for his mom and dad. He's having a hard time balancing himself on the step ladder and hanging the picture straight. He nearly falls into his mother's antique porcelain clowns that sit on her favorite table. What a nightmare that would be.

"Stupid picture! I hate doing this!" grumbles Fred with a nail in his mouth.

Patricia walks into the living-room and sees her brother struggling.

"Need any help?" asks Patricia.

"Ahhh!" screams Fred as he falls, nearly missing the porcelain clowns.

"Are you okay? I didn't mean to scare you. Here, let me help you," insists Patricia as she straightens out the ladder.

Fred brushes himself off and is shocked that Patricia would offer to help him. The first thing that comes to his mind is that she wants something. Fred believes that every family member only offers help with an ulterior motive. There's no way that she'd help him unless she wanted to use his bike or borrow one of his games.

"I'm okay, really. What's up with the help? All right, what do you want in return?" asks Fred with beady eyes.

"I don't want anything. Can't a sister help her brother just because you're my brother?" asks Patricia, stepping closer.

"What are you talking about?! You've never helped me with anything before. Come here, let me feel your forehead," says Fred as he reaches for Patricia's head.

Patricia brushes off Fred's delusional presumption of her wanting to help. She lays Peggy down and begins to help her brother to hang the picture.

"I don't want anything," says Patricia, smiling. "I just want things to be different between you and me, that's all."

Fred scratches his head, confused because Patricia hasn't requested a thing. Patricia knows that there's no greater repayment for evil than to treat a person who's teased her, treated her poorly or made her feel small, than to be nice to them and mean it.

"You *must* want something! This is too weird for me to handle," mutters Fred, flustered.

"Nope, don't want a thing," says Patricia as they hang the picture nice and straight on the wall. "There. That wasn't so bad, now, was it?"

Meanwhile, Chuck and Derek are watching a movie at

SCARED STRAIGHT

Derek's house. Mr. and Mrs. Flue can't believe how quiet the two boys are in the living-room. Mr. Flue is bald with graying hair on the sides of his head. He loves to play practical jokes on his son, yet has a low tolerance for foolishness. Mrs. Flue is lean, has big hair, and is very smart. She stops her husband from getting carried away with Derek and his youger sister, Tonia. Together, Mr. and Mrs. Flue make a hip couple. The silence coming from the living-room has their skin crawling. Usually, Chuck and Derek would be teasing each other or laughing about something stupid that had happened at school. Chuck's smiles are starting to get on the Flues' nerves as he turns to show his appreciation for their hospitality again.

"Something's not right with those boys," mutters Mr. Flue as he peeks out from the kitchen. "That smile on Chuck's face is giving me the 'hee-bee-gee-bees'."

"Leave them alone. Their behavior is strange, but you should be happy that they're not running around the house like usual," says Mrs. Flue.

"I guess you're right," says Mr. Flue as he takes one last peek into the living-room.

Chuck and Derek are staring at the TV and not paying attention to the movie. Each one is having a moment, reflecting on what had happened on Maccabus.

"What just happened?" asks Derek, snapping out of his trance.

"I don't know. I was about to ask you the same question," replies Chuck as he places a cookie back on the table.

"We have to get over this. My parents are going to grill me if we don't change our attitudes. You haven't eaten us out of house and home like you normally do. My Dad is very suspicious," says Derek as he notices that his parents are peeking into the living-room.

"Would you kids like some potato chips?" asks Mrs. Flue, embarrassed that she got busted for spying.

"No thanks!" reply the boys.

Mr. Flue pulls Mrs. Flue back into the kitchen.

"See, I told you that something's not right! They turned down potato chips. Chuck would eat the TV if it tasted like food!" mutters Mr. Flue, tapping his foot.

"I guess you're right. What are we going to do?" asks Mrs. Flue.

"We need to talk to Derek after Chuck leaves. He'll crack under pressure from the both of us," replies Mr. Flue as he peeks back into the living-room, hoping to catch the boys whispering.

"Dad!" mutters Derek. "Quit peeking out of the kitchen!"

Mr. Flue jumps back into the kitchen, respecting Derek's request for privacy.

As Derek reaches for the remote, the phone rings.

"Hello?" answers Derek. "Hi, Tammy…. Chuck and I are trying to watch a movie."

"What is she doing?" asks Chuck as he leans closer.

"Okay. Really … mine, too. All right, talk to you later," says Derek as he hangs up the phone.

"What did she say?" asks Chuck.

"She wanted to know how we're doing and if my parents are bugging us about last night," replies Derek as he raises the volume.

"I can't wait until all this blows over. I feel like a bomb is about to go off," mumbles Chuck as he bites into a cookie.

It was only a matter of time before Chuck would break his fast.

"Me, too!" says Derek.

Chuck looks at the clock and decides that he'd better get home. He knows that his mom is probably waiting anxiously for her Chucky to get home. Besides, the cookie has reignited his appetite and he knows that there's a feast fit for a king waiting for him.

SCARED STRAIGHT

"I've had enough of the movie, I'll talk to you later," says Chuck as he brushes off cookie crumbs from his shorts.

"Remember Chuck, we can't tell anybody!" warns Derek as he walks with Chuck to the front door.

"I know, I know," mutters Chuck. "Call me later."

Chuck heads out the door and Derek heads back into the living-room to deal with his parents. Both boys are wondering how long the gang can keep this secret.

CHAPTER TWO

DEREK'S BORED

Mr. Levy, Bucky and Derek's laid back, humorous English teacher with a wild hairstyle, is going over last week's writing assignment while his class finishes their reading assignment. He enjoys the delicious green apple that Bucky gave to him as he marks up his students' papers. Mr. Levy shakes his head, perplexed by the sudden change in Bucky and Derek's attitudes. If he only knew about their journey to the island of Maccabus, he'd probably choke on his apple. Oh well, Tommy and his friends have vowed to take that story to their graves. All the students in the classroom have their heads dutifully buried in their books with the exception of Derek, Lucy and Ronnie.

DEREK'S BORED

"You did what?!" whispers Ronnie, looking up to make sure that he didn't envoke Mr. Levy's attention.

"I slayed a three-headed dragon and destroyed Orin," replies Derek proudly.

"How did you do that?" asks Lucy softly.

"I did it with a magic sword. Tommy was badly hurt and Chuck had broken his arm. It was up to me to be the hero. I was fighting six or seven demons at once. When Orin jumped into the picture, I wielded the sword in his direction and released its power. I'm telling you the truth, I swear," rambles Derek.

Derek has a smile that extends from one ear to the other. His classmates are amazed that he could save his friends from a certain death. Never before have the kids heard of such an epic story of bravery among their peers. Derek is a hero.

"Derek! I thought that this was our secret! We're not supposed to tell anybody!" whispers Bucky as he realizes what Derek is talking about. "How could you?!" asks Bucky, shaking his head.

Derek lowers his head like a puppy dog that just got in trouble for chewing the furniture. Bucky's glare makes him feel guilty.

"Sorry. I couldn't help it," whispers Derek, realizing that Mr. Levy is about to look their way. "We'd better stop talking or we're going to get in trouble."

"Wait until the others hear about you blabbing your mouth," whispers Bucky disapprovingly as he pretends to read. "You'll be an outcast."

Mr. Levy notices that his class is still working on their assignment. Well, at least most of them are.

As Derek starts to defend himself, Janet, a frumpy little girl with an attitude, interrupts Bucky and him.

"Bucky … I heard that you and your friends found an island full of adventure," says Janet. "Teresa said that you rescued your friends as well."

DEREK'S BORED

Derek's eyes light up, becoming angry that Bucky would make him feel bad for breaking the gang's promise when he obviously did the same thing. Bucky begins to sweat. Janet has given him away. He needs to do something quickly or else he's going to look like a fool in front of his classmates.

"I don't know what you're talking about!" denies Bucky defensively, burying his head in Mr. Levy's assignment. "Janet, you need to mind your own business!"

Janet frowns at Bucky. How dare he give her and attitude, epecially with the information she has. Janet notices Derek becoming upset and decides to really get Bucky in trouble with his friend.

"What do you mean?" asks Janet. "You've been blabbing about your trip all morning! Sarah told me that you were the one who got your friends off the island of Macaroni."

"*Maccabus*," say Bucky and Derek in unison, correcting Janet and looking at one another, concerned and a little angry.

Across the hall in Mrs. Peachtree's class, it's no different. The promise that Tommy and his friends made to each other at Bucky's tree fort has been thrown out the window. A secret this big was waiting to be exposed. Mrs. Peachtree, a young math teacher with a perpetual expression of kindness, is finishing her business with Principal Barnes in his office. She's known to shock many students when she raises her voice.

Chuck is surrounded by a large audience of his classmates hanging on to his every word. They've been fascinated by his version of what had happened on Maccabus. By the looks on the kids' faces, one would think that Chuck had discovered America. Patricia watches in disbelief and shakes her head. She wishes that Tommy or Tammy would be here to straighten him out.

"I had two or three gargoyles flattened under me!" mutters Chuck with peanut butter crackers flying out of his mouth. "The fighting on the island was intense, but not for me. It was like I had supernatural strength. I could bend trees so that my friends could walk through the swamp. I even knocked-out a giant gorilla!"

"Then what?!" asks Timmy excitedly, not able to let Chuck finish.

The kids' eyes and mouths are wide open as Chuck tells his version of what had happened on Maccabus. Many of the kids visualize themselves on the island with Chuck and his friends. He has given his classmates a real treat by opening their imaginations to a whole new world. Several girls giggle as they watch Chuck loading up on his snacks, preparing to continue his tale. The students love him; he's kind, funny and always has a story that keeps them glued to their seats. Little Bobby, a smaller version of Chuck, almost falls off his seat as he leans in, not wanting to miss a word.

"I took out all the gargoyles and found the treasure," replies Chuck.

"You found a 'treasure'?!" asks little Bobby.

Patricia shakes her head and laughs with Peggy.

"What a liar," says Patricia to Peggy.

"Yeah ... and lots of it! They even crowned me king of Maccabus!" mumbles Chuck with a mouthful of crackers. "I had all the children on the island bowing before me."

He gives Patricia the "keep-your-mouth-shut" look. As Chuck is about to finish his story, Mrs. Peachtree enters the classroom. Their eyes meet as time stands still for Chuck, knowing that he'd been busted.

"Chuck! What are you doing now?!" asks Mrs. Peachtree. "How many times have I told you not to eat in my classroom?"

Chuck looks at the floor and sees his pile of crumbs and empty cracker wrappers. It looks like a miniature dump around his feet.

"Sorry, Mrs. Peachtree," replies Chuck, cowering.

Patricia and Peggy giggle at their friend getting in trouble once again. Not only is Chuck the heavy-set kid in class, but he's

DEREK'S BORED

the one that gets scolded the most by Mrs. Peachtree. Chuck is the butt of many of his classmates' jokes. However, the students know that without him, class wouldn't be as much fun.

"Are you telling that Macadamia story again?" asks Mrs. Peachtree as she heads to her desk.

"You mean, *Maccabus*," say Chuck and Patricia.

Down the hall in Ms. Roosevelt's class, Tammy, Jimmy and a few other students are talking in a loud whisper about the gang's amazing weekend. Tammy, of course, has on her wrestling mask as she tells her side of the story. Jimmy listens intently as he sees that Tammy is serious.

"How did you do that?" asks Jimmy.

"I grabbed Orin's magic staff and used it on him. It was amazing! There were five or six giant men who tried to take me down, but they couldn't!" replies Tammy, starting to pant like a dog. "There was even a giant goblin … but I took care of him!"

Jimmy and the other two students are captivated by Tammy's animated version of Maccabus.

"Then what?" asks Jimmy, edging closer with his desk.

Tammy glances up to make sure that Ms. Roosevelt is still writing their assignment on the board. Ms. Roosevelt is a robust teacher with cheeks that could hold a small cake. When she speaks, everyone listens; she's not to be taken lightly. The last thing that Tammy needs is for Ms. Roosevelt to interrupt her while she's on a roll. Tammy can sense that her social status among the students is rising and wants to ride the wave while it's still there. One boy smiles at Tammy as if she's the coolest kid in the world.

"I made Orin disappear," replies Tammy.

Freddie, a small freckle-faced, blonde-headed friend of Jimmy's decides to get in on the conversation, although being late for class caused him to miss most of the story.

"Where were you when this happened?" asks Freddie.

"We were on the island of Maccabus," replies Tammy, frustrated for repeating herself.

"Where's that?" interrupts Freddie.

"It's under Tommy's bed!" replies Tammy impatiently.

The kids start laughing at Tammy, slowing the flow of her tale. Ms. Roosevelt hears the laughter and turns around and sees Tammy in the middle of her story.

"Tammy!" warns Ms. Roosevelt.

Tammy quickly rips off her wrestling mask and is gripped with fear. She knows that Ms. Roosevelt hates it when she brings her homemade wrestling mask to class, but there's no way that she'd be able to talk about Maccabus without it. Images of the giant warlock in the swamp have been haunting Tammy all morning.

"Yes, Ms. Roosevelt," answers Tammy, cowering.

"How many times do I have to tell you not to bring that ridiculous mask to my classroom?" asks Ms. Roosevelt, frustrated. "And I warned you about disrupting my class with your Story Time ... remember?!"

The kids giggle because they know that Tammy is in trouble.

"I'm sorry about 'disrupting' your class, Ms. Roosevelt. I won't bring my wrestling mask to class again, either," replies Tammy as she quickly puts it in her backpack.

"Good. Now quit talking and start writing! ... All of you!" instructs Ms. Roosevelt as she sits back at her desk.

The students quickly obey Ms. Roosevelt's command.

A large group of kids is gathered in the back of Tommy's class, and it's no different. As a matter of fact, it's much worse. Tommy is taking advantage of the fact that Mr. Bells left the classroom. Mr. Bells had to go to the teacher's lounge to wash the food coloring off his shirt from an experiment gone awry. Mr. Bells is an eccentric science teacher that has black and gray streaks through his hair. Many students believe that he works in the city morgue on his days off.

Becker, a genius with bad luck and a smaller version of Bucky, sits anxiously awaiting Tommy's next words. Tommy's tales have his classmates yearning for more. Robert and James quarrel with each other over which one of them would've been the hero on Maccabus. The students have forgotten about their assignment and Tommy has now become the teacher. Becker's intense blue eyes pierce through Tommy as images of Maccabus flash through his imagination.

"There were five or six demons! I don't know to be exact … I was too busy kicking their butts to count! Once I finished them off, I grabbed this magical dagger and destroyed the giant praying mantis. It had three offspring that needed to be destroyed as well. Oh … did I mention how I rescued the princess?" asks Tommy, excited and almost out of breath.

"Wow!" mutters Becker, shaking his head

Karen, a small girl with lots of freckles and long pigtails decides to get in on the conversation. She's never been one to miss out on an exciting story. In fact, some of the kids call her, "Nosy Karen" because she has a tendency to poke her nose into everyone else's business.

"What about the others?" asks Karen with an attitude.

"Who? Bucky, Tammy and Derek? They were frozen in their tracks. I saved my friends' lives!" replies Tommy as he puffs out his chest like a proud rooster.

"You're the coolest," says Becker, totally amazed by his new hero.

Mr. Bells enters the room.

"I knew it! Can't even leave for two minutes without you misbehaving!" says Mr. Bells as he dries off his hands.

Tommy seems to shrink in his desk from getting busted.

"But I didn't …," explains Tommy.

DEREK'S BORED

"Don't 'but' me, Mister! Take your seat and be quiet!" says Mr. Bells as he adjusts his glasses.

"Yes, Mr. Bells," mutters Tommy, signaling to the others that he'll finish his story later.

"Good. Now let's pick up where we left off. Becker, since you want to participate in class discussions, come up to the front of the class and help me mix the contents of this container again," insists Mr. Bells as he grabs two beakers from a drawer.

Becker's face is washed with fear as he recalls what had happened the last time Mr. Bells mixed the food coloring in the container.

"Yes, Mr. Bells," mutters Becker as he reluctantly walks to the front of the class.

It's finally lunchtime, and Mindy and Patricia are walking toward the cafeteria. As they walk past the library, they notice all the kids looking at them and whispering. A sense of uneasiness washes over Mindy and Patricia as Alex, Martha and Jeremy point at the girls and snicker to one another. By the expressions on their peers' faces, Mindy and Patricia can tell that one of their friends has leaked their secret. They stop dead in their tracks as they overhear Betty and Melinda talking about their friends.

"I heard that Bucky killed a *dragon!*" states Betty. "And he did it with his bare hands!"

"Oh yeah, well I heard that Derek and Tammy saved the island from an alien attack! I think the aliens took Chuck in for an experiment, but he escaped," says Melinda.

Patricia giggles at the girls' comments. Mindy, however, doesn't find them amusing.

"Patricia, this is serious! Kids have been talking about our nightmare on Maccabus all morning. Do you hear how far off the truth has gotten?" asks Mindy as she motions for the girls to keep walking.

"Sorry. I know that it's serious. What are we going to do?" asks Patricia, trying to hold back her laughter as she envisions Chuck surrounded by small aliens.

"Look, we have to call an emergency meeting at Bucky's today!" replies Mindy.

"You're right. We can't let this get out of control. If my parents find out, I'm never going to be allowed to hang out with you guys again," says Patricia.

"At lunch, I'm going to tell the gang to keep quiet until we get to Bucky's. Hurry, we need to stop the leak before it gets worse," says Mindy.

Patricia giggles with Peggy as Mindy races toward the cafeteria. Mindy can't wait to give her friends a piece of her mind and let them know how disappointed she is in them. Patricia knows that Mindy will unleash on her friends once she finds them.

"I still think that it's kind of funny, don't you?" asks Patricia.

"Yeah. Your friends are silly," replies Peggy.

Mindy notices Bucky and Chuck talking outside the cafeteria. She wonders which one of her friends has been blabbing his or her mouth and making up these ridiculous stories that are spreading around the school. The girls can see Bucky and Chuck's guilty looks from a mile away as the boys look up and notice Mindy marching their way.

"Hey, guys! Don't go in yet!" yells Mindy, hurrying Patricia along.

"Oh boy, we're in trouble," mumbles Bucky.

"I bet that she's going to tell us off," mutters Chuck as he finishes a donut.

"Deny everything! Let her go and interrogate everyone else," advises Bucky as he backs away from Chuck.

Mindy and Patricia finally make it to Chuck and Bucky. Mindy catches her breath before the tongue lashing. This type of gossip could land the gang in serious trouble. The boys haven't seen Mindy this worked up since the time that they broke Tony's bicycle. Patricia revels in Mindy's authoritative demeanor.

"You guys started a mess!" says Mindy, examining the boys with a stern look.

"What are you talking about?" asks Chuck as he wipes off the filling from the side of his mouth.

Bucky holds back his laughter.

As Mindy is about to answer Chuck, Becker walks up, having just come from the boys' bathroom. Becker has always had poor timing. One time he walked between two students arguing over a game of chess and got hit in the face with a piece of pie.

"What happened to you?!" asks Bucky.

"Mr. Bell's experiment went bad again, and I was the guinea pig," replies Becker, pulling on his shirt.

Chuck and Patricia chuckle at Becker's stained clothes and wet hair.

"Are you okay?" asks Mindy.

"Yeah. Say, what really happened to you guys on Maccadew?" asks Becker.

"*Maccabus!*" say Bucky and Chuck in unison.

"See what I mean?" mutters Mindy as she grows increasingly frustrated because of Becker's comment. "This is ridiculous!"

Bucky and Chuck wish that they could shrivel up as Mindy turns back their way and glares into their eyes. The whole school knows about their adventure under Tommy's bed. Now everyone will want to see Orin's castle or meet Omit. For some strange reason, kids enjoy scary stories and adventures until they actually experience one, themselves.

"Becker, this is a private conversation. You'll have to talk to the boys later," says Mindy.

"Sorry. I'll see you two inside," says Becker as he walks away.

Mindy looks around to make sure that there are no more surprises.

"We need to meet at your place today!" says Mindy sternly. The comment catches Bucky by surprise. The gang has never used the tree fort on a Monday. Monday is usually the day that Tommy and his friends recover from their weekend of mischief and fun. Besides, Mondays are also a day for the kids to take a break from one another; it's an unspoken rule among the gang. As close as they are, they know how it gets when they see too much of each other. Tommy and his friends can make each other's skin crawl if they're not careful.

"You want to come to my place ... today?" asks Bucky as he seeks Chuck's help.

"Don't look at me," says Chuck, looking toward the ground. He bites into his candy bar as if it's Mindy's head.

"Yeah ... your place, today," replies Mindy as she turns to Patricia for support. "We need to end the rumors and discussion of our trip to Maccabus."

"Why? I don't ...," mutters Bucky.

"You know 'why!' I've heard all the stories about aliens, dragons and treasures that are floating around school! We need to reinstate our code of silence and do damage control, that's why!" replies Mindy.

"She's right, Bucky. I guess things have gotten out of control with our adventure," says Chuck, giving in to Mindy's demands.

"Good. Let's go in and tell the others," insists Mindy.

Chuck, Bucky and Patricia follow Mindy to tell the rest of the gang about their plans. Chuck and Bucky walk with their heads hung low, knowing that Mindy means business. Amazing how little Mindy can turn even the toughest of boys into pudding in her hands.

DEREK'S BORED

The gang is sitting huddled together at their usual table. They remain quiet, waiting for Mindy to give them their lecture. The occasional teacher passes by to make sure that the gang isn't planning trouble. Ever since their giant food fight that practically started World War III, they've been under close watch by the school's administration. Tommy and his friends notice several kids pointing and murmuring to one another about their fabled tales. Nicholas, the school artist, walks by Tommy's table and holds up a large drawing of the gang surrounded by wizards and dinosaurs. Several kids follow Nicholas, snickering, trying to figure out who was the true hero on Maccabus.

Tommy and his friends know what the topic of discussion will be. Tammy and Derek have a hard time controlling themselves from laughing. Tommy sits in his seat, guiltily, knowing that he said too much. Bucky's attention deficit disorder (ADD) kicks in as he gazes out the window, off in his own thoughts. Chuck, on the other hand, is packing his peanut butter and jelly sandwich with cookies and jelly beans.

"Do you guys hear what the other students are saying?" asks Mindy, disappointed. "We've become the joke of Franklin Thomas School!"

Her friends' lower their heads as if they are a bunch of dogs getting scolded for peeing on the carpet.

"How bad is it?" asks Tommy reluctantly.

"I heard one boy saying that Chuck ate some wizard," replies Mindy.

"That's nothing. I heard some girls talking about Tammy flying a plane off Maccabus. And if you think that's bad, I also heard Reggie talking about Bucky, commandeering the giant praying mantis and destroying Orin's castle with it," adds Patricia.

"Bucky!" yells Derek as he notices Bucky not paying attention.

"What? Did I do something good?" asks Bucky as he snaps out of his trance.

DEREK'S BORED

"No, Bucky, it's the complete opposite! We're talking about the fabricated stories we each told today," replies Derek.

Bucky looks at his plate, wishing he could forget that he even came to school today. Tommy and Tammy look at each other, embarrassed. They realize that everything's out of control and that something needs to be done before Principal Barnes takes action against them.

"Sorry, Mindy, you're right. What do we do now?" asks Tommy.

"We meet at Bucky's after school. We need to recommit to our oath of silence and do damage control," replies Mindy as Patricia gives her a smile of encouragement. "We need to come up with a plan to reverse these horrible rumors."

Tommy stands up and regains his composure. After all, he's the head honcho of the gang. But more importantly, Tommy knows that he must take responsibility for dragging his friends into this mess.

"Look guys, we can't let this go any further. We broke our promise and things are messed up. I admit that I got carried away in my own little world, but Story Time is over. From now on, we tell everyone that it didn't happen," says Tommy convincingly.

"We don't need to tell everyone that we didn't go to Maccabus. Kids don't believe it happened anyway. We've become the butt of everyone's jokes. Just like we said would happen if we told anyone," states Derek, shaking his fist at a boy at the next table.

"You get 'em, brother!" mutters Chuck with a mouthful of chips.

"It doesn't matter what everyone else is saying or believing," says Mindy, eyeing each of her friends. "We need to tell everyone that we made it up … and that's *final!*"

The gang agrees to Mindy's plan.

Across town at city hall, Mr. Duncan is sitting in his big

office staring at a bulletin board full of pictures. Mr. Duncan, a heavy-set, older man with thinning gray hair, is the town mayor. He's the no-horse-play-type that takes his job very seriously. No one in town can remember the last time that they'd seen him smile. The bulletin board is plastered with pictures of Tommy and his friends. It resembles a board seen in the post office requesting information for wanted criminals. Tommy is at the top, with his six friends underneath.

"You're not going to *ruin* my parade this year!" mutters Mayor Duncan as he throws a dart at the board. "The time has come for justice!"

Mayor Duncan presses the buzzer on his phone.

"Lilly, would you come in here, please," requests Mayor Duncan as he puts away the remaining darts.

Lilly, a tall, skinny woman with straight black hair and matching black glasses enters the office immediately. The tone of the mayor's voice through the phone has her adrenaline flowing. She'd ask Mayor Duncan, "How high?" if he were to ask her to jump.

"Yes, Mayor Duncan, what is it?" asks Lilly nervously.

Mayor Duncan points to the bulletin board. He feels his pulse race as he glares at the kids' mug shots on the board. He has visions of them cleaning his parks and streets after being apprehended.

"These kids have *ruined* our parade every year. So far, we haven't been able to catch them red-handed in order to do something about it. This is our year!" states Mayor Duncan as he slams his fist on his desk.

"Ooooh!" says Lilly as her eyes light up from Mayor Duncan's confidence in catching Tommy and his friends. "What do you plan to do?"

"Nothing," replies Mayor Duncan.

She drops her pencil, surprised at Mayor Duncan's comment.

DEREK'S BORED

"Excuse me, Sir?" asks Lilly as she braces herself.

Mayor Duncan realizes that he needs to explain his plan; Lily has never been very bright.

"Every year we approach the kids at their homes or school, warning them about our tactics to catch them. This year we go *undercover!*" declares Mayor Duncan with beady eyes.

Lilly gets excited about going undercover. She loves to watch TV and her favorite shows are about police stories.

"How will you do it?" asks Lilly excitedly.

"First, I will have the kids followed to learn exactly where they'll be watching the parade. Next, I will have staff on the floats watching the kids' every move. Finally, I will have spotters on the roofs, getting a bird's eye view of the gang," replies Mayor Duncan, almost cracking a smile. "These kids are going down!"

"Excellent plan, Sir!" exclaims Lilly.

"Thank you, Lilly. Please ask Mr. Thompson and Ms. Hart to come in here on your way out," says Mayor Duncan as he shuffles through some papers on his desk.

"Yes, Sir," says Lilly as she leaves his office, filled with excitement.

Frankie, Jimmy and the gang are at Bucky's tree fort, stuffing their faces with snacks and waiting for the meeting to begin. Chuck, of course, is out of control, waiting to swallow his mouthful of Silk Worms, his favorite candy, before indulging in the chocolate donuts and potato chips that are in his hands.

"Slow down, Chuck!" says Jimmy, not getting too close. "You're going to choke!"

"Don't worry about him, Jimmy. He's an eating machine. Go, Chuck, go!" says Derek, cheering. "I wouldn't get too close to him if I were you."

"All right, guys, everyone sit down. The meeting is about to start," says Tommy.

Everyone grabs a last snack and takes a seat on the floor.

DEREK'S BORED

Frankie and Jimmy have been asked to attend the meeting for damage control. It looks as if Tommy, Chuck, Derek and Bucky are the ones to get an "earful" from the girls at this meeting. No longer will the7 boys be able to blame the girls for blowing their cover, due to blabbing their mouths about Maccabus. Tommy, to redeem him and his buddies, figures that Frankie and Jimmy can be the gophers to do the legwork necessary to straighten out this mess. Frankie and Jimmy, however, have agreed to come under different pretenses.

"Look, Frankie and Jimmy ... the stories that we told you, today, about Maccabus aren't true. We made them up ...," says Tommy, putting down his soda.

"*What?!* What do you mean they're 'not true'?" asks Frankie, upset that he told so many people.

"No way!" declares Jimmy.

"Yeah, we made them up. Do you really think that someone can go to the nether world from under their bed? Let's be real!" pitches Tommy, cool as ice.

The gang marvels at his demeanor. Frankie and Jimmy look at the others, confused and disappointed. They were expecting a different meeting altogether. How are they going to explain their stories to their classmates? Their credibility will be flushed down the toilet and they'll be sitting all alone in the cafeteria if they have to tell everyone that the stories aren't true.

"That's right guys, it was one, big lie," says Bucky, trying to keep a straight face. We're sorry that we put you in this predicament."

"Sorry, guys. We got carried away with our Story Time and should've never let it get this far. No harm, no foul. What do you say?" asks Mindy, winking at Tammy.

"Yeah, guys, you know that we have Story Time up here. Well, this one went over the top ...," says Chuck with a donut hanging out of his mouth.

"But this was the best story yet!" mutters Frankie. "It seemed so real!"

DEREK'S BORED

"Well, it wasn't. Look, to make it up to you … we'll let you guys come to the movies with us this weekend," offers Tommy, shaking his head for the others to agree.

Frankie and Jimmy are disgruntled by the kids' omission of truth. The boys stare helplessly at Tommy and his friends as they hold firm in their decision to change their story. Frankie and Jimmy realize that they've been invited to Bucky's tree fort for something other than Story Time. Their dreams have been smashed by a meeting to cover-up the exaggerated stories that were told in school about the gang's adventure on Maccabus.

"But the whole school is talking about this!" claims Jimmy. "We…."

"I know, I know. That's why we have you here. We need both of you to help us squash this story," says Tommy.

"How?" asks Frankie.

"We need you to tell the kids at school that it didn't happen. You guys are good at making up stories … you'll think of something good to say. We also need you to get them thinking about the upcoming Hummel County Parade," replies Tommy.

Tommy's friends watch their fearless leader handle Frankie and Jimmy. Tammy smacks Chuck's hand for trying to steal her gum as Mindy motions for Derek to remain quiet. Frankie and Jimmy look at each other and realize that this is an opportunity for the gang to owe them a favor. The momentum of the meeting is changing in Frankie and Jimmy's favor.

"I don't know …," says Frankie, playing hard to get.

"Come on, guys! We've done so many things for you in the past," declares Mindy.

"Yeah, but you haven't done anything this big. You're going to owe us, *big time!*" states Frankie as he nudges Jimmy.

"Yeah!" declares Jimmy.

"Fine, we owe you a favor. Now are you happy?" asks Tommy.

"I think that we need to think about it," replies Frankie, smirking.

Tammy stands up and walks toward the boys. She's finished playing nice and wants to use her muscles to persuade Frankie and Jimmy to change their attitudes. The boys' eyes light up as they see Tammy twitching.

"Okay guys, we'll do it!" mutters Frankie as he shakes Tommy's hand.

Derek slouches down, depressed. He knows that this year's parade won't be the same. Derek is usually the one that comes up with the ultimate plan that ruins the Hummel County Parade. The rotten kids at school look up to him for his craftiness and elusiveness that keep him and his friends out of trouble. Frankie and Jimmy, however, become excited and rush out of Bucky's tree fort. The gang now owes them a favor and they have the Hummel County Parade to plan for. Tommy and his friends aren't the only kids in town with a couple of *tricks* up their sleeves.

It's Saturday morning and the streets are beginning to fill up with families trying to get a good spot to watch the parade. The Hummel County Parade isn't a joke! Each year, the crowd gets larger as Mayor Duncan delights the people from Hummel County with new surprises. This year, they're expecting a mini-rollercoaster for everyone to enjoy. Kids run excitedly next to the floats, pretending to beat them while they cross the street.

"I made it!" screams Omar.

Parents lose track of their children with all the chaos. Dads get frustrated when their wives blame them for the kids' reckless behavior. Families play the blame game until little Johnny or little Suzie runs back into their arms.

"You were supposed to watch Jackie!" screams Mrs. Thompson to her husband.

Dogs are barking wildly at all the commotion. It's clear that another Hummel County Parade is about to take place.

DEREK'S BORED

Back at city hall, Mayor Duncan has his undercover task-force lined up, waiting for their leader to take them into battle. Many in his team are equipped with binoculars, portable radios and even disguises. The tension is thick as each member knows how important the taskforce is to Mayor Duncan and how the mayor has anticipated this day for weeks. Several guys want the same revenge on Tommy and his friends as the mayor does; especially the town's sanitation department. They've worked overtime cleaning up the gang's assault on Mayor Duncan's parades. No one wants to be responsible for botching his plan because of negligence.

"Tom … is your team ready?!" asks Mayor Duncan, checking over his plans.

"Yes, Sir!" replies Tom.

"Good. Sally … is your team ready?!" asks Mayor Duncan.

"Yes, Sir!" replies Sally, holding back her nervous stomach noises.

"Okay then, let's go and get them!" declares Mayor Duncan enthusiastically.

The undercover taskforce gathers their things and heads to their positions.

Tommy and his friends are in for quite a surprise. All they want to do is have some good clean fun, and all the mayor wants to do is pounce on them as if they'd stolen his son's bicycle. It's a battle of the wits; who can outsmart who? In Mayor Duncan's eyes, there's no way Tommy and his friends are going to get by him this year. Maybe it's Mayor Duncan and his undercover taskforce who are in for the surprise.

Bucky's tree fort is packed with the gang and all their gear. For the most part, Tommy and his friends had enjoyed their new attitudes and the pact that they'd made with each other. The gang thought it was amusing that most of their classmates were frustrated with their lack of entertainment and mischief in their classrooms.

Tommy and his friends hum a tune, smiling, as they check their backpacks that are filled to the brim. They look like they're ready for war and not a parade. Water bottles are strapped to Tammy and Bucky's waists. Chuck is carrying so many snacks that he looks like a walking vending machine. Tommy and Derek wear head-bands, symbolizing their readiness to endure the heat. Even dainty Patricia and Mindy are loaded to the hilt, trying to figure out just what it is that they're carrying.

Usually, their backpacks would be full of firecrackers, horns, marbles, shaving cream and any other items that could dis-rupt the Hummel County Parade. This year, their backpacks are filled with enough snacks to feed the entire town. They have candy, gum, lollipops, chips and cookies; everything a kid could want and then some.

"We're actually going to *share* our snacks?!" inquires Chuck, hoarding a bag of candy. "Isn't there something else that we could give to the kids?"

Chuck breaks out in a nervous sweat as he envisions his friends tossing their snacks at the children of Hummel County.

"That's right, Chuck. We swore that we'd change our ways," replies Tommy. "Come on, buddy, let go of the bag."

Bucky and Derek shrug their shoulders and hesitantly agree with Tommy. Mindy and Patricia smile at one another. Mindy gently takes the bag from Chuck, careful not to get her hands too close to his mouth. She winks at him, indicating her approval of his cooperation.

"Okay, guys, let's head to the parade," says Tommy as he finishes tying his shoelace. "Don't worry … I'll make sure that we have fun."

"Yeah, right! This year's parade is going to be *boring*. I don't know if I can handle it," mutters Derek as he smiles through his teeth at Patricia.

"I know, but we don't want to see Orin again … do we?" asks Chuck as he looks toward the window. "Look, if I have to give up my food, you can handle it. Now suck it up!"

DEREK'S BORED

The gang leaves Bucky's tree fort and heads for the parade. Derek is the only one who really doesn't want to go this year. He's hiding it pretty well, but deep down inside, his gut yearns to start a little trouble.

I don't do what I want to do, but what I hate to do, I do. And when I want to do good ... I do bad. And when I don't want to do bad ... I do it anyway, thinks Derek, as he exits the tree fort last.

These friends have used Story Time to discuss the struggle of "good-versus-evil" within their innerselves. They know that this battle has plagued men, women and children since the beginning of time. In a weird way, this reality fascinates them. They use this as an excuse for the misbehavior, mischief, and rebellious attitudes that make them so popular among their peers.

Across the street from Bucky's is a member of Mayor Duncan's undercover taskforce. Mr. Lowsan, a timid, middle-aged man with short hair, is posing as a mailman. He's carefully watching the gang as they emerge from Bucky's backyard. This so-called mailman fumbles through his bag, pretending to organize the mail for his route.

"I have the gang in sight," speaks Mr. Lowsan discretely into his two-way radio.

"Hi, Mr. Mailman!" screams Mindy, waving.

Mr. Lowsan gets nervous and almost drops his mailbag. This is his first undercover assignment. If he blows his cover, he'll be sweeping the floors of city hall for the next twenty years.

"Hi, kids!" says Mr. Lowsan as he reviews the address of a letter.

Mayor Duncan's mailman follows the gang down the street, documenting their every move.

Over at Frankie's house, he, Jimmy and Tosha are gathering their things for the big day. Tosha blends in real well with all of the boys. She's very athletic and can horseplay with the best of them.

DEREK'S BORED

She'd give Tammy a run for her money, but their mutual respect has deterred them from exchanging blows. Tosha's older brothers have contributed to her toughness. Frankie, Jimmy and Tosha are loading up their backpacks and preparing for the Hummel County Parade. This year, it's their turn to shine and be the kids that all the other children look up to at school. Frankie tucks some rope back into Jimmy's bag as Tosha shakes a can, making sure that it's full.

"How do I look?" asks Jimmy as he adjusts his backpack.

Frankie and Tosha giggle because Jimmy looks like a ninja.

"You 'look' ridiculous!" replies Frankie as he shoves Tosha.

"What do you mean, 'ridiculous?!' I think that I look the coolest out of all of us!" declares Jimmy as he crawls against the wall, playing the ninja. "Can you guys see me?"

Frankie and Tosha crack up at their friend and his black ninja outfit.

"You'll stick out like a sore thumb! We're not going to a fight ... we're going to a parade! I think you'd better borrow some of Frankie's clothes and blend in with us," replies Tosha, shaking her head.

"She's right. Here, take these," says Frankie as he hands Jimmy some clothes.

"Fine! You guys are just *jealous!*" mutters Jimmy, grabbing the clothes.

The streets of Hummel County are completely lined with families waiting for the parade to start. Security is clearing a few people from the streets so that the parade can take place. Kids are eating cotton candy and popcorn as they eagerly wait for the sound of the marching band to begin. Each year, the Hummel County High School Marching Band starts the parade with a new song. The kids love the loud music that sends chills up their spines.

"When is the parade going to start, Mommy?" asks a little girl as she pulls her mother's blouse.

"Soon, dear, soon," replies her mom.

"Look, Mommy, a clown!" yells the little girl, pointing down the street.

It's Mayor Duncan. This is the undercover disguise that he plans on using to catch the gang. No one in the crowd has any idea that the clown is the town mayor.

They're around here somewhere! thinks Mayor Duncan.

He continues to walk down the street, waving and smiling to the crowd as he looks for Tommy and his friends. Underneath that fake smile is a man on a mission, hungry for justice. Mayor Duncan canvasses the area, making sure that all of his agents and taskforce are ready to take down Tommy and his friends. Mayor Duncan has given his personnel the permission to use all means necessary to bring the gang to justice. A person might think that Mayor Duncan is tracking a serial killer by the man hours and scheming put into this plot to catch Tommy and his friends as they try to ruin this year's parade.

On top of the ice cream shop stands Mr. Reynolds, admiring the beautiful day. He's a tall man with glasses who loves to hunt, and is part of the mayor's undercover taskforce. Mr. Reynolds is careful not to let anyone see him as he uses his hunting binoculars to spot the gang from the rooftop. His heart races as he combs the street, looking for the would-be-hoodlums; a new hunting experience that'll make a great story around the campfire one day.

"I don't see them yet," speaks Mr. Reynolds into his two-way radio.

He has his eyes on Pete's Pet Store. That's where Tommy and the rest of the gang usually watch the parade. The kids of Hummel County fight over this spot. There's a donut shop and video arcade next to the pet store that Tommy and his friends visit during the parade. Pete usually has exotic animals on the sidewalk that add to the excitement as well.

"Kevin, come in. Do you see the kids?" asks Mr. Reynolds into his two-way radio.

DEREK'S BORED

Kevin, a college student who aspires to work for the mayor, is disguised as a meter-man. He's walking carefully through the neighborhood, stopping occasionally to read meters for the power company. Kevin's doing an excellent job for the mayor. He wipes the sweat from his glasses as he notices the gang approaching from down the street.

For the first time, Tommy and his friends are going to be late for the parade. They're walking briskly through the neighborhood, unaware of the watchful eyes upon them. Tammy and Bucky stop, waiting for Chuck to catch-up.

"Yes, Frank, I have the kids in my sight, over," replies Kevin into his two-way radio.

As the kids see the crowds, they stop. Something is missing.

"What's wrong?" asks Tommy, adjusting his backpack.

"I have a *bad feeling* about the parade. It's the same feeling that I had on Maccabus when Orin was watching us," replies Tammy.

The gang looks around to make sure that Orin isn't watching them. Kevin quickly checks a meter, pretending to be working so as not to blow his cover. His face warms up as he feels several sets of eyes glancing his way.

"Yeah, I agree with Tammy. I'm not into this parade, at all. What are we going to do for fun?!" asks Derek, frustrated.

"Hey, guys, the parade is cool ... so quit complaining," says Bucky as he takes a sip of water. "They've got great food, lots of candy, and plenty of rides."

"Yeah! Come on, Derek, lighten up," says Mindy. "Maybe you can win another giant stuffed tiger like you did last year!"

"Look, guys, enough with the bickering. We'll have plenty of fun, trust me," says Tommy. "Isn't that right, Chuck?"

Chuck is daydreaming about all the junk food that is served at the parade. There are smiling vendors at every corner, pitching their products to anxious kids and their parents. They have hotdogs, hot pretzels, honey-glazed peanuts, candy apples, taffy, cinnamon twirlers, cotton candy and plenty of soda. The food is marching around Chuck's head like a parade as he smiles at the sky.

"Chuck! Wake up!" screams Tommy.

"What happened? … Sorry," says Chuck as he wipes the drool from his mouth.

"Come on, guys, we're already late," says Tommy as he motions for everyone to move along. "No more complaining, Derek. Besides, I have a feeling that something big is going to happen at this year's parade. I think that Bosco's and Pete's…."

"Hey, guys, that guy has been following us ever since we left Bucky's house," says Patricia, turning abruptly.

"Yeah, I saw him, too," adds Mindy as she walks next to Patricia.

Tommy turns and looks toward Kevin. The tension can be felt a mile away as Tommy and Kevin make eye contact. Kevin frantically pulls out a map and rushes over to the gang.

"Excuse me, kids, but can you tell me where Jackson Street is? I'm new to this town and my boss will fire me if I don't finish my work," rambles Kevin.

"Yes, it's two blocks that way," replies Tommy as he points toward Jackson Street.

"Thank you. You kids enjoy the parade," says Kevin as he walks away.

Kevin has enough butterflies in his stomach to fill a room. The gang buys Kevin's lie and heads into the crowd, looking for a spot to watch the parade. Kevin turns around and watches the gang head toward Pete's Pet Store. Now is his chance to help foil Tommy and his friends' plan to ruin this year's parade and earn some serious brownie points with Mayor Duncan.

"They're here! … Yes. The kids have bags that are full of something. They probably have horns and rope! It looks like they're prepared for war! Better call for backup," speaks Kevin into his two-way radio.

DEREK'S BORED

He lets the gang walk further into the crowd before he continues to follow them.

The Hummel County High School Marching Band is now ready to begin its march down Main Street. Mr. Jenson, the band leader who looks like he should be playing the tuba instead, lifts his conductor's stick and prepares to blow his whistle. The band lifts their instruments, ready to play, following the lead of their instructor. Mr. Jenson adjusts his hat and turns to face Main Street, full of excitement and ready to give the town a show. He wipes the beads of sweat from the sides of his large cheeks as he faces his band.

"One ... two ... one, two, THREE!" screams Mr. Jenson.

The band starts to play and begins their march down the street. The crowd sees the band marching out from Kent Street moving in formation. Everyone rises to their feet and begins to cheer, happy that their annual parade has finally begun. The kids are ecstatic and jump up and down, driving their parents crazy. The sugar from all the junk food is starting to take effect on the children.

"The band, the band!" screams a little boy, tugging on his mother's arm. "Come on, Mommy, let's get closer!"

"Look, Daddy, it's starting!" screams another boy. "Daddy, please pick me up! I want to see the band!"

As Mr. Jenson turns and heads down Main Street, people can see the first float moving into its position to follow the band. The float is full of animals sponsored by Pete's Pet Store. There are furry cats, barking dogs and squawking birds of all types, crying out to their adoring fans. Pete usually has exotic, live animals for the kids to pet as well. And to add to his splendor, he's probably the nicest guy in all of Hummel County.

Frankie, Jimmy and Tosha watch from across the street as Tommy and his friends settle along the sidewalk. Frankie and his goons are standing behind a group of spectators, waiting patiently for the opportunity to present itself for their reign of terror to begin. Jimmy scares away a little boy who was examining their bags.

"Look at those guys! Chickens!" declares Frankie as he checks his bag.

"Yeah! Boy are they going to miss out! They'll be coming to us to play after school when this is all through!" states Jimmy, smiling.

Tosha looks at her watch and gathers her share of the trouble.

"Guys, we're going to be late," says Tosha. "Let's move."

Frankie and Jimmy follow her through the crowd to find a sweet spot to start their trouble. The kids move among the people like snakes moving through the grass, looking for their next meal. Their moment of glory has arrived as they anticipate releasing their wrath on Hummel County and becoming the new heroes at school.

Bucky notices Frankie and his crew disappearing into the crowd. He senses that something isn't right by the paranoid look on Jimmy's face. Bucky nudges Chuck and points across the street.

"Hey, look at Frankie!" says Chuck as he grabs Tammy.

The gang looks over and notices Frankie, Jimmy and Tosha sneaking through the crowd, carrying their stuffed backpacks.

"They're up to something," says Tammy.

Little do Tommy and his friends know that they're being watched by Mr. Reynolds from the top of the ice cream shop. He watches them like a hawk, unaware of Bucky's discovery. Mr. Reynolds notices the gang's stuffed bags and is overcome with an adrenaline rush like never before. He mentally prepares himself for the upcoming confrontation.

"Everyone get ready! The kids have their backpacks full of trouble!" speaks Mr. Reynolds into his two-way radio.

Down the street, Mayor Duncan signals for his undercover taskforce to head toward Pete's Pet Store and grab the kids before they start their mischief. His blood begins to flow like a raging river as he anticipates catching the kids red-handed. Mayor Duncan begins to fantasize about the celebration that will take place once Tommy and his friends are brought to justice. He quickly shakes off the visual as a kid screams for more ice cream.

"Thank you, Frank. Keep your eye on them, we're coming," speaks Mayor Duncan into his two-way radio.

Mayor Duncan blends into the parade and heads toward Tommy and his friends. The Hummel County High School Marching Band is slowly approaching the gang and playing much better than last year. The people of Hummel County are being treated to a real show as the band members play their hearts out for the crowds. The sound of drums beating loudly has kids dancing on the sidewalks. Even the parents join in, trying to show some rhythm as they move to the sounds of the trumpets and tambourines. Even with the jubilant atmosphere, the spirit of doom settles over the town. The poor citizens of Hummel County have no idea what's about to hit them as they continue to have fun.

"They're so loud, Mommy!" shouts a little girl. "Look, there's a clown juggling!"

Girls toss batons high into the air as they pass the crowd. People *whistle* and *cheer* for the band, waiting for the floats to come.

"Look, Dad, there's Pete's Pet Store! It's finally here!" yells a boy as he jumps up and down like a chimpanzee. "Yeeeaaahhh!"

The float from Pete's Pet Store has dogs walking next to it and barking at the spectators. There are beagles, Labrador retrievers, hound dogs and bulldogs that occasionally try to break away from Pete's employees, wanting to play. On the float, there's a snake handler with a large snake around his arm. There are also parrots and toucans of all sizes, screeching and talking from their cages. The employees of Pete's Pet Store are dressed in cat and dog costumes. This is their time to let loose, goof off with the kids, and enjoy the parade. Pete thinks that some of his employees actually wish that they were dogs and cats instead of humans. His employees wave and throw candy to the kids as they pass the crowds.

The next float behind Pete's is the Sweet Tooth Candy Factory float. Chuck begins to pant like a dog as he sees his favorite float coming down the street. His friends wonder if he's more excited to see this float than his own mother.

"Guys! Sweet Tooth is coming! Sweet Tooth is coming!" shouts Chuck with his tongue frolicking in his mouth like one of the bulldogs from Pete's float.

Tommy and the gang look down the street at Chuck's request. They like that float as well, but not nearly as much as Chuck does. No one in Hummel County likes that float as much as Chuck. Chuck pushes his way through the crowd to get a better look.

"Chuck, take it easy! Here, take this," says Derek.

He reaches into his bag and hands Chuck a candy bar.

Mr. Reynolds sees Derek and Chuck make the exchange.

"Hurry, guys, they're about to start! I just saw one of them reach into his bag for something," speaks Mr. Reynolds into his two-way radio. "I think it's a flare! You'd better take precaution!"

Across the street, Jimmy turns and notices the gang watching the parade. He stops suddenly, causing Frankie and Tosha to run into the back of him.

"*Hey,* why did you stop?" asks Frankie as he picks up his water bottle.

"It's Tommy and the gang. Something's going on with them … look," replies Jimmy, pointing.

Frankie and Tosha notice that Tommy and his friends have stuffed bags as well. They immediately become suspicious, thinking that they're carrying the same arsenal as them.

"Look, they're going to ruin the parade!" declares Tosha.

"I knew they'd change their minds! There's no way that they'd let this year go by without some kind of trouble," says Jimmy as he hides behind a family.

"Let's sit here and see what they do," suggests Frankie.

As Frankie, Jimmy and Tosha sit and watch the gang, the Sweet Tooth Candy Factory float passes in front of them. On the float are several members of Mayor Duncan's undercover taskforce; the women are dressed in colorful dresses and the men are dressed like giant elves. They're throwing candy to all the kids, acting as if they'd done this for years. On the other side of the float is Mayor Duncan. The gang is cheering him on as he does his act. By the looks of it, a person might think that Mayor Duncan was a rodeo clown on his days off. Tommy and his friends don't realize that they're cheering for a man who's obsessed with catching them in the act of destroying his parade.

Across the street, Kevin and Mr. Lowsan are posed to catch the gang in the act. Their hearts race and their mouths begin to dry up as they wait for the mayor's signal. All *eyes* are on Tommy and his friends. The scene resembles a war movie in which an army battalion is about to be ambushed by the enemy.

The unsuspecting gang is enjoying the festive mood of Hummel County. The music from the band has Tommy and his friends bobbing their heads and dancing to the beat. They smile and wave to several kids, showing off their new outlook on life. Maccabus really did a "number" on the gang. Bucky and Chuck whistle at the passing floats, feeding into the joyful spirit of the parade. Derek joins in with his buddies and begins to horse-around, dancing to the music. Thoughts of evil have left their minds as they embrace the true essence of clean fun.

"Guys, let's share some of our snacks with these kids," says Tommy as he begins to open his bag.

"You know, it feels pretty good to do good deeds," says Tammy as she begins to open her bag. "It's a weird kind of good."

"Not too much!" declares Chuck as he reluctantly opens his bag.

Chuck quickly inhales several pieces of candy and some cookies. He figures that he'll feel less guilty if he gives less away. The gang reaches down into their bags and prepares to distribute their goodies. Derek motions for several kids to come over for some free snacks. It's as if time stands still as Tommy pulls out a snack and Mayor Duncan unleashes his crew.

"Now!" screams Mr. Reynolds into his two-way radio.

Mayor Duncan's undercover taskforce converges on the spot where Tommy and his friends are standing. The crowd *disperses* as several participants from the Sweet Tooth Candy Factory float fly through the air to subdue Tommy and his friends. Kevin and Mr. Lowsan break through the crowd and grab Patricia and Bucky. The rest of the gang drop their backpacks and brace for an attack. For the first time, they're on the opposite side of an undermining plan to ruin the parade.

"Got you!" screams Mayor Duncan, feeling that his day has come. "Come here, Mr. Puddin!"

"Ahhh!" screams Tammy as she tries to fight off one of Mayor Duncan's officers.

"What did we do?!" asks Tommy, petrified with fear. "It's okay, Patricia, don't worry!"

The crowd backs away from Tommy and his friends. The citizens of Hummel County watch in bewilderment as the gang is apprehended by Mayor Duncan and his undercover taskforce. A group of clowns and entertainers in the parade notice the ruckus and stop walking. Mr. Jenson blows his whistle and raises his hands, silencing the band. Everyone is looking at Tommy and his friends as if they had robbed a bank. The spectators who came out to watch the parade can almost hear a pin drop through the dead silence. A somber spirit falls upon the crowd as families huddle together, trying to figure out why Tommy and his friends are in trouble.

DEREK'S BORED

"What's going on, Mommy?" asks a girl, frightened.

"I don't know, dear, but stay close to me," replies her mother.

Tommy and his friends are in total shock, realizing that they've halted the parade and become the center of attention. For the first time in history, the gang is in trouble for doing absolutely nothing wrong. Tommy and his friends are silenced by the overwhelming presence of police and undercover agents as they're led toward city hall.

Back across the street, Frankie, Jimmy and Tosha are celebrating the fact that Tommy and his friends are in trouble. They're careful not to draw attention to themselves and meet the same fate. They watch with gleaming smiles as the gang is shuffled away from the parade by Mayor Duncan and his crew. Frankie smiles at his counterparts, witnessing for the first time, the gang's agony of defeat.

"Guys, this is our chance!" states Jimmy as he unzips his backpack. "All security is focused on them!"

"Let's do it!" exclaims Frankie as he pulls out a pair of sunglasses from of his bag.

With Tommy and his friends distracting everyone, Frankie and his crew have free reign of the parade. They look down the street and see the rest of the parade catching-up with the front. Frankie canvasses the street, looking for the best location to start their assault.

"I've got it! The clowns! Jimmy, empty your bag of marbles on the clowns!" instructs Frankie, bubbling with excitement. "With them falling all over the street, that'll give me a chance to do my thing!"

"That's an excellent idea! I'll see you guys later!" mutters Jimmy as he disappears into the crowd.

Mayor Duncan notices that the parade has stopped and that people are starting to leave. The disappointed looks on the parents' faces as they explain to their children that it's time to go home, breaks his heart. With the gang in his custody, he quickly signals for the parade to continue.

"All right, everyone, we have things under control! *Let the parade begin!*" shouts Mayor Duncan as he blows a whistle.

The people in the crowd realize that the clown is Mayor Duncan. Their faces light up as they feel the triumphant spirit of their mayor overshadow the melee caused by Tommy and his friends. Mr. and Mrs. Lutz grab their children and head back toward the curb to finish what they started. Other families join them and move toward the street, anticipating the resumption of the parade. Mr. Jenson smiles at the crowd and blows his whistle, signaling for the band to resume playing. More people slowly move back along the streets as the music picks up tempo. Families walk by the gang and glare at them as if they had committed a felony. Tommy and his friends hold their heads low, trying not to make eye contact with anyone.

"I knew that Smart boy was no good," mutters Mrs. Walsh to her husband.

"See, son, that's what happens when you hang out with the wrong crowd," says Mr. Walsh.

Tommy and his friends are herded down the street like cattle.

"What's going on?" asks Bucky as he begins to cry. "Why are we in trouble?"

"Yeah, we didn't do anything!" states Tommy, almost tripping over Tammy's foot.

Mayor Duncan turns around and signals for everyone to stop. He walks in front of the gang to address them as to why they're in trouble. This is the day that he'd been waiting for since last year's parade. Not one minute had passed that Mayor Duncan didn't fantasize about bringing Tommy and his friends to justice. Almost like a prisoner, he'd marked his calendar off to this very day.

DEREK'S BORED

"You kids have destroyed my parade, every year! You've gotten away with so much in your short lives! I hear about what goes on in school ... the food fight, the teasing and so forth and so on. I've never caught you red-handed until now. Kevin, open their bags!" says Mayor Duncan with authority. "Frank ... would you help Kevin, please?"

Kevin begins to open the kids' bags.

"*What's this?!*" asks Kevin. "You've got to be kidding!"

"Where are the horns?! What about the rope?! *Jelly beans?!*" asks Frank as he pulls apart Derek's bag.

Mayor Duncan can't believe his eyes as he gasps for air. His world is turned upside down as the thought of being wrong crosses his mind. The undercover taskforce shakes their heads in disbelief as the crowd looks on, shocked by their discovery. One year of preparation and anticipation only to catch Tommy and his friends with snacks. What a waste.

"Candy?! Brownies?! Soda?! *Where* are the firecrackers?!" demands Mayor Duncan as he pulls out the contents of Tommy's backpack.

The undercover taskforce looks on with embarrassment as Mayor Duncan fumbles through the kids' backpacks, looking for trouble. He still believes that they have things hidden in the junk food. Mayor Duncan will never be able to live this one down if he doesn't find something.

Jimmy has made his way to the curb, positioning himself to empty his bag of marbles. The group of clowns who are coming up the street have no idea what's about to hit them. The kids laugh as small, colorful clowns walk under the legs of the giant clowns who are walking through the streets on stilts. The clowns are dancing to the beat of the band, totally obnoxious and out of rhythm.

"Oh boy, is this going to be great!" exclaims Jimmy, looking around to make sure that no one's watching him.

As the clowns get close, Jimmy empties his bag onto the street. Marbles race toward the clowns in every direction, flooding the street. It's like a million tiny bowling balls barreling toward a bunch of pins. The first group of clowns flies high into the air as they step on the marbles. Mr. and Mrs. Rouse, along with their seven children, buckle over laughing as they watch the clowns tumbling to the pavement. At first, the crowd doesn't realize that the clowns are falling to the ground because of the marbles.

"Look at the clowns, Mom! Aren't they silly?" asks a little girl.

"The way they fall, it seems so real," says her brother.

The clowns try very hard to keep their balance, which is next to impossible because the marbles have taken over the street. Jimmy's prank causes a chain reaction; clowns fall into each other, which leads many of them to fall into other entertainers, which leads them to fall into the crowd. Some clowns split their pants as they try not to fall. Others fall flat on their backs, hoping not to get trampled.

Frankie has made his way to the float for Hank's Furniture Store. This float has two large hot-air balloons shaped like Hank and his wife. Frankie checks to make sure that the coast is clear for him to put the icing on the cake. He's bubbling with excitement as he envisions the kids at school congratulating him and his friends.

Wait until everyone sees these balloons over the city, thinks Frankie, as he pulls out a pair of scissors from his backpack.

The crowd's attention has now shifted entirely to the chaotic clowns. Frankie takes a deep breath and runs to the back of Hank's float, cutting the ropes that are fastening the balloons. Quickly, he disappears into the crowd as the balloons break away and rise toward the sky.

Back down the street, Mayor Duncan and the gang witness the parade falling apart before their eyes. The hot air balloons are rising into the air. Clowns are tumbling to the ground, falling on top of each other. The citizens of Hummel County scramble for cover, trying to figure out what's going on with their beautiful town. Kids *screaming* and *crying* can be heard throughout the streets.

DEREK'S BORED

"WHAT'S GOING ON?!" demands Mayor Duncan as he grabs Tommy.

The undercover taskforce looks at each other, confused. One of the balloons gets snagged on a banner that stretches across the street. The banner's ropes give way to the balloon, sending the banner crashing to the ground. Several families run for cover screaming as they feel the presence of danger. The town is in total chaos as parents grab their children and head home.

Tommy and his friends chuckle to themselves, as they now have become spectators to this year's mischief. They watch as Frankie and his crew exit the parade, unnoticed, and head home. Mayor Duncan throws Tommy's backpack to the ground, frustrated and enraged. Once again, he's been outsmarted. The gang doesn't realize that they'll relive this moment on their next adventure; a *prophecy* is waiting to be fulfilled on the other side of the nether world.

Tommy and his friends are back at Bucky's tree fort, safe and sound, out of harm's way. The gang has escaped trouble by the skin of their teeth. The kids in the neighborhood can't quite figure out their stroke of luck. That probably explains the reason why they're so envied by all the kids in Hummel County. Well, that's part of the reason. The real reason everyone envies the gang stems from their so-called unprecedented journey to Maccabus through the nether world under Tommy's bed, bringing to life their dreams and nightmares. Their exaggerated stories about escaping near-death experiences have kids around school fantasizing about the island. The gang also has Bucky's tree fort in which to talk about it and create even greater adventures.... They're the coolest kids on the planet.

"I can't believe that Frankie and Jimmy pulled it off!" mumbles Chuck with pieces of pie flying out of his mouth. "Did you guys see that fire?!"

DEREK'S BORED

"Those two are going to be in big trouble! ... *Ewww!*" mutters Mindy as she wipes a piece of Chuck's pie off her hand.

"'*Trouble?*' They got away with it. Everyone was looking for us," says Tommy.

Tammy is pacing back and forth.

"They stole our glory!" declares Tammy, full of jealousy. "We should've been the ones to ruin the parade!"

"Yeah! If we have to live like this, we'll never have any fun!" states Derek, still frowning about his day. "No more Mr. Nice Guy!"

"Calm down, Derek. Did we forget about Maccabus all of a sudden?" asks Tommy as he motions for Bucky to pay attention. "We agreed to be nicer so that something worse doesn't happen to us."

"Yeah, guys. We said that we were going to change ...," says Mindy.

"'Change' is *boring!*" mutters Derek as he stands up. "Did you see the smiles on Frankie and Jimmy's faces when they left the parade!? I want to smile like that!"

"I'm not bored," says Patricia to Peggy.

"I agree with Derek! What are we going to do up here? Watch Patricia play with her doll?" asks Chuck as he stuffs his face full of cookies. "We need some action!"

"Hey, that wasn't nice, Chuck!" says Patricia defensively.

She quickly cowers, for fear of getting yelled at.

Bucky is in the corner trying to catch an ant, not really paying attention to the heated discussion. He catches one and down the hatch it goes. Yummy!

"Bucky! Do you want to get in on the conversation?!" asks Tommy as he smells his sweaty headband.

Bucky is startled by Tommy and loses another ant.

"Tommy, you scared me. What is it?" asks Bucky.

"Quit trying to catch ants and join us! This is important!"

mutters Derek as he shoves Chuck for trying to steal some snacks from his backpack. "I said no!"

Bucky kicks his feet in frustration and joins his friends.

"Guys, I don't know how long I can last being nice. It's not in my blood. We were born rebels!" declares Derek.

"I'm with Derek!" adds Tammy.

Derek and Tammy high-five each other and make a face at Mindy. The spirit of mischief and deviance flies around the tree fort, touching Chuck, Derek and Tammy. It was only a matter of time before their true colors would resurface. Chuck puts down the apple pie he was about to inhale and joins Derek and Tammy. He must have something important to say, considering that he's willing to put down a scrumptious apple pie.

"I'm kind of getting bored, too. What about Old Man Jones' house? What about our adventures at the beach?! We've had so many good times … and those usually involve trouble," says Chuck, eyeing his pie to make sure that no one touches it.

"Look, you three, let's give it some thought," suggests Tommy, knowing that he's in an uphill battle. "I know that we can still have fun without all the trouble…."

"The kids at school are going to call us nerds if we continue this behavior!" states Tammy as she punches Derek in the arm. "Gotcha! You want a piece of this?!"

"We're 'nerds'?" asks Bucky, looking toward Mindy and Patricia.

"No, you stupid …," replies Chuck.

"Okay, refrigerator!" says Bucky sarcastically.

"That's it! You're dead meat!" yells Chuck as he lunges at Bucky.

Tommy and Tammy grab Chuck and stop him from giving Bucky a steamroller.

"Guys, stop it! No one's a 'nerd' and we're not 'boring'!" says Mindy as she sets her drink down. "Haven't we learned our lesson about reaping what we sow? If we do bad things, then bad things are going to happen to us."

"*Whatever!* You sound like my teacher! I'll see you guys later! I'm going to find Frankie and Jimmy. They know how to have fun!" mutters Derek as he leaves the tree fort.

"Wait for me!" shouts Chuck as he gathers his food.

"Fine, go ahead and leave! Tammy, are you in or out?" asks Tommy with an attitude.

Tammy looks at Mindy, Patricia, Bucky and Tommy. They look back at her, hoping that she'll stay. She bites her lip, knowing that Bucky can banish her from his tree fort. Obviously, Derek and Chuck don't care. As long as Chuck has a stash of junk food like the one in his backpack, he'll be just fine. No matter where he is!

"I'm with them," replies Tammy sadly. "I'm sorry, guys, it's in my blood."

She grabs her things and follows Derek and Chuck to Frankie's house.

"*Fine!* The three of you will be begging us to take you back!" mutters Tommy, frustrated.

Frankie, Jimmy and Tosha are heading to Bucky's house, thinking about how they were the ones who ruined the Hummel County Parade and not the gang. Gloating is an understatement to describe the expressions painted on their faces. If their heads were any bigger from pride, they'd float away.

"Hey look! Here come, Derek, Chuck and Tammy!" says Jimmy.

"I wonder where they're going," says Frankie as he waves to Derek.

Derek notices Frankie waving and gets excited, seeing his new heroes. A strange sensation washes over Derek's body, chasing the friendship of their archrivals. He takes the lead and rushes across the street. Chuck and Tammy follow close behind; now the shoe is on the other foot.

DEREK'S BORED

"Frankie, where are you guys going?!" yells Derek as he lets a car pass. "Wait for us!"

"We were headed to Bucky's!" replies Frankie as he senses a weakness in Derek's voice. "Something happened to them ... look. Chuck can't keep it together," whispers Frankie, shaking his head.

"Where are you guys heading?!" shouts Jimmy as Frankie gives him a nudge.

"We were coming to see you guys!" replies Derek.

Derek, Chuck and Tammy let the last car pass and run across the street to meet their new best friends. Chuck has to stop, careful not to leave a fallen cupcake behind. He blows off the dirt and kisses it, thinking that it's good as new. Frankie and Jimmy can't believe that Derek and his friends would be so happy to see them. The boys can see Derek and Tammy's eager eyes staring at them, crying out for excitement. This is definitely a first and something they won't forget for a long time.

"You guys were great!" mutters Chuck, out of breath. "I can't believe how high the balloons sailed away!"

"Thanks. It was nothing," says Jimmy, smiling.

"No one stopped you?! What happened? We saw some of it, but Mayor Duncan made us leave," says Tammy as she tries to grab a candy bar out of Chuck's bag.

"Rrrrrrrrrrrr!" growls Chuck.

Tammy backs away. Frankie, Jimmy and Tosha take in the moment, looking at Derek and his friends as being weak. They puff out their chests, proud, expecting to be treated like royalty. Amazing how one event changed the attitudes of Frankie, Jimmy and the gang.

"I take it that you guys want to hang out with us ... is that why you're here?" asks Tosha as she nudges Frankie.

"What happened to you guys?" asks Frankie. "I'm sure that you got an earful from the Mayor. There must have been thirty of his men surrounding you guys!"

DEREK'S BORED

"'Mayor' Duncan thought that we had stuff to ruin the parade this year. Do you believe that he setup a sting operation to catch us?" asks Derek, shaking his head.

"How did they know when you were going to be there?" asks Jimmy.

"I don't know," replies Derek as he offers Frankie some of his snacks.

"All I know is that before we knew it, we were jumped by security," says Tammy, shaking her head.

"I know ... we saw the whole thing. Look, it's the police!" declares Frankie as he grabs Derek and pulls him into a bush. "Everyone hide!"

Tammy and the others duck into the bushes as well.

"What 'police?' Where?" asks Derek as he examines a scratch on his arm.

"You didn't see the police car that was driving up the street?" asks Jimmy, panicking.

"No. You guys are *running* from the cops?" asks Derek, feeling like he and his friends have just entered into a movie. "This is so cool!"

The kids hide and wait for the heat to pass. Thoughts of being brought home to their parents in the back of a police car race through their heads. The voices of their parents yelling at them send chills down their bodies. Now they have great motives to not get caught. The police car disappears and the kids slowly emerge from behind the bushes.

"What are you kids up to now?!" asks Old Man Jones.

"Ahhh!" scream Chuck and Frankie.

"*It's a ghost! Run!*" screams Jimmy as the kids take off running.

Frankie, Jimmy, Tosha, Chuck, Tammy and Derek, all run in different directions.

"You'd better run! Hey, you're the kids who papered my

house last week! I'll find you!" yells Old Man Jones, checking his heart and waving his fist at the kids.

Derek makes it down the street and turns back to see if Old Man Jones is chasing him. Unlikely, but Derek is taking no chances. As he turns around to head home, **something** flies by him very fast. Derek is bewildered by the flash of green light that disappears into thin air. The **something** resembled some kind of flying creature and left behind a mist that showers Derek and places him under a trance. Derek is overcome with a sense of déjà vu as he recalls the magic dust used by Tammy on Maccabus. Derek is overwhelmed with a tingling sensation as the world around him begins to spin. He stumbles to keep his balance and notices a drastic change in the temperature.

What was that? Could it have been an alien? **What's happening to me?** thinks Derek, as he shivers, falling to his knees.

He remains still and tries to figure out what just left him this wonderful present. Images of strange lights and foreign places flash before his eyes, creating a distorted film in his imagination. The tingling sensation and dizziness leave Derek's body as the sound of kids laughing echoes in his head. Derek shakes off the trance and notices David Skooner and a few of his friends walking across the street. Derek waves and acts as if nothing had happened as David shows him his new skateboard. As David and his crew take off running, Derek stands up and lets out a deep breath, disappointed.

"I can't believe Tommy and those guys want to be boring! No more fun for them. Oh well. Frankie and Jimmy have the police after them. Now that's action! I'm going to start hanging out with them from now on," says Derek to himself.

Derek continues his walk home, daydreaming about what he would've done to ruin the Hummel County Parade. Thoughts about the gang breaking up cross Derek's mind, but are soon erased by images of Chuck and Tammy reminding him of his sense of adven-

DEREK'S BORED

ture and need for action. *Derek has no idea what just happened with the flying creature, or that this event will lead him and his friends on their next adventure.*

CHAPTER THREE

ELECTRONIC

The cafeteria at Franklin Thomas School is filled with kids who seem to have had too much sugar during the morning hours. Tommy and the gang are sitting in their normal section, somewhat quiet and still trying to figure out their status with one another. Chuck, however, is pleading with the rest of the gang to share their lunches. Mindy, Bucky and Patricia cover their lunches and turn their chairs, protesting Chuck's walkout on Saturday. The wounds of division from their episode at Bucky's tree fort have been haunting the gang all morning. Teachers continue to keep a watchful eye on Tommy and his friends. Derek and Chuck notice Mr. Tuggle and Mrs. Grims murmuring about the gang. The boys crack a fake smile and wish that the teachers would disappear.

ELECTRONIC

Frankie and Jimmy are going from table to table, boasting about what they did on Saturday. They're rejoicing as several kids shower them with praise for their deeds against Mayor Duncan. Like typical kids, they can't keep their mouths shut and the story changes each time that it's told. As Frankie and Jimmy make their way around the cafeteria, their story about the Hummel County Parade gets better and crazier with each table visitation.

"Do you want to come over and play video games after school?" asks Derek as he takes a bite of his sandwich.

"Sure," mumbles Chuck with sloppy Joe stains on the sides of his mouth. "Tammy, are you going to eat that?"

"What about us?" asks Tommy as he sets down his fork. "Since when did we turn into *chopped liver?*"

"You guys are too boring for me. I need action!" replies Derek as he slaps Chuck five. "Oh, man, you got sloppy Joe on me!" mutters Derek as he wipes his hand. "This nice attitude of yours makes my skin crawl."

Mindy and Bucky frown at Derek's comment. Even though the kids fight like cats and dogs, the gang loves each other like brothers and sisters. This is the first time that there's been division among Tommy and his friends. The kids have been like seven peas in a pod; inseparable for years. The chemistry won't be the same if they split up.

"Oh yeah, well, you can't come to my tree fort anymore!" declares Bucky.

"That's okay! We didn't like that 'tree fort' *anyway!*" mutters Chuck with a mouthful of applesauce. "We have better places to go now!"

The war is on.

"Tammy, are you with us?" asks Derek, sneering at Tommy.

Tammy looks at the rest of the gang and then back at Derek. "I'm in. I'll see you guys after school," replies Tammy as she stands up. "I'm sorry, guys, but I agree with Derek. I need action, too," says Tammy as she heads to class.

"This isn't good. Tommy, do something!" insists Mindy as Derek and Chuck follow Tammy out the door.

"What do you want me to do? Everyone has free will. I can't change their minds. Besides, they'll be back. I feel it," says Tommy as he pushes his tray to the center of the table.

Tommy, Bucky, Patricia and Mindy continue to discuss Derek and the others' threat to form an alliance with Frankie and Jimmy. Tommy is confident that the boys aren't enough to keep Derek and Chuck happy. He reminds Mindy about the way that Frankie and Jimmy get on Tammy's nerves and make her skin crawl. The group is temporarily relieved by Tommy's words, but the spirit of resentment quickly pops up by the end of lunch.

Bucky and Derek are sitting in Mr. Levy's class, giving each other the silent treatment. As a matter of fact, they won't even look at each other. Bucky feels scorned that Derek, Chuck and Tammy would abandon their friendship over Frankie and Jimmy. He believes that Frankie, Jimmy and Tosha used no skill in their mischief at the parade on Saturday; it was pure luck!

"Okay, class, put your things away so that we can watch the movie," instructs Mr. Levy as he rises from his desk. "The sooner you finish, the sooner we watch the movie."

His students scramble to put their books into their desks and get ready for the movie. Mr. Levy brought in an animated film about a prince and a princess trapped in an evil castle. He's famous for bringing the coolest movies to school.

"Is everyone ready? … Good. Now remember, you'll have a writing assignment based on this movie … so pay attention!" explains Mr. Levy as he walks toward the TV.

He looks around the classroom and sees his students sitting up in anticipation of the movie to begin. The kids love it when he brings a movie to class. For some, it means naptime. For others, it's a break from Mr. Levy's boring lectures. As for Bucky and Derek, the darkness of the class will give them even more separation and a time to ponder their future relationship.

"There, now we're ready. Bart, would you please get the lights for me?" asks Mr. Levy, inserting the movie into the DVD player.

Bart, a lanky kid with curly hair, gets up and shuts off the lights. The students sink their heads onto their desks as the movie begins. Several kids' bulging eyes pierce through the darkness of the room, watching the movie intently.

Across the hall in Mrs. Peachtree's class, Chuck and Patricia are having words about what had happened at lunch. Students laugh at Chuck as he picks a piece of dried sloppy Joe from his shirt and eats it. Chuck gives Sam the fist, motioning for him to mind his own business. He thinks that Sam has some nerve laughing at him. Just yesterday, Sam was caught by his classmates picking his nose and eating it.

"I don't think that you guys are being nice," says Patricia, frowning.

"'Nice?' Derek is the one with the video games, not me," says Chuck as he sneaks a bite of a cookie. "All we want to do is have some fun, but you guys want to be are a bunch of *goody-two-shoes* and *boring!* How do you expect us to have fun if we can't tease each other or play practical jokes on people?"

"But we're supposed to be friends, *no matter what.* How can you throw away years of friendship over a stupid parade? We made a promise to change. Do you want Orin to come back?" asks Patricia as she clutches Peggy.

"We are friends, just not now. And as far as Orin goes, I'd like to see him try to come back! I would …," says Chuck as he sneaks a donut into his mouth.

ELECTRONIC

"*Chuck!* Are you eating again?!" asks Mrs. Peachtree, startling him.

"Ahh! Orin's here!" declares Chuck as he wrestles with his desk, trying to stand up.

The students laugh at Chuck.

"Everyone, settle down and get back to work!" scolds Mrs. Peachtree. "And Chuck ... no more eating!"

Patricia shakes her head at Chuck, disappointed with his attitude. Peggy taps Patricia on the shoulder to whisper something into her ear.

"Patricia, ask him about Tommy's cookout," whispers Peggy.

"Chuck, what about 'Tommy's cookout'?" asks Patricia, making sure that Mrs. Peachtree isn't looking. "Do you plan on coming and eating all that yummy food?"

Chuck chokes on his donut as a vision of Tommy's backyard flashes before his eyes. Tommy's cookout is coming up and Chuck knows the menu even before it starts. It's another one of the gang's favorite events of the year. Chuck wishes that they'd have it more often. They have eating contests ... of course, Chuck is always the winner ... and games and music. Tommy's family really knows how to throw a party! The kids get a kick out of Mr. Smart's ridiculous cooking outfits. Chuck also knows that Tommy's little cousins have a crush on him. They sit and watch him do his thing the entire cookout.

"What about it?" asks Chuck as he snaps out of his trance and wipes his mouth.

Patricia has him right where she wants him. She sees his eyes light up like headlights. Chuck is at her mercy, knowing that he wouldn't miss this event for the world.

"Well, if we're not your friends, then I guess you guys won't be coming to the cookout," replies Patricia, smiling out the side of her mouth.

ELECTRONIC

Chuck almost begins to cry at the thought of being excluded from this year's festivities.

"No, wait! I'm sure that we can work this out!" says Chuck frantically. "Please, not the 'cookout'!"

"Does this mean that you'll talk some sense into Derek this afternoon?" asks Patricia.

"Yes! Yes, I will!" replies Chuck, panting like a dog.

"Chuck!" scolds Mrs. Peachtree. "What are you doing now?!"

Chuck falls out of his desk, startled once again. A cookie that was in his hand shoots across the room.

"Yes, Ma' am," mutters Chuck as he tries to straighten himself out.

"Quit talking and finish your math problems!" warns Mrs. Peachtree.

"Yes, Ma' am," says Chuck, reaching under his desk as he pretends to start working.

Instead of pulling out some paper, he pulls out a large chocolate bar. With the coast clear, he inhales it. Chuck feels that he'll need the energy to confront Derek later that afternoon.

Back in Mr. Levy's class, Derek is falling asleep as he watches the movie. A combination of a full stomach, dark room and cool air conditioning, have presented the perfect sleeping environment for Derek. He knows that all environments are good sleeping environments, but this is perfect. Derek gently puts his head onto his desk and begins to dream.

His dream takes him on an adventure to find the princess that's trapped in the evil castle. The adventure starts off in a place named Gibeon; it's a virtual-reality city. This "City of Lights" looks as if it was designed by futuristic architects. The people there are friendly and always busy. Even during the day, the flashing, colorful lights make the city look alive and festive. There's more fun than a boy or girl could imagine in Gibeon; even the adults find themselves reliving their childhoods daily. Between the virtual-reality game centers, arcades, movie theaters, electric parade and spectacular fireworks show, there's something for everyone.

Derek finds himself walking through the heart of Gibeon in total amazement. He gazes at the lightbulbs and light fixtures around each home and store. All the buildings have odd shapes and appear to be moving. The multicolored properties and lights give Derek a feeling of being trapped in a giant rainbow.

"Wow, I wonder how this place looks at night!" says Derek as he marvels up at a tall building.

"*It looks beautiful,*" says a voice.

Derek turns around to see **something** fly away, very fast. It's the same flying creature that flew by him and showered him with mist after Old Man Jones scared him and his friends. This time, Derek catches a glimpse of its small green body, wings, and glowing light.

"Hey, wait! No, come back!" calls Derek.

Derek runs down the street chasing the flying creature. Whatever it is doesn't listen to Derek's request and vanishes in the distance. Once again, Derek finds himself becoming dizzy after being showered by the same strange mist. He shakes it off and continues down the street until he sees a boy sitting on the curb, eating an ice cream cone.

"Hi, there. My name is Derek. What's yours?" asks Derek, jolting one last time from the mist.

"Toby," replies the boy.

The manner in which Toby is eating the ice cream cone reminds Derek of Chuck. But his appearance reminds him of Tommy; similar big ears and straight hair. As a matter of fact, he could pass for Tommy's brother with no problem.

"Where am I?" asks Derek, looking toward the sky.

"You're in Gibeon, the City of Lights," replies Toby as he stands up.

ELECTRONIC

Derek gets excited as he notices video games in every store along the street.

"*Cool!* You guys play video games too?" asks Derek as his adrenaline begins to rush. Derek sneezes all over Toby's ice cream cone. "Sorry about that!" mutters Derek as he wipes his nose.

"Of course we play video games, but only at night," replies Toby as he places the rest of his ice cream cone in the trash. "What's wrong?"

Derek looks at Toby, confused by his response. He's never heard of video games only being played at night. The only time that Derek has heard of a restriction on playing video games was when Tommy got in trouble for breaking a window. Something doesn't seem right.

"'Only at night?' Why?" asks Derek, checking to see if the flying creature is still nearby.

"In Gibeon, we have to live by the rules of the city. Sometimes Mayor Messa bends the rules for his own children and special guests. Other than that, video games are only played at night. Besides, that's when the parade starts," replies Toby as he waves to one of his friends.

"'*Parade?*' I love 'parades'!" exclaims Derek excitedly.

Derek has a flashback of the recent Hummel County Parade, recalling who stole the show. Images of Frankie and his crew sneaking through the crowd appear before his eyes.

This year's 'parade' wasn't that great. Oh well, next year's will be different, thinks Derek.

"Do you like video games?" asks Toby. "You look like a gamer."

Toby catches Derek's full attention.

"I *love* to play 'video games!' By the looks of your city, I could live here forever!" replies Derek, spinning in circles, gawking at all the different types of games that are in the storefront windows.

"What's your favorite kind of video game?" asks Toby, shaking his head and chuckling at Derek's zeal for his city.

"I like racing games the best!" replies Derek. "What about you?"

At that moment, Toby's parents walk up with their pet dog. Their benevolent smiles overwhelm Derek. The mother is taller than the father, which brings a smirk to Derek's face. He's never seen a wife this much taller than her husband. Derek almost wonders if the altitude is different between the two.

"Hi, dear, is this your new friend?" asks Toby's mother.

"I guess so, Mom," replies Toby as he looks at Derek.

"Good. My name is Mrs. Robinson and this is Mr. Robinson," says Toby's mom, extending her hand out to Derek.

He reaches out to shake her hand. As Derek does, he's blinded by Toby's mother's smile and kindness. His parents almost seem surreal.

"It's nice to meet you Mr. and Mrs. Robinson. My name is Derek," says Derek as he reaches over to shake Mr. Robinson's hand.

"Stay and play," says a voice.

Derek looks around and sees the flying creature zipping by again. It went by so fast that Derek can't identify it. He does, however, sense that he's seen it before.

"Did you guys hear or see that?" asks Derek, looking toward the sky.

The Robinson's look at Derek as if he's crazy.

"'Hear or see' what?" asks Mr. Robinson as he looks at his wife and Toby. "Another one7 of these types, huh," he whispers.

Derek peers up at the buildings to make sure that the flying creature isn't watching him. He begins to feel foolish for dragging the Robinsons into his delusional vision. Or is it?

"I guess it was nothing," replies Derek, surrendering his theory.

"Would you like to stay for dinner?" asks Mrs. Robinson.

After discovering that Derek is asleep in class, Mr. Levy

sneaks up on him, motioning through the dark room for the other kids to back away. He has no idea that Derek's dream has taken him to a far off land. The class braces for Mr. Levy to strike a large bell that's placed next to Derek's head. Several kids chuckle and murmur, glad that it's not them who will be embarrassed by Mr. Levy. *"Ding, dong! Ding, dong! Ding, dong!"*

"Wake up, sleepy-head!" yells Mr. Levy as he strikes the bell.

"Ahhhh!" screams Derek as he jumps to his feet.

Derek examines himself as he tries to figure out where he's at. The students snicker at Derek for getting busted napping during the movie. He finally realizes that he's not sleeping in his room and becomes embarrassed. Bucky shakes his head, glad that Derek got in trouble.

"Sorry, Mr. Levy," says Derek as he wipes the drool from his mouth.

"That should teach you not to fall asleep in my class again. You wouldn't listen to my warnings, so I had to use this…. I'll be watching you," says Mr. Levy as he points at Derek, moving his fingers. *"Eh, eh!"* mutters Mr. Levy as he returns to his desk.

The students take their seats and continue watching the movie.

Derek takes his seat and feels something strange in his hand. Upon opening it, he discovers a small, **blue lightbulb**. It's not a typical lightbulb, either. It looks like one that he saw in *Gibeon*. His hand begins to tremble as visions of Gibeon appear in his mind. Derek's body is overcome with the same strange sensation that he experienced in his dream.

What the heck? thinks Derek, as he examines the blue lightbulb.

He quickly closes his hand. Derek checks to make sure that no one else sees him with the lightbulb. Derek would never hear the end of it if he told his classmates where he got it. His farfetched stories of Maccabus were enough. Now Gibeon?

ELECTRONIC

"Psst, Derek!" whispers Bucky as he decides to break the silent treatment, figuring that Derek had enough.

He startles Derek, almost to the point of tossing the light-bulb into the air.

"Ahhh!" yelps Derek, clasping the blue lightbulb. "What do you want?"

He quickly puts it into his pocket until he can figure out where it came from.

"What's wrong with you?" asks Bucky.

Derek starts one of his sneezing episodes from being nervous. There's no way to explain the lightbulb or his dream. Visions of Gibeon dance in his head, creating even more confusion for Derek. Mr. Levy turns around as Derek's sneezing episode gets out of control.

"Derek, why don't you go to the bathroom," suggests Mr. Levy.

"That's a good idea, Mr. Levy, I'll go right now," says Derek as he heads to the door. "*Ah-chew!*"

The Smarts are rushing to the dinner table, drawn by the aroma of Mrs. Smart's cooking. She has outdone herself again, with baked lasagna, homemade meatballs and a fresh garden salad. The steam rising from the hot and bubbling lasagna has Matt mesmerized. The bright red tomato sauce for the meatballs calls Tommy's name. Mr. Smart plays the parmesan song, shaking the cheese in the container, making sure that there's plenty for his lasagna. Mrs. Smart walks in with a fresh-baked apple pie that steals the attention away from the other food. Waiting in the freezer is vanilla ice cream; the perfect match for her apple pie.

"Okay, Ned, time for grace," says Mrs. Smart as she takes her seat.

The boys bow their heads and smile, waiting to hear how badly their father will flub the prayer this time. Mr. Smart clears his throat and bows his head. He peaks one last time to make sure that everyone has their eyes closed. Mr. Smart feels embarrassed enough that they have to hear his prayer, let alone see him struggle to find the words.

"Father, please keep us clean. I mean, please keep us safe. Thank you for the food, Amen," prays Mr. Smart.

Tommy and Matt dive into dinner.

"So, Tommy ... how was school today?" asks Mrs. Smart as she prepares a salad for her husband.

"Fine ... why?" asks Tommy as he blows on his lasagna.

"I don't know. Patricia's mom said that some of the kids at school were responsible for the disaster at the Hummel County Parade. I just wanted to make sure that you weren't a part of it," replies Mrs. Smart.

Mr. Smart coughs and tries not to choke on a meatball. Thoughts of his son wreaking havoc with his friends on Saturday have his blood boiling. Matt puts his food down, waiting to see if Tommy gets in trouble.

"*Excuse me?!*" mumbles Mr. Smart, putting his fork down and sipping on water.

"Dad, it wasn't me. I swear!" mutters Tommy as he swallows his lasagna.

"It had better not be!" says Mr. Smart as he resumes scarfing down his wife's cooking.

"It's a shame that some kids have to ruin a good time for others," says Mrs. Smart, shaking her head. "I hope they find the kids who did it."

The phone rings as Tommy is about to comment. He jumps up to answer it, knowing how angry his father will be for the rude interruption. Mr. Smart doesn't understand why kids call each other during dinnertime. Tommy makes sure to answer it promptly. Each ring reddens Mr. Smart's ears like a Tasmanian devil.

"No calls during dinner!" barks Mr. Smart with a mouthful of food.

ELECTRONIC

"Honey. What did I tell you about speaking with your mouth full?" asks Mrs. Smart as she grabs her husband's hand to slow him down.

Mr. Smart yields to his wife's request.

"I'll tell them to call back later!" shouts Tommy as he runs into the living-room.

Derek sits on his bed, fidgeting, and waits for Tommy to answer the phone. His escapade at school has left him traumatized. Derek stares at the blue lightbulb in his hand, still trying to figure out how it got there. He glances over toward his bedroom door, making sure that his parents don't come in.

"Come on, Tommy, answer the phone!" mutters Derek impatiently.

"Who's on the phone?" asks Mrs. Flue as she enters the bedroom unexpectedly.

Derek quickly closes his hand, startled.

"Mom! It's Tommy," replies Derek, hoping that his mother didn't see the lightbulb.

"Come into the living-room when you're finished. I want to show you something," says Mrs. Flue with a smile.

"Okay, Mom," says Derek, motioning for his mother to give him some privacy. "Tommy, it's me, Derek!" says Derek as his mother leaves the room. He inspects the lightbulb to make sure that nothing had happened to it. "We need to talk. Can you come over?"

Derek opens his hand, once again, to analyze the blue lightbulb while Tommy has him on hold. He holds it up to the light, trying to figure out if the lightbulb came from his classroom. Waking up abruptly and Mr. Levy's "hawk-eyes" didn't give Derek the opportunity to investigate the scene of the crime. Derek was still feeling the effects of the mist showered over him by the flying creature.

"Okay. Please hurry!" says Derek desperately as he hangs up the phone.

ELECTRONIC

Mindy is sitting down to another wonderful dinner with her grandparents. Mrs. Rose has prepared meatloaf with mashed potatoes and gravy. Hot, buttered corn on the cob garnishes each plate. Of course, there's a homemade dessert sitting on the table as well. Mindy smiles at her grandfather as she watches the steam rise from the fresh-baked rolls. The love between the Rose family is something that Mindy's friends envy.

"How was your day, sweetheart?" asks Mrs. Rose as she serves Mindy a plate of food.

"Someone's going to buy a car?" asks Mr. Rose as he puts in his false teeth so that he can eat.

Mindy and her grandmother chuckle at Mr. Rose's question. Mrs. Rose leans closer to her husband so that he can hear her speak. Mindy winks at her grandfather and smiles.

"No, dear, I asked Mindy how her day was," replies Mrs. Rose.

Mr. Rose gets embarrassed.

"Oh, sorry, sweetheart," says Mr. Rose as he grabs Mindy's hand.

Mrs. Rose motions for them to say grace.

"May I say grace, today, Grandma?" asks Mindy as she raises her head.

"Why of course you can, dear," replies Mrs. Rose, smiling.

"Heavenly Father, please let my friends get along and bless this food. Amen," prays Mindy.

As Mindy is about to dig into her plate of food, she notices that her grandfather has fallen asleep while praying. This is nothing new for Mr. Rose.

"Grandpa, wake up," says Mindy as she shakes her grandfather's arm.

Mr. Rose jumps up, forgetting where he's at.

"Someone say, *'bingo'?!*" asks Mr. Rose, looking for his marker.

ELECTRONIC

Mindy laughs hysterically while Mrs. Rose shakes her head at her husband's question.

Chuck is practically drowning in the spaghetti and meatballs that his mother made for him. Ms. Puddin uses a special recipe for the sauce that her sister-in-law from Italy gave to her. It's made from fresh tomatoes, fresh garlic and onions, sausage, ground beef, mushrooms and some secret ingredients that Ms. Puddin won't reveal to anyone. It's the kind of sauce that Chuck runs his finger across the side of his bowl and licks his finger. The garlic toast that's made with today's fresh bread is glistening with butter. Chuck can't remember when he's ever felt so hungry, since he ran out of snacks half-way through school.

"Chuck! Get your head out of the bowl," mutters Ms. Puddin as she reaches for a piece of garlic toast. "You know that's not the way I taught you to eat."

Chuck lifts his head from his large bowl and has pasta sauce all over his face. He looks like a raccoon that's been going through a trash can, looking for something to eat.

"Sorry, Mom," says Chuck as he wipes off his face. "You know how much I love your cooking. I couldn't help it."

"Mrs. Tilly called me today about the parade. Did you kids have anything to do with that?" asks Ms. Puddin as she puts down her fork.

"No, Mommy, we're innocent," replies Chuck as he spears a couple of meatballs with his fork.

"Good. Now finish up so that we can eat dessert," says Ms. Puddin.

Ms. Puddin finishes her last bite and heads to the kitchen. Chuck becomes excited, knowing that his mother will return with four trays of various desserts.

Derek is walking past the living-room, heading to the front

porch for his meeting with Tommy. He's desperately in need of serious advice and can't wait to tell Tommy about the blue lightbulb and his dream. Derek knows that Tommy will have good discernment and give him sound advice. Derek grasps the lightbulb, making sure that he doesn't lose it.

"Where are you going?" ask Mr. Flue as he steps out from the family-room.

"Ahhh! I'm not going anywhere, Dad. Why?" asks Derek as he begins to sweat.

Derek's parents look at each other, concerned.

"Derek, did you forget to come in here like I asked of you?" asks Mrs. Flue.

"Sorry, Mom, I forgot. I'm meeting Tommy outside. He wants to talk to me about something. I think it's concerning a girl that has a crush on him. What did you need to show me?" asks Derek as he heads into the living-room.

He notices a box that's beside his father's chair. Derek's eyes light up as watches his parents trying to hide the box. Now they're the ones who are acting weird. Maybe they went to Gibeon too.

"What's that by your chair, Dad?" asks Derek, straining his neck.

Mr. Flue pushes the box in front of him and his wife.

"Is that what I *think* it is?!" asks Derek as he begins to pant like a dog.

Derek bobs up and down, waiting to attack whatever is in the box. Mr. and Mrs. Flue smile at each other, knowing how happy Derek will be once he opens it. Mr. Flue takes his time as he turns the box around toward Derek; he loves teasing his son.

"Yes, it's … *surprise!*" replies Mrs. Flue as she pushes the box toward Derek.

"It's a Dokken Game Station!" screams Derek as he charges his gift.

ELECTRONIC

Derek appears to be in slow motion as he dances around his new video game set. He envisions his friends playing all their favorite games with him. Derek's dream and the blue lightbulb have changed his stony heart toward the gang. Mr. and Mrs. Flue embrace the moment as they witness their son's joy because of their surprise.

"Consider it an early birthday present," says Mr. Flue as he hugs his wife.

Derek runs over and hugs his mom and dad, one eye still on the Dokken Game Station. Not many kids in the neighborhood have this video game set; it's the top of the line. The graphics make the games seem so real, almost as if a kid is in the game itself. With the Flue's big screen TV and his new Dokken Game Station, Derek will no doubt be the envy of the gang.

"All the kids will want to play at my house from now on!" declares Derek as he begins to open the box. "You guys are the best!"

Mr. and Mrs. Flue stare at each other with their mouths open. The thought of entertaining all the kids in the neighborhood worries them. Mrs. Flue has images racing through her head of kids spilling their drinks on the floor. Mr. Flue is overwhelmed by the notion of kids jumping on his furniture, cheering for Derek as he plays his new game. What a nightmare for a parent, but a good time for a child. For a minute, Derek forgets about the blue lightbulb as he tries to read the manual to his new Dokken Game Station. His jubilant celebration is short-lived by the sound of the doorbell.

"That's Tommy! I've got to go! Thanks, Mom and Dad!" yells Derek as he rushes out the door.

Derek leaves behind the giant mess that he made opening his new gift. Mr. and Mrs. Flue embrace and smile upon the mess, appreciating the happiness that the gift has brought to their son. Little do they know that Derek has *discovered* something that no other kid in the world has ever seen. This blue lightbulb makes the

Dokken Game Station look like a game of rock-paper-scissors; no big deal. Mr. and Mrs. Flue are overcome by a sudden chill in the air, similar to the one that Derek felt when he was showered by the mist from the flying creature.

"Do you feel that?" asks Mrs. Flue as she picks up a piece of cardboard.

"Yeah. I'd better check the thermostat," says Mr. Flue as he carries the box toward Derek's room.

Tommy is standing on Derek's porch, ringing the doorbell. He looks at his watch and shakes his head, somewhat disappointed that he didn't go over to Bucky's instead. He still can't believe that he gave in to Derek's request to come over; especially after the way that Derek treated him and the others over the weekend. But Derek's crackling voice on the phone sparked Tommy's curiosity. He backs away as Derek opens the door.

"It's about time that you answered the door!" states Tommy, noticing Derek's facial expression. "Wait, where are we going?" asks Tommy as Derek shuffles him to the side of the porch. "What's wrong with you, Derek?" he asks, sensing that something's weighing heavy on Derek's mind.

Derek looks around to make sure that no one else is looking or that no one can hear the two of them. If he had to explain to someone how the lightbulb mysteriously appeared in his hand, Derek wouldn't know where to begin. Tommy looks around as well, totally confused.

"Promise me that you won't tell anyone!" mutters Derek nervously.

"I 'promise.' What is it?!" asks Tommy, with great curiosity.

Derek slowly opens his hand and shows Tommy the blue lightbulb. He acts as if he had found a pot of gold or a hidden treasure. Tommy, on the other hand, isn't the least bit impressed with Derek's surprise.

ELECTRONIC

"*That's it!* You had me rush all the way over here for a stupid lightbulb! What do you want me to do with that? I'll tell you what, maybe you can work part-time at the circus and hold it up for everyone to see!" teases Tommy as he heads off the porch.

"No, wait! You don't understand!" exclaims Derek, frazzled.

"You're right, I 'don't understand.' I'm leaving. I passed on a wrestling challenge from Matt for this?" asks Tommy, disappointed. "I'm leaving!" mutters Tommy as he tries to break Derek's grip on his arm.

"Wait, Tommy, let me explain! This lightbulb ended up in my hand after I had a dream about being in Gibeon. It happened this morning in Mr. Levy's class, during his movie ...," explains Derek.

Tommy looks at Derek like he has three heads. He's never heard of a city named Gibeon in school before.

"'Gibeon?' What's 'Gibeon'?" asks Tommy, somewhat intrigued.

"It's the City of Lights that has lots of video games, movies and cartoons. They have virtual-reality game centers and giant arcades ... oh yeah, they also have an electric parade!" replies Derek excitedly.

Now Tommy looks at Derek like he has twelve heads. He knows that there's no such place like this on the planet. If there was, every kid in the country would bug their parents to move there.

"Yeah, right! Do you have another bad fever or something?" asks Tommy as he checks Derek's forehead.

Derek pushes Tommy's hand away as he teases him.

"No, I'm serious!" replies Derek, frustrated.

"Look, Derek, there's no such place as Gibeon and I have to go. It's getting late. I'll see you at school tomorrow. Who knows, maybe I'll see you in Gibeon," says Tommy, laughing.

Tommy leaves his friend behind, confused and rejected.

ELECTRONIC

Derek takes a seat on a chair and gazes at the sunset, watching the day turn into night. He holds the lightbulb up and tries to figure out its meaning. As darkness begins to fall on Hummel County, the blue lightbulb begins to glow. The lightbulb appears to be breathing in Derek's hand; the glowing light fades in and out. Derek's eyes grow as the blue light dilates his pupils.

"Oh, boy!" mutters Derek as he checks to make sure that no one else can see this supernatural manifestation. "How am I going…?"

"*Derek!* Come in here and help your father assemble this video game station!" yells Mrs. Flue from inside the house.

The lightbulb stops glowing upon hearing Mrs. Flue's voice. Derek quickly puts it into his pocket, wondering what just happened. Images of Gibeon flash across his mind.

"Yes, Mom, coming!" mutters Derek as he shakes his head.

As Derek grabs the doorknob to head into the house, he's distracted by a flash of light zipping by the front yard. It reminds him of the flying creature that keeps haunting him, both here and in his dream about Gibeon. This time, the flying creature is luminous and makes a strange humming noise.

"Come back!" shouts Derek as he watches the flying creature light up the trees and disappear into the neighborhood.

Derek stops and shakes off the dizzy spell left by the flying creature. In his head, he hears a voice say, "*Stay and play.*" It's the same voice that he heard in his dream about Gibeon. Now Derek is totally freaked-out and rushes into the house to help his father before something else bizarre happens.

Bucky has just finished brushing his teeth and is now getting ready for bed. As usual, he looks toward the bottom of his bed, making sure that nothing's there. Bucky, of course, has every light on in his room as he does this. Flashes of Maccabus still haunt him. After checking his bed and realizing nothing is waiting for him, he looks out the window at his tree fort.

ELECTRONIC

"I hope that Derek, Chuck and Tammy change their minds. Story Time isn't going to be the same without them," says Bucky as he closes his window.

"Goodnight, Bucky!" yells Mr. Hogwash from down the hall.

"Goodnight, Dad!" yells Bucky.

He walks over to the lights, shuts them off and sprints toward his bed. Bucky screams as he sails through the air, trying to avoid the so-called monsters that live under his bed. This is a ritual that he and his friends go through every night as they go to bed. Bucky knows better than to give whatever is living under his bed a chance to grab his feet. Having landed safely on top of his bed, Bucky quickly tucks his blankets around his feet, tightly, and makes sure that they don't hang over the edge of his bed. With a few quick prayers and some heavy breathing, Bucky finally falls asleep.

Tammy finishes playing a video game while her older brother Ralph observes her. Ralph, now attending college, came over for dinner and brought his hand-held video game called Dragons & Swords. He wasn't as lucky as Derek to get the Dokken Game Station to play the game. The object of Dragons & Swords is to slay as many dragons as a player can by using the different types of swords that are hidden in the castle and the various fighting arenas. This is the most popular game among the kids at school.

"I'm going to win!" screams Tammy, kicking Ralph by accident. "Sorry, bro!"

Ralph shakes his head watching Tammy become overzealous over the game. He knows that she's taking this friendly competition too seriously. Tammy has always been that way and Ralph can't do anything but smile at his younger sister.

"All right, sis, you win. I have to go," says Ralph as he reaches for his game.

Tammy jumps up and does a victory dance around the living-room. Sarah and Susan, Tammy's twin sisters, join their older sister in the dance. They don't fully understand the madness of Tammy's celebration, but continue to act silly and scream at the top of their lungs. The Tutu house becomes a sports arena when there are games to be played; every man for himself.

"I am the champion! I am the champion!" declares Tammy, dancing with her arms high in the air.

She even makes the I-beat-you-face at her brother.

"Whatever. I'll see you girls later," says Ralph as he shakes his head.

Mr. and Mrs. Tutu smile as they watch their daughter's kookiness. Ralph kisses his parents goodbye and quietly leaves.

"Is she ever going to change?" asks Ralph as he opens the door. "Never mind. I'll see you next week."

Tammy finishes her victory dance and heads upstairs for her nightly pushups.

"Goodnight, Mom and Dad!" shouts Tammy as she rushes up the stairs.

Back at Derek's house, Derek is staring at the blue lightbulb, inanimate on top of his bed. He walks around the bed, ready to dash out of his room should something strange happen. A million thoughts race through his mind about its origin. He tries to recall all the video games that he'd ever played. With no revelation about the mysterious lightbub, Derek checks the bottom of his bed, making sure that there's nothing under there waiting to attack him.

"Come on, do something," pleads Derek as he inches closer toward his bed.

He sees that nothing's happening and with the lights on, kneels before his bed to get a better look. Derek flicks the lightbulb and flinches back, as if it's hot. Suddenly, it happens; the blue lightbulb comes to life. A fluorescent blue light dances around his room, almost like a tornado of color. The magical, mystical light puts Derek into a trance as he follows the different beams of light around his bedroom. This is definitely the weirdest thing that he's ever seen in his life.

"W-o-w!" mutters Derek, dazed. *I hope Mom and Dad don't come in!* thinks Derek.

"*Stay and play!*" says a voice.

Derek looks toward his window and sees the flying creature bolting from his windowsill; the same flying creature that's been haunting him since Old Man Jones'. He looks back at the lighbulb and recalls his close encounters with the unknown creature in Gibeon and on the front porch. Derek's trance ends as the illuminating blue lightbulb quits glowing. His attention is drawn to his window once again. The flying creature is back and hovering in one position, smiling at Derek.

"It's a giant firefly! No, it's a fairy!" states Derek, covering his mouth.

Derek checks to make sure that his parents didn't hear him.

The flying creature stares at Derek, knowing that he's afraid to get any closer. Derek can't believe his eyes, staring in awe at this creature that resembles a futuristic angel, about a foot tall. Her green body, pointy nose and ears, and big hair captivate Derek as he tries to figure out what she is. Derek looks back at the blue lightbulb; it remains lifeless on his bed.

"Hey!" screams Derek as the blue lightbulb *explodes* with color, lighting up the room.

Derek glances back toward his bedroom window. Without hesitation, he dashes to the window with an adrenaline rush strong enough to fight an army. Derek may have discovered one of the oldest legends of Hummel County.

Man, where did you go? thinks Derek, as he canvasses the yard.

The flying creature is nowhere to be found.

Derek heads back toward his bed, walking through the light show created by the blue lightbulb. It's as if Derek has been transported back into the sixties and walked into a hippie's room. Derek waves his hands in the kaleidoscope-type light. He stops dead in his tracks as he hears a knock on his bedroom door. The light show ceases.

"Who is it?!" asks Derek with eyes like saucers.

"It's your Mother!" replies Mrs. Flue from outside the door. "You forgot something downstairs."

They're not ready for this! I'm not ready for this! thinks Derek, as he looks for a safe place to hide the lightbulb.

"I'm coming, Mom!" says Derek, scrambling around his room.

Derek grabs the lightbulb from his bed and stares at it, totally confused. First, it was the blue lightbulb ... then the unknown flying creature ... and now, he knows what the flying creature looks like and that she controls the blue lightbulb. Derek slides the lightbulb into his pocket and opens the door for his mother.

"What's all the commotion about?" asks Mrs. Flue, snooping.

"Nothing, Mom, why?" asks Derek nervously.

Mrs. Flue looks into Derek's eyes with the I-know-you-are-up-to-something look.

"Don't try to *fool* me! I can sense trouble a mile away," replies Mrs. Flue.

"I swear! Nothing!" mutters Derek as he heads toward his desk, pretending to do some homework.

"It had better be nothing. Here are your instructions for Dragons & Swords," says Mrs. Flue, checking over his shoulder one last time.

"Thanks, Mom. Goodnight," says Derek as he examines the instruction manual.

"Goodnight, dear," says Mrs. Flue.

Mrs. Flue kisses Derek goodnight and heads back to the kitchen for cleanup.

ELECTRONIC

Derek does his ritual of making sure that there's nothing under his bed as he prepares to call it a night; he's exhausted. With no creatures in sight, Derek climbs into bed and begins to read the instructions for his new game.

"This is cool," says Derek as he flips through the pages.

He checks the window, again, to see if the flying creature has returned. Nothing. Derek continues reading about Dragons & Swords and falls into a deep sleep. While sleeping, Derek dreams about his new video game. In his dream, Derek finds himself entering a giant fighting arena through a long, dark tunnel. The crowd goes crazy as Derek sees a small dragon entering the fighting area from the opposite side of the arena. The dragon lets out a giant screech and blows fire high into the sky, trying to break its chains. Derek is gripped with fear, not knowing how he's going to fight this wicked beast. Before exiting the tunnel, the flying creature appears, hovering in front of Derek and smiling.

"Hey, how did you get into the game?!" asks Derek, amazed.

"I'm everywhere," replies the flying creature with an Irish accent.

"You can talk?! *Cool!* What's your name?" asks Derek as he glances over toward the dragon.

"My 'name' is Matilda," replies the flying creature.

"Cool, my name is …," says Derek.

"I know … your name is Derek," says Matilda as she backs away from the tunnel.

She dances in the air like a ballerina.

As Matilda glides through the air, she creates a *massive* light show that puts the blue lightbulb to shame. Derek steps out of the tunnel and is caught up in Matilda's exposition of light and power. The crowd is mesmerized by Matilda's angelic song that's belting out of her tiny mouth. Derek is paralyzed in a state of euphoria as Matilda displays her musical talent, as well as her multicolored show of lights. Matilda flies through the fighting arena and sprays the entire crowd with a blue mist. Now Derek knows where the mist came from.

"How did you know my name?" asks Derek as Matilda finishes her song.

"I know many things about you," replies Matilda, smiling.

Derek is shocked by her statement, but fear washes that feeling away as he notices that the match is about to begin. He feels an instant connection with Matilda and doesn't want his new friend to get hurt by the raging dragon. Silly Derek; Matilda has the power to slay many dragons.

"You'd better watch out ... the other dragons are about to come out!" warns Derek as he grabs a mystical sword from a table. "This one should do!" mutters Derek as he wields the sword, similar to a medieval warrior.

"Be watchful for the huge red dragon! It will have seven heads and ten horns," warns Matilda.

Before Derek has a chance to comment, Matilda disappears. He jumps back, startled by Matilda's sudden disappearance. Derek has only seen this type of magic on television. Little does he know where this so-called magic comes from. Her *source of power* could destroy a legion of huge red dragons.

"Where did you go, Matilda? Come back!" demands Derek as he focuses his attention toward a side tunnel of the fighting arena. "Whoa!"

The huge red dragon with seven heads and ten horns bursts through the massive door that covers the tunnel. The spectators of the fight go ballistic and focus their attention on poor Derek as he trembles, wielding his sword.

"*Kill him!*" screams one boy.

"Did you think that was cool?" asks Matilda as she appears behind Derek.

"Ah! Yeah, but the dragon! I can't fight this alone!" shouts

ELECTRONIC

Derek over the chanting crowd. "Now I know that I can't fight this alone! Look at that huge fighter!"

Several warriors enter the arena.

"Be not afraid, Derek. My source of power will never abandon or forsake you. Take refuge through me and he shall be your strength," says Matilda. "Do you want to see something *glorious?*"

Matilda makes a cloud, brighter than the sun, appear over the red dragon. The red dragon, blinded by the cloud, lets out a giant screech.

"Wow!" mutters Derek as he looks away from the cloud.

His eyes grow wide, awestruck by Matilda's power. Matilda is by far the coolest thing that he's ever seen or known. She's more fascinating than Orin or Omit from Tommy's first trip to Maccabus.

"What do you mean by 'glorious'?" asks Derek as the red dragon retreats back into the tunnel.

"Bring your friends over to your bed … and I'll meet you on the *other side.* You will return to Gibeon through the nether world under your bed. There, you and your friends may play video games until your hearts' content. I'm sure that the girls will enjoy the electric parade," replies Matilda, serenading Derek with a hymn that silences the crowd.

Derek closes his eyes and covers his face as the fighting arena is overshadowed by a bright, blue light. A magnificent spectrum of color shoots out of Matilda's body, giving her the appearance of a supernatural strobe light. This display of light and color blinds the crowd as well. Matilda's angelic melody woos the spectators to sleep and puts Derek into a trance.

As Derek removes his hands from his face and opens his eyes, he finds himself in his bedroom, awakened by the blue lightbulb. The light in his bedroom is exactly the same as the one Matilda created in his dream. Once again, the mystical blue light dances around his room.

"Oh, man, what a dream!" mutters Derek as he rubs his eyes.

ELECTRONIC

He looks into the tornado of light coming from the lightbulb and sees images of Gibeon. Derek watches Toby and several children riding their bikes and waving at him. He can even hear the kids talking and laughing. Derek then sees several kids playing video games in an enormous game center. Finally, a giant firework explodes over the city of Gibeon in front of Derek's eyes.

"No, wait!" says Derek as the light disappears.

Derek gets out of bed, exhausted, and walks over to the light switch. His dream has worn him out. Derek turns off the light and dashes toward his bed, ready to sleep for a month. He has no idea what he uncovered by falling asleep in Mr. Levy's class.

The gang is standing in front of Franklin Thomas School, huddled around Derek, waiting for him to explain his big emergency. Derek paces back and forth, nervously, trying to formulate a plan how to tell his friends about Matilda. Without proof, he knows that they'll tease him without measure. Derek senses that his friends are growing impatient and stops his pacing.

"This had better be good, Derek! I'm missing the bake sale!" mutters Chuck, checking to make sure that he has enough food for the day.

"Yeah, Derek, I had to wake up early to be here!" complains Tammy as she peeks over at Chuck's bag. "Sorry, dude!"

"Look, guys, I had a dream about Gibeon ...," says Derek.

"Not that Gilbert story, again!" mutters Tommy as he throws up his hands.

"It's Gibeon! The place I went to is called *Gibeon!*" exclaims Derek.

The gang looks at Derek like he's a madman. Tommy shakes his head, disappointed. He can't believe that Derek would bring up that story again and tell the others.

"'Gibeon?' What's 'Gibeon'?" asks Tammy, envisioning what the place might look like.

ELECTRONIC

"It's the City of Lights that has virtual-reality game centers, arcades and an electric parade …," replies Derek convincingly.

"Where's this 'Gibeon' located?" asks Bucky, joining the conversation. "My teacher never mentioned 'Gibeon'."

"It's under my bed," replies Derek, nodding his head.

He checks to make sure that no one's coming their way.

The kids draw back from Derek, recalling their last adventure under Tommy's bed. Chuck stops eating his donut and relives his nightmare with Tuga and his people. The tribal drums beat in his head. Tommy realizes that Derek is serious and that this isn't a joke.

"No way! We're not going back under!" declares Tommy as chills travel down his spine.

"But Matilda promised me that we'd have fun!" states Derek.

"'Matilda?!' Who's 'Matilda'?!" asks Chuck with a mouthful of cookies.

"Matilda is the flying creature who's been following me around for the past couple of days. She looks like a cross between a giant fairy and a firefly. Matilda brought me into the world of Dragons & Swords," replies Derek.

"Zip it!" mutters Tommy, motioning for Derek to close his lips.

Derek's conversation is overwhelming. Mindy stands away from her friends, trying to discern what Derek is talking about. Patricia discusses with Peggy her input about Derek's dream. One thing is for sure … the gang thinks that Derek has lost it. No one has ever met a talking fairy/firefly. There are plenty of giant fireflies that come out of the woods at night, but none this big and none of them talk. And a giant fairy/firefly named Matilda? … This one should go down in the record books as the craziest story yet. Mindy walks up to Derek and feels his forehead.

ELECTRONIC

"Are you sick again?" asks Mindy.

"No, I'm not 'sick'!" replies Derek as he sneezes.

"What *exactly* did 'Matilda' say?" asks Tommy as he wipes Derek's snot from his shirt. "Next time, cover your nose and your mouth when you sneeze!"

"Matilda said that we could meet her in Gibeon and play all the video games we want. She also said that we could watch the electric parade before we go home," replies Derek.

Derek sparks Tammy and Chuck's interest at the thought of playing video games. Patricia looks at Peggy, interested in the electric parade.

"I bet there are lots of lights," says Patricia as she envisions a walking Christmas tree.

Bucky shakes his head, undecided.

"Guys, I don't know if this is a good idea. Remember what happened on Maccabus?" asks Bucky. "Did we forget about Orin's dungeon?"

As the kids withdraw from Bucky's question, Matilda flies by the gang, sending everyone to the floor but Derek. Derek watches in awe as Matilda displays her dispensation of power and love. She creates a magnificent light show for them in broad daylight. Students pass by Tommy and his friends, but don't see Matilda. It's a visitation only for the gang. The students stare curiously at Tommy and the others, watching them slouch down to the ground, hiding from an imaginary object.

"Look at those idiots!" says a boy, pointing.

"Matilda!" screams Derek as he lifts his fist toward the group of boys.

Matilda flies back and lands on Derek's shoulder. Derek smiles at her and shakes his head at his friends. Tommy and the others are amazed, watching Matilda's green body illuminate in the morning sun. Her smile mesmerizes the gang and eases their curiosity.

ELECTRONIC

"Derek's not crazy and this is no Maccabus," says Matilda. "Gibeon is pure fun."

"I've never heard such beautiful music. Where's it coming from?" asks Mindy as she humbles herself before Matilda.

"She talks!" states Chuck, opening his mouth as if he's going to catch a fly.

"That's right, and I do much more than sing and talk. But you'll have to go to Derek's Friday night to find out what else I can do for you," says Matilda as she sprays a mist over the gang with her mini-staff.

Derek and his friends become *transfigured* by Matilda's mist and find themselves caught up in Matilda's musical light show. The gang spins around and around, almost as if they're in a tornado. Images of strange animals and children playing on a mountainside appear in the light. A giant Rusk, similar to a ram, bleats out aggressively toward the gang. Derek and his friends then see Toby and a friend, holding up a welcoming sign and waving cheerfully. The gang shakes their heads as they watch a preview of Gibeon in the tornado of light. Matilda ends the music and Derek and his friends find themselves in Gibeon.

The gang is standing atop a large dam, gazing at the iridescent blue sky that's filled with puffy, white clouds. The kids can almost touch the clouds as they pass before their eyes. The air has a distinct smell to it; it's pure and filled with the scent of fresh flowers. A vast mountain range backdrops the city of Gibeon, giving it a view only seen in Heaven. Derek and his friends gawk at the lively city in the middle of paradise.

"Holy mackerel! Where are we?!" asks Chuck, still frozen and clenching a candy bar in his hand. "What happened to Franklin Thomas School?"

"How do we get down there?!" asks Bucky as he takes a whiff of the cleanest air in the world.

"Did you see that?! Was that a bird?!" asks Tammy, fidgeting with her wrestling mask.

"No, that was a friend of mine. You'll meet him when you come back to Gibeon. You guys do want to come back, don't you?" asks Matilda, smiling.

"This place is the *greatest!* I can feel it. Can we stay?" asks Mindy as she notices some strange animals on the mountainside. "Is that a bear?"

"No, it's a Hoader. And no, you can't 'stay.' There's something that Derek left behind that I need," replies Matilda.

"*What?!* I didn't do anything! What do you need from me, Matilda?" asks Derek as he shoves Chuck.

"I need you to bring the blue lightbulb," replies Matilda.

"What's up with this 'blue lightbulb'?" asks Tommy. "Why does...?"

Matilda ascends into a small cloud and spins around.

Tommy and his friends back away as Matilda puts on a spectacular light show; it's filled with pink and gold lights. Her celestial song and soothing music put Tommy and his friends to sleep. Matilda smiles upon her special guests and flies off as she finishes her ballad. She leaves behind a golden mist that showers the gang. Suddenly, the music stops and the sound of kids' laughing replaces it.

As Tommy and his friends open their eyes, they find themselves huddled around a tree in front of Franklin Thomas School. The gang remains dazed and speechless, still under Matilda's power. There's a large group of students laughing at them, trying to figure out why they're so scared. Derek looks around for Matilda, but she's nowhere to be found. Chuck realizes that two girls are laughing at him because his zipper is down.

"What just happened?!" asks Tommy as he looks for Matilda in the tree.

ELECTRONIC

"All right, kids, break it up!" scolds Principal Barnes. "Mr. Smart and Mr. Flue ... get your friends to class, *now!*"

The students who were laughing rush to their classes.

"Yes, Mr. Barnes," say Tommy and Derek in unison.

"All right, guys, we'll talk about this at lunch," says Tommy, grabbing his backpack off the ground.

The gang shakes off their rapture and disperses.

Tommy and his friends are left with a sense of adventure from Matilda's brief presence and their quick journey to Gibeon. Snapshots of Gibeon begin to preoccupy the kids' imaginations as they head to class. Some envision meeting the kids of Gibeon while others envision nature trails and giant waterfalls.

"See, I told you that Matilda was real!" says Derek with a giant smile.

"I'm sorry that I doubted you, brother. We need to make a major decision about Gibeon. Do you think that they'll have tree forts in Gibeon?" asks Bucky.

"'Tree forts?' You already have a 'tree fort'. We're going there to play video games and test our skills in their virtual-reality game centers," replies Derek as a vision is given to him by Matilda.

"*What's wrong?!*" asks Bucky, grabbing Derek's arm.

"It's Matilda. She needs our help when we get there. She'll tell me what's wrong at lunch," replies Derek as he snaps out of his trance and continues walking. "I'll be okay. What are you looking at, chump?!" mutters Derek as he shakes his fist at Grover.

Grover makes a face at Derek and takes off running.

"Hey, wait for me! Take it easy, Derek!" yells Bucky, running.

Derek and his friends are standing outside the cafeteria, waiting to start their special meeting. They know that the teachers inside the cafeteria won't give them the privacy that they need. The gang is still trying to shake off their early morning trip to Gibeon.

ELECTRONIC

Many of the kids couldn't pay attention in class, still feeling the effects of Matilda's mist. Her angelic compositions continue to ring in the kids' heads.

Tammy got in trouble for trying to emulate one of Matilda's songs. Patricia and Chuck kept hallucinating, thinking that Mrs. Peachtree was Matilda. Tommy failed to complete his assignment, still amazed that his friends passed through the nether world without venturing under his bed. The gang knows that this trip will be one for the ages. They'll reach a whole new level of stardom upon returning from Gibeon; *if they return*.

Tommy steps in front of his friends as the last students enter the cafeteria. He notices that his friends look different. There's an aura of peace and light that surrounds each one of them. His friends stare back at Tommy, thinking the same thing.

"Look at you, Tommy! There's a light coming off you," says Tammy as she reaches to touch it. "This is so cool!"

"What are you talking about? It's you that has the light!" says Tommy, swiping his hand over Tammy's head.

Tammy snaps out of her trance as she watches the last trail of light from Tommy's hand disappear.

"Hey, sucker! Don't make me!" mutters Tammy as she pulls away from Tommy. "I'll put you in a headlock before you can say, 'uncle'!"

"Guys, stop it! What about Gibeon?!" asks Derek as he steps next to Tommy.

The gang is overwhelmed with a tingling sensation. It's as if Matilda heard Derek say, "Gibeon," and dowsed them with her mist again. Something's very strange. Derek and his friends somehow have a connection with Gibeon that's eternal. How could this be? They were only in Gibeon for such a short time.

"Do you guys feel what I'm feeling?" asks Chuck as chills travel down his body.

"Do you feel cold, too?" asks Mindy, wiggling her arms.

ELECTRONIC

The gang backs away as Derek bends down on one knee.

"*Derek!* What's wrong?!" asks Tommy as he checks to make sure no one else is coming their way.

"It's Matilda! Her friend that she was going to introduce can't meet us on Friday. Now she wants us to be the *Grand Marshals* for the electric parade!" replies Derek. "And she wants me to be the *Master of Ceremonies!*"

He snaps out of his trance and stands to his feet.

"'Grand Marshals?' Are you serious?! Do you know how cool that will be?!" asks Tammy as she pumps her arm in the air.

"Wow! 'Grand Marshals' ... I can see it now!" states Chuck as he envisions the gang on a float, tossing candy and toys to all the kids.

"Did you hear that, Peggy?" asks Patricia, holding Peggy close to her heart. "We get to be 'Grand Marshals' in a parade!"

"What are you doing, Patricia? This is no time to be talking to Peggy. We have to plan for the parade!" says Derek as he shoves Chuck.

Chuck dives for the cupcake that was knocked out of his hand by Derek.

"Chuck! What's wrong with you?! ... All right, guys, I take it we're going to Gibeon," says Tommy with a smile from ear to ear.

He has his own thoughts about being the Grand Marshals.

"What about the *vote?* You guys know that we vote on everything we do," says Mindy, stepping to the front.

"Mindy is right ... we need to 'vote.' How many of us are in favor of going to Derek's Friday night to go to Gibeon?" asks Tommy, raising his hand.

Chuck, Derek, Tammy and Patricia raise their hands without hesitation. Mindy and Bucky leave their hands down. Even though they were affected by Matilda and have the opportunity of a lifetime, they still have a sense of fear from their last adventure.

ELECTRONIC

"Well, I guess that settles it … five to two. We go to Gibeon!" declares Tommy cheerfully.

Mindy and Bucky look at each other, disappointed. They know the rules of engagement to be part of the gang; majority rule wins. Amazing how soon kids forget about trouble or danger when tempted by excitement and fun. Matilda's plan to bring the kids to Gibeon is working. There's no way any kid could pass on the opportunity to be the Grand Marshal of a parade; especially an electric parade. Matilda's pursuit of Derek has paid off and her powerful mist has worked its charm.

"All right, guys, we meet at my house on Friday at seven o'clock," says Derek as he takes in a deep breath.

Chuck breaks out the cookies, celebrating their next adventure. Hands to mouth he stuffs his face, anticipating his trip to Gibeon. Tammy adjusts her wrestling mask and waves her hands in the air, pretending to lead a float. Patricia dances with Peggy while Bucky pretends to be tossing beads to the kids of Gibeon. His friends' excitement has taken away his anxiety. Derek watches like a proud father as his friends embrace the trip.

"I'm ready!" exclaims Tammy. "The kids of Gibeon are going to love us!"

Mindy shakes her head, still feeling as if they're making a big mistake. Her friends' pleading eyes get the best of her.

"What? … I'll go, I'll go!" says Mindy, surrendering to her friends' peer pressure. "Whoopee … are you happy?!" mutters Mindy sarcastically.

Chuck and Derek hug their friend, excited. Mindy brushes off Chuck's chocolate cookie crumbs from her shirt and smiles out the side of her mouth. The kids' celebration is cut short by an approaching Principal Barnes.

"I'll see you guys inside!" says Tammy as she races into the cafeteria.

"Matilda, here we come!" declares Derek as he heads to the restroom.

ELECTRONIC

The rest of the gang enters the cafeteria, recalling their visitation to Gibeon atop the large dam. Tommy, Mindy, Patricia, Chuck and Bucky begin fantasizing about their return to the City of Lights. Their appetites have been suppressed by anxiety and visions from Matilda.

Derek is on his front porch pondering which story to tell his parents. Having told his friends it was okay to have a sleepover without permission is a big "NO NO" in the Flue household. Derek remembers how upset his parents became when Tonia did it with three of her friends; he has six. Matilda's voice saying, "Friday night," plays over and over again in his head as he paces the porch. That voice seems to drown out his father's yelling that echoes in the back of his head saying, "Don't even think about it!"

I know ... I'll ask my parents to celebrate my birthday party early. They gave me my present early, so why can't we have the party early? thinks Derek.

He musters up some courage and heads into the house, seeking his mother. Derek knows that he'll have better luck with her than his father. Something about a child with puppy-dog eyes, pleading for a favor, melts the heart of any mother. As Derek passes the living-room, he notices his Dokken Game Station sitting in front of the TV. He envisions all the kids in the neighborhood becoming jealous once they see it.

"It will be a party to break in my new gift," says Derek proudly.

"Hi, dear. How was school today?" asks Mrs. Flue as she walks out from the kitchen, drying her hands.

"Awesome! Say, Mom ... can my friends come over this Friday for a sleepover?" asks Derek with a twinkle in his eyes. "*Please* ... pretty please!"

"You want them to come over 'this Friday?' I'll have to talk to your father first before I say yes," replies Mrs. Flue, scratching her head. "Oh, no, don't start that!"

Derek cuddles up to his mother, trying to butter her up. She's always been a sucker when Derek gets this way; especially around his birthday. Her heart begins to soften as she looks into her son's gleaming eyes.

"Please, Mom. It can be part of my early birthday present," begs Derek as he points to the Dokken Game Station. "I'll clean your car!"

Mrs. Flue looks at the video game set, then Derek, realizing how cute her son looks. She remembers last year's party when Chuck's head got stuck in the container of ice cream. The visual causes her to chuckle softly.

"All right, you can have the 'sleepover.' But make sure that you behave until then … and talk to your father about helping him in the yard. Remember, he wants yard of the month," says Mrs. Flue as she smiles at her son.

"You're the best, Mom!" proclaims Derek as he embraces his mother and jumps up and down with excitement. "I'm gonna have a *p-a-r-t-y!*"

Derek celebrates the fact that his friends are coming over to travel to Gibeon from under his bed; his mother thinks otherwise. Now Derek will really have something to brag about with his friends and classmates. No longer will Tommy be looked upon as the cool kid with the nether world under his bed. Little does he know that he'd be *wise* to calm his emotions. Derek doesn't realize that he might be biting off more than he can chew by taking his friends to Gibeon.

Mrs. Flue continues to shake her head as she watches her son dance around the house like a baboon. She thinks that his excitement is pertaining to the newly purchased Dokken Game Station and his early birthday party. Derek kisses his mother and rushes off to his room, thinking about Matilda and Toby.

ELECTRONIC

Chuck, Frankie and Jimmy are standing in front of Chuck's house, fighting over the last cookie that Tosha's mom gave to them. Chuck, of course, is fighting over the cookie as if his life depends on it. There's no way that he's going to lose this battle. In fact, he's never lost a battle over food in his life, and it shows.

"How about I sit on the both of you? What do you think about that? That's what will happen if you don't let go of my cookie!" warns Chuck.

"*Your* 'cookie?!' Tosha's mom made this one for me!" mutters Frankie defensively.

Jimmy realizes that Chuck is beginning to sweat and becoming agitated with him and Frankie. The last thing that he needs is to be squashed by a hungry Chuck.

"Let him have the 'cookie,' Frankie," insists Jimmy as he backs away.

"Listen to your friend!" mutters Chuck as he begins to lose his patience. "I'm warning you one last...."

Chuck finally pulls the cookie away from Frankie. He holds it high in the air, observing the cookie as if it's a trophy.

"I won, I won!" states Chuck, gloating.

Tommy strolls up to the ruckus, still thinking about their upcoming trip to Gibeon. Matilda did a "number" on him by flooding him with visions of Gibeon's arcades and the types of games that he'll be playing; his curiosity is at its peek. He's been daydreaming about how different this adventure might be in comparison to his first trip to Maccabus. For some strange reason his mind has blocked out the second adventure to Maccabus with his friends.

"Hey, guys. Chuck, I need to talk to you, alone," says Tommy sarcastically, waving goodbye to the others.

Jimmy and Frankie step back as if Chuck is in trouble. Usually when Tommy requests a private conversation, it means serious business. The last time that Tommy and Chuck had a meeting that was confidential it was about Mrs. Walker's broken window.

ELECTRONIC

"He's not in trouble, you guys," says Tommy as he observes Jimmy and Frankie's hush-hush conversation.

"Fine! If we can't be included in your conversation, we'll leave!" mutters Frankie jealously.

As Frankie and Jimmy turn to walk away, Frankie grabs the cookie from Chuck's hand. He sprints off like a thief who had just robbed a bank. Chuck doesn't stand a chance of catching Frankie with the head start that he got. He glances down at his empty hand, then Frankie; Chuck feels chafed.

"I'll get you tomorrow!" yells Chuck, waving his fist.

"Forget the cookie, let's talk about Friday," says Tommy as he puts his arm around his buddy. "I'm sure that they'll have plenty of unique cookies in Gibeon."

Tommy and Chuck walk away from his mother's house. Chuck's eyes light up at the thought of what's going to happen Friday night. Matilda had paid him several visits in his imagination. Earlier, Chuck dreamt that Matilda brought him to the world's largest chocolate factory. There, he was able to eat candy that doesn't exist in Hummel County. Not only that, Matilda allowed him to bring some home; four truck loads to be exact!

"What about 'Friday'?" asks Chuck as drool begins to form on the sides of his mouth. "We're still going, aren't we?"

"I wonder if Derek can bring Matilda back. I have a few questions for her before we go," replies Tommy.

"Like what?" asks Chuck, intrigued.

"I want to make sure that there are no wizards or demons in Gibeon. And, that we won't encounter Zanders or strange creatures once we get there. Mindy has a gut feeling that something's waiting for us on the other side," replies Tommy.

Chuck freezes, remembering his ordeal with Orin and his ghouls. As tough as Chucks seems, his bark is greater than his bite. It's only a matter of time before someone calls his bluff. There's no amount of chocolate in the world that could entice Chuck to relive his nightmare on Maccabus. Chuck would consider going on a diet before facing Tuga and Orin again.

"I agree. I don't want to see any of them ever again! Let's ask Derek," says Chuck as he puts a candy bar back into his pocket.

All this talk about wizards, Zanders and demons has ruined his appetite. Without hesitation, Tommy and Chuck march over to Derek's house. Unsuspected by them, Matilda was watching from a nearby tree.

"'Wizards, Zanders and demons' ... I'll fix them," says Matilda.

Matilda disappears in a whirlwind of light.

As Tommy and Chuck make their way to Derek's house, Derek sits in his room, staring at the blue lightbulb. Thoughts of grandeur about Gibeon race through his head. But with those thoughts come images of trouble, mischief and chaos for the gang as they venture through the City of Lights. The lightbulb remains inanimate, not glowing at all. Derek is waiting for it to give him another light show and reveal to him some hidden secret about Gibeon. He's been preoccupied with the lightbulb ever since Matilda told him to bring it with him on Friday as if his life depends on it. Derek picks it up and tries to figure out its meaning, but to no avail.

"I need to ask Matilda why I have this blue lightbulb.... Let me see what happens if I rub it," says Derek as he rubs the lightbulb like it was some kind of magic lamp. "Ouch, that's hot!" mutters Derek as he drops the lightbulb back on his bed.

He walks over to the window and sees Tommy and Chuck walking up the sidewalk. Derek senses that something's wrong by the manner in which they're walking. He turns back to check on the lightbulb; nothing. Derek then looks toward the sky, hoping that Matilda will show up again.

ELECTRONIC

I wonder what they want, thinks Derek.

He grabs the blue lightbulb and puts it into his pocket. Derek heads to the front door to meet his friends. Several thoughts come to mind as to why Tommy and Chuck are coming over unannounced; the first one concerns the gang. Before Derek leaves his room, he stares at the darkness under his bed. A flash of light startles him and he ducks out the door. Derek peeks back into his room, only to be disappointed.

"What the heck? Matilda? Please don't do this to me," pleads Derek as he steps back into his room.

The doorbell rings.

"Oh, well. I got it, Mom!" shouts Derek as he rushes downstairs.

Derek opens the door and pushes his friends outside. He's not taking any chances in ruining their plans to go to Gibeon. The last thing Derek needs is for his parents to catch wind of Matilda, the blue lightbulb or Gibeon. He knows how snoopy his parents become when his friends come over to visit. Derek checks back through the door to make sure that his mom is nowhere in sight.

"The coast is clear. What's up, guys?" asks Derek quietly.

Chuck signals for Tommy to ask the question. He's afraid that he'll mess it up and ask Derek something completely different.

"Can you bring Matilda back?" whispers Tommy as he nudges Chuck for chewing too loudly.

"Why are you picking on me?! Why don't you pick on Derek for the runny nose that he hasn't wiped yet?" asks Chuck as he gags. "Clean that thing!"

"Sorry…. Why do you want to see Matilda?" asks Derek as he wipes his nose on his shirt. "If you don't stop making faces at me, Chuck, I'm going to wipe it on you!"

Tommy becomes repulsed, watching Derek's snot dragging across his sleeve.

"We wanted to ask her some questions about Gibeon.

ELECTRONIC

Mindy has a bad feeling and so do I," replies Tommy.

Chuck begins to swallow marshmallows as if they're mints and moves his head back and forth, watching Tommy and Derek's discussion. His anxiety is getting the best of him.

"I never call Matilda, she just shows up," says Derek as he motions for Chuck to settle down. "What's bothering you about Gibeon?"

"Aren't you the least bit curious about the giant mountain that we saw from the dam?" asks Tommy.

"What 'mountain'?" asks Derek as he reaches for a marshmallow. "Okay, I'm sorry! Just wait until the next time you want some of my food, Chuck!"

"You know ... the one with the intense cloud around it," replies Tommy.

"Hi, kids ... are you looking for me?" asks Matilda, standing at the opposite side of the porch.

"Ahhh!" scream Chuck and Derek as they grab onto each other.

"Where did you come from?" asks Tommy, looking around to make sure that no one else is nearby.

"I had a hunch that you kids wanted to see me," replies Matilda, smiling.

She flies over to be close to the boys.

Derek and his friends settle down with the presence of Matilda. The tingling sensation returns, similar to the one from her mist. Matilda's dainty little body and big eyes have them mesmerized. Her cute little accent is soothing to the ear as well.

"We have some questions for you," says Tommy as he gazes into her eyes.

"What are they? Wait, let me guess. You want to know about 'wizards, Zanders and demons,'" replies Matilda.

Tommy and Chuck almost drop to the floor. How could she have possibly read their minds and known what they were talking about a short time ago? They look at each other bewildered, yet intrigued as to how she knows so much.

"That's amazing! How did you know that we were talking about demons and wizards?" mumbles Chuck with a mouthful of marshmallows.

"I know much more than you can handle," replies Matilda confidently.

Her statement gives Chuck and Derek the creeps.

"Well, are there wizards, Zanders and demons in Gibeon?" asks Tommy reluctantly.

Matilda hesitates. The kids stand motionless as they anticipate Matilda's answer; an affirmative answer could nullify the trip. Matilda hovers in front of each kid, waiting to see who will buckle under pressure first.

"Derek, pull out the blue lightbulb, please," insists Matilda as she pulls out her mini-staff.

"How did you know that I have the lightbulb in my pocket?" asks Derek with his mouth hanging to the floor.

"Like I said, 'I know ...,'" replies Matilda.

"EVERYTHING!" say Chuck and Tommy in unison.

The boys cower, fearing that they've disrespected Matilda.

Derek reaches into his pocket and pulls out the blue lightbulb. As he holds it up, Matilda waves her mini-staff and begins to serenade the boys. The front porch is lit up with an extravagant light show, seen only by the boys. The blue and aqua light is generated from the blue lightbulb and not Matilda. She looks on like a proud mother as Derek and his friends follow the mystical beams of light around the porch. The kids are amazed at how the lightbulb breathes and changes colors. Derek and the others can't believe how in sync the lights are to the music.

"This is what you can expect in Gibeon," says Matilda, waving her staff like the conductor of a symphony orchestra.

ELECTRONIC

"Is there a chocolate factory?" asks Chuck as he watches a beam of light bouncing off Tommy's forehead.

"No, but there's lots of candy. You do like candy, don't you?" asks Matilda, moving her hands through the light.

She knows that Chuck loves candy and just wants to see Chuck flustered. Chuck nods his head and remains speechless. Derek and the others gawk as they see images of Gibeon in the tornado of light. The boys see kids running though the street as the electric parade begins. An image of a giant fun house appears and disappears in the blink of an eye. Chuck then focuses on a large virtual ice cream parlor while Tommy watches two boys fencing in a giant arcade. Matilda decides that the kids have seen enough to whet their appetites. She winks and the blue lightbulb goes out. The music stops as well.

"Hey, what happened?!" asks Derek as he stops dancing. "Please bring back the show!"

"That's enough for now. Bring the blue lightbulb with you Friday. And whatever you do ... don't let anything happen to it," says Matilda with an eerie tone.

At that moment, Mrs. Flue opens the front door. Derek quickly puts the lightbulb back into his pocket, hiding it from his mother. Matilda, of course, disappears into thin air. Chuck and Tommy quickly pull themselves together, ready for the questioning.

"I thought I heard you kids out here. Would you boys care for some lemonade?" asks Mrs. Flue. "Are you okay, Chuck? You look like you saw a ghost."

Tommy looks over and notices Chuck's pale complexion.

"I'm okay, Mrs. Flue. I guess I'm just hungry, that's all," says Chuck as he tucks in his shirt.

"If that were the case, you'd be pale all the time," teases Derek.

Chuck lunges for Derek, but is quickly met by Tommy.

ELECTRONIC

"Now I know that you kids are okay," says Mrs. Flue, shaking her head.

"'Lemonade' would be great, Mom," says Derek as he motions for his mother to give them privacy.

Mrs. Flue, still feeling a bit suspicious, reluctantly heads back into the house to fetch the kids their lemonade. The kids canvass the front porch and yard, searching for Matilda. Realizing that she's gone, Derek pulls out the blue lightbulb once again. Matilda created a mental image of Gibeon for the boys that they'll never forget. If curiosity killed the cat, then these three boys don't stand a chance. The visions of Gibeon are soon washed away for Derek, realizing the weight he must carry on his shoulders. Not only does he have the pressure of making sure that his friends have a good time in Gibeon, but he's also responsible for the integrity of the blue lightbulb.

"Why do you think Matilda wants me to bring this?" asks Derek as he carefully maneuvers the lightbulb in his hand. "Do you think that it leads us to a treasure?"

"I don't know," replies Tommy as he moves closer to Derek to get a better look.

Derek moves away from Tommy, protecting the lightbulb as if the future depends on it.

"Better yet, what did she mean by, 'don't let anything happen to it'?" asks Chuck as he takes a bite of beef jerky.

The kids look at each other, perturbed. A million possibilities race through their minds as to the significance of the blue lightbulb. Unfortunately, there's no time to discuss Matilda's visitation. Mrs. Flue is returning with their lemonade.

Over at Mindy's house, Mindy is talking on the phone with Bucky. She paces the room anxiously as she talks to her friend. The idea of going to Gibeon has her thinking about Maccabus again. The subtle voice playing the devil's advocate wouldn't leave her alone all day.

ELECTRONIC

"I don't know if we should trust this Matilda. It's written not to trust all spirits, but test them to see their source," says Mindy into the phone.

"Where is that written?" asks Bucky on the other end of the telephone. "I don't remember learning that."

"I don't have time to explain now, I'll show you later. You'll be surprised who the author is," says Mindy as she turns around, thinking that she hears her grandmother. "Look, we shouldn't take any chances … *especially* with what we just went through."

Bucky stops pacing, himself, as a flashback of Maccabus enters into his head. He nods his head in agreement with Mindy's recommendations. Her negativity is causing him to have second thoughts about Gibeon as well. Mindy's reminder of Maccabus causes the mental factory that exists in Bucky's head to open for business. He walks over to his window and looks out at his tree fort.

"This is going to break up our friendship again, you know," states Bucky into his phone as he taps his foot nervously.

"I know, I know…. If we back out, the others will be mad. I don't want to ruin our friendship," says Mindy from the other end of the telephone.

Bucky agrees with Mindy and doesn't want to break up the group either. He's thinking of ways to convince himself and Mindy that their friendship is worth the risk of going to Gibeon.

Mindy is now standing at her window, listening to Bucky's rationalization as to why they should go to Gibeon with the others. Her heart races with each of Bucky's ideas. She turns back toward her bed and visualizes the tunnel ride to Gibeon.

"I agree…. I'll be praying hard until then…. Okay, I'll talk to you later," says Mindy as she hangs up the phone.

Immediately, Mindy drops to her knees and begins to pray.

ELECTRONIC

There's a large number of strange sheep grazing on the hillside of Mount Chrome. The brown and red sheep are careful not to wander too high up the mountain. A heavy white cloud surrounds the entire top of the mountain. The peals of lightning and thunder in the heavy cloud act as a shield for uninvited guests. As a matter of fact, no one journeys up the mountain past the dense cloud unless called upon.

The scenery around Mount Chrome is picturesque. There are many smaller mountains in the range; some with giant waterfalls that produce the most brilliant rainbows ever seen. Other mountains have intense foliage, feeding several types of animals not seen in Hummel County.

Mount Chrome is the mountain that struck a nerve with Tommy. Too bad he never got to ask Matilda about the mountain while he was on the dam with his friends. The citizens of Gibeon travel to the dam to take in its spectacular views. They also venture to Mount Chrome at the end of the week, seeking strength and wisdom from their Great Mountain.

From the base of the mountain, Matilda flies toward the heavy cloud, stopping by several mountain goats to say, "Hello."

"Matilda, you have done well to come as commanded," says a sonorous voice from the heavy cloud.

The animals scamper down the mountain, scared by Mount Chrome's voice. Matilda flies to a sacred stone that's made just for her. The stone's brilliant colors weave between the large rock, creating a work of art. She humbles herself at the edge of the heavy cloud; her light decreases so that the light of Mount Chrome may increase.

"This Mindy is a worthy child. She doesn't trust you yet. She would do well in Gibeon. Her prayers shall be answered. Go and visit with her ... I will be with you," says Mount Chrome.

"As you wish, Great Mountain of mine," says Matilda.

ELECTRONIC

Lightning flashes across the sky, indicating the will of Mount Chrome being accomplished.

Mindy concludes her prayer and glances up at a large picture on the wall. The picture was taken at Tommy's annual cookout; the gang looks so happy. It brings a smile to her face, but that is short-lived as the thought of the gang breaking up enters into her mind. It's as if her friends walked out of the picture and went home.

"No! Please, God ... don't let this be!" says Mindy, shaking her head at the picture.

She prepares herself to pray again. As Mindy bows her head, she notices Matilda on her windowsill. Matilda smiles down on her and whistles a tune that leaves Mindy speechless. A sense of peace washes over her as she watches Matilda's display of soft light dance around her bedroom. Mindy and Matilda's spirits connect in a way that no words can describe.

"What are you doing here?" asks Mindy as she gets off her knees.

"I came to answer your prayer. You don't trust me, I know. I hope to instill trust in you by giving you this," replies Matilda as she lights up the window.

Matilda extends her hand out to Mindy. She can't help but grab the gift from Matilda, succumbing to Mount Chrome's changing powers. Mindy is overwhelmed with love and peace that she's never experienced before. The boys wouldn't be able to handle this moment; it would turn them into a bunch of softies.

"What is it?" asks Mindy as she pulls out the gift from a small cloth bag.

"It's a Gratchin," replies Matilda as she flies into the room.

"It looks like a candle. What am I supposed to do with it?" asks Mindy, looking for a place to put it.

"Place it over there," replies Matilda as she secretly winks.

"*Wow!* How did you do that?" asks Mindy as she walks toward her desk.

ELECTRONIC

She places her gift on a beautiful gold candleholder.

"Don't worry about how. In life you have to get the *'how'* out of everything and just believe," replies Matilda as she waves her mini-staff. "That's the essence of faith."

"Wooowwww!" mutters Mindy, watching a flame rise up from her Gratchin.

Along with the flame, the Gratchin plays a melody similar to Matilda's angelic songs.

"I saw you praying. Are you scared to go to Gibeon?" asks Matilda.

"To be honest, yes," replies Mindy as she follows the smoke from the Gratchin. The smoke dances to the music. "Wait, how did you see me praying?"

Matilda flies over to Mindy and displays her gift of light, comforting her uncertain heart. She also breathes a delicate mist over her as commanded by Mount Chrome. Matilda knows that Mindy has power within the gang to make things happen. By gaining a friendship with her, Matilda is almost guaranteed that things will go smoothly on Friday. She notices Mindy's transfiguration and ceases with her aerial acrobatics. Now Matilda has a messenger.

"Look, trust me. There's nothing but fun in Gibeon. We have video games, movies, cartoons, candy and an electric parade," says Matilda convincingly. "Not to mention the citizens of Gibeon as well. You kids will love them."

Mindy sees that Matilda is being sincere and making every effort to assure her about the safety of her friends. Matilda's efforts are slowly taking affect on her.

"Okay, Matilda, I'll go," says Mindy as she watches Matilda's light glow.

"Who are they?" asks Matilda, pointing her mini-staff toward a picture on the wall.

"Those are my Grandma and Grandpa Rose," says Mindy proudly. "Do you have…?"

ELECTRONIC

Mindy turns around and discovers that Matilda is gone. She immediately rushes to the window, hoping to catch a glimpse of her leaving, but it's too late. Matilda has vanished to the next dimension, preparing for the arrival of Derek and his friends.

It's Friday evening and the gang is sitting in Derek's livingroom, impatient and ready for their next adventure. Tommy and his friends have barely survived the week. Chuck's tales of what he thinks is waiting for them in Gibeon and Tammy's visions of grandeur had the kids on edge. Even Patricia had her friends spooked when she shared her dream about a boy named **Jonathan**. She saw him in a *dark place*, far away from Gibeon. He was surrounded by *wicked kids* and *grotesque creatures*, huddled around a fire. Tammy, of course, was quick to discount her credibility. If only Tammy knew how real Patricia's dream was, the gang might reconsider taking this trip.

Mr. and Mrs. Flue are serving Derek's friends fruit punch, watching the kids devour a table full of fresh-baked goodies. There are sugar cookies, chocolate chip cookies and fudge brownies. Chuck, of course, is out of control in the corner. He's not only stuffing his face with cookies, but he's stuffing his pockets as well.

"*Chuck!*" scolds Derek. "What are you doing?!"

Chuck freezes like a deer in headlights as the gang stares at their friend. A half-eaten cookie hangs out of his mouth as he tries to hide the fact that he's hoarding Derek's snacks. Mindy shakes her head in disappointment while Mr. Flue chuckles. Chuck reminds him of himself when he was his age.

"What?" mumbles Chuck with his mouth full of cookies. "Come on ... it was only a couple of cookies and brownies."

"Save some for the others!" replies Derek as he looks at the half-empty plate.

Tammy marches over to Chuck and drags him by the ear in front of the TV.

"Ouch!" yelps Chuck, embarrassed by Tammy's gesture.

Patricia shakes her head and smiles at Peggy.

Mr. and Mrs. Flue are enjoying themselves as they continue playing chaperone. What's not to like about Tommy and his friends? Most kids in Hummel County think that they're a walking circus. Many people believe that Tommy and his friends should be in the movies.

"Eat up, everyone, there's plenty more in the kitchen," says Mrs. Flue, smiling.

Mr. Flue almost loses it as he watches Chuck bend over to pick up a cookie.

"You kids behave yourselves when we leave now," says Mr. Flue, making sure that he lets them know who's in charge. "I don't want to have to send anyone home early."

"Yes, Mr. Flue," says the gang in unison.

Mr. Flue smiles and feels the respect of the kids.

Tommy and his friends are great actors, as are most kids. They tell their parents and other adults what they want to hear, yet have a grocery list of ulterior motives. The kids' facade of kindness and truth is bought by Mr. and Mrs. Flue; hook, line and sinker.

Little do the Flues know where the kids are going tonight and what's in store for them in Gibeon. If they did, they would put a stop to it right away. Mr. Flue sees Chuck whispering to Tammy and turns back to patrol the living-room. Mrs. Flue, however, signals for him to join her in the kitchen so that the kids can have some privacy.

"I don't know about you guys, but I'm too excited to do anything," states Derek.

"Yeah, let's go now!" adds Tammy, grasping her wrestling mask.

Tommy and his friends can't sit still and begin to pace around Derek's living-room. Each kid has a movie about Gibeon dancing around his or her head.

"We'd better settle down before your parents start questioning us," suggests Bucky as he notices the gang doing laps around the living-room.

"Bucky is right. Let's go into the family-room and play with my birthday present," says Derek, checking to make sure that his parents aren't spying on them. "Someone grab what's left of the snacks and bring them with us. Not you, Chuck!" mutters Derek as he heads toward the family-room.

"Whatever! Last one there is a rotten egg!" screams Chuck as he shoves Tommy and zips by Derek, hoping to get a good seat in front of the TV.

Derek and his friends are now in front of the big screen TV. For some reason the television seems much bigger than usual, almost surreal. Bucky cautiously walks up to examine the TV as if it's going to swallow him whole. Chuck senses Bucky's fear and seizes the opportunity.

"Ahhhh!" screams Bucky as Chuck grabs him from behind.

The gang laughs at Chuck's horseplay with Bucky. Bucky, however, doesn't find it amusing. There are still large butterflies having a field day in his stomach, anticipating tonight's event.

"Sorry, Bucky," says Chuck as he smears chocolate on Bucky's shirt.

Derek finishes setting up his new Dokken Game Station for his friends to play. He stands over it like a proud father and smiles. Tommy and the others look on with envy as he grabs the remote for the TV. They know that Derek will use his new video game set as leverage at Bucky's tree fort to get his way.

"All right, guys, who wants to play me first?" asks Derek as he turns on the TV.

Derek's friends are silenced, staring into his television as if they're looking at a ghost. An illuminating, deep blue screen blinds the gang; it's brighter than any blue that they've ever seen. The kids are blasted with a tingling sensation from their heads to their toes, as if a giant hand reached out from the TV and sprinkled them with magic dust. Derek's friends cover their eyes from the brightness as he steps back, waiting for the television to explode.

"Is that you, Matilda?" asks Derek as he lowers his hands.

"Yes, Derek, it's me," replies Matilda from the light. "It's okay, everyone, you can look now."

Tommy and his friends lower their hands as the blue light disappears from the TV screen. The screen now shows Matilda standing in the middle of Main Street in the heart of Gibeon. Behind Matilda, kids are running around making preparations for the electric parade. Many of the kids have candy or funny looking lights in their hands. Weird looking clowns come in and out of the picture, teasing the gang. Fireworks explode in the distance, bigger and better than any fireworks show in Hummel County. Derek and his friends remain speechless as they watch "Matilda TV."

"Wow!" mutter Chuck and Bucky, totally amazed.

The rest of the gang smiles as they catch a glimpse of their next adventure. Patricia notices a girl talking to her doll on the street corner.

"Look, Peggy, a friend," says Patricia, clutching Peggy.

All life in Gibeon freezes as Matilda flies closer to the screen to address Derek and his friends. The gang gets closer to the TV, anticipating Matilda's next words.

"This is only a preview. Are you kids ready to see Gibeon in person?" asks Matilda.

A spectacular display of light illuminates from Matilda.

"Yeeeaaahhhhhhh!" declares the gang, filled with awe.

Derek and his friends grab each other and jump up and down, filled with excitement. Chuck and Tammy dance around one another as if they're at a hoedown. Chuck gets dizzy and falls into a table. Derek looks toward the kitchen to make sure that his parents aren't going to break up their moment with Matilda. Tammy and Mindy laugh as they watch Chuck stand up and struggle to keep his balance.

ELECTRONIC

"Yes, we are!" states Tommy as he touches the TV screen.

"Good. Derek, where's the blue lightbulb?" asks Matilda as her light goes out.

Derek pulls it out of his pocket, only to have it light up the room. This time, a red light shoots from his hand and dances off the faces of his friends, placing them under Matilda's power.

"It's right here ... whoa," replies Derek, as if he's falling asleep.

"All right, Derek, remember ... don't let anything happen to that lightbulb," says Matilda with an eerie tone. "It's an *essential* part of your journey."

The gang looks intently at the blue lightbulb in Derek's hand.

"Hey, where did Matilda go?!" asks Chuck, shaking his head at the pitch-black TV screen.

"I don't know," replies Derek as he snaps out of his trance. "Matilda, come back!"

"What does she mean by, 'don't let anything happen to that lightbulb'?" asks Mindy as she walks up to the TV.

Derek places both hands on the lightbulb, protecting it like a mother hen with her eggs. Tommy realizes that the blue lightbulb is an essential part of their adventure.

"Maybe you ought to let me hold that," suggests Tommy as he steps closer to Derek. "Come on, Derek, hand it over!"

He pulls the lightbulb close to his chest, keeping it out of Tommy's reach. There's no way that Derek is letting any of his friends take his glory from him. Like a German shepherd guarding its dinner, Derek begins to growl at his friends as they approach. He now understands its importance, but doesn't understand its meaning.

"I don't think so! Besides, Matilda told *me* to bring the lightbulb with us, not you guys!" mutters Derek snobbishly.

The kids scatter as Mrs. Flue enters the room with their

lemonade. Derek's friends change their demeanor instantly and take their seats on the floor. They don't want to alert Mrs. Flue about their plans with Matilda. If she finds out, Mr. Flue will never let the kids come over again. Tommy, Bucky and Patricia murmur about school and Lenny and Edward's mishap at the bus stop, watching Mrs. Flue's every move. Chuck and Tammy look like they fell down the "tree of confusion" and hit every branch along the way. Little do the kids know that their faces have guilty written all over them.

"You kids are acting like you've never been here before. What's up?" asks Mrs. Flue as she places the lemonade on the table. "Chuck, close your mouth."

"Sorry, Mom, we were arguing over who's playing the first game," replies Derek. "You know how it gets sometimes."

"I don't *understand* you kids and those games. Play nice or else your father will come in ... and you know what that means," says Mrs. Flue as she looks toward the kitchen.

Chuck rushes over to help Mrs. Flue with the lemonade. The longer she stays with the kids, the more likely she'll find out about Matilda and Gibeon. Mindy and Patricia help Chuck to distribute the lemonade.

"*Chuck?* Now, Ms. Rose and Ms. Quiet ... I can accept their help. But you, Chuck, wanting to help? Now I know something's wrong!" says Mrs. Flue as she hands Chuck a tray of cookies.

"Nothing's 'wrong,' Mom. Can you please leave now? It's kids' time," pleads Derek.

Mrs. Flue gets the hint that she's not welcome and heads back into the kitchen.

"Let me know if you need anything else," says Mrs. Flue, walking through the kitchen door.

"Thanks, Mrs. Flue," says the gang in unison.

Derek waits until his mother is gone and pulls out the blue

ELECTRONIC

lightbulb. Like curious monkeys, his friends walk over to look at it, waiting for it to light up again. The kids are frustrated, wanting to know why it's so important and what will happen to them should Derek break it. Tammy takes precaution as she steps behind Chuck, letting him be the guinea pig should anything strange happen.

"I've never seen one like that before," says Patricia.

"Yeah, I wonder what's so important about this stupid lightbulb," says Tammy as she pushes Chuck forward.

"Hey!" screams Chuck, shoving Tammy back. "I'm not scared of you!"

"Guys, quit it! It's not a 'stupid lightbulb'!" mutters Derek as he twirls it around.

"Be careful!" warns Mindy as she reaches for the lightbulb. "Matilda told you not to let anything happen to it!"

Derek quickly cups it in his hand, protecting it from the others. The blue lightbulb has given Derek a sense of power that he's never felt before. He gloats over the fact that his friends don't have a blue lightbulb of their own. The kids are somewhat envious, but know that Derek is the gatekeeper to their next adventure. Not only has this lightbulb changed his status with the gang, but it has somehow taken away his allergies and silenced his sneezing episodes.

"Look, this is *my* adventure and I make the rules!" says Derek sternly.

Tammy immediately takes offense at Derek's attitude. It's one thing to have power and favor from Matilda, but a cocky attitude? No way. She steps forward as if she's going to put Derek in a headlock.

"I was just kidding!" says Derek, backing away. "Come on, guys, let's break in my present!"

The gang regroups in front of the TV to play Dragons & Swords. Derek and Mindy grab the joysticks and take their positions next to the Dokken Game Station. The rest of the gang watch intently as Dragons & Swords begins. Derek smiles as he recalls the dream that he had while reading the manual for the game. He realizes that now isn't the time to reveal his formal introduction with Matilda to his friends. Derek's friends marvel at his skills as he plays the game and slays several dragons; not knowing that his dream gave him the insight to win.

It's finally bedtime. The boys are in their pajamas, staring at Derek's bed from a distance. Tommy, Chuck, Bucky and Derek can hear their hearts beating through the silence of the night. Not a word is spoken as Derek and his friends envision their ride to Gibeon. Chuck has a half-eaten donut hanging from his mouth as he stares into the darkness under Derek's bed. Tommy has a flashback of the lit tunnel he traveled through on his return trip from Maccabus.

"Hi, boys," says Matilda from the windowsill. "Are you ready to go?"

Her unannounced visit sends the boys crashing into each other, as they seem to think that something from Gibeon has made it to the other side to get them. Matilda chuckles as she watches the chaos.

"Ahhh!" screams Bucky as he collides with Tommy.

The boys finally realize that the noise came from the window and not from under the bed.

"Matilda, what are you doing here?!" mutters Derek as he stands up.

"Sorry, boys.... Where are the girls?" asks Matilda.

"They'll be here shortly. They're waiting for my Mom and Dad to go to sleep," replies Derek.

At that moment, the door creeps open. The boys turn around abruptly, expecting Derek's parents to bust them for talking to Matilda.

"*Is it time?*" whispers Mindy as she pokes her head into the room.

ELECTRONIC

Derek signals for the girls to come in and be quiet. Mindy, Patricia and Tammy slowly tiptoe into his room as if they're a pack of thieves in the night. They're dressed in their pajamas as well. Chuck scarfs down the last of the donut and checks his bag, making sure that he has plenty of snacks; he learned his lesson from his trip to Maccabus.

"What do we do next, Matilda?" asks Derek as he turns back toward the window.

"Hey, where did she go?" asks Chuck as he looks around the room. "How come she always disappears when we need her the most?!"

"Great! Now what?!" asks Tammy sarcastically.

"Hey, guys … Derek will lead us to the bed the same way that I did last time," replies Tommy as he nudges Derek.

"Hey!" yelps Derek, startled. "Yeah, this is *my* adventure!" says Derek as he clutches the blue lightbulb. "All right, let's do this!"

Derek and his friends look at one another, making sure that they're ready to go to Gibeon. The gang gives each other the "okay" signal and locks hands, waiting for Derek to turn off the lights.

"All right, Derek, do your thing," says Tommy.

Derek takes in a giant gulp of air and trudges toward the light switch. His stomach feels like it's about to jump out of his body; his nerves are shot. Even though Matilda has promised the gang fun and excitement, Derek can't relax. Visions of Orin's wicked army flash before his eyes, and the loud cries of the giant praying mantis sound in his head. Derek makes it to the light switch and turns to see his friends embracing each other with eyes wide open. The tension in the room is thick as everyone waits for the lights to go out.

"Here it goes," says Derek as he shuts off the lights.

The room turns pitch-black. The kids squeeze each

other's hands as their heartbeats pulsate throughout the room. Chuck swallows the last of his candy bar and prepares himself for the ride. Derek slowly walks past his friends toward his bed, clenching his fists. Tommy and his friends follow close behind, prepared to be sucked under Derek's bed and taken to Gibeon.

"I'm scared!" whispers Patricia.

"Don't be 'scared,' Patricia. Everything's going to be okay," whispers Mindy. "Here, hold my hand."

The gang travels toward Derek's bed, huddled together like a school of fish. Derek realizes that he's within a few feet and stops; a million thoughts race through his head. His friends sense that something's wrong and are gripped with a paralyzing fear. The kids start to have second thoughts about their trip, as every horror movie that they've ever seen comes to life before their eyes.

"Hurry, Derek, before I change my mind!" whispers Chuck as his stomach growls.

"Ah! Chuck, quit it!" mutters Tommy.

"Well, here it goes," says Derek quietly. "Gibeon, here we come."

His friends hold on tighter, anticipating what's about to happen. Derek finally reaches his bed and lets out a sigh, thankful that nothing horrible has happened yet. Mindy and Patricia clench their eyes so hard that they see stars. Patricia almost squeezes Peggy's head off as well.

"Ouch!" yelps Derek as his leg smashes against his bed frame.

The gang crashes into Derek like a seven-car-pileup.

"What happened? Why aren't we going?" whispers Tommy, thinking that the trip to Gibeon has been cancelled. "All right, Chuck, you can let go now!"

"I don't know 'what happened'!" replies Derek as he tends to his leg. "Maybe we're not supposed to go."

ELECTRONIC

At that moment, Matilda appears in the window and lights up the room for the kids to see her.

"Matilda, what happened?" asks Derek as he steps away from his bed. "How come we're not on our way to Gibeon?"

"Tommy must lead you. It's he who possesses the power to reach Gibeon," replies Matilda, playing angelic music.

"*Me?!* Why me?" asks Tommy, confused.

"You were chosen to bring 'Good News,' were you not?" asks Matilda as she waves her mini-staff toward Tommy.

Tommy steps back as a tornado of light appears in front of him.

Staring into the bright dancing light, Tommy's friends are shown a scene from his experience at summer camp. Tommy is standing on the side of a mountain, gazing at the shooting stars. His friends gawk as they watch him being blinded by an *exploding star*. A voice then asks Tommy, "Tommy, Tommy, why are you persecuting me and my children?"

"When was that?!" asks Tammy as Bucky clutches her side. "Bucky, let go!"

"That was four years ago," replies Tommy, dismayed. "Remember when my parents sent me away?"

The gang huddles together as Matilda's music intensifies.

"Whose voice was that?" asks Derek.

"It was Orin's," replies Tommy as chills travel down his body. "He...."

"I see that 'Orin' has misled you. So that you know, 'Orin' is the father of all lies. That voice was the same voice that came out of the Wise Well," explains Matilda.

The gang is flabbergasted that Matilda knows about the Wise Well. It was the Wise Well that saved Tommy and his friends from Orin after he was turned into a giant, evil warlock. The island of Maccabus was set free of Orin's reign by the Wise Well.

"Jamie told you that 'Orin' came to him as an angel of light, but realized that there was nothing but darkness in him," explains Matilda as she hovers in front of Tommy.

"How do you know about the 'Wise Well' and 'Jamie'?" asks Tommy.

"As I told you, I know more than you can handle. Listen, forget about what lies behind and press forward to what lies ahead," replies Matilda as she waves her mini-staff toward the bottom of Derek's bed.

A flash of light illuminates under Derek's bed.

"More will be revealed later. Hurry, you're going to be late," says Matilda as she flies away.

"'Late' for what?" asks Bucky.

The room becomes dark.

"I don't know, but let's go!" exclaims Tammy excitedly.

The gang regroups in front of Derek's bed with Tommy in the lead. He grabs his friends and slowly walks toward the bed. As Tommy pauses at the bedside, Derek's pajama pocket lights up from the blue lightbulb. Blue and hazel lights dance around the room, blinding the kids as they try to follow the moving lights. The kids are overwhelmed with a strange sensation over their entire bodies; a strong vibration.

"What's going on?!" asks Chuck, covering his eyes.

"*AHHHHHHHHHHHHHHHHHHHHH!*" scream Tommy and his friends.

Tommy and his friends are sucked under Derek's bed and begin their journey through the nether world toward Gibeon. Once again, the kids find themselves screaming down a dark tunnel, tumbling over one another. Lights and images of Gibeon flash on the walls of the tunnel. Tommy notices a strange cartoon character that he's never seen before; it looks like a porcupine-type superhero. Mindy notices a superhero that looks like a giant frog. Tammy and Bucky watch the flashing lights of the storefronts appear on the walls. Strange dogs with giant heads bark at the gang; one looks like a lion.

"I want to go back!" screams Bucky as he tries to grab onto Chuck.

The gang notices the light at the end of the tunnel approaching rapidly.

"We're here!" screams Tommy as he braces himself for a crash landing.

"*AHHHHHHHHHHHHHHHHHHHHH!*" scream Tommy and his friends as they prepare to land in Gibeon.

Toby and Matilda are standing on a street in Gibeon, staring at a black prism suspended in midair. Matilda has cleared this section of the street for her guests to arrive. It's decorated with balloons, signs and streamers, showing the gang the true spirit of hospitality. Several kids have horns and various noise makers to welcome Derek and his friends. Matilda even padded the street with a giant mattress for Tommy and his friends to tumble down. Toby backs away as he hears the kids' screams getting closer.

"LOOK OUT!" yells Tommy as he tumbles out of the prism first.

One by one, Derek and the others exit the prism and tumble down the mattress.

"Whoopee!" screams Chuck as he exits the prism last.

The black prism disappears. Matilda laughs with Toby as they watch Chuck plow down his friends like a bowling ball. Derek and Tammy immediately jump on Chuck and rub his head on the mattress. The three of them roll around in the middle of the street, but Chuck emerges victorious.

"These kids are too much," says Matilda as she shakes her head.

Tommy and his friends brush themselves off and immediately spot Matilda.

ELECTRONIC

"We made it!" declares Derek, raising his hands. "See, guys, I told you so!"

The conversation is cut short as the gang notices the splendor of Gibeon. Its unique buildings and display of lights overwhelm the kids. Mindy notices a spectacular building that resembles a church; the steeple is as high as the sky.

"Wow, look at that!" says Mindy, pointing at the building.

The kids stare in awe as light reflects off the top of the steeple. Matilda knows that this will be one of Mindy's favorite places to visit.

"Looking down from the dam, I knew this place was going to be awesome! There's nothing like this back home," says Tommy as he stares up into the sky.

"Derek, aren't you going to say, 'hi' to me?" asks Toby.

"I'm sorry, Toby," replies Derek, turning around. "Everyone, this is my friend, Toby. I *told* you that the dream was real!" mutters Derek.

Chuck moves through the gang to get a closer look at Toby. He becomes jealous, feeling threatened by Toby's presence. Chuck makes it obvious that he's ready to battle over Derek's friendship. His mouth starts twitching as he flares his teeth.

"You must be Chuck," says Toby, smiling. "Don't worry … I'm not here to steal your friend."

Chuck is caught off guard with Toby's comment. He ponders whether or not Toby is some kind of wizard. There's no way that he could know his name without being one; especially since he's never met him before.

"How did you know my name?" asks Chuck, examining Toby like a dog.

"Derek talked about you in his dream," replies Toby. "He told me that you would appreciate this."

Toby walks up to Chuck and hands him some candy. The gang continues to like Gibeon more and more as they see Chuck smiling.

ELECTRONIC

"You read my mind!" states Chuck as he begins to peel the wrapper off the candy. "Wow! You guys have to try some of this! … Never mind!"

"Matilda, what's first?" asks Mindy, still amazed at the giant church.

"Yeah, where are the games?" asks Tammy as she pulls out her mask. "Where's the giant arcade?"

Matilda sees that the kids are becoming impatient. She can feel their sense of urgency to experience Gibeon and all that it has to offer. Matilda waves her hands back and forth, causing the kids to feel a sense of peace that they've never felt before.

"Hey, what did you do?!" asks Tommy as he breathes in the fresh air. "I feel like I'm floating. Guys, wave your arms like a bird."

"I want you to enjoy Gibeon on Gibeon's terms, not yours," replies Matilda.

"Relax, friends. All who come to 'Gibeon' never forget the experience," says Toby. "We don't want you to miss a thing."

Derek remembers how often he pondered about Gibeon from his brief stay. Mindy and Patricia smile at one another as they notice some children heading their way. Toby's comment catches Tammy off guard.

"We're not the first kids to come to 'Gibeon'?" asks Tammy.

"No, sweetheart, you're not. We even have some kids living here that have made Gibeon their new home," replies Matilda as she belts out a melody.

Tommy and his friends follow the display of lights coming from Matilda as it heads toward the sky. The light dances to her music as she sings to the gang. Her futuristic opera is soothing to their ears. Matilda's melody touches the hearts of Tommy and his friends; their gleaming smiles blind each other. The kids are overwhelmed with love and joy as they embrace their adventure.

Mindy and Bucky point at a store full of TVs that are playing all kinds of movies and cartoons. There's an animated film that catches their eye. The flat screen TV shows superheroes in action, fighting an evil force of aliens from the planet Hulken. Mindy and Bucky walk over to the store window to get a closer look at the action.

"Hey, where are they going?" asks Patricia.

Chuck notices an ice cream shop that looks similar to the one in his dream. His eyes practically bulge out of his head at the thought of some vanilla ice cream topped with hot fudge. A little boy comes out and waves Chuck over.

"I'll be right there!" yells Chuck as he takes off running. "I-c-e … c-r-e-a-m!"

Mindy and Bucky watch Chuck zip by them and begin to laugh.

"The last time I saw Chuck move that fast was on … never mind," says Mindy.

Matilda notices that the group is falling apart. She decides that she'd better do something before she gets in trouble with her Superior. Matilda's first enchantment wasn't enough for these kids; their mischievous spirits could use several. She's never had a group of kids like this, so full of energy and rebellion. Without another moment to waste, Matilda belts out a tune that freezes Tommy and his friends. The tune has no words, but its hypnotizing pitch could make an army go to sleep. The music coming out of Matilda's mouth sounds as though a full symphony is playing.

"What are you going to do, Matilda?" asks Toby as he looks into Derek's eyes.

"These kids are wild … I sense it. I need to take some of their energy away before they damage something and upset the others," replies Matilda as the melodious music stops. "Don't worry, Toby … everything will be just fine."

"Whatever you say, Matilda…. I love this," says Toby as he waves his hand in front of Derek's face.

ELECTRONIC

Matilda lights up the street corner and begins to sing another tune. The light is green and dances around the street, bouncing off each store and into the sky. The citizens of Gibeon walk to their storefront windows to watch Matilda's show.

"We must have some new visitors," says one woman, holding onto her husband as she stares toward the sky.

Toby dances in the middle of the street to Matilda's singing. Her music is soothing to the ear, and soulful to the feet. Other kids come out from their parents' shops to join in on Matilda's welcoming song.

"Hi, Toby," says one little boy.

"Hi, Dirk," says Toby, smiling as he twirls around. "These are the kids that I told you about."

Dirk walks up to Chuck and notices his intense ice cream face and begins to chuckle. Chuck's eyes are as big as saucers and he's biting his tongue, pointing toward the ice cream shop.

"I've never seen a kid this big, before," says Dirk. "Does he bite?"

Matilda comes out of her light show and notices that the streets are filled with kids. This is her sign to start the adventure. Matilda's new song should have Derek and his friends tamed and ready to be obedient to her requests. Matilda slowly ends the song, which then causes the light to disappear. The kids of Gibeon love it when Matilda sings to them and uses her powers. Matilda has a way with children that sends them into another dimension; freeing their young imaginations.

"Okay, kids, I want to introduce you to Derek and his friends," says Matilda. "Remember, Mount Chrome says, 'If you receive these children in his name, then you receive him.' Take care of them, so that you may honor our Great Mountain."

The kids run over to Derek and his friends, waiting for the gang to snap out of their trance. Matilda sees that her children are ready and snaps her fingers. Slowly the gang comes back to life with the biggest smiles on their faces. Derek and his friends look around, confused, trying to figure out where they are.

"What happened?" asks Chuck, looking at Dirk. "What are you looking at? Is there something on my face?" asks Chuck as he cleans his face like a cat.

"Where are we?" asks Tommy, scratching his head.

The kids of Gibeon giggle at Tommy and his friends for their strange behavior. Derek reaches into his pocket and pulls out the blue lightbulb. He holds it high in the air for everyone to see. All the kids of Gibeon bow toward Derek, knowing that it's he who possesses power and magic.

"Why is everyone staring at me?" asks Derek innocently.

At that moment, the blue lightbulb illuminates and begins its own show, sending light beaming out of Derek's hand and bouncing off everyone. It almost resembles a giant strobe light. Red, yellow, green, purple and unique colors comprise this heavenly masterpiece that illuminates out of Derek's hand. The illumination turns into a tornado of light, swirling its way into the sky. This tornado of spectacular measure can be seen throughout Gibeon.

Children across town know that they have visitors and pay homage to the light. The kids can see the purple and yellow lights swirling around their city. Matilda's song echoes between the buildings, bringing a smile to her children's faces.

There's a large group on top of the dam watching the light rise from the city of Gibeon. These families have the best view of the light show. They, too, pay homage to the light, knowing Matilda has new guests.

Derek's friends are paying homage to the light as well. Matilda's last song has transformed their souls. They now have a true connection to the light.

"Wow, look at that," says Patricia as she points Peggy toward the light.

"Why does Derek get to have all the fun?" whispers Bucky.

ELECTRONIC

Bucky quickly bows his head as he realizes that a little girl overheard his question.

Matilda flies into the tornado of light and spins around, exhibiting her own light show. The children of Gibeon get up to watch Matilda put on an exhibition for Derek and his friends. No laser light show in the world could compete with the light show displayed by Matilda and the blue lightbulb. The plethora of colors stimulates Derek and his friends' senses to the point of no return. Mayor Messa appears in the light, waving at his special guests. Images of giant waterfalls and a large zoo with strange animals flash before the kids' eyes.

"She's amazing!" says Tommy to Chuck.

Chuck can't comment. As he stood gawking at Matilda, Chuck opened his mouth so wide that it got stuck. He continues to observe Matilda's acrobatics, astonished, forgetting about the ice cream shop and all its goodies.

"This is the *coolest* place in the world!" says Tammy as she puts on her wrestling mask.

A little girl immediately pulls out her own mask and puts it on. The mask looks like a lion's face. It's obvious that she's imitating Tammy. Tammy looks over and notices the girl with her mask on. She instantly feels a kindred connection with the girl that she's never felt before with anyone. Tammy immediately walks up to her. The girls check each other out, like two stray dogs meeting each other for the first time. Tammy is definitely curious.

"Hi, my name is Tammy. What's yours?" asks Tammy gingerly.

Derek and the others hear the tone of Tammy's voice and realize that something had happened to her.

"Did you hear, Tammy? This is a miracle!" says Mindy, smiling.

"Yeah. Does this mean, no more wrestling?" asks Bucky as he watches a strange bird fly by. "I can't believe how good I feel!"

ELECTRONIC

"My name is Tina," replies the little girl as she kicks her feet, looking at the ground. "I think your mask is cool."

Tammy immediately falls for Tina and feels a sense of friendship that's completely new to her. She can feel Tina's love and sincerity and wants to be part of it. Behind the mask, Tammy has a gut feeling that she just made a new friend that will be her exploring companion while in Gibeon. Unfortunately, Tammy has never heard of the parable about the wolf dressed in sheep's clothing.

"Tina, will you show me around?" asks Tammy, as if this is the first time that she'd ever asked someone to be her friend.

"Sure. There's so much to see and so little time for you to see it all," replies Tina as she glances at the dark forest at the end of the street.

She's careful not to alert Tammy of her intentions.

Tommy notices a little boy watching Tina intently from inside one of the shops. The boy's discerning eyes glow through the store window, giving Tommy the creeps. Tommy senses that something's not right with the boy by the way he's looking at Tina. The boy watches very carefully as Tammy shakes Tina's hand.

"Don't look, but there's a kid in the window, behind us, that's giving me the creeps," whispers Tommy to Derek.

Derek slowly turns around.

"What 'kid'?" asks Derek as he canvasses the storefronts with his eyes.

Tommy whips around and notices that the boy is gone. Canvassing the sidewalk with his eyes, Tommy sees the boy running into the crowd; he occasionally turns back to make sure that Tommy isn't chasing him.

"There! There he is!" shouts Tommy, pointing frantically.

Matilda notices Tommy and Derek making a scene in front of the other children and decides to investigate. She flies down to see what's wrong with Tommy.

ELECTRONIC

"Is everything all right?" asks Matilda as her light goes out. "I noticed that you were bothered by something across the street."

Tommy's friends rush over to see what's going on. Tommy scratches his head, wondering why the boy would've taken off like that.

"There was a *kid* staring out the window over there. He gave me the creeps," replies Tommy as he points in the direction of the store. "When he noticed me looking at him, he took off running."

"I don't see a 'kid,'" says Bucky as he accepts a piece of candy from a little boy. "Thank you."

Matilda knows exactly which kid that Tommy is talking about. The store he was pointing at is Bobbie's Bicycles. She was hoping that little Bobbie would've listened to her warning. Matilda knows that she must contain Bobbie's identity and confront him about his breach of security.

"Don't mind Bobbie, he's harmless," insists Matilda as if nothing's wrong. "Well, I guess we're ready."

The gang is once again mesmerized by her glowing light. Their bodies are overwhelmed by a chilling vibration as Matilda breathes a mist over them. Her new ballad causes Tommy and the others to forget that Bobbie's name was even mentioned. Matilda is almost ready to take her special guests on their adventures through Gibeon.

"Single file, everyone ... good," says Matilda as she slowly flies backwards toward the heart of Gibeon. "I need you to stay close to each other. That way no one will get lost or stray away from the group."

Tommy and his friends line up behind Matilda and nudge each other, excited to venture into the city. Chuck and Bucky fight over their position in line. With one hip check, Bucky didn't stand a chance. Mindy shrugs her shoulders at Toby, apologizing for her friends' behavior. Once Matilda sees that they've complied with her request, she turns around to address the gang. The kids' enthusiasm to begin their adventure is halted by the serious look on Matilda's face. It's as if her face transfigured before their eyes.

"Kids, I want you to listen very closely. No one is to venture off into *Zevon Forest* that's located on the outskirts of Gibeon. The forest is full of wicked children and wild creatures that will hurt you. These children once lived in Gibeon, but were expelled for their disobedience. Only *evil* is found in the forest. It's forbidden for any of you to go there," orders Matilda with a serious tone that causes a stir in the kids' hearts.

Derek and his friends observe the dark forest from a distance. Without Matilda's warning, the kids would've been oblivious to any evil coming from the beautiful scenery that lines the city. The trees are deep green and the flowers are in bloom. Birds can be heard chirping through the forest as if they're on a holiday.

"You mean … that forest?" asks Tommy, pointing.

"How could anything bad come from something so nice?" asks Mindy, confused.

"That looks like the forest from my dream. I saw an evil boy who lived in it. He was the leader. His name was *Jonathan* …," says Patricia as she clutches Peggy.

The music stops. The area of the street where Matilda has the gang gathered becomes silent at the mentioning of Jonathan's name. Kids on the curb mumble to one another and shake their heads, recalling the battle that took place between Jonathan and the mayor. Girls rush back into their parents' stores and shops. Derek and his friends look around, confused.

"Why is everyone leaving? What did she say?" asks Derek as he looks at Patricia.

"'Jonathan' is the ruler of Zevon Forest. He was the most beautiful kid in all of Gibeon. He was musically gifted beyond measure and played music for Mount Chrome. One day, he decided to venture up the mountain and walk into the sacred cloud of

Mount Chrome. He wanted the powers of our Great Mountain so that he could rule Gibeon. There was a battle with Mayor Messa's army and he was cast out to Zevon Forest. With him went his followers," explains Matilda.

Derek and his friends stare at Matilda with eyes like saucers and mouths touching the floor. The gang huddles together as if Jonathan is going to charge out from Zevon Forest; they're spooked and frightened to say the least. The presence of evil has permeated from Zevon Forest with Matilda's story of Jonathan.

"Is 'Mount Chrome' the mountain that we saw from the dam?" asks Tommy as chills travel down his spine.

"Yes, it is. He's the power that I mentioned to you, Derek, which would never abandon or forsake you. How else do you think Gibeon is able to maintain such beauty and light? Mount Chrome is the source of all true light," replies Matilda, bowing her head.

The families that still line the street bow their heads, as well. Derek's friends are bewildered about her comment, regarding their private conversation. Before they can find out more details about Matilda and Derek's secret rendezvous, a powerful gust of wind sends their heads bowing faster than they can blink an eye. The tingling sensation in their bodies has them in a state of euphoria. Never before has the gang felt such serenity and bliss.

Matilda knew that the kids' curiosity about Jonathan and Zevon Forest would damper their trip to Gibeon. She immediately turned it over to Mount Chrome in her mind. Mount Chrome knows everything and was the one who sent the gust of wind.

"Look, you've been *warned* about Zevon Forest. Take this warning to heart.... Now lets see what Gibeon has in store for you," says Matilda as massive lights shoot from her open hands.

Matilda serenades Derek and his friends with music and a light show that's intense. Derek and the others look toward the sky and away from Zevon Forest. Matilda's ballad has the kids remembering her promises back home. She points the lights in the direc-

ELECTRONIC

tion of Main Street. The scene resembles Mardi Gras. The citizens of Gibeon are running through the streets with not a care in the world. Everything they need is provided for them by Mount Chrome. The gang stares at the different storefronts and their vivid décors. Many of them practically call out Derek and his friends' names, inviting them to play video games or watch animated movies.

"Hey, look!" mutters Chuck with a mouthful of candy.

Derek and his friends look toward a tall building in the distance. The kids gawk and poke one another as they watch themselves on a giant video screen in the middle of town. It's as if the gang has become movie stars overnight.

"*Cooool!*" says Chuck as he watches the lights dancing around the sky.

"I can't believe I'm on TV!" states Tammy, noticing that Tina has disappeared. Hey, where did she go? wonders Tammy.

"We're famous! I look pretty handsome, don't I, Bucky?" asks Derek, puffing out his chest.

"I think I 'look' better! What do you think, Mindy?" asks Bucky as he fixes his hair.

"I think both of you need to settle down before you float away with those inflated heads of yours," says Mindy as she chuckles with Tommy and several other kids.

"Where's the arcade?!" asks Derek.

"I want to see the parade!" exclaims Patricia as she squeezes Peggy.

"Now that's more like it! Follow me," says Matilda as she leads them into town.

She continues her journey into the heart of Gibeon. Derek and his friends follow Matilda, dancing through the streets as she plays her music. The kids of Gibeon leave their parents and join Matilda and her guests. The jubilant march toward Main Street is one that the gang will never forget. And the adventure hasn't even begun!

ELECTRONIC

Tina emerges from the darkness of an alley located between Fred's Electric and Dom's Donuts. She, on the other hand, has different plans for Derek and his friends. Tina keeps out of sight as Matilda leads her guests toward the heart of Gibeon. With beady eyes, she looks toward Zevon Forest and sees a wicked boy holding a leash to a giant wild boar. The wild boar looks as if it could eat Derek and his friends in one bite. The boy is careful not to leave the boundaries of Zevon Forest; the dense shrubbery hides him well. Tina and the boy make eye contact; his job is done. The wicked boy retreats back into Zevon Forest with his beastly animal as Tina disappears back into the darkness of the alley.

CHAPTER FOUR

PICK YOUR FUN

Derek and his friends are awestruck as they walk down Main Street, glaring up at the tall buildings. The city of Gibeon is much bigger than any other city that the kids have seen in their short lives. The gang is overwhelmed with excitement; the sounds of Gibeon ring in their ears. Matilda stops Derek and his friends in front of Arnold's Arcade and Mollie's Movie Theater, knowing that this is where they'd have her stop first. The gang is swarmed by another wave of kids, welcoming them to their city.

Derek practically has a panic attack as he looks in the window of Arnold's Arcade and watches the kids having fun. The sounds of the arcade games can be heard through the glass. He sees that Arnold's has every video game category: sports, fighting, war games, trivia and alien adventures. Any game he could want is in there. Like a puppy dog, Derek fogs up the glass as he envisions himself playing against the children of Gibeon. Derek waves Chuck and Tommy over to join him.

Mindy and Bucky glance up at Mollie's to see what movies are playing. With fifty titles to choose from, they shake their heads at one another and smile. Bucky has visions of eating popcorn and watching "Chargers." Mindy has visions of slurping a soda and watching "Lost in Love."

The gang is in Heaven, realizing that their parents are nowhere to be found. They also rejoice, knowing that they won't hear those famous words, "Finish playing, it's time to come home!"

"Now, kids, this is where the fun begins," says Matilda as she smiles over her flock.

"Do we have to stay together?!" asks Tammy, contemplating watching a movie or playing video games.

"Yeah … what if we don't want to do what you choose for us?!" asks Bucky, panting like a dog. "Can we pick our own 'fun'?"

Matilda sees that the kids are over-excited and want to be let loose.

"First, I must ask Derek if he still has the blue lightbulb. Well, Derek, do you?" asks Matilda.

The gang immediately focuses their attention on Derek, as if their lives depend on the lightbulb. Derek notices his friends glaring at him and becomes nervous. Without hesitation, he pulls it out from his pocket and holds it in the air for everyone to see.

"Good," says Matilda. "Let me see … what should we do first?" asks Matilda, spinning around.

Chuck's stomach growls, sounding like a herd of elephants stampeding down Main Street. Several children that are standing outside of Arnold's Arcade laugh at him; they've never heard such a noise. Tommy and Mindy smile and shake their heads, knowing what the noise means.

PICK YOUR FUN

"Sorry, guys, I'm hungry," says Chuck as he shrugs his shoulders, embarrassed.

"How about a hamburger first?" asks Matilda as she turns her head toward Chuck. "I bet that would settle your stomach."

Chuck's eyes light up brighter than her light show. He licks his chops, fantasizing about what kind of hamburgers they might have in Gibeon. The thought of a good hamburger and French-fries has the gang diverted from their plans at Arnold's and Mollie's. Tommy and Bucky rub their bellies and smile, approving Matilda's suggestion.

"That sounds pretty good to me, Matilda," replies Tommy, nodding his head toward his friends. "I think that I'll have a triple-decker with onion rings."

"Yeah, I'm pretty 'hungry' myself," says Derek, rubbing his stomach. "Besides, I can't let my buddy eat alone. I'm going to have a double-cheeseburger with chili."

"Do they have chocolate shakes?" asks Patricia.

Chuck takes out some cookies from his pocket and starts inhaling them as an appetizer.

"Guys, you're killing me with all this food talk! Let's go!" mumbles Chuck with crumbs flying out of his mouth.

"Okay, then, let's go eat!" says Matilda as she points to Hank's Hamburgers.

The kids take off running toward Hank's.

"Last one there is a rotten egg!" screams Tammy as she takes the lead.

Back in Zevon Forest, Jonathan and Mable are sitting on a tree stump having a serious discussion. The raging fire in front of them lights up the dark forest as they await the return of their messenger. Jonathan has been transformed into a skinny, freckle-faced, red-headed kid with a serious attitude. He is now much different than Matilda's description to the gang. The evil within Jonathan and his grudge against Gibeon have manifested boils, skin abrasions and many other disorders that have given him an aura of wickedness that could scare the dead. Mable, a frumpy little girl with black hair, was expelled from Gibeon after Jonathan and his followers. Mable has always looked up to Jonathan and tried to start a rebellion against Mayor Messa for sentencing him to Zevon Forest. Fortunately, none of the kids took her seriously and exposed her plans to the mayor. Together, Jonathan and Mable have been plotting revenge on Mayor Messa.

The citizens of Gibeon stay clear from the borders of Zevon Forest. The sounds coming from the evil swamp echo through the dark woods. People are scared from the legends that are told about what lives in the forest. Giants and disfigured mongrels are believed to roam the forest, looking to devour any stray man, woman, child or pet. The teachings of Gibeon's sacred book, the *Tobit,* have revealed to its citizens the wickedness and evil that now exists. It was foretold of Jonathan's demise, and his fate that will take place in the upcoming battle with Mount Chrome. Jonathan and his *sorcerer* are fulfilling all that's written in the Tobit.

The wicked boy and his giant wild boar appear out of the darkness of the forest. They're followed by several evil kids and their wicked creatures. One particular creature, a Rundar, is so ferocious that it's muzzled and contained by three boys. It has the body of a small bear and the head of an alligator. The wicked boy approaches Jonathan with fear and trembling. He knows that his life depends on the information that he's about to give to his master.

"Well, Rampart, what did you discover?" asks Jonathan as he tosses another log onto the fire.

"There are seven kids with Matilda, and Tina has made her contact ... it's a girl," replies Rampart. "I believe that I heard her friends call her, 'Tammy.' Matilda has placed the kids under her power and they're eating at Hank's."

"Very good, Rampart … you shall be recompensed for your work. I'll see you in the swamp," mutters Jonathan.

Rampart tosses his boar some meat, rewarding him for a job well done. He then motions for his cronies to follow him toward the swamp.

"It's been a long time since we've seen new kids come to Gibeon," says Mable.

"This is our time, I feel it," says Jonathan with an evil overtone, rubbing his hands together. "Our plan is working. *Revenge* shall be ours!"

"What are we going to do next?" asks Mable, intrigued.

Jonathan stands up; the thought of revenge gets his blood pumping.

"We must contact Tina. She will bring us the girl," replies Jonathan.

Mable stands up as well, seeing the intensity in Jonathan's eyes. She knows that Tina will do anything that Jonathan asks her. His followers and their creatures of the swamp begin to howl and grunt, celebrating their master's plan of revenge on Gibeon.

Unlike Zevon Forest, Hank's Hamburgers has an atmosphere that's joyous and festive. The music is playing loud and the citizens of Gibeon are still welcoming their new guests with open arms. Derek and his friends have new additions to their gang and are tossing down some serious hamburgers, especially Chuck. He has an audience of kids watching in awe as he loads up his second triple-decker hamburger with all the fixings.

"Can he really *do* it?" asks one little girl.

"He could eat a whole cow if you let him. Get 'em, Chuck!" shouts Derek.

Chuck ignores the crowd and seems to inhale the hamburger as if it's the first thing that he'd eaten all day. Chuck sounds more like he's drowning than eating. Girls move away as juice squirts out of Chuck's mouth. Several kids shake their heads, amazed, wondering where all the food goes.

Matilda watches like a proud parent and smiles upon her children. The kids all seem to get along with one another as they finish their meals. Tommy struggles to finish the last of his ice cream float; his slurping makes Derek's skin crawl. Chuck finishes the last bite of his hamburger and licks his fingers clean. Matilda shakes her head at Chuck and signals for Toby to take care of the bill. Toby reaches into his pocket and pulls out a gold coin.

"Here, Mr. Hank," says Toby. "Thank you for taking care of us."

"You're welcome, Toby. I'm sure glad that you enjoyed the burgers," says Hank as he watches Chuck wipe off the ketchup and mustard from his face. "At least I know that *he* enjoyed his meal."

"Okay, kids, let the games begin!" says Matilda as she flies to the front of the store. "Please, hurry. We have so much to do before the parade."

Toby and the gang jump from the table and wish everyone goodbye. With Matilda sending flashes of light their way, Derek and his friends break away from their fans and head toward the exit. They can hardly wait for their fantasies to begin; the kids recall their visions of Gibeon prior to making the trip.

"What are we doing first?" inquires Derek, checking on the blue lightbulb.

"Be patient, my child. Good things come to those who wait. Haven't you ever heard that before?" asks Matilda, smiling.

"Yeah, yeah, yeah ... I know. My Mom tells me that all the time," replies Derek.

"You kids sure ask a lot of questions," whispers Toby to Tommy.

"You haven't seen anything yet," whispers Tommy.

"Where are we going?" asks Patricia as she checks out a picture on the wall.

"I don't know … but I can't wait to see a movie," replies Mindy.

The picture that gets Patricia's attention shows Mayor Messa giving a speech. She tilts her head, trying to figure out where she has seen a resemblance of Mayor Messa before. Patricia has no idea that Mayor Messa and Mayor Duncan are related.

Matilda and the gang are standing in the middle of Main Street, watching several kids converge along the sidewalks. They're hoping to get a better look at Derek and his friends. Bucky gets embarrassed as he notices two girls pointing at him. Rumors have been spreading around the city about the gang ever since they arrived in Gibeon. Already, Chuck and Tammy have made a name for themselves; his wolflike eating habits and her wrestling mask are to blame.

Jeffrey, a twelve-year-old boy with lots of muscles, walks up to Derek and hands him a present. Derek smiles while he examines the gift, sensing Jeffrey's friendly spirit. It's customary in Gibeon for the one who has the blue lightbulb to receive a gift before his or her adventure begins.

"Go ahead, open it," insists Jeffrey, smiling.

Derek can't believe all the attention that he's getting.

"You guys see this?!" asks Derek excitedly as he shows his gift to his friends. "I bet it's a…."

"Just open it, Derek!" demands Chuck.

Tommy and the others shake their heads, letting Derek enjoy his time in the spotlight. He rips open the package to see what Jeffrey has given him. Out of the box emerges a necklace with a small crystal, shaped like a star.

"*Cool!*" says Derek as he puts it around his neck. "Look at me, everybody! This is *soooo* bad!"

Mindy immediately walks up to Derek and puts the charm in her hand, wanting to get a closer look. She admires the crystal as the light sparkles off its facets.

"This is beautiful, Derek," says Mindy as she smiles at him. "You are truly blessed."

Chuck becomes a little jealous.

"Hey, what about *me?!*" asks Chuck as he bites into a candy bar as if it's Derek's head.

"You had your moment back at Hank's," replies Tommy, shaking his head.

Derek walks over and hugs his best friend, letting him know that he's still loved.

"Yeah, Chuck, you ate more than all the kids of Gibeon put together!" says Bucky, chuckling.

"Sorry, Derek, if I'm ruining your moment. You deserve it," mutters Chuck as he brushes his shoes across the ground.

Tammy notices Tina staring at her from a distance. Jonathan's sorcery has given Tina the power to pierce Tammy's soul through her eyes. Tammy finds herself practically hypnotized, but is quickly jarred free by Matilda's ballad. She wants to prepare her special guests for their upcoming adventures. Something within Matilda tells her that these kids need more of her music to change their attitudes. Once again, Derek and his friends are caught up in bliss as they dance in the streets with the children of Gibeon.

Tina wants no part of Matilda and disappears, knowing that it won't be long before she brings Tammy to Jonathan.

"Okay, kids … who wants to play video games?" asks Matilda as her light fades away.

Derek, Chuck, Tommy and Patricia raise their hands high in the air. Derek waves his back and forth as if he's trying to flag down a passing car.

"Jeffrey, please show our guests a good time," says Matilda as she waves her mini-staff and a trail of violet light appears.

"Wow!" mutter Derek, Chuck, Patricia and Tommy as they gawk at the trail of light that leads them to Arnold's Arcade.

Matilda motions for the kids to get going. Derek takes off running through the violet light and waves for the kids of Gibeon to join him. His friends cover their eyes from the explosions of white light that surround Derek as he runs. Tommy finally takes off running and is followed closely by his friends and a large group of kids.

"And you two … the movie is waiting," says Matilda as she waves her mini-staff toward Mollie's Movie Theater.

A giant stairway appears.

"Holy, mackerel! Can we really walk up there?" asks Bucky with his jaw dropped.

"Yes, you can. Now go before you miss the beginning of the movie," replies Matilda.

Mindy is speechless as she walks toward the stairway, gawking. Bucky grabs Mindy and follows several kids up the magnificent stairway of light to the second floor of Mollie's Movie Theater. The kids can't help but watch their feet as they walk, staring at the unique shade of purple and green light that leads them to their movie. Bucky and Mindy smile and wave to their fans below as they enter the movie theater; it's as if they're movie stars. If only Frankie and Jimmy could see them now, they'd pay to play with the gang.

"Toby, I must go and see Mayor Messa. Please watch our guests!" says Matilda as she flies away.

"You can count on me!" shouts Toby as he watches Matilda disappear.

Toby notices that Tina and Tammy are walking toward Alice's Ice Cream Shop. He's overcome with a sense of *uneasiness* as he watches Tina acting strangely. Toby's discerning spirit tells him that he'd better go and investigate what's going on with Tina.

"Come on, Toby, lets go!" shouts Derek as he covers his eyes from the blinding light. "I came back to Gibeon to hang out with you … remember my dream?!"

Toby stops, frustrated.

"Be right there!" shouts Toby.

Several kids grab Toby and rush him toward Arnold's. Derek snatches his new friend from the other kids and leads him into Arnold's. Before Toby enters the arcade, he looks back at the girls wishing he could say something to Tammy.

Mayor Messa, who's passive yet firm, and his lovely assistant, Joyce, are standing at his window, overlooking the entire city of Gibeon. His office is located on the top floor of the tallest building in the city. There are windows on all sides of his office, giving him an excellent view of Gibeon and the fireworks show. When he's not at the parade, he enjoys keeping and eye on his city from his office. Mayor Messa needs to spend most of his time in the office, paying special attention to Mount Chrome. Mount Chrome displays its power and sends the mayor messages by lighting up the sacred cloud that surrounds the mountain.

"Ah, Joyce, another day in paradise," sighs Mayor Messa, twirling a pencil.

"Yes, Sir, it's beautiful," says Joyce as she watches the clouds roll by the window.

"I can't wait to meet this new group of kids," states Mayor Messa as he holds a printout of their picture. "There's something about them that I can't put my finger on…."

"I hope they're not like the last group," says Joyce, with a hint of disappointment. "That would be a disaster."

"The initial report is that they're okay. Here, this is what they look like," says Mayor Mesa.

Joyce mulls over the picture of Derek and his friends; their smiling faces are deceiving. The mayor and his assistant are unsuspecting of the gang's true nature. Even though he knows that evil is sometimes masked with kindness and good intentions, Mayor Messa can only try his best to weed out trouble; so far he's been successful. That record, however, is about to be tested. Suddenly, Joyce and Mayor Messa are startled by a knocking on the door.

"Who is it?" asks Mayor Messa, looking toward the door.

"It's little Bobbie," replies Bobbie from the other side of the door.

Mayor Messa sighs and signals for Joyce to open the door for his little friend. Bobbie has been a spy for the mayor for the last four years. Ever since Jonathan's expulsion from Gibeon, Mayor Messa has taken no chances. Bobbie monitors the citizens of Gibeon for plots to possess the power of Matilda or Mount Chrome and take over the city. The mayor's army is on standby around the clock, ready to wage war and defend Gibeon.

"Well, hello, Bobbie," says Joyce as she opens the door.

"Good morning, Ms. Joyce. Good morning, Mayor Messa," says Bobbie as he enters the large office.

"Good morning, Bobbie. Well, what's the latest?" asks Mayor Messa.

"Tina's making a move on one of our guests. Her name is Tammy," replies Bobbie as he looks toward Mount Chrome. "They're headed to Alice's."

Mayor Messa walks over to a window that overlooks the part of Main Street where Matilda and the gang began their day. He scratches his head, pondering what to do about Tina since her father is one of the most respected citizens of Gibeon.

"I was hoping that this day would never come. How do I weigh happiness in my city? One child's life or thousands of people.... Go and tell the others," instructs Mayor Messa sadly.

Bobbie runs out of the mayor's office.

Derek and his group are now in Arnold's Arcade, gawking at how many different video games and table games the arcade has. Bells and lights go off throughout the building, making it hard for anyone to hear themselves think. The atmosphere is electrifying. The expressions on the kids' faces tell it all. The sound of tokens crashing out of the change machines has the kids' adrenaline rushing. Derek and his friends are in Heaven.

"Look, there's a Battle Zone!" yells Chuck excitedly. "I can't believe that they have one of those here!"

"Wow, they have a ton of pinball machines!" yells Tommy, pointing to his left.

Derek zones in on the racing section of the arcade and freezes; this is a dream come true for him. He glances over at the machines and notices several racing games that include cars, motorcycles, skiing and boats.

"I'll see you guys later!" yells Derek as he races off to play.

Toby and a few of his friends follow Derek to watch him try his skills behind the wheel.

Chuck notices the giant snack bar and becomes excited. The junk food that's in the glass counters practically calls his name. He decides that he'd better go and scope out what they have in case one of his friend's is hungry. Yeah, right! A large "slushy" machine grabs his attention which causes him to trip over his feet. With his tongue hanging out, Chuck dodges through the kids as they play their favorite video games. Chuck, of course, doesn't lose his grip on his candy bar as he races toward the counter.

"That kid doesn't need to eat," says one boy as Chuck rushes by like a freight train.

"That's not nice, Albert," says Matilda with a motherly voice.

"Sorry, Matilda," mutters Albert, embarrassed.

Matilda sees how happy Derek and his friends are with the children of Gibeon.

"I'd better remind Derek about the blue lightbulb," says Matilda, closing her eyes.

Derek is overcome by a dizzy spell, as if he's going to pass out. He grabs onto the Downhill Race Game, trying to keep his balance. Derek then grabs his head and closes his eyes, listening to Matilda's instructions.

"Remember … whatever you do while in Gibeon, don't let anything happen to the blue lightbulb. You're going to need it tonight," says Matilda in Derek's head.

"Are you okay?" asks one little boy as he walks around Derek. "Someone get some help!"

Matilda's voice and melody drown out the boy's cry for help. Derek immediately checks his pocket and feels around for the lightbulb. Grabbing it and realizing that it's safe, Matilda's power wears off. Derek snaps out of his trance and sees several kids staring at him as if he's a freak of nature.

"What did I do now?" asks Derek.

"You looked like you got dizzy. Are you okay?" asks Toby as he breaks through the crowd. "Everyone, give him some room to breathe!"

"I'm fine, really," replies Derek as he puts several tokens into the game. "All right, Toby, let's see what you got!"

Matilda watches from a distance and determines that everything's under control for now. It brings a warm smile to her face, watching her children getting along with her guests as they play their favorite video games. Derek waves and smiles back at Matilda, touching her heart. Matilda glances over and sees Chuck smiling and waving at her. She shakes her head, watching the snacks in his hands move back and forth and the food falling from his mouth as he smiles. Matilda zaps Chuck with a flash of orange light and flies off to visit with Mayor Messa.

Across the street at Mollie's, Mindy and Bucky are standing at the snack counter with Kris and Jack. Kris is an eleven-year-old girl who's somewhat of a busybody, and Jack is a ten-year-old boy who's laid back. The movie theater is packed with kids rushing to get to their movies and find a good seat. The atmosphere is chaotic, as if someone fired a gun at a cattle ranch and the cows are charging across the field. Mindy, Bucky and their new friends ignore the screaming kids and focus on getting their snacks before the movie starts.

"What are you guys getting?" asks Kris as she mulls over the selection.

"I'm getting popcorn and a chocolate bar," replies Jack as he motions for more butter.

"Jelly Bears and soda for me," replies Mindy, pointing.

"How about you, Bucky?" asks Kris, staring over at the girl that's next to her. "What kind of snacks are you getting?"

"I'm going to order the Chocolate Covered Ants," replies Bucky as he wipes the drool from the side of his mouth.

Only in Gibeon is Bucky able to find Chocolate Covered Ants.

Mindy and the others grab their snacks and head into the theater to watch the movie, "Ben." The kids stumble as they walk, trying not to drop their junk food as they search for good seats in the dark theater. Of course, the kids do the "movie-theater-shuffle" as they climb over other kids to get to their seats.

"Hey, watch out!" yelps one boy as Jack steps on his foot.

"Sorry," says Jack as he takes his seat.

Mindy and the others finally make it to their seats.

"What's this movie suppose to be about?" asks Bucky, inhaling his Chocolate Covered Ants.

"It's about a boy who gets lost on a hiking trip. He tries to make it back to town in an old abandoned car," replies Jack as he munches on popcorn. "I think that his family is terrorized by a giant bear as well."

The other moviegoers get hungry smelling Jack's hot, buttered popcorn.

"Is this a true story?" asks Bucky excitedly.

Bucky remembers when Frankie and Jimmy got lost while camping with Frankie's parents. They made it back to town, but not without poison ivy and a good scolding from Frankie's dad for leaving their campsite.

"No," replies Kris as she swallows a Jelly Bear.

Bucky and the others practically get run over by last minute stragglers trying to find some seats. The kids finally get comfortable and wait for the everlasting commercials to start playing on the movie screen.

Down the street by one of the parks sit Tammy and Tina talking on a bench. Kids walk their animals past the girls, smiling at Tammy as if she'd been a citizen of Gibeon forever. Tammy, unaware of Tina's deception, looks around and takes in the scenery. A sudden remembrance of Jonathan's story shakes off her nostalgic spirit. Tina pretends to be enjoying the scenery and checks to make sure that no one followed them to this spot.

"What do you do for fun back home?" asks Tina with a piercing smile.

"I like to wrestle with Frankie and Jimmy and hang out at Bucky's tree fort," replies Tammy.

"What's a 'tree fort'?" asks Tina, playing dumb.

The question catches Tammy by surprise. She holds back her laughter, not wanting to offend her new friend. Tammy wonders how any kid wouldn't know about a tree fort. Matilda's power is still working through Jonathan's curse, but is fading away.

"It's a small house in a tree. We meet at Bucky's tree fort every week, telling stories about our dreams and nightmares. We call it, 'Story Time.' We also plan our adventures in there," replies Tammy, passing on the opportunity to make fun of Tina.

"What else do you do in the 'tree fort'?" asks Tina, checking the streets one more time.

"Well, we talk about our fears of what's under our beds at night. Do you kids have that fear as well?" asks Tammy.

"What do you mean?" asks Tina as her eyes light up.

"Well, we like to tell stories about things that we're afraid of …," replies Tammy.

"So … you like *storytelling,* do you? I have a story that you've never heard before," says Tina as her eyes grow beady. "Would you like to hear about it?"

Tammy becomes mesmerized by Tina's piercing eyes and intrigued by a good story.

"Yeah ... what's the 'story' about?" asks Tammy, starting to soften.

"Come ... follow me. We have a bungalow that's probably similar to what you're talking about. That's where we tell our stories," replies Tina with a sinister overtone.

She stands up and continues to maintain her smile and intense glare into Tammy's eyes. Tammy looks at Tina, confused, not knowing what a bungalow is. The part about telling stories, however, has her imagination running wild.

"Where is the 'bungalow' at? Why can't you just tell the 'story' here?" asks Tammy.

Tina starts walking toward Zevon Forest.

"I can't tell the story here because I want to introduce you to some of my friends, first. They're part of the story. Isn't it better to tell a story and have the people who are in it with you?" asks Tina, playing mind games with Tammy. "You should know better."

"Yeah ... I guess you're right," replies Tammy as she starts to feel the effects of the ice cream.

She should've paid closer attention to Tina and not befriended her so quickly. As Tammy turned her back to speak to Dorothy, Tina dosed her ice cream with Jonathan's mystical powder. Tammy has no idea who she's following; all she knows is that there's a story to be told.

"We'll be there shortly. It will be so much fun, *I promise,*" replies Tina as her face turns evil.

Tammy is blinded by Jonathan's spell and is being lead into the pit of evil. Tina plots her entrance into Zevon Forest as the two girls walk down the street. Tammy continues to nag Tina for her story, but to no avail. Jonathan uses his sorcery from the wicked swamp and enters the girls' minds. He knows that Tammy is his ticket to reach Derek and the others. Jonathan also gives them visions of grandeur about Gibeon to appease them while the walk toward his temporary home.

Back in the arcade, Patricia is playing air hockey with an older girl named Samantha. Samantha has blond hair, a big smile, and could give Tammy a run for her money if the two girls were to wrestle. She's good friends with Kris and Jack. Samantha noticed that Patricia was extra shy and was waiting for someone to initiate a conversation with her. Mount Chrome has taught the citizens of Gibeon well, regarding hospitality and the concern for others. The gang has been overwhelmed by the way that they've been treated since arriving in Gibeon. Tommy and his friends feel like royalty.

"Thanks for playing with me, Samantha," mutters Patricia as she smashes the puck against the side.

"No problem!" groans Samantha, returning the puck.

"Tell me about the parade that we're going to see later. I heard that it's the best ever. Matilda showed us a preview before we got here and I love the fireworks that go with it," says Patricia, out of breath.

"It's an *awesome* 'parade.' Every float is lit up with bright colorful lights, and the music that comes from the band can be heard throughout the city," explains Samantha as the puck flies by her head.

"Sorry!" says Patricia, smiling.

"No problem. How about we get some ice cream?" asks Samantha, signaling that she's finished playing air hockey.

Patricia nods her head. The two girls head over to the snack bar for some ice cream and to discuss their plans to watch the parade.

Tommy is fighting off aliens and space monsters with his spaceship, playing Alien Blitz III with his new friend, Ron. Ron is a skinny kid who loves to hang out with his friends. He's always looking for something fun and exciting to do; he gets bored very easily. Ron watches in awe as Tommy exhibits exceptional playing skills; especially for a first timer. Tommy gloats, feeling the attention of many onlookers and admirers.

"You're awesome! Are you sure that you don't have this game back home?" asks Ron as he rocks his body, watching Tommy play the game.

"Yup!" replies Tommy with his tongue hanging out as he pounds the fire button.

"What's it like where you live? Do they have a parade everyday, like here?" asks Ron, waving at a friend. "Watch out, Tommy!"

Tommy destroys the last alien ship and lifts his hands, celebrating his high score.

"Thank you! Thank you! ... What's it like back home? ... It's pretty fun. We hang out a lot and get into all types of trouble, usually. Our big thing is Story Time up in Bucky's tree fort. As far as the 'parade,' we only have one once a year. You guys are lucky to have one every day," replies Tommy as he enters his initials into the game.

"I heard Bucky talking about his 'tree fort' and it sounds pretty cool. As far as 'trouble,' we don't have trouble here, though. The only 'trouble' in Gibeon history was a few years ago when Jonathan tried to take over the city. That's a time that no one will ever forget," says Ron as if he's telling a fairy tale.

Tommy has a flashback of Bobbie running out of the store when the gang arrived in Gibeon.

"What happened?" asks Tommy, wanting to hear his version of the story.

Ron looks around to see if anyone can hear their conversation. Mayor Messa gave explicit orders to the people of Gibeon not to talk about Jonathan or Mable's expulsion from Gibeon. Tommy looks around, confused, troubled by Ron's change in demeanor. Ron pulls Tommy aside to answer his question.

"Jonathan used to be one of the most talented kids in all of Gibeon. He played music for Mayor Messa and Mount Chrome, and was loved by all. Matilda used to make him jealous because of her powers …," explains Ron, turning back to make sure that no one is listening.

"*Go on!*" demands Tommy as he edges closer.

"Jonathan knew that if he had the same powers as Matilda and Mount Chrome, he could control Gibeon. You haven't seen the full extent of Matilda's powers yet," explains Ron.

"How did Matilda get her 'powers'?" asks Tommy anxiously.

"They were given to her by Mount Chrome. You've seen that heavy cloud that lingers around the mountaintop, haven't you?" asks Ron.

Tommy nods, intrigued by Ron's seriousness.

"No one in all of Gibeon can explain how or why they were administered to her, but they were. She's the only one that can go into the sacred cloud. Rumor has it that Mayor Messa also has a connection with Mount Chrome. The citizens of Gibeon love the Mayor, but he usually keeps to himself and only comes out for the parade," explains Ron with his heart beginning to race.

Ron's conversation has reminded Tommy of Orin and his magical powers.

"There's no evil in Matilda, *is* there?" asks Tommy reluctantly.

"No, my friend, why do you ask?" asks Ron, chuckling.

"The last time that my friends and I went on an adventure under my bed …," replies Tommy hesitantly as he glances over at a video game.

He has second thoughts about bringing up Maccabus

because they'd be there all day. Tommy doesn't want to ruin his day by talking about Orin and Omit. Ron notices that the subject of evil has affected Tommy.

"What happened last time you went 'under your bed'?" asks Ron as he moves closer to Tommy.

"Nothing happened! Let's forget that I brought it up ... it's not that important," replies Tommy, fumbling to find the right thing to say.

As Ron moves in for the kill to uncover Tommy's experience on Maccabus, Chuck charges up with a handful of tokens and an ice cream cone that's melting all over his hand. Chuck uses his giant tongue to lap up the melted ice cream.

"Hey, guys, let's go and play some basketball! They have the coolest basketball game that I've ever seen!" exclaims Chuck, out of breath. "The entire basket spins around!"

Ron laughs at Chuck; he looks like he went to war with the snack bar.

Tommy's eyes light up at the thought of playing basketball; he loves a mean game of basketball. Tommy also knows that this will get him out of his conversation with Ron.

"Can you guys really play 'basketball'?" asks Ron as he checks out Tommy and Chuck. "I think that you guys are going to have your hands full," boasts Ron as he shuffles his feet and pretends to shoot a basket.

"Heck yeah, I can play!" declares Tommy as he shoots an air ball.

"I know that I might not look like a ball player, but I can throw the brick!" proclaims Chuck, dribbling an imaginary basketball. "Oh, sorry!" says Chuck as snacks fly out of his pockets. "I got it.... No, really, I got it!"

"Good. Last one to the hoop smells like a dog!" mutters Ron as he races toward the basketball games.

Tommy and Chuck follow close behind, dodging between video games to catch-up with Ron. As Tommy pulls ahead of Chuck, he thinks that he sees Bobbie hiding behind a game. He immediately stops and Chuck crashes into him, spilling his tokens and even worse, dropping his ice cream cone.

"What's wrong with you?!" asks Chuck as he mulls over the wasted ice cream cone on the floor. "Look what you made me do!"

"I'm sorry! Did you see Bobbie behind that game?" asks Tommy, pointing.

Chuck looks around the arcade and sees a bunch of kids having fun and playing their favorite video games. Not able to locate him, Tommy realizes that Bobbie is gone. A suspicious spirit washes through Tommy's body as he envisions him starting trouble with his friends. An image of Bucky and Bobbie fighting snaps Tommy out of his trance.

"Never mind," mutters Tommy as reaches down to help Chuck pick up the tokens.

Tommy glances over one last time, hoping to see Bobbie. With Bobbie out of sight, Tommy quickly shifts his attention back to Ron.

Mindy, Bucky, Kris and Jack are going to war with their snacks as they wait for the beginning of their movie. Crunching and slurping can be heard throughout the movie theater, annoying some of the moviegoers. It seems like an eternity for the previews to finish. The city of Gibeon does a lot of advertising in their movie theaters, which frustrates Bucky. The kids trade their snacks back and forth, making sure that everyone gets a taste of what each one bought.

"How much longer until the movie starts?" whispers Bucky as he picks a piece of candy from his shirt. "See … that was the dumbest commercial that I've ever seen."

"Yeah, I don't know why they show dancing pencils, either. The 'movie will start' soon," mutters Jack, fighting to get a popcorn kernel out of his teeth with his tongue.

"This is great. Thank you for coming along with us," whispers Mindy as she finishes her last Jelly Bear.

"Look, the movie!" states Bucky excitedly.

"Shhhhhhhhh!" signal several kids.

Bucky sinks into his chair, embarrassed that the other kids had to tell him to be quiet. The movie finally starts and Mindy, Jack and Kris get comfortable in their seats. The theater lights up with the opening scene. On the screen, there's a spectacular mountain range with a beautiful meadow down below; it reminds Mindy and Bucky of home. A gust of wind gives the flowers the appearance that they're dancing. The kids can practically smell the colorful flowers of the field in the movie theater.

"Doesn't that look familiar?" whispers Mindy.

"Yeah…. I'm starting to miss my Dad," whispers Bucky as he glares at the screen.

A little girl holds her finger to her lips.

The kids watch as Ben and his family drive down the highway, heading toward Chattem's Bluff Campsite. Ben and his sister, Lucy, look out the car window toward the sky, admiring the clouds and sun casting shadows on the mountainside. Ben and Lucy look like twins and appear to be twelve-years-old. Their giant smiles radiate off the screen as they stare out the window. Mrs. Hopkins watches the rolling fields of grain dance back and forth to the force of God's power. She's an overbearing mother who loves her family beyond measure. Mrs. Hopkins plays with her long hair as she stares out the window as well.

"Are we there yet, Dad?" asks Ben, acting as if he has to go to the bathroom.

"Almost, son," replies his father as he looks at Ben through the rear-view mirror.

Mr. Hopkins is a hardworking man with tough skin who

cherishes his family vacations. He smiles to himself as he watches his family take in the spectacular views.

"Where are we going first, Dad?" asks Lucy.

"We're going to unpack 'first,' then have lunch," replies Mrs. Hopkins.

Ben and Lucy become excited about lunch. Mr. Hopkins sees that his family is hungry and speeds up, racing down the winding country road toward Chattem's Bluff.

Tammy and Tina are standing on the outskirts of Zevon Forest, staring at a beautiful strawberry plant full of the largest strawberries that Tammy has ever seen. Her mouth begins to water as she imagines what they'll taste like. Tina has preoccupied Tammy with empty promises of her visit to Gibeon. She told Tammy that her friends could perform their Story Time at the amphitheater for all the children of Gibeon.

"Wait, Matilda told us not to go into Zevon Forest," says Tammy as she backs away from the luring plant. "I don't want any trouble!"

Even though Tammy is walking away, she can't take her eyes off the scrumptious strawberries.

"Don't worry, we're not going into the 'forest.' Here, take one. This strawberry will make you *feel* powerful," states Tina as she picks a strawberry.

She glares into Tammy's eyes and places her under a spell. Tammy is rendered powerless and falls for Tina's temptation, grabbing the strawberry. The strawberry glistens with juice as she moves it around. The thought of becoming powerful is something Tammy isn't ready to pass up. Softly, she hears a voice say, *"Eat it."*

This is okay. We didn't have to go into Zevon Forest to get it, thinks Tammy.

"Go ahead, eat it," says Tina with an evil smile.

Tammy is hypnotized by her smile and takes a bite out of the strawberry. She immediately falls into a trance as she chews the forbidden strawberry. The world around her begins to spin out of control, as if she's in a tornado. Tammy finds herself flying around a whirlwind of light. The light, however, is quite dark; reddish-orange to be exact. Tammy sees her past as she twirls around in the tornado of light, revisiting times in her life when she was mean. She sees herself attacking Frankie and Jimmy and making them cry. Tammy also sees herself teasing her friends and talking behind their backs. The tornado of evil light penetrates Tammy's body and changes her. Before Tina's eyes, Tammy's face appears to be withdrawn and her eyes turn red. Images of the wicked forest appear in the whirlwind as well. Several kids on the backs of monstrous, wicked snapping turtles wave their torches toward Tammy and Tina. The kids are very dirty and have a look of death on their faces. Their ragged clothes look as if they've been worn forever.

When the dust and light settle, Tammy and Tina find themselves in the middle of Zevon Forest. They're standing in front of Jonathan and Mable; their faces are lit up by a large fire. There are several evil kids just inside the light of the fire, prowling around and waiting for their fearless leader to speak. One boy looks like a small gorilla. He beats his chest, honoring Jonathan. A wicked orange breeze passes through the dark forest; in it are several ghostly faces that glare at Tammy and call out for Jonathan's revenge.

"Hey … what happened? Why are we here?! And who are *you?!*" asks Tammy, dazed and confused.

"Hello, Tammy…. Welcome back to your old self," replies Jonathan as a swamp animal cries out. "My name is Jonathan and this is Mable. We brought you here knowing how much you love mischief and adventure. We're also here to help you bring back your friends. Being good is no fun … and you *know* it!"

Tammy is gripped with fear from Jonathan's appearance. Something tells her to strike first if she wants to survive. Tammy looks around and reaches for her wrestling mask. A crow's call makes her jump.

"I'll take on the three of you!" threatens Tammy, flinging on her mask. "You want a piece of me? Come and get me!" mutters Tammy, flexing her muscles and hoping that they won't call her bluff.

She moves back and forth like a crab, trying to figure out which one she'll take down first. Jonathan nods his head and backs away.

"Okay, I was just kidding!" declares Tammy as she notices more evil kids coming out of the darkness of the swamp. "You guys are fine just where you are! See ... I give!"

"Slow down, Tammy ... we're on your side," says Jonathan.

Jonathan's suave demeanor sends chills down Tammy's spine.

"Yeah ... we're here to *help* you, not *hurt* you," says Tina, moving toward Tammy.

Tammy grabs her head and tries to gather her thoughts. The forbidden strawberry and her evil journey to Zevon Forest have her seeing red. Matilda's anointing of peace and love has worn off; she now feels irritable and discontent. Tammy feels a bond with Jonathan's wicked spirit and begins to savor the evil of Zevon Forest.

"What's in there?" asks Tammy as she points to a bag. "I bet you that it's voodoo!" mutters Tammy, recalling the time on Maccabus when she played a witch doctor to save Chuck and Derek from Tuga's villagers.

Jonathan looks down at his hand and shakes the bag. He knows that Tammy is hooked and that the effects of the strawberry have taken hold of her. It's only a matter of time before Jonathan's plan of revenge on Mayor Messa and Matilda come to fruition. Mable walks over and hands Tammy a book.

"This is what I have learned since being cast out of Gibeon," replies Jonathan as he opens the bag in his hand. "I've been patiently waiting for this day to come for a very long time. The wait is over!"

Jonathan sprinkles some dust over the book and mumbles to himself. The book lights up, almost like fire.

"'Cast out of Gibeon?' Why?" asks Tammy as her hands begin to tremble.

A strong gust of wind blows through the wicked forest.

The book opens up in Tammy's hands to a page entitled, *BABYLON*. It reads:

BABYLON

The inhabitants of Gibeon shall be amazed when the beast comes again. There will be power and authority given to the beast for one hour. The inhabitants and beast will have one mind and rise up, together. The faithful will rejoice as the Power from above, destroys the beast.

Tammy looks up from the book, totally confused yet curious as to what she just read.

"My time is coming, but will have its limit," says Jonathan as he walks over to the fire. "I need to destroy the power from above."

"There are beasts here, too?" asks Tammy, shivering with fear. "Tina, what's going on?"

Jonathan throws a handful of dust over the fire and backs away. An explosion lights up the dark forest, sending several kids and animals scurrying toward the swamp. The fire changes color; red to purple to black to orange. Screaming and moaning can be heard from the raging flames, as if there are people in the fire.

Over the fire appears a large cloud of white smoke, perfectly shaped. In it, Tammy watches Jonathan walking up Mount Chrome. Jonathan is clean-cut with tanned skin, and has distinct facial features that drive the young girls crazy. Tammy sees him ascend into the sacred cloud that surrounds the mountain. Several of his followers wait below the cloud. There are kids of all sizes and colors that anticipate their fearless leader to speak.

"Whoever you are, *I* have come to scale this mountain! Above you, I will set up my throne! I will take my seat in the recesses of the North!" shouts Jonathan through the heavy cloud. "I will be like Mount Chrome! The people of Gibeon will bow to *me!*"

Jonathan's followers celebrate on the mountainside.

A thunderous *boom* startles his followers as the mountain begins to tremble. Mount Chrome is upset that someone would journey into his sacred cloud, uninvited, and disrespect him in such a manner. Jonathan's blatant arrogance is something that Mount Chrome hates and will destroy. Several animals scamper down the mountain, terrified. Lightning flashes across the heavy cloud and the sky above as Mount Chrome prepares to speak. Mayor Messa's army appears from the base of the mountain.

"You are condemned to Zevon Forest, Jonathan! To the recesses of the pit you shall go!" declares Mount Chrome with a voice that sounds like thunder. "When people see you … they shall stare. They will wonder who you are. As you raise up tyrants and wickedness … I will be there to destroy the work of your hands!"

Jonathan tumbles down the mountain; his appearance changes in front of his followers' eyes. Jonathan transforms into a skinny, freckle-faced, red-headed kid with boils and skin abrasions. A seed of wickedness and evil is planted within Jonathan's soul that will allow him to rule Zevon Forest for a time.

"*Noooooo!*" screams Jonathan as he stumbles into one of Mayor Messa's officers.

The heavy cloud descends over Jonathan's followers, transfiguring them as well. They are given contorted faces with large evil eyes. The kids look as if they were raised from the swamp. A war breaks out between Jonathan, his followers, and Mayor Messa's army.

Tammy watches the intense *battle* taking place in the cloud of white smoke. Her jaw drops as she witnesses Mayor Messa's army having their way with Jonathan and his followers. The grunting, screaming and moaning send chills throughout her body. Bloodied images pass through the cloud and disappear. Jonathan realizes that this display is too deep and needs to end. He waves a crooked cane over the fire and the cloud of white smoke disappears.

"No, wait! I can handle it! Please let me see more!" insists Tammy as she shakes her head. Not many kids have seen this event or read from Jonathan's book. "Who's the beast?" asks Tammy as she takes off her mask. "And when is all of this supposed to take place?"

This is a topic that's not open for discussion to anyone in Gibeon or Zevon Forest, especially her. Without another moment to waste, Jonathan snatches the book from Tammy. He grabs it before Tammy gets hurt or releases an unknown spirit.

"Hey!" mutters Tammy as she watches the book leave her hands.

"You're asking too many questions!" mutters Jonathan with a villainous voice as he hands the book back to Mable. "Besides … you don't know the power of this book. In the wrong hands and we'd all be *dead*."

Tammy's mouth drops open and she quickly brushes her hands clean of any residue from the book. She realizes that she has struck a nerve with Jonathan, watching his facial expressions changing. Tammy's thoughts are redirected, wondering what her friends are doing. Having them around would ease her troubled heart. Images of Chuck and Derek playing a video game appear before her eyes.

"Don't you want to get back to your friends?" asks Jonathan as he rubs his hands.

Tammy is stunned that he could read her mind. Jonathan glares into Tammy's eyes, almost putting her back into a trance. He senses her feisty spirit and knows that it could jeopardize his plans if he doesn't do something about it.

"Yeah, how do I get 'back'?" mumbles Tammy as she dozes off. "My ... friends...."

Mable grabs a bag of forbidden strawberries and hands them to Jonathan, who grabs the bag and places it in Tammy's hand. Jonathan winks at Mable and backs away from Tammy, preparing for one of his spells.

"*Kuta, Dobet, Num!*" chants Jonathan with his hands over Tammy.

A whirlwind of reddish light surrounds Tammy, preparing her to re-enter Gibeon. Jonathan sprinkles some of his magic dust in the whirlwind, causing it to change colors. His new spell erases Tammy's memory regarding their conversation about the beast and what she saw on Mount Chrome. Jonathan's sorcery will enable him to reach her in the city, through her mind, and give her visions. He snaps his fingers. Tammy wakes up and finds the bag in her hand. She shakes her head, trying to gather her senses; her friends' voices start to ring in her head. Tammy looks around sheepishly, and then quickly opens the bag upon hearing Jonathan's command in her head.

"Strawberries!" exclaims Tammy, popping one in her mouth.

Jonathan nods and Tina eats a strawberry as well. Tammy and Tina find themselves in the same tornado of light that brought them into Zevon Forest. Images of wicked, prehistoric birds and kids banished to the swamp appear in the light as Tammy and Tina spin through the air. Tammy squeezes her eyes shut; Jonathan's spell takes hold of her body. Little does Tammy know what she *possesses* as she travels back to Gibeon.

Mayor Messa, his assistants, and Matilda are busy in his office making plans to ensure that tonight's parade is extra special for his guests. The mayor knows that Derek and his friends have traveled a long way to Gibeon; he doesn't want to disappoint them. The reports on the kids' behavior from Arnold's and Mollie's have brought joy to Mayor Messa. He and Matilda are trying to decide which float to bring out for Derek and his friends. The mayor slowly turns the pages of a giant book that's filled with all the floats of Gibeon

"This one!" says Matilda, pointing. "I think that Derek and the others shall be pleased with this float. With a couple of changes it should remind them of home."

Mayor Messa smiles and agrees with Matilda.

"They sure will be surprised to see 'this one.' I don't think that we've ever used this float before," says Mayor Messa as he scratches his head. "Then it's settled. I'll tell Richard to get on this right away."

Mayor Messa has a worried look wash over his face as he closes the book. With his hands folded behind his back, he heads toward the window. Matilda notices that Mayor Messa is bothered by something as he stares at the street below. His sudden silence and grim look on his face give her an unsettling feeling. She motions for the others to leave and flies over to be next to him.

"What's wrong, Mayor Messa?" asks Matilda.

"I hope that these kids behave while the parade takes place. Something's not sitting right with me," replies Mayor Messa as he turns to face Matilda. "You know how you sometimes get that gut feeling that trouble is lurking? Well, that's how I feel now."

"Don't worry, Mayor, they'll 'behave,'" says Matilda confidently. "Their hearts and minds were altered when they first got here … remember? We also have Bobbie and his crew making sure that nothing happens. Did you forget about that too?"

"No, I 'remember.' But I also 'remember' how kids usually go back to their former ways once they've tasted a bit of kindness. For some reason they seem to get bored being nice. Don't you remember Donnie Buckly?" asks Mayor Messa.

Matilda has a flashback of when Donnie visited Gibeon. He was held in the city for an extra day to help clean up the fountains that he messed up by adding food coloring and soap to the water. The town hasn't forgotten that event and would prefer that another incident of that nature never happens again.

"Speaking of Donnie, where's that little Bucky character?" asks Mayor Messa as he pours himself a glass of water.

"Bucky and Mindy are with Kris and Jack in the movie theater," replies Matilda.

"And the others?" asks Mayor Messa, wiping the side of his mouth.

"They're at Arnold's," replies Matilda, chuckling at Mayor Messa's sloppy drinking.

"Okay … see to it that they make it to the parade early so that we can talk about the rules for leaving Gibeon on time," instructs Mayor Messa. "And please keep your eyes and ears open. I'll see you soon."

"Yes, Mayor," says Matilda as she flies out an open window.

Mayor Messa watches her fly away. He walks over to the window, still thinking about Derek and his friends and what could possibly go wrong. No matter how confident Matilda is, he's not taking any chances. Mayor Messa calls in the head of security to do some precautionary planning.

Over at Mollie's, Mindy and her crew are slouched in their seats, watching Ben and Lucy try to catch some lunch in Bear Creek. Ben is sitting on a log next to the shore with his fishing rod held high in the air. His sister is picking up shells and rocks to throw into the creek. She loves bothering her brother while he tries to enjoy himself.

"Hey, you're going to scare away all the fish!" scolds Ben.

"There are no fish in this stupid river," mutters Lucy.

"It's a creek, silly," states Ben. "Why don't you go and throw the rocks at a tree."

Ben's sister makes a face at her brother, as if it made a difference what she called the flowing water, considering that he hasn't caught a thing. As Lucy rises from picking up another rock, she sees two eyes peeking out of the dark woods. She slowly gets up and walks next to Ben.

"There's something in the woods!" whispers Lucy.

Ben slowly turns his head to where his sister is pointing and notices the eyes. He gently puts down his fishing pole, ready to make a run for camp.

"Let's walk away, very, slowly. Maybe it will leave us alone if we're quiet," whispers Ben in a calming voice.

As Ben and his sister back away from the log, the "eyes" that were watching them lunge out from woods.

"It's a *bear!* Run for it!" screams Ben as he takes off running. "Hurry, Lucy, hurry!"

"M-o-m-m-y, help us!" screams Lucy, running ahead of Ben.

Ben and his sister run toward camp, unaware that the bear is more interested in taking a bath than messing with either one of them. Lucy pulls away from Ben and heads down the trail leading to their camp. Ben looks back to see where the bear is, unaware that his sister is running down a different path. His anxiety and fear of the bear have Ben's blood pumping so fast that he doesn't notice his sister's absence. As Ben turns to see where Lucy is, he falls down an abandoned well.

"Ahhhhhh!!!" screams Ben.

His scream echoes down the dark well while he tries to grab hold of something to break his fall.

Mindy and Bucky look at each other, reminded of their journeys to Maccabus and Gibeon from under Tommy and Derek's beds.

"That looks familiar, doesn't it?" whispers Mindy with her eyes wide open.

"Yup. How will he get out?" asks Bucky as he finishes his popcorn.

The other kids in the movie theater signal for Mindy and Bucky to be quiet with a chorus of "Shhhhhhhhhh!" Jack and Kris sink further down in their seats, filled with embarrassment. Bucky and Mindy resume their positions and watch Ben trying to cry out for help from his sister.

Over at Arnold's, Tommy and Chuck are fighting each other in a martial arts video game called Sako Warrior II. The kids watch in amazement as Chuck manages to eat an ice cream sandwich and maneuver the joystick to play the game. Even with all the distractions, Chuck pulls ahead of Tommy in points.

"You'll never beat me!" mumbles Chuck with his mouth full. "Get him! ... Yeah!" mutters Chuck as he plays the game. "See, Tommy ... you're no match for me!"

"Do you think he eats this much back home?" whispers one kid curiously.

"He probably could eat the game if he wanted to," replies another kid, grinning.

Tommy and Chuck kick each other as they try to outfight one another in the video game. Tommy chose to fight Chuck with "Jensin," one of the great warriors in the land. Chuck chose "Tibi" as his fighter. Grunts, groans and smacks ring out from the game as Chuck's fighter finally defeats Tommy's warrior.

"That's it, I win!" declares Chuck as he raises his hands, victorious. "Y-e-a-h!"

Tommy pushes Chuck as he backs away from the game. He notices Derek next to a pool table staring at the blue lightbulb. Derek holds the lightbulb up to the light, trying to bring back its radiance and make it come to life.

"What's up with Derek?" asks Tommy.

Chuck inhales a snack given to him as a prize for beating Tommy. His celebration with Toby's friends is cut short, noticing Tommy walking over to investigate what Derek is trying to do with the blue lightbulb. Derek's piercing eyes grab Chuck's attention. Chuck motions that he'll pass on the next game and heads over to be with his friends.

"Hey, Derek … what's going on with the lightbulb?" asks Tommy. "I saw you acting weird with it. Is everything okay?"

"Yeah, Derek, let me see it!" demands Chuck.

Derek quickly pulls it away.

"Easy! Matilda said for nothing to happen to this … and I know how clumsy you can be sometimes!" mutters Derek, protecting the lightbulb.

"Whatever!" says Chuck, biting into a cupcake as if it's Derek's head.

"Why do you think that Matilda told you to bring it with you?" asks Tommy.

"I don't know. All I know is that she told me to 'bring it' and to make sure that nothing happens to it," replies Derek.

"Maybe it's what gets us home," says Chuck as he stares into a game of Alien Fighters.

"Yeah, right!" mutters Derek, twirling the lightbulb. "How's this lightbulb going to 'get us home'?" asks Derek sarcastically.

Chuck's comment has sparked Tommy's curiosity. He stops and ponders Chuck's statement about getting home, very intently. This particular topic was never brought up between the gang. They were caught up in bliss from Matilda's light shows, music, and the stimulating atmosphere of Gibeon. Matilda failed to mention the most important part of their adventure as they walked through the city streets. Even Omit disclosed this information when Tommy and his friends inquired about it.

"No, wait ... how *do* we get home?" asks Tommy worriedly.

A messenger from Mount Chrome appears out of nowhere and walks between Chuck and Derek. Tommy steps back, shocked, and looks around to see where the boy came from. Chuck talks to himself under his breath, trying to figure out what just happened. It's as if the boy stepped out of one of the video games.

"Matilda will 'get you home,' don't worry. No one has stayed in Gibeon that didn't want to stay," replies the boy. "Although ... we've had a few that were *delayed* in going home due to mischief. This wouldn't apply to you, now would it?"

Derek and his friends don't like the tone of the boy's voice. He said it as if they're never going home.

"You don't have to worry about us!" declares Chuck, throwing his hands to his sides.

"Say, where's Tammy?" asks Tommy, looking around.

"She went off with Tina. I saw her walking down the street when we were coming in here," replies Derek, gingerly putting the blue lightbulb back into his pocket. "Why do you want to know?"

Several boys back away after hearing Tina's name mentioned. The boys murmur about what they saw Tina do while she and Tammy were in the ice cream shop. One of them saw Tina pull out Jonathan's bag, but couldn't exactly see what she did with it. Tommy takes notice of their conversation and believes that Tammy might be in jeopardy.

"This isn't like her to miss out on video games. I have a funny feeling that something's not right," replies Tommy worriedly. "Shouldn't we go and look for her?"

"Relax, she'll be fine," replies Derek as he glances over at a video game. "I know that Matilda did something to her when she sprayed us with her mist ... but Tammy is Tammy."

"Who7 will be 'fine'?" asks Matilda with the voice of Chuck's fighter from Sako Warrior III.

"Ahhhhh!" screams Chuck as he tries to hide behind Derek. "It's a warrior, run!"

Matilda and the other boys giggle at the sight of Chuck and his friends looking for a place to hide.

"Sorry, guys, it's just me!" says Matilda, standing on top of Frog Catcher.

Matilda plays a soft melody and gives the children a show. Derek and his friends come out from behind a video game, realizing that it's only Matilda and not a warrior. They brush themselves off as if they weren't scared in the first place.

"There you are. Where have you been?" asks Derek as he looks at Tommy and Chuck, acting as if he had protected them.

"I've 'been' downtown with Mayor Messa going over tonight's parade. Are Mindy and Bucky still at the movies?" asks Matilda as her light goes out.

"I guess so," replies Derek.

"Good. You kids are in for a big treat tonight. We're using a float that's never been seen by the citizens of Gibeon," says Matilda. "Who knows ... maybe you'll be able to fly with it."

Derek and his friends' eyes light up, trying to envision what the float might look like. Tommy suddenly recalls their conversation about getting home. His stomach drops, nervous as to what Matilda might say. Flashes of never returning home appear in his imagination. Even though other kids have stayed, they haven't seen enough to leave Hummel County. Matilda senses Tommy's concern and smiles at her guest.

"Matilda, how do we...?" asks Tommy.

"Get home?" asks Matilda as she finishes the question.

PICK YOUR FUN

"Yeah. You read my mind," mutters Tommy, shocked.

Derek and Chuck smile at each other and wonder if she knows what they're thinking about. Chuck quickly changes his thought about sliding down a giant slide into a pool of chocolate. Toby and several children who were in his daydream disappear; they're replaced by Matilda's warning about Zevon Forest. Derek shakes his head and clears the vision of an admiring fan smiling at him when he walked into Arnold's.

"Derek ... do you still have the lightbulb?" asks Matilda.

The lightbulb comes to life as Derek pulls it out of his pocket. The blue light dances around the arcade while Matilda sings a hymn. This show is completely different. Not only are there blue lights twirling around the arcade, but there are sliver, aqua, green and yellow lights shooting out of Derek's hand like a laser gun. A sudden mist falls from the ceiling of the arcade. In it, are images of the parade and the band playing for the gang. The kids in the arcade are getting quite a show. The Gibeon Electric Band is jamming before their eyes. Derek and his friends become mesmerized by the light show and Matilda's singing.

The other kids in the arcade stop playing their games to join in on the song. They perform a synchronized dance for Derek and his friends; arms waving to the music and ballerina-type spins. Tommy floats around the light as if he's made of rubber. Not a care in the world could bring him out of this incredible experience. Chuck tries to eat the bubbles of light that are coming out of Derek's hand. His giant smile indicates the joy and fun that he's having in Gibeon. Kids waltz around, moving to the beat of Matilda's ballad. The production put on by Matilda and the children would be good enough for Broadway.

"What do we do with this?" asks Derek as he stares into the lightbulb.

Matilda realizes that the kids have had enough and stops her extravaganza.

"Don't let anything happen to it … no matter what! You'll find out why you brought it this evening!" replies Matilda as she flies off to check on Mindy and Bucky.

"But, wait! What about the…?" yells Derek as he tries to catch Matilda.

She disappears.

The movie has definitely picked up its pace. Mindy is grabbing onto Bucky's arm as they watch the giant bear terrorizing Ben's family at their cabin. His family is screaming, bracing for the bear to break down the cabin door. The bear is growling as it stands on its hind legs and flairs its large teeth. The kids in theater are in suspense as they watch to see if the bear will attack Ben's family.

"I hope nothing happens to them!" whispers Mindy with one eye closed.

"They'll be okay," says Matilda from behind them.

Mindy and Bucky practically jump out of their seats.

"Matilda! You scared us!" whispers Bucky.

"Are you kids enjoying the movie?" whispers Matilda.

Mindy and Bucky nod their heads and quickly turn their attention back to the movie; the cry of Mr. Hopkins calling out for help sends chills down their arms. Matilda sees that the kids are engrossed in the movie and heads back to the mayor's office. Kris grabs hold of Jack as she watches Mr. Hopkins slam down the dead phone.

"They should try to run for the car!" whispers Kris.

"Shhhhhhh" rings out around Mindy and her friends as the other kids motion for them to be quiet. They sink further into their seats, knowing that there's nothing worse than being told to be quiet in a movie theater. The kids have eyes like saucers as they continue to watch the film.

The next scene of the movie lights up the theater. The bear is on the outside of the cabin, trying to figure out a way to get inside. The sunlight reflects off the bear's shiny coat as he walks around the porch, growling and smelling the fear of Ben's family.

"What are we going to *do?!*" asks Mrs. Hopkins, clinging to Lucy.

"I'll distract the bear and you two get the car ready!" replies Mr. Hopkins as he throws a lamp at the door, trying to scare off the bear.

"What about *Ben?!*" cries Lucy. "We can't just leave him!"

Mr. Hopkins hugs his daughter while his wife holds on for dear life. They brace against each other, expecting the bear to come crashing through the walls at any moment.

"Don't worry, sweetheart. Your brother is probably at the ranger's office getting us some help," says Mr. Hopkins.

The family embraces in one last hug before Mr. Hopkins runs onto the front porch to confront the bear.

Mindy, Bucky and Kris have one eye closed and clutch onto each other in suspense. They can't believe how courageous Mr. Hopkins is as they watch him break away from his family. Jack opens his eyes and sees Mr. Hopkins heading toward the window, ready to battle with the bear. Mr. Hopkins grabs another lamp as a weapon; he doesn't stand a chance.

"I can't believe he's going out there!" whispers Mindy as she digs into Jack's arm.

As the four kids watch the movie and wait for Mr. Hopkins to distract the bear, the scene changes to Ben climbing his way up the abandoned well. The hole is becoming brighter as Ben makes his way to the top. There are several roots and holes along the way that make it possible for Ben to get footing.

"I have to make it!" says Ben, straining to grab the next root. "I'm coming, Lucy!"

As he reaches for the root, it comes out, causing Ben to slip back.

"Oh no!" whispers Bucky as he squeezes his empty box of popcorn.

"Please, let him make it!" prays Mindy.

The group continues to wiggle in their seats as they watch the movie. Kids *ooh* and *aah* as they watch Ben catch himself slipping and regaining his composure. Ben has no room for mistakes, and he has no idea what his family is going through back at their cabin. All Ben can think of is an image of his sister alone in the woods with a monstrous bear.

I've got to save her! thinks Ben, as he regains his footing.

Ben finally reaches the top of the well and pulls himself out. The sound of kids cheering erupts in the movie theater as the audience roots for Ben to save his family.

Tammy and Tina are standing outside of Arnold's Arcade, watching the others play their favorite video games. Tina checks around to make sure that no one's watching them. She knows that her life depends on this mission; reuniting Tammy with her friends and bringing them back to Zevon Forest. If Tina fails, she'll be collecting snails from the wicked swamp for Jonathan's sorcery for the rest of her life. Tammy becomes excited about joining the rest of the gang and challenging them to her favorite fighting games.

"Can we go in yet?!" asks Tammy anxiously. "Come on, those kids don't know how to play!"

"We'll go in shortly! I want to make sure that you have the strawberry tarts, and that you understand the plan," replies Tina with a sly overtone. "You'll offer the tarts to your friends when I tell you...."

"Yeah, yeah, I have 'the tarts,'" mutters Tammy. "I remember 'the plan.' I'm to give them the tarts when you scratch your nose."

Tina notices Bobbie peeking out from around the corner of

a building. Bobbie, spying for Mayor Messa, makes eye contact with her; if looks could kill, they'd both be dead. He was alerted by his crew of her whereabouts and wants to find out what's in Tina's bag; the one spotted in Alice's. Tina knows that Bobbie will report to the mayor that the girls were apart from the rest of the group. Jonathan sends Tina a message in her head and a dose of his black magic to deal with Bobbie. A wicked chill travels from across the road and strikes Bobbie's inner core. He tries to shake it off and realizes that he's going to need help dealing with Tina and Tammy. Tina quickly schemes up a plan.

"Quick, ask Bobbie to come here!" mutters Tina.

"Why?" asks Tammy as she notices Bobbie walking away.

"It's customary for the citizens of Gibeon not to offend our guests by rejecting their offerings," explains Tina. "Offer him a strawberry tart! Hurry, do it now!"

"Come here, Bobbie! I have something for you!" shouts Tammy convincingly.

Bobbie walks from around the corner and heads their way. He has a bad feeling wash over his body, but knows Gibeon's customs. No one wants to answer to Mount Chrome for breaking his decrees. Bobbie grudgingly walks over to Tammy and Tina and prepares himself for evil. If only he knew where the two of them had been, he'd risk answering to Mount Chrome.

"What's up, Tina?" asks Bobbie as he eyes Tammy's basket.

Tina can see that Tammy is nervous.

"Go ahead, Tammy, offer him one. That's what you wanted to do, wasn't it?" asks Tina, smiling through her teeth at Bobbie.

"Here, Bobbie, we made these for my friends. But you can have the first 'one,'" says Tammy as she pulls out a strawberry tart from her basket.

Tammy offers Bobbie the sweet-smelling strawberry tart. Bobbie's stomach turns because he feels the presence of evil growing. Reluctantly, he takes hold of the strawberry tart and is overcome with a strange feeling. Cold sweat begins to pour down the sides of his head. Images of Jonathan's battle with the mayor appear before his eyes. Bobbie is blinded by the reflection of light coming off the sugar-coated surface of the tart.

"Thank you, Tammy," says Bobbie.

Tammy hands Tina a strawberry tart as well. Tina and Tammy watch as Bobbie enjoys the tart that was made from a recipe in Jonathan's book. He begins to choke and the Zevon Forest tart sends Bobbie into a trance. Tina and Tammy bite into their tarts, knowing what's about to happen.

The three of them find themselves in a wicked tornado of light; this one being more powerful than the other two. On the walls of the tornado, Tina and the others can see Jonathan's followers celebrating their arrival around a large fire. Bobbie's past appears in the light as well. He sees himself and Jonathan playing together when they were younger. Jonathan's laughter numbs Bobbie's entire body. Caveman-like faces, melting, and swamp creatures flash before Bobbie's eyes. His body shakes and trembles as his brain is pulled back and forth from the spinning tornado of purple light. Even Tammy and Tina are terrified as the screams of wicked kids and animals hurt their ears.

As the tornado of light settles, Bobbie and the girls find themselves in the middle of Zevon Forest with Jonathan, Mable, and his henchmen. Bobbie shakes off his trance and is startled by a snake that attaches to his leg. Jonathan waves his crooked stick ... and the snake is gone. The dark forest comes to life as birds of the night sing their welcoming songs. A light fog sets in that brings with it a warm mist that numbs Bobbie and the girls. Bobbie tries to shake off Jonathan's curse, but can't. His appearance changes before the girls' eyes.

This is so, cool! thinks Tammy, as she watches a boy cooking something in a kettle. I am under no authority but

200

Jonathan's! thinks Tammy, who is now entirely brainwashed by Jonathan's evil.

"Welcome, old friend," says Jonathan with an eerie smile.

Bobbie stares intently at Jonathan through the foggy mist. It's been a long time since he's seen his former friends. Even though Mount Chrome has transformed them, Bobbie suddenly feels a bond to their evil spirits. Bobbie, himself, is now evil due to Tammy's offering and Jonathan's magic through his whirlwind of light.

"How did I get here?" asks Bobbie, looking around the dense forest.

"You ate from the forbidden fruit and now you're one of us," replies Jonathan as he extends his hand. "Come on, Bobbie, live a little. Welcome to *my* world."

Bobbie shakes his hand and the two boys lock eyes.

"When did I eat the 'fruit'?" asks Bobbie, still dazed and confused.

"It was in the tart," replies Tina as she moves closer to the fire. "You're now part of Gibeon's history."

Mable walks up to Bobbie and gives him a hug. He backs off like he always does when girls touch him.

"Ewww, don't touch me!" mutters Bobbie as the others laugh.

"Well, my friend, we have a lot to go over. You're going to help me ...," says Jonathan as he points his crooked cane at Bobbie's chest.

"How do you three know each other?" asks Tammy.

Jonathan, Mable and Bobbie look into the fire and reminisce about each other.

"We used to play hockey with Mayor Messa's son, Richard. The four of us were inseparable. After each game we'd go to the lake and fish or swim until it was dinnertime. But that ended abruptly!" replies Jonathan, stabbing his cane into the ground.

"Why did everything end?" asks Tammy, confused.

"Richard and I became close buddies. I was closer to him than anyone in Gibeon. One day we were in his dad's office getting something for his father. When Richard went into the other room, I stumbled upon the secrets to Gibeon and Matilda's powers ...," replies Jonathan, watching Tammy's eyes light up.

"That's when all the trouble began," states Bobbie, interrupting.

Jonathan approaches Bobbie in a threatening manner.

"Thanks, Bobbie ... that will be all. Anyway, I wanted to have those same powers so that all the other kids would look up to *me* instead of Matilda. I discovered the Tobit, the sacred book of Gibeon. In it, are all the secrets to Gibeon. It pointed to Mount Chrome as the source of all power. I then formed an alliance with a large group of kids to march up Mount Chrome and attempt to capture this power. And the rest, you already know," explains Jonathan as he walks around the fire.

Now Jonathan has Tammy's full attention. The information about the Tobit struck a nerve with her. She envisions some large spell book like the one back on Maccabus. Images of Omit and Orin around his magic pool appear in her imagination.

"Tell me more about the 'Tobit'!" insists Tammy as she shakes off her trance.

"It's the sacred book of Gibeon that only Mayor Messa and Matilda have access to. The city's entire history and its secrets lie in that book. It explains the power that lies in the Altar Room, as well," replies Jonathan with beady eyes. "With that book ... *we* will rule Gibeon and be free to do *whatever* we want!"

In his mind, Jonathan envisions what he'd do if he had his hands on the Tobit.

"How do you expect to get the 'Tobit' from Mayor Messa? You guys were expelled from Gibeon. You can't just walk into his office and grab it," says Tammy, noticing some wicked kids and their creatures exiting the dark swamp.

"She's right…. Mayor Messa has secured that book like never before," says Bobbie, shaking his head. "There's no way…."

"That's why we brought *you* here," says Jonathan, standing face to face with Bobbie. "You're the key for us to get the Tobit."

Jonathan's evil cronies lift their torches and clubs, celebrating their fearless leader's plan for revenge. A whirlwind of yellow light rises up from the fire and lights up the dark forest. Images of children playing in the parks appear in the light. The children in the whirlwind of light are transfigured into evil kids and the sky becomes dark; a sign of things to come.

"How can *I* help you?" asks Bobbie, feeling like his stomach dropped out of his body.

"*Igor,* come here!" shouts Jonathan.

An evil looking kid, beastlike with a disfigured head, walks in from the darkness of the swamp; it's Igor. He's so *grotesque* that Jonathan keeps him in the swamp, almost like a caged animal. Igor has been working on his magic and waiting for this day forever. The evil inside Igor has been leaking from his body and is the source of all darkness in the wicked swamp. Igor has several gouges on his arms which cause the girls' stomachs to turn. The wicked kids of the swamp move out of Igor's way as he heads toward the fire. They talk among themselves, glad that Jonathan is with them. No one talks to Igor but Jonathan, and no one looks at Igor's enlarged eye. Some say that his eye will turn anyone into stone who looks at it.

"Igor, show them your sorcery," insists Jonathan as he walks up to the fire.

"*AAAAARRRRRRRRRRRR!*" bellows Igor as he cuts off a piece of his flesh and throws it into the fire.

Several animals and kids retreat into the swamp. The presence of evil is overwhelming; groaning and screeching voices cry out from the fire. Tammy passes out as a large reddish cloud appears over the fire. Images of people flash before their eyes through the well-formed cloud, giving Jonathan and the others a show. Igor takes off running toward the swamp to recover from his wound. As Tammy comes to, Tina helps her up off the ground just as Jonathan shows the group what he sees in the cloud of smoke.

"See, my friend ... from here I have been able to keep tabs on you. Igor's sorcery allows me to see present and future events," explains Jonathan, pointing to the cloud. "This was your meeting with Mayor Messa that took place last week. As you can see, I hear everything as well. Watch and listen."

In the cloud, Jonathan and the others watch Bobbie meeting with Mayor Messa in one of his conference rooms. Several security officers walk into the room to join the meeting. They're discussing the arrival of the gang and listening to Matilda's report on Derek.

"I know that you spy for Mayor Messa and help him watch over Gibeon. I've heard your conversations and know about his paranoia regarding visitors to his city. He has given you access to all the rooms in his office.... This is how I will get my revenge!" shouts Jonathan with his hands raised in the air.

The fire flares up, lighting the dark forest once again. Tammy watches as Jonathan's wicked army surrounds their fearless leader. Several large kids that look like they eat dirt for breakfast hold back their wolflike creatures. These creatures smell blood and can sense the upcoming battle.

"How did you become a spy?" asks Tammy.

"The Mayor and my Father are old friends, and my Dad suggested that I help his buddy secure the city," replies Bobbie, nodding his head as he envisions his own little plan. "Now I can see why you brought me here. He'll never suspect me trying to steal from the Tobit."

"Awesome! Our day has come!" exclaims Mable.

Tammy realizes that something big is about to happen that

involves plenty of mischief and possibly trouble. Bobbie's tone and Mable and Tina's rejoicing have Tammy's blood beginning to flow like a raging river. She begins to visualize the upcoming *war* between Jonathan's army and the city of Gibeon.

I can't wait until the others hear about this! thinks Tammy.

"We need to bring in Tammy's friends," says Jonathan as he glances over at Tammy. "Isn't that what you're thinking about? You didn't think that we'd forget about them, did you?"

The comment catches Tammy by surprise. The thought of Jonathan reading her mind grips her with fear.

"What's next?" asks Mable as she takes a seat on a log.

"Come, let us sit. We need to get ready. The time of redemption draws near!" sneers Jonathan.

All those present in the dark forest gather around the fire, waiting for Jonathan to reveal his master plan. Orbek, a large, wicked kid with pointed ears, brings over his evil lizard that looks like a miniature dragon. He walks up to the fire and hands Jonathan another bag from Igor. The sounds of the swamp come alive in the flames as Jonathan sprinkles some dust over the raging fire.

Mayor Messa has no idea what's about to hit him and his city. Jonathan has no idea what's about to hit him from Mount Chrome. The upcoming battle is not of the flesh, but of the principalities, powers and spirits that have been foretold since the beginning of time.

Back at the movie theater, Mindy and the others are watching Ben's family try to organize a search team for Ben. They're sitting at the park ranger's office where he and his assistants are mapping out their strategy to find Ben.

"Please tell me that we're going to find him!" pleads Mrs. Hopkins as her husband hands her a handkerchief.

"Yes, Ma'am ... we know these woods like the backs of our

hands. I'm sure that he's snug somewhere, waiting for us to get him," says the ranger, resting his hand on her shoulder for reassurance.

"I want to go!" insists Lucy.

"No, honey, you stay here with your Mother. She needs you," says Mr. Hopkins.

"Let's not waste more time and head out!" declares the ranger as he grabs his hat.

Mr. Hopkins kisses his wife goodbye and heads out with the search team to find his son.

Mindy and Kris' eyes begin to tear up, thinking that Ben will never make it home again. They watch helplessly as Ben's family and the rangers leave for the woods.

"Ben will be okay. See ... they have so many people looking for him. And look, they even have dogs," whispers Bucky.

Bucky reaches over and hands Mindy a piece of chocolate. She smiles and accepts the chocolate, realizing that it's only a movie.

"I wonder how the others are doing," whispers Mindy as she wipes her nose.

"Do you want to go and see how they're 'doing'?" asks Kris, fidgeting in her seat.

"No, I want to finish the movie first," whispers Mindy.

Once again, the kids are told to be quiet by a chorus of "Shhhhhhhhhh!"

Across the street at Arnold's Arcade, Tommy and Toby are competing in a medieval fighting game called The Dueling Knight. Toby's knight knocks Tommy's knight off his horse for the third time. The kids of Gibeon cheer for Toby as he beats another visitor at his favorite game.

"I bet I'd beat you if this was real!" states Tommy as he steps away from the game.

"Oh, yeah?!" mutters Toby as his eyes light up. "This sounds like a challenge to me."

"I'm the best swordsman in my neighborhood!" brags Tommy, pretending to fight. *"Bring it on!"*

"Well, I'm the 'best swordsman' in all of Gibeon," says Toby humbly. "You'd better think twice if you want to duel...."

"How about we take this game outside?" asks Tommy, smiling.

The sound of the arcade is drowned out by the crowd's reaction to the challenge. Chuck slams down his sandwich and pumps his fist; a real duel has his blood pumping. He gets energized, visualizing Tommy stuffing Toby's words back into his face. Little does Tommy know what he just agreed to. Toby walks away from the game, smiling, accepting his friendly challenge.

"Are you sure you want to do this?" asks Toby confidently.

"Of course I 'want to do this' ... that's why I asked!" replies Tommy, smiling toward Chuck and confident that he'll win.

"Okay, then ... so be it!" says Toby as he points toward the dueling cage.

Tommy and Chuck look toward the other end of the arcade. Their mouths drop to the floor as they stare at a giant dueling cage. Surrounding the cage are bleachers for the kids to watch each match. Suddenly, Tommy develops a lump in his throat. The thought of a dueling competition with the entire city watching is overwhelming. Tommy has flashes of what the match might be like. He sees himself being embarrassed by Toby, stretched across the floor, defeated.

"What the heck is that?!" whispers Chuck as he takes a bite of candy. "I've seen one of those on TV ... and the fighters didn't look so good when they finished their match."

Toby senses that Tommy is nervous and elbows his friend Jacob. Toby wants to show-off for his friends as he teaches Tommy a lesson. Jacob, a small boy with thick glasses, waves for his friends to come over to watch Toby make a spectacle out of Tommy. The kids chuckle as they watch the expression on Tommy's face changing by the second.

"You've been in one of those before, haven't you?" asks Toby, smirking.

"Sure I have!" replies Tommy, gulping.

Tommy has enough butterflies in his stomach to fill an entire exhibit at a museum.

"You've never 'been in one of those before'!" whispers Chuck.

"Shut up! I can't let him know that!" whispers Tommy. "I'm *trying* to bluff! See how the kids are looking at me like I'm some kind of chump?"

"Well, you are!" teases Chuck as he throws up his hands.

"Look over there," suggests Toby, pointing toward a wall. "That should give you an idea of what to expect when we enter that cage."

Tommy lets Chuck loose and looks toward the wall. The pictures on the wall are of Toby winning various dueling tournaments. Tommy glares at a picture that has Toby with the tip of his sword pressed against an opponent's throat. The boy is lying on the floor and looking up at Toby as if he sees a ghost. That image stains Tommy's mind and sends chills down his back.

"That's great!" mutters Tommy, wanting to vomit. "What did I get myself into, Chuck?!"

"This is all you, brother!" replies Chuck as he backs away from his friend. "I'll be over there!"

"Do you want to wear blue or red?" asks Toby.

Tommy sees the red uniform and envisions himself bleeding from Toby's quick swordsmanship. Tommy has a flashback of his bloody sword fight with Omit in Orin's backyard of his castle. Images of his face and arms being cut by Omit's sword, race through his mind. Suddenly, the room begins to spin and

PICK YOUR FUN

Tommy clams up; the blood was too much for him to handle. Chuck realizes that Tommy is about to pass out and watches him fall to his knees. Tommy glances up at him with a look of desperation. Chuck's heart breaks as he sees his friend's eyes starting to water.

"*I'll* challenge you instead!" exclaims Chuck as he squeezes a snack to pieces. "No one hurts my friends and gets away with it! Now give me the 'blue' uniform!"

Toby notices that Tommy's complexion has changed to pale white.

"Are you all right, Tommy?" asks Toby as he pulls out the fencing uniforms. "I didn't mean to scare you like that," says Toby as he chuckles softly toward his friends.

"Sure, I just need a minute," replies Tommy as he buckles over.

"Never mind him ... you need to worry about me! I see how you're teasing my friend behind his back! You're not fooling anyone but yourself! *It's time to pay the piper!*" mutters Chuck with his teeth showing.

He looks like a wild dog trying to intimidate another dog before they fight.

Toby sizes up Chuck, realizing that his overweight body will be great for practicing some of his new techniques. Chuck recognizes Toby's tactics and bites into a candy bar as if it's Toby. Without hesitation, Chuck sucks in his stomach, hoping to appear in better shape and intimidate his opponent. Chuck is about to burst as he holds in the air, trying to impress the gathering crowd.

"What are you doing, Chuck?!" mutters Tommy as he stands to his feet. "You're going to get hurt!"

"No, I won't! I'll give him one of my steamrollers! That will fix his attitude problem! He'll be out before you know it!" replies Chuck, exhaling.

Toby and Chuck enter the dueling cage, walking to opposite

sides. Chuck psyches himself up by breathing extra heavy and mashing his fists together. Every fighting movie that he'd ever seen flashes through his mind. Toby smiles at Chuck as he turns around and shakes his head, ready for the challenge. He throws him the blue uniform to put on. As the uniform flies through the air in slow motion, Chuck has an epiphany and charges Toby, hands raised forward.

"*Ahhhhhhhhhhhhhhhh!*" screams Chuck.

Toby shakes his head at Chuck's foul play. He quickly throws down his red uniform like a bull fighter and prepares to manhandle Chuck. Chuck raises his head and sees Toby waving the uniform like a cape, inviting him to join the party. Toby's smile irritates Chuck and makes him grind his teeth and run faster. Chuck braces himself for the impact and digs in; making sure that his revenge for Tommy isn't in vain.

"*Ole! Ole!*" screams Toby, pulling the uniform up and down.

Chuck tucks his head down, ready to knockout Toby. The crowd cheers as they watch Chuck become a human freight train on its way to do some serious damage. The pounding of Chuck's footsteps drives the spectators crazy. The kids lean in their seats and prepare for a massive collision between Toby and Chuck.

"This one is for Tommmmmmmmyyyyyy!" declares Chuck with his hands reaching forward.

Derek, after hearing all the commotion, breaks through the crowd and realizes that his best friend is in the dueling cage.

"*Noooooooooo!*" screams Derek, holding onto the cage.

Toby moves his red uniform high in the air and Chuck passes under it. The crowd watches in awe as Chuck flies through the exit of the cage and *sails* through the air. It appears that Chuck is swimming through the air as he prepares for the inevitable. Derek watches with his mouth wide open as Chuck heads toward the crowd. Toby cringes; he didn't plan for this to happen.

PICK YOUR FUN

"Ahhhhhhhhhhhhhhhhhh!" screams Chuck as descends onto the bleachers.

The kids freeze in horror as Chuck, the flying bowling ball, spreads his arms out, hoping to take out as many kids as he can. No sense in wasting this one! It appears that Chuck is positioning himself for a giant belly flop. Tommy and Derek watch with their faces partially covered as Chuck knocks down an entire section of bleachers. Kids go flying everywhere as Chuck's human splash *mushrooms* through the crowd. Some kids tumble over one another as they try to escape the wrath of Chuck. Without realizing it, Chuck has accomplished his largest steamroller. The arcade erupts into laughter while several kids lie under a floundering Chuck. Several of them are flattened like pancakes. The poor victims of Chuck's steamroller begin to laugh as well, realizing that they're still alive.

"Can you believe that he did that?!" asks Derek, chuckling. "He must've taken out forty kids! Where's a camera?!"

"Wait until the others hear about this!" replies Tommy, laughing.

Chuck pulls himself out of the mess and raises his hands in victory. In his mind, he's a hero for doing something that not many kids could accomplish. The crowd cheers for Chuck as he surveys the area, smiling to himself, proud of his super steamroller. Chuck quickly pulls up his pajama pants, realizing that several girls are laughing at his large underwear that's hanging out. Toby looks on as Chuck struggles to tuck in his underwear, and can't help but laugh himself. The kids don't realize that their laughter will be short-lived because of the evil that's brewing outside of Arnold's.

CHAPTER FIVE

DEREK'S RIDE

Derek, Tommy and Chuck have decided to adhere to Toby's recommendation and take a break from Arnold's Arcade. They have ventured next-door to Cindy's Ice Cream Parlor where each of them are enjoying a hot fudge sundae. Chuck, however, has two sundaes for himself; a treat for taking on half of Gibeon on behalf of his friend.

"Where did you find him?" asks Toby jokingly as he watches Chuck consume the sundaes like a dog. "I've never seen anyone eat like that!"

"He's my best friend," replies Derek, smiling. "That a boy, Chuck! Show them how to eat!"

"Hey, what about me?!" asks Tommy jealously. "Since when did I get pushed to the back of the line?"

"Take it easy, you're my next best friend," replies Derek.

Toby envies the boys' friendships.

"I used to have friends like you guys," says Toby as he scrapes the last of his sundae out of the bowl. "But now they're gone."

Toby's saddened demeanor strikes Derek in the heart. The first thought that comes to his mind is that Toby's friends are dead. Derek motions for Tommy to take over the conversation; he doesn't handle death too well.

"What happened to your 'friends?' Where did they go?" asks Tommy as he puts down his sundae.

Derek cringes in his seat as he envisons a funeral.

"One of my friends got kicked out of Gibeon ...," replies Toby.

"'Kicked out of Gibeon?' You can get 'kicked out of Gibeon'?" asks Derek, somewhat relieved.

"Yes, you can, my friends," replies Toby, pushing his bowl to the center of the table. "But it's something that we don't talk about."

The thought of getting kicked out of Gibeon grabs Chuck's attention.

"How do you do that?" asks Chuck, looking up from his bowl, hot fudge covering his face. "I know you don't talk about it, but I *need* to know!"

"There are two rules that we must follow here in Gibeon. The first is this: Mount Chrome is the one and only authority in Gibeon. We must love Mount Chrome with all of our heart and strength. Gibeon shuts down at the end of the week and we pay homage to Mount Chrome; we rest as well. The second is this: We must love each other as we love ourselves," explains Toby.

DEREK'S RIDE

"Tommy, what's wrong?" asks Derek.

"It just dawned on me that Toby was talking about Jonathan," replies Tommy as he drops his spoon.

The name of Jonathan makes the hairs on the backs of the boys' necks stand up straight.

"How are my children treating you boys?" asks Matilda, appearing out of thin air.

"Whoa! Toby and his friends are the best, Matilda! Where have you been?" asks Derek as he smacks Chuck's hand. "Get your paws off my ice cream!"

"Yeah, you missed all the excitement!" says Tommy, shaking his head at Chuck.

Matilda waves her mini-staff and creates a window of light in the middle of the ice cream parlor. The kids gawk watching the city of Gibeon coming to life in the prism of silver light; it's as if they're watching TV.

"As you can see, boys, I've been preparing your special float. Remember, you're the Grand Marshals for tonight's parade. Look at all the kids of Gibeon … making all those provisions for you and your friends. There's so much to prepare and so little time to do it. Goodbye, Rusty and Veronica," says Matilda as the prism disappears. "Now that I've given you a glimpse of tonight, I must go to Mount Chrome. There's something happening that I need to tend to before I rejoin the Mayor."

Matilda's statement about Mount Chrome leaves an uneasy feeling in the kids' stomachs. Tommy and Derek see images of Zevon Forest flash before their eyes.

"But, wait, Matilda!" shouts Toby as Matilda flies toward the exit.

Matilda turns around and sprays the entire ice cream parlor with a blue mist. Her new enchantment brings a smile to the kids' faces. She sensed their tension and doesn't want some rumors to ruin the rest of the gang's time in Gibeon.

DEREK'S RIDE

"Oh, Derek … do you still have the lightbulb?" asks Matilda, smiling.

All eyes are on Derek as he reaches into his pocket to see if it's still there. A lot has happened since the last time he checked. Chuck's tidal wave had Derek jumping for his life. Tommy watches nervously, thinking that Derek is going to pull out broken pieces of the lightbulb.

I bet it's not there! thinks Chuck.

I knew I should have taken it from him! thinks Tommy.

The kids hear tokens rattling around his pocket as his fingers try to separate what's in there. Matilda flies back toward the boys, watching Tommy and Chuck become agitated.

"That's it, he broke it!" whispers Chuck to Toby. "That wouldn't have happened if I was holding it!"

"Come on, Derek, just pull it out. You 'broke it,' didn't you?!" asks Tommy, gulping.

Derek pulls out a pile of junk from his pocket and sprinkles it onto the floor.

"Oh, wrong pocket," replies Derek, quickly reaching into his other pocket. "Ta-dah!" shouts Derek as he raises the untouched blue lightbulb into the air.

Chuck and Tommy let out a sigh, still not knowing the purpose of the lightbulb. Chuck frowns at Derek for giving him a panic attack for nothing.

"See, it's still in one piece!" exclaims Derek, waving it in his friends' faces. "You guys need to chill!" mutters Derek as he gingerly puts the lightbulb back into his pocket.

"Why do we need this lightbulb?" asks Tommy.

"I told you, you'll find out tonight," replies Matilda. "Are you kids ready to return to Arnold's so that I can head to Mount Chrome?"

"Yeeeeeaaaaaaaaahhhhhhhhh!!!" scream the kids.

Matilda spins around and exhibits a spectacular light show

that dazzles the kids. Cindy's Ice Cream Parlor appears to be spinning with her. Matilda's display of green, purple, red and yellow lights puts Tommy and the others into a trance. Her music intensifies as the ice cream parlor transfigures before the kids' eyes. Matilda's music is replaced by the sounds of tokens crashing out of machines and talking video games. Kids' screaming and bells dinging begin to ring in Derek and Chuck's ears.

Tommy, Toby, Chuck and Derek open their eyes and realize that they're standing in the middle of Arnold's Arcade. The boys remain speechless as kids run by to play their favorite video games. Matilda has transported them to Arnold's with her awesome power; even Toby shakes his head, bewildered. For some reason, the atmosphere in Arnold's is more intense; high-energy music and laser lights drive the kids crazy.

A racing game from across the arcade catches Derek's attention. Derek is overcome with a feeling that he can't explain; a feeling of excitement and adventure that makes his eyes twitch. Somehow, the video game subliminally calls his name; he hears, "*Derek, come and play,*" in his mind. Its glowing screen puts Derek into another trance. Chuck and Tommy turn and notice that their friend is hypnotized by the racing game.

"I'll see you guys later," mutters Derek as he walks over to the game like a zombie. "I ... must ... play ... that ... game."

"Is he good?" asks Toby.

"'Is he good?' Derek could beat any one of you with his eyes closed!" replies Chuck, biting into a sandwich. "No one beats Derek in racing!"

"Oh, yeah? This I got to see!" exclaims Jeffrey as he takes off running.

Tommy and the others follow Jeffrey to watch Derek play the game. As the boys run through the arcade, images of the characters from each video game fly through the air; they look like ghosts. Tommy and Chuck shake their heads as superheroes, warriors, monsters, and athletes zip by and disappear before their eyes. This second round of video game action will take their skills and excitement to a whole new level.

Over at Mollie's Movie Theater, the action has heated up as well. Mindy, Bucky, Kris and Jack are practically biting through their lips as they watch Ben being chased by a wild dog. He struggles through the dense woods, looking for the nearest tree to climb.

Run, Ben, run! thinks Mindy, as she squeezes her empty soda cup.

Just as Ben passes through some thick shrubs, he hears a loud growl.

"I can't watch anymore!" whispers Kris, grabbing onto Bucky's arm and squeezing it.

Bucky glances down at Kris' hand and thinks the same thing. He looks back at the movie screen and sees the bear walking out of the shrubs, standing on its hind legs and baring his teeth.

"*Rooooaaaarrrr!*" growls the bear, waving his giant paws in the air.

The kids in the theater seem to shrink into their seats, as if the bear is going to jump out of the movie screen and attack them. Mindy squints her eyes, trying not to watch what she thinks will happen to Ben. Bucky takes a deep breath and passes out in his seat; the drama is too much.

"Wake up, Bucky, wake up!" whispers Jack, looking over at a lifeless Bucky.

The kids look back up at the screen and see the bear facing off with the wild dog. It's as though the bear is defending Ben.

"Yeah!!" scream the kids in the theater.

Kids throughout the movie theater rejoice and hug one another while the bear scares away the wild dog. Bucky throws a box of Chocolate Covered Ants into the air, waking up from all the commotion.

"What?! What?!" asks Bucky, looking around to make sure that the bear isn't inside the movie theater.

Mindy and the others laugh at Bucky.

"Ben's going to be all right," whispers Jack, noticing several kids looking their way. "Are you all right, Bucky?"

"Somebody, help me!!!" shouts Ben as he pumps his arms.

The group turns back toward the movie screen and sees Ben running for his life. His cry for help echoes in the canyon, to no avail. Ben's parents and the search team are still organizing their efforts to find him.

Down on Main Street, Mayor Messa and his crew are carefully walking by each float, making sure that his people's work is satisfactory. He wants perfection for tonight's parade. The mayor stops by one particular float; it's a giant swan. Mayor Messa smiles, watching the lights beam out of the swan's eyes and its wings moving up and down. He turns abruptly as one of his workers plays the massive electric organ on the Zadok Music float. The lights on the float dance perfectly to the music.

One of the mayor's assistants is standing before the Henry Fire Starter float. Edward, a humble older man, gazes up toward the sky, awestruck by this particular float. Inside Henry's hat is a large arsenal of amazing fireworks, enough to entertain an entire state. Mayor Messa has a remote control that operates Henry and initiates the fireworks show. He takes great pride in this particular float, knowing how much his citizens enjoy it.

"Do we have Henry loaded up yet?" asks Mayor Messa, smiling.

"Yes, Sir!" replies a man, adjusting a rope.

"I hope it's better than last year," says Mayor Messa. "Don't forget about the Bonya Rocket."

"It's there, Mr. Mayor. We've added three Super Bows and two Centipedes as well. You and your guests will be very pleased," says the man, smirking.

"Good. Come on, everyone, let's go and see how the animals are doing," insists Mayor Messa.

Mayor Messa turns around and looks toward the heart of Gibeon.

I wonder where Bobbie is, thinks Mayor Messa, as he checks his watch.

"Everything okay, Mayor?" asks Louis. "You have a concerned look on your face."

"Yeah ... for now," replies Mayor Messa, looking toward Mount Chrome. "Come, let's not keep Casey waiting. You know how he gets with his animals."

He motions for everyone to follow him.

"I wonder which animals Mr. Casey will bring out tonight," whispers a little girl. "I hope he has a Rafflin. Those birds have the prettiest colors."

"I hope he brings out the Lungar!" says a little boy. "That would be cool!"

The Lungar is the most beautiful animal in all of Gibeon. Its long, shiny hair and crystal blue eyes captivate the children. The kids also enjoy this animal due to its massive size and obnoxious behavior. The thought of the Lungar is short-lived as Mayor Messa stops abruptly.

"Are we finished with Derek's surprise float?! If not, when will we finish?" asks Mayor Messa.

"Don't worry, Mayor. Everything's under control," replies Edward. "Hunter radioed me with the status."

Mayor Messa lets out a sigh and continues leading his group toward Casey's.

Derek is staring with his eyes and mouth wide open at the

video game that was calling his name. There's a large crowd around him, murmuring and waiting for him to play. The game is called Street Speed III. Everyone except Derek and his friends knows about the legends of the game. More kids begin to gather around Derek, anticipating the big race. Tommy and Chuck can't figure out the strange looks on the kids' faces as they walk up to Derek. Derek grabs Chuck and the three boys watch the previews for Street Speed III; the game appears to be vibrating.

"Okay, Derek, let's see what you've got," says Tommy as if he's challenging Derek to a race. "We didn't come all the way to Gibeon for you to lose."

"Yeah, Derek, show everyone how good you are!" mumbles Chuck with a mouthful of chocolate. "Beat the fastest time! You can do it!"

"Toby, why are there so many kids watching Derek? And why are they pointing?" asks Tommy, concerned.

"This game is *full* of surprises. Many visitors have played this game and ... well, let's just say that they weren't the same after they played," replies Toby, smiling. "All right, Derek ... you have an audience waiting for you. Get ready for the ride of your life."

"Derek! Derek! Derek! Derek!" chants the crowd.

"Well, here it goes," mutters Derek as he walks up to the game.

The kids watch the video screen intently as the game goes over the different race tracks. The first track is called Metropolis. This race takes place in a busy city at night. There are plenty of spectators lining the streets, cheering for their favorite racers. The Metropolis track is for the advanced racer due to its dark streets, winding tunnels and speeds that each car can reach. The second track is called Suburbia. It takes place in the outer city limits, racing through rural roads and highways. The last track is called Trax. This race takes place within a standard racetrack; the winner has to complete twelve laps in the fastest time.

DEREK'S RIDE

There are six different cars that race against the player. Each player has three Extended-Time lines that they can cross, extending his or her racing time. The player has an option to drive the race car using the stick shift; it has four speeds. There's also a Nitro Button that supercharges the car. A cloud of smoke appears over the screen, displaying the different tracks.

"Which game are you going to play?" asks a little boy, nudging through the crowd to get a better look at Derek.

"Metropolis of course!" replies Derek, starting to feel a little pressure.

He reaches down to put a token into the machine. The kids back off to give Derek some room, noticing the intensity in his eyes; a look that could scare even Jonathan. Derek cracks his knuckles, showing everyone that he means business. Toby shakes his head and smiles to his friends, excited for his new buddy to prove himself in front of the crowd.

"Get 'em, Derek!" calls Chuck with a mouthful of cookies. "Now, everyone, give him plenty of room to race!" mutters Chuck, squeezing his bag of cookies and spilling some on the floor. "Oops! Sorry!"

"Yeah, Derek, make us proud!" yells Tommy, pumping his fist.

The noise in the arcade silences as the game begins.

"Do you think that he's better than Jack?" whispers one little girl.

"No way!" whispers her friend.

"I bet he could take on 'Jack' with one eye closed!" states Chuck, hovering over the two kids.

"Ahhhhhh!" cries the little girl as she imagines Chuck's head looking like a giant kickball.

"Chuck, leave them alone!" warns Tommy, shaking his head. "Sorry girls."

"But I didn't do anything," says Chuck defensively.

DEREK'S RIDE

"Good luck, my friend," says Toby as he watches Derek get positioned in his racing car. "Oh, by the way ... you only have half of the city *watching* you. No pressure!"

Derek ignores Toby's cheap shot and settles into the car. He pushes the start button and grabs hold of the steering wheel firmly with both hands. Derek stares intently at the video screen, waiting for the game to begin. The crowd watches Derek turning the steering wheel and selecting the Metropolis track. The video screen then prompts Derek to select a car for his race. There's a Tarri, a Florcei, a Stallion and a Zetal.

"Pick the Stallion!" shouts Chuck, almost knocking over a little boy. "Sorry, dude!"

"No, pick the Florcei," says Tommy, calming down Chuck with a pat on the back.

Derek moves the steering wheel until the prompt stops on the Tarri. The Tarri is sleek and looks as if it could outrun any car in Hummel County.

"Sorry, guys," says Derek, smiling as he pumps the gas pedal to make his selection.

The next screen displays the different types of accessories that a player can add to his or her car. There's a Nitro Tank, a Supercharge Engine, Racing Stripes and Tires. Derek moves the steering wheel back and forth between each selection, teasing everyone.

"Make up your mind, would you?!" yells Randy.

Chuck turns around and stares as if he's going to swallow the kid whole.

"Sorry," mutters Randy, cowering. "Take your time, Derek!"

The crowd follows the prompt around and around. Derek finally steps on the gas pedal and selects the Nitro Tank.

"Cool!" says Derek. "Now I'm ready!"

The screen shows a count down until the race starts. There's a large white "Ten" flashing in the middle of the black screen. Then there's a "Nine."

"*Eight! Seven! Six! Five! Four! Three! Two! One!*" scream the kids in unison.

The video screen shows Derek's car lined up with the other six racers. The Tarri's engine revs up as the starter girl holds up a green flag. The starter is a blond-headed girl who looks as if she just walked off the beach.

"Get them, Derek!" shouts Tommy over the rowdy crowd. "Show us who's the man!"

The kids of Gibeon and Derek's friends become silent and stand still. The starter girl smiles at Derek through the video game and drops the green flag. For an instant, Derek is overwhelmed by her smile, feeling as if he knows her. But that feeling is quickly smashed by the sound of screeching tires. Derek uses his lead foot and presses down on the gas pedal. He begins to shift gears and jump around his seat, acting as if he's driving a real race car. Derek looks like a professional; one hand on the steering wheel and one hand on the stick shift. The crowd in the arcade is going ballistic.

Tommy and the others watch the video screen and see smoke rising from Derek's tires as he peels out from his starting spot. Derek's Tarri races down the street, weaving through the pack of cars and almost crashing into an old, souped-up Stallion. The people in the game are cheering for their favorite racers from the sidewalks that line the city streets.

"This game is so real!" says Chuck, staring at the video screen.

"The graphics are amazing! This game is much cooler than any that we have back home!" states Tommy, extending his neck to get a better look.

"Derek is pretty good, so far," says Toby, shaking his head.

"'Pretty good'?!" mutters Derek as he gnashes his teeth, steering his car around the others. "You haven't seen anything yet!"

DEREK'S RIDE

Derek's Tarri is almost pushed off the road by one of his opponents.

"Derek, look out!" yells Chuck as he grabs onto the little boy that's in front of him. "Drive your car to the right!"

The video screen shows a split tunnel up ahead. Derek quickly maneuvers his car, avoiding a collision with the barrier that separates the tunnels. His car's headlights offer the only light throughout the tunnel. From a distance, the kids can see other cars heading in Derek's direction as he accelerates his Tarri.

"Move to the left!" screams Tommy. "You're going to crash!"

"Watch the yellow car!" warns a little boy.

"I got it!" screams Derek, gliding in and out of on-coming traffic. "*I'm* driving, not you!"

Derek shifts the gears up and down, adjusting to the corners of the tunnel. The lights on the signs barely give a player enough time to react and not crash. Derek makes it out of the tunnel without a scratch. Tommy and the others cheer and wipe the sweat from their foreheads.

"See, I know how to drive!" brags Derek as he shifts gears.

Two boys shake their heads, disapproving of Derek's cocky attitude. Before Derek's arrogance can set in, he smashes into a lamppost along a street corner. The crash sends Derek's car spinning out of control. The Tarri smashes into another car which sends his opponents crashing into each other. The kids behind Derek cringe as they watch smoke and twisted metal emerge from the pileup.

"Go, Derek, go!" screams Chuck as he squeezes a sandwich in half.

Derek quickly turns the steering wheel and tries to straighten out his car. He's sweating profusely, knowing that his Tarri is only seven seconds behind the leader. As Derek approaches a straightaway, the kids see the Extended-Time cross line in the distance.

DEREK'S RIDE

"Punch the Nitro Button!" yells Tommy. "Come on! Beat these guys!"

Derek punches the Nitro Button and grabs the steering wheel with both hands. The Nitro Tank kicks in and sends Derek's car screaming down the straightaway, passing the other cars. Derek's Tarri zooms through the Extended-Time cross line and gives him more time to race.

"All right!" screams a little boy, cheering for Gibeon's new hero. "Go, Derek! You can do it!"

The crowd in Arnold's watches as three cars approach Derek's Tarri to ruin his game. Derek quickly shifts down into second gear and steers his car out of the path of a blue car. He rocks back and forth in the seat of the game, biting his tongue and bobbing his head; if he could, he would enter the game. The Tarri barely dodges each car and heads toward the finish line. A monstrous roar from the kids of Gibeon sends chills down Derek's arms; he's overwhelmed with support to win the race.

"Oh no!" screams a little girl.

"Push the Nitro Button!" screams Toby. "Do it now!"

Derek smashes the Nitro Button and nothing happens.

"What's wrong?!" asks Jeffrey. "Push it again!"

"The Nitro Tank is empty! I guess I used it up the last time I punched it!" replies Derek as he races his car. He puts a death grip on the steering wheel. "Come on, come on!" mutters Derek, driving neck-in-neck with the Zetal.

"Cut him off, Derek!" mumbles Chuck with a mouthful of potato chips. "Use a cheap shot if you have to!"

The Zetal and Tarri are driving down the straightaway; one car pulls ahead, then it falls back. The finish line is getting closer and closer, driving the spectators crazy. Tommy and the others watch a large group of boys and girls cheering at the finish line. Derek sees the reflection of Tommy, Toby and Chuck cheering for him on the video screen.

Derek leans his body toward the right, moving the Tarri

away from the Zetal. The maneuver, however, doesn't throw off his opponent. Several kids are practically grabbing Derek's neck to help him drive. The crowd in Arnold's is chaotic; whistling and screaming drown out all other sounds of the arcade.

"I can't watch!" says Rusty, covering his eyes.

"Hold on, Derek!" screams Tommy. "Don't let him beat you!"

The Tarri and Zetal cross the finish line simultaneously as the starter girl waves the checkered flag back and forth. The two cars skid and come to a complete stop on the other side of the finish line. The video screen shows a large crowd of people pouring onto the street to congratulate the drivers.

"Who won?!" asks a little boy.

Derek is panting like a dog, staring at the kids in Arnold's. Tommy, Chuck and the rest of the onlookers remain silent, waiting for the results of the race. Chuck is holding a cupcake in mid-bite as he waits for the screen to change. Toby stares with his mouth open, not knowing how to react should Derek lose the race.

The video screen displays the Tarri and Zetal racing toward the finish line in slow motion; it will be judged by a photo finish. Tommy and his friends hold their breath while the replay finishes. Hearts pound and palms become sweaty as the kids watch the finish line approaching.

"This is too much!" whispers a little girl, turning away.

"I bet he didn't win," whispers her friend.

Chuck looks over at the two, ready to pull another belly flop.

"Derek 'won'!" shouts Tommy as he grabs Toby and hugs him. "I knew it!"

"*Yeeeeaaaaahhhh!*" roars Chuck.

Derek jumps out of the seat of the car and raises his hands, victorious.

"I 'won'! I 'won'!" declares Derek, almost crushed by his new fans. "I told you that he didn't stand a chance!"

The kids of Gibeon celebrate with Derek, smothering him.

DEREK'S RIDE

Toby smiles as he watches Derek shine in his moment of glory; he's happy that his new buddy came through with his trash-talking. He winks at Tommy and gives him a thumb up, approving their visit to Gibeon. Toby notices Patricia making her way through the crowd to congratulate her friend. She's prevented from reaching Derek by a swarm of girls wanting to congratulate her for Derek's victory.

Over at Tina's house, it's a completely different story. Tammy, Bobbie and Tina are sitting on her front lawn, recovering from their return trip from Zevon Forest. Jonathan has7 given them plenty to think about and plenty to do. His plot for revenge is brewing in the midst of all the fun that the others are having at Arnold's and Mollie's. Evil *radiates* from Tina and her counterparts; kids rush by, not wanting to make eye contact.

"Are you sure that you can handle it?" asks Bobbie, concerned.

"My friends and I have been doing this for years," replies Tammy confidently. "*Trouble* is our middle names!"

"How do you plan to get the remote from Mayor Messa?" asks Tina.

"Well, if these strawberries work half as much as they did on me, Patricia will be our girl," replies Tammy, smiling.

"'Patricia'?!" ask Bobbie and Tina.

"That's right, Patricia. She's so sweet that the Mayor can't help but trust her. She'll have 'the remote' for the Henry Fire Starter float before you know it," replies Tammy. "Her puppy-dog eyes are too much to resist."

"What about the band?" asks Tina. "How will you lead them out of the city?"

"I'll leave that to Chuck," replies Tammy. "We'll dress him up like a tuba player and stick him in 'the band.' Once he's in, he'll do the rest. Don't let his weight fool ya! Chuck is pretty crafty and quick on his feet when he wants to be," says Tammy, envisioning Chuck playing the tuba.

"What about you, Bobbie? Won't the Mayor expect you to walk with him?" asks Tina.

"No. He'll have me on Undercover Service apart from him and expect me to keep my eyes open. That will give me the opportunity to help you guys and monitor him and his security force," replies Bobbie with a sinister grin. "I can see it now!"

"Excellent! Jonathan will be pleased when I tell him what's going on," says Tina.

"We need to start planning our meeting locations and times, soon," says Bobbie as he checks his watch. "I think that Tammy should bring these tarts to her friends right away."

"When they ask me where I was, what do I tell them?" asks Tammy.

"You can 'tell them' you were with me. Most of the kids of Gibeon know that I'm a loner and keep to myself. You can 'tell them' we were walking in the Garden of Gesham," replies Tina, looking over to make sure that no one's spying on them.

"Good idea," says Bobbie as he stands up. "I'd better get back to Mayor Messa's office and see how Matilda and the others are doing. Besides, I don't want them to get suspicious."

"Don't forget about the Tobit!" says Tina, rising from her seat. "That's the most important part of our mission!"

"Relax, I know. Besides, Jonathan just reminded me in my head," says Bobbie, shaking off the vision.

Tammy grins and rubs her hands together. A plan of this magnitude is beyond her wildest dreams. Jonathan's plan for revenge will give a new meaning to the word sabotage. Visions of the wicked swamp flash through her imagination. Tammy shakes them off and tries to unwind; her blood races in anticipation.

"All right, you two, I'll see you later," says Bobbie as he heads back into the city.

Tina checks Tammy's basket, double-checking that there are enough tarts for her friends.

"They're all here! Let's get this party started!" states Tina as she gives Tammy a high-five. "You haven't seen *trouble* yet. When you go back home, no one will ever mess with you again!"

Tammy embraces Tina's lie, and the two girls head toward the city. Tina continues to feed her false promises and Jonathan continues to brainwash Tammy while they walk. The rest of the gang has no idea what's heading their way.

Mindy and Bucky, oblivious to what's going on with their friends, are huddled together watching the movie. It keeps getting more intense by the minute. Kids' eyes light up the theater as they wait for something scary to happen. No one dares to make a noise during this part of the movie, especially those that slurp the last bit of their sodas and make that annoying sound.

Mindy and the others are watching Mr. Hopkins walking in a dark abandoned cave looking for Ben. He has two park rangers with him in case there's trouble. The giant movie screen is pitch-black, with an occasional flash of light moving through the dark cave. The light is coming from Mr. Hopkins and the park rangers' flashlights.

"Ben? Are you in here?!" asks Mr. Hopkins. His voice echoes in the cave. "Son, it's your father!" shouts Mr. Hopkins.

Mr. Hopkins turns the flashlight toward the two rangers to make sure that they're okay. He sees the rangers checking other paths in the cave. Suddenly, a group of bats flies out from their homes and begin to attack the three trespassers. Mr. Hopkins and the others swat wildly at the bats.

The kids in the movie theater cringe and grab hold of each other. Girls squirm in their seats and swat their hands in the air. It's as if the bats are heading into the theater. Some kids even cover their eyes, waiting for the bats to disappear.

"Ahhhh!" screams Bucky as he spills his drink.

"Make them go away!" says a girl as she tries to hide in her seat.

"It's only a movie, you guys!" says Kris, shaking her head. The kids in the movie theater settle down as they watch the bats exiting the cave.

"Are you kids enjoying yourselves?" asks Matilda, suddenly appearing out of thin air.

"Ahhhh!" yelps Kris as Jack throws his popcorn into the air.

"It's the bats!" mutters Bucky as he grabs Mindy.

Matilda's untimely visit adds to the suspenseful movie. The kids gather themselves together, realizing that it's only Matilda. Jack knows that Matilda didn't appreciate the way they were mocking Mindy and Bucky's fear.

"Sorry, kids. Look," whispers Matilda.

The kids turn around and see Mr. Hopkins and the two rangers run out of the cave.

"Look familiar, Mindy?" whispers Matilda as her eyes begin to glow.

Matilda's glowing eyes put Mindy into a trance and bring her back in time when she ran out of one of the tunnels in Orin's castle. Mindy's world begins to spin.

"How did you know I was there?" asks Mindy, emerging from Matilda's trance.

"That's not important right now," replies Matilda. "I came to remind you to be at Hank's before sunset...."

"What about the others?" asks Bucky, interrupting.

The kids in the movie theater turn around, frustrated.

"Is this how you behave at home?" whispers a little girl.

"Shhhhhhh!" signals a boy to the left.

"Sorry," whispers Mindy.

Mindy turns back and sees that Matilda is gone. Her and Bucky look over and notice Jack and Kris captivated by the movie, staring at the screen with their eyes wide open. They join their friends and sink back into their seats to continue watching the film.

DEREK'S RIDE

On the movie screen, a park ranger, Mrs. Hopkins and Lucy are checking Lake Jordan, looking for Ben. A couple of the ranger's assistants join them to make sure that he hasn't drowned. Mrs. Hopkins and her daughter are standing on the shore, totally distraught. Heading their way is a large alligator, looking for something to eat.

"Are you sure he's a good swimmer?" asks the park ranger.

"Yes, I'm sure. Please, I beg you, help me find my son!" pleads Mrs. Hopkins.

"We're going to 'find' him, Ma'am. We'll walk over to the docks and take out one of the boats. From there we'll get a good look at the shore of the lake," says the park ranger.

"*Ben! Ben!*" calls Mrs. Hopkins.

Mrs. Hopkins breaks down and cries. One of the park ranger's assistants comforts her with a tissue.

"Here. We'll 'find him' … I just know it. Don't give up hope because hope doesn't disappoint. Stay strong in your faith and keep praying," says the assistant.

Mrs. Hopkins takes the tissue and smiles at the assistant's kind gesture. The moment is short-lived.

"*Alligator!* Run to the docks!" shouts the park ranger, shuffling Mrs. Hopkins and Lucy away.

The alligator snaps its mouth open and lunges onto the shore.

The park ranger and Ben's family spoil the alligator's plans for dinner as they take off running toward the docks. As the group approaches the docks, they see Mr. Hopkins kneeling on the edge of the dock, holding his hands together as if he's praying. Mrs. Hopkins's heart pounds with anticipation, feeling that her husband will be the bearer of bad news. She pulls ahead of the park ranger and his assistants to find out what her husband knows.

"*Sweetheart!*" shouts Mr. Hopkins, rising to his feet to greet his wife.

"Any news on Ben?!" asks Mrs. Hopkins while the two embrace in a hug.

Ben's sister joins in on their moment of sorrow, knowing that Ben is still out in the woods somewhere. The park rangers let them have their moment as they comfort one another.

"Are we ever going to see 'Ben,' again?" asks Lucy, teary-eyed.

"You bet, pumpkin!" replies Mr. Hopkins, wiping away her tears and caressing her cheek.

Mindy, Bucky, Kris and Jack huddle next to each other in their seats. The emotional family reunion without Ben has them in tears. The sappy music from the movie has the audience in tears as well. By the sound of it, a person might think that each kid in the movie theater just lost a family member.

"I hope they find him soon," whispers Mindy, wiping a tear.

"I can't take this much longer," whispers Bucky, blowing his nose.

"He's in the woods," whispers Kris, all choked up.

"Yeah, but is he still alive?" asks Jack.

Mindy, Bucky and Kris glare at Jack, shocked that he'd make such a comment. The kids in front turn around as well and give Jack a nasty look.

"Sorry," says Jack, sinking back into his seat.

Things aren't so sad over at Arnold's Arcade. In fact, the energy and jubilant vibe of the kids could light up a football stadium on any given Sunday. Matilda is on top of Street Speed III, observing her children still celebrating Derek's first place finish. Two kids finish playing the game and shake their heads, wondering how Derek finished the race so fast.

"Did you hear that I won?" asks Derek, breaking away from the crowd.

"Yes, but that's not why I'm here," replies Matilda. "I'm here to remind you of the electric parade and our meeting place. We don't want to keep Mayor Messa waiting. Remember ... he has something special planned for you and your friends."

"I know, I know. We meet at Hank's before sunset," says Derek impatiently.

"Good. Continue on, my children," says Matilda.

"I want to play next!" mutters Chuck jealously. "I can win, too, you know!"

"Don't forget the lightbulb," says Matilda as she flies away

Tommy and Chuck glare at Derek, fearful that he may have crushed it during the race. Derek was rocking back and forth in his seat as he played the game, totally focused on winning and not paying attention to the great mystery hidden in his pocket. All the excitement and sudden movement could've easily crushed the lightbulb. Derek reaches into his pocket as the kids back away. The kids become tense, awaiting certain disaster.

Please be there! thinks Tommy, as he taps his foot.

We're never going to get home! thinks Chuck.

"There's no way the 'lightbulb' is still in one piece," whispers Toby's friend.

"Wrong pocket," states Derek, shrugging his shoulders.

The crowd sighs with relief.

"What happens if it's broken?" asks Tommy hesitantly.

"You don't go home," replies Matilda's voice out of thin air.

Tommy and the others look around for Matilda and realize that she spoke to them from another location. Patricia looks at Peggy and Chuck with a tear in her eye. As much fun as they've been having in Gibeon, it's not enough to keep them here forever. Chuck begins to sweat, thinking of never seeing his mom again. Tommy swallows hard, thinking about his family worrying about him and searching for him.

Derek pulls his hand out of the other pocket and slowly

opens it. A bright blue and white light beams up to the ceiling from Derek's opened hand. The kids of Gibeon back away and bow down toward Derek.

"It's not 'broken'!" exclaims Chuck as he squeezes Tommy. "Matilda, you're back!"

"We get to go home!" says Patricia to Peggy.

"But how *does* this get us 'home'?" asks Tommy as he breaks away from Chuck. "I can't take it anymore, please tell us about the lightbulb."

"That's something you as a group will have to find out," replies Matilda as she waves her mini-staff. "Ye of little faith ... how long will I be with you? It's Mindy's faith that will prevail."

Tommy and the others are overwhelmed with a tingling sensation.

Derek slowly turns around and gives everyone a show from the blue lightbulb; dancing images of the band march out from his hand and head toward the exit. Tommy and Chuck gawk as they watch the Gibeon Electric Band disappear into thin air. Matilda joins Derek and belts out a melody that brings a smile to every face. Derek, filled with joy and happiness, turns back toward Street Speed III to show his gratitude to Matilda. Suddenly, Derek's allergies kick up and he tilts his head back for one of his obnoxious sneezes. The blue lightbulb did something to Derek as it radiated in his hand. He begins breathing to the beat of the music and motioning for everyone to back away.

"What's wrong with him?!" asks Patricia as she squeezes Peggy.

"Oh no, he's going to sneeze!" replies Chuck, motioning for two boys to back off. "Look out!"

"*Someone grab the lightbulb!*" screams Tommy.

Derek takes one last, deep breath and closes his eyes. Before his friends can rescue the lightbulb, Derek lets out the loudest and hardest *sneeze* of his entire life.

DEREK'S RIDE

"Ahhhhhhhhhhhh, Cheeeewwwwwwwww!!!!!!" bellows Derek as he sneezes.

A gust of wind blows through the arcade.

The dancing blue light stops as the lightbulb flies high into the air. Tommy and his friends watch in suspense as it twists and turns over, almost hitting the ceiling. Before anyone can make a move to catch the blue lightbulb, a giant cloud of smoke appears in front of Street Speed III. Suddenly, the *roar* of a race car's engine sends several kids retreating even farther away from the game. The sound of the engine is coming from the thick cloud of smoke. Tommy, Chuck and Toby back away themselves, waiting for the smoke to clear. Tommy watches helplessly as the blue lightbulb disappears into the cloud.

"What the heck is going on?!" asks Chuck, pulling Derek to safety.

"It sounds like one of the cars from the game!" replies Tommy as he holds onto Patricia. "Everyone stay back!"

Matilda smiles, knowing one of her friends has come out to play with her special guest. As a result of Derek's super sneeze, Thunder, an older, souped-up hot rod, was called out of Street Speed III. As the smoke clears, Thunder smiles at Derek and idles his engine. Derek is speechless; his eyes light up brighter than the lightbulb.

"*Cool!*" declares Derek as he breaks loose of Chuck's hold. "Do you guys see this?! There's a race car in the arcade!"

He walks up to the car cautiously.

"Be careful, Derek!" warns Tommy, concerned. "Chuck, hold Patricia."

"Looking for this?" asks Thunder as Derek peeks into the car.

Derek jumps back, blinded by the blue lightbulb. A thunderous cheer rings out throughout the arcade.

"Yea, Thunder!" scream several kids. "He found the blue lightbulb!"

236

DEREK'S RIDE

"You can talk too?!" asks Derek, shocked.

"Of course I 'can talk,'" replies Thunder. "Hop in! Don't you want your blue lightbulb back? Remember ... Matilda warned you not to lose it."

Tommy and the others look at each other, dumbfounded that Thunder would know about the importance of the blue lightbulb. Derek, however, is preoccupied with the fact that a race car was birthed from a video game and is now idling in the middle of Arnold's. He walks around Thunder, admiring his bright red paint and fancy racing stripes. The extra-large racing tires and crash bar get Derek's blood pumping. Thunder smiles at Derek as he passes the front of the car.

"Number Seven! That's my favorite number!" shouts Derek, noticing the large number on Thunder's hood. "I bet you're faster than the Tarri!"

"All right, kids, you're in good hands now. Thunder, be easy on my guest," says Matilda as she winks at her friend.

"You got it, Matilda," says Thunder, winking back.

Tommy and his friends walk up to Derek and examine Thunder as well.

"Wait until Frankie and Jimmy hear about this!" states Chuck, continuing to eat his candy bar. "Forget them! Wait until we tell the kids at school that we saw a race car jump out of a video game!"

"No one's going to believe it!" says Tommy, flabbergasted.

"Get in, my friend. It's time to go for a ride. You like to play video games ... how would you like to *become* a video game?" asks Thunder.

"*No way!* How is that possible?!" asks Derek with eyes as big as Thunder's tires.

"Anything is 'possible' to the one who has faith. Jump in. I'm going to take you for a ride in Street Speed III," replies Thunder as he revs his engine.

DEREK'S RIDE

Derek looks toward the video game and envisions himself being in the game. Tommy and Chuck also look at the video game and shake their heads. They, too, envision their friend racing the other cars while he drives Thunder.

"Now I'm starting to freak out! This is too much! We're going to watch our friend 'become' part of a video game?!" asks Chuck as he drops his candy bar to his side.

"Isn't that dangerous?" asks Patricia, hugging Peggy close to her body.

"No, Patricia. Your friend will be safe with me as long as he listens," replies Thunder.

"Oh great, he has to 'listen'!" says Chuck sarcastically. "Goodbye, Derek!"

Derek stares at Chuck and pumps his fist, bothered by Chuck's negative attitude.

"I can 'listen' … I promise!" swears Derek as he jumps in Thunder's driver's seat.

Thunder revs his engine, sounding as if a rocket is going to take off. The kids immediately fall to the floor and cover their ears. Before another word is spoken, a heavy cloud of smoke rises out of Thunder's exhaust pipe. The smoke builds up thicker than when Thunder exited the video game. As the smoke dissipates, the sound of the engine disappears; Thunder and Derek are gone. Tommy and Chuck immediately run to the front of Street Speed III and see their friend waving at them from the winner's circle.

"I can't *believe* that he's in there!" declares Tommy, pointing to his friend. "D-e-r-e-k!"

"This is too cool!" exclaims Chuck as he leans in toward the video screen. "Be careful, Derek!"

"You haven't seen anything yet," says Toby, walking through the crowd.

"What do you mean?" asks Tommy, concerned.

DEREK'S RIDE

"You guys get to race him," replies Toby, smiling. *"How cool is that?!"*

Tommy and Chuck look at each other in disbelief. Realizing that Toby is being serious, they grab each other's hands and jump up and down, filled with excitement. This is by far the coolest thing they've ever seen in their lives. They rush over to the adjoining Street Speed III games that will allow them to race their friend and race each other.

"Patricia, would you like to play, as well?" asks Toby.

"No thanks, I'll just watch," replies Patricia as she shies away.

"Come on, Patricia ... live a little! How often do you get to do this?!" asks Chuck, having trouble squeezing into one of the cars. "What are you looking at, punk?!"

Patricia mulls over the thought of racing Derek. The proposition is quickly smashed by a thought of her crashing into him.

"That's okay, you guys 'play.' I'd only slow you, two, down," replies Patricia, forcing out a smile.

"I wouldn't 'play' either," whispers a little girl, noticing how uncomfortable Patricia has become. "Don't worry. You can watch the race with me."

"Suit yourself, Patricia!" mutters Tommy as he climbs into his car.

Several kids chuckle as they watch Chuck's large body squeezing into his car. Poor Chuck has no idea that the kids are laughing at his expense.

"Come on, Chuck! Hold your breath!" instructs Tommy, smiling.

Chuck inhales and sucks in his stomach. Those extra inches are barely enough to let him get situated in his seat.

"Maybe he should go on a diet or something," whispers one little boy.

"That's not nice!" says Patricia, defending her friend.

DEREK'S RIDE

Tommy and Chuck are now seated and ready to play Street Speed III. They glance over at each other, waiting for the game to begin. Toby walks up to each machine and deposits enough tokens for them to race Derek.

"There you go. Now you're ready," says Toby as he backs away from the machines. "Good luck, guys!"

Tommy and Chuck push their start buttons and grab hold of their steering wheels. The arcade becomes silent. Tommy and Chuck's screens indicate that the two boys are ready to race their friend. The video screen shows the different race tracks to choose from. Tommy and Chuck contemplate between Metropolis, Suburbia and Trax.

"I say that we race on the Metropolis track!" exclaims Chuck excitedly.

"I don't know ... we already saw the 'Metropolis track.' Why don't we try something different?" asks Tommy. "Come on, let's spice it up!"

"Can I make a suggestion?" asks Toby, stepping forward.

"Sure," reply Tommy and Chuck.

"Select the 'Metropolis.' You won't be sorry," says Toby in an insinuating tone.

Tommy and Chuck's curiosity level reaches an "all-time-high." The smirk on Toby's face leaves the boys wondering what's waiting for them in Metropolis.

"'Metropolis' it is!" declares Tommy, turning back to the video screen.

Tommy grabs the steering wheel and maneuvers the prompt until it reaches the Metropolis track. He then presses the gas pedal to make his selection. Chuck follows Tommy's lead and does the same.

I wonder what Derek's doing now. He'd better not make any friends while he's in there! thinks Chuck.

The next screen shows the types of racing cars to select. Chuck remembers that Derek chose the Tarri last time and won.

"I want the Tarri!" shouts Chuck as he mashes the Nitro Button.

"That's the car I wanted!" mutters Tommy.

"I called it first!" claims Chuck, smirking.

"Fine, take the 'Tarri!' I'll take the Fork!" states Tommy, grinning.

"That's Florcei!" shouts the crowd.

Tommy sinks down in his seat, feeling embarrassed that he mispronounced the car he had chosen for the race.

"Sorry, 'Florcei,'" says Tommy as he makes his selection.

The next screen shows the accessories that each player can add to his car. Tommy and Chuck look at the selections very intently, trying to figure out whether the Nitro Tank, Supercharge Engine, Racing Stripes or Tires would help them win the race.

"I'm going to take the Supercharge Engine," says Tommy as he makes his selection. "What are you selecting?"

"I'm going to take the Nitro Tank," replies Chuck.

"You picked the same, exact setup that Derek chose! That's pretty original!" says Tommy sarcastically.

"*Jealous?!*" asks Chuck with chocolate in his teeth.

"Ewww!" says a little girl, grossed out by Chuck's mouth.

Chuck smiles even bigger for the girl.

"Sorry, Toby," says Patricia as she shakes her head.

"Don't worry. It's not your fault that he's obnoxious. Personally, I think Chuck is hilarious," says Toby, watching Chuck fight for the last sip of his slushy drink.

The crowd gathers closer to the video game, anticipating the race to begin.

"Who do you think will win?" whispers Tony.

"Derek, for sure!" replies his friend.

DEREK'S RIDE

"What about Toby?" asks Tony. "How can we not cheer for Toby?"

The kids of Gibeon react to Toby's name and turn around. "'Toby!' 'Toby!' 'Toby'!" chants the crowd.

"Yeah, 'Toby,' jump in!" insists Tommy, waving his hand.

A concerned look washes over Chuck's face. After all, it was Toby who made a fool out of him in the dueling cage. Toby notices that Chuck is less than thrilled with the kids cheering for him. Chuck turns around and mumbles to himself.

"I will have to decline, my friends," says Toby humbly.

"Come on, Toby!" coaxes Tommy, wanting revenge for what he did to him earlier. "It will be...."

"If he doesn't want to race, *don't* force him!" mutters Chuck, squishing a cupcake.

Tommy realizes that Chuck is still sore about the way Toby man-handled him in the dueling cage. Chuck's beet-red cheeks give it away. Chuck's friendship is more important than Tommy's personal vendetta.

"Maybe you're right, buddy. We'll play something else after the race, Toby," says Tommy.

"Deal," says Toby, smiling. "You guys better pay attention. The race is starting!"

All eyes are focused on the start button, illuminating brighter than before. The crowd is eagerly awaiting Derek and Thunder to appear on the screen. Tommy and Chuck turn back toward the screen and grab hold of their steering wheels and stick shifts. Tommy reaches over and pushes the start button a second time. Once again, the screen shows a count down until the race starts. There's a large white "Ten" flashing in the middle of the black screen. Then there's a "Nine."

"*Eight! Seven! Six! Five! Four! Three! Two! One!*" scream the kids in unison.

The crowd freezes.

DEREK'S RIDE

The video screen shows Tommy and Chuck's cars lined up next to each other. Derek and Thunder are sitting at the front of the pack. Derek turns around in his car to see where his buddies are at. The spectators in the game pour onto the streets, ready for the race to begin.

"Hey, why does Derek get to be in front of us?!" asks Chuck as he bites his lip.

"He's there because he won the last race," replies Toby.

Tommy, Chuck, Toby, and all the kids in the arcade stare intently at the video screen, wondering what it's like to be in the world of a video game. The kids envy Derek.

Inside the game, the engines are revving up as the starter girl walks over to Derek's car. Derek turns around and waves to his friends back in Gibeon. He stands up in Thunder and waves to the racing fans as well.

"Okay, Derek, focus on the race!" says Thunder.

"I am 'focused!' I just want to make sure that my friends can see me!" mutters Derek as he grinds the gears, nervous from the starter girl's presence.

"Hey, that hurt!" mutters Thunder as Derek misses a gear. "Take it easy, pal!"

"Go get them, Derek," says the starter girl as she walks to her position.

"How did you know my name?!" asks Derek, surprised.

The kids along the city street jump up and down, cheering for Derek to beat his friends. Somehow, the crowd in the game has knowledge that Derek is in a race against his friends. Derek is overwhelmed by the attention that he's getting from the spectators. He looks back and sees Tommy and Chuck's cars revving their engines.

"Are you ready, Derek?!" asks Thunder.

"I'm 'ready'!" replies Derek as he puts on his helmet. "Those suckers are going down!"

DEREK'S RIDE

The starter girl backs off and lifts her green flag. All eyes in Metropolis are on Derek and Thunder. Derek looks over and sees another driver giving him the eye.

"What's his problem?!" asks Derek over the roaring engines.

"The guys out here mean business!" replies Thunder. "This may be the hardest race of your life!"

Derek quickly looks ahead at the starter girl and places both hands firmly on Thunder's steering wheel. The girl looks intently into Derek's eyes, giving him a sense of déjà vu. It's the same glaring look that she gave him when he was playing the game from the outside. Once again, this feeling is lost as she drops the flag to begin the race. The cars spin their wheels and take off through the thick smoke, jockeying for position.

The crowd inside Arnold's is out of control, cheering for their favorite racers. A sea of bodies shuffles to get a better look at the race. Snacks and hands go flying into the air as the kids watch Tommy and Chuck race toward Derek's car.

"Get them, Tommy!" shouts a little boy. "You can do it!"

"Hurry, Chuck, hurry!" scream two little girls.

Chuck quickly turns around and notices the girls. Becky has black hair, strawberry freckles and a chubby face. Barbie has straight, blonde hair and a giant smile. They're the same two girls who wouldn't leave him alone when he first arrived in Gibeon. They return his glance with flirtatious smiles, reminding him of Tommy's cousins.

Ewww! thinks Chuck, as he swerves to miss a car.

"Come on, Derek, take it home!" yells Alan, jumping up and down.

Toby and Patricia shift their attention to Bobbie. He's staring at all the excitement from the corner of the arcade. Toby notices something different about Bobbie, but can't put his finger on it.

DEREK'S RIDE

"That boy gives me the creeps," whispers Patricia.

"Don't worry about him, he's harmless," says Toby. "A little strange, but harmless."

Bobbie notices their conversation and decides to wave as a sign of peace. Toby and Patricia wave back at Bobbie, unsuspecting of what he, Jonathan and the others have been up to. Bobbie smiles as if everything is okay.

"Why doesn't he come over and join us?" asks Ricky as he walks up to Toby.

"Watch out!" screams a little boy.

Toby and Patricia's attention is shifted back on the game. The crowd watches Tommy and Chuck vigorously moving back and forth in their chairs, trying to out-maneuver one another to win the race. Toby looks back to invite Bobbie over for some fun, but he's disappeared. He canvasses the arcade with his eyes … no Bobbie.

"Tommy's winning!" shouts Erica. "Come on, Tommy, you can do it!"

Toby turns his attention back to the race. He moves through the crowd to get a closer look and see why his buddy, Derek, isn't winning. Toby focuses on Tommy's screen where his Florcei has just pulled ahead of Thunder and Chuck's Tarri. The cars race in and out of on-coming traffic. Each car is reaching speeds of up to one-hundred-thirty-five miles-per-hour. The engines and tires squeal as they reach maximum speed. The boys approach a divided, open tunnel that runs under a large group of railroad tracks. There are many barricades in front of the tunnel, signifying that work is being done on the road. Tommy and Chuck pull their cars into the left tunnel as the first train passes overhead.

"Cool, a train!" shouts Chuck as he takes his eyes off the road. "I wonder if you…."

"Look out, Chuck!" screams a little boy.

Chuck's Tarri hits a concrete pillar and spins out of control, knocking over several barricades. The crash sends workers running for their lives and out of Chuck's way.

"Nooooooo!" moans Chuck as he regains control of his car.

Toby and Patricia try to move closer, hoping to see how Derek is doing. Patricia is still in shock that her friend is inside Street Speed III.

Derek and Thunder are weaving in and out of the barricades, barely escaping several crashes. They also avoid smashing into the work trucks that are moving under the overpass. As Derek drives, he looks between the concrete pillars to see where Tommy is. A barrel of paint slips out of a worker's hands and into his path.

"Turn right!" yells Thunder.

Derek quickly turns around and sees the barrel of paint bouncing his way.

"Ahhhhh!" screams Derek as he steers Thunder to the right. "Oh, no, look out!"

Derek's hard turn to the right sends Thunder onto a ramp leading to the highway above. Thunder's tires screech and almost lose traction as Derek tries to maintain his speed. He drives the car onto the bypass highway and regains control of the road. Derek glances down to the highway below and sees Tommy emerge out of the tunnel, ahead of him and in first place. His aerial view of Tommy's Florcei and Chuck's Tarri has him at an advantage. Derek guns it and quickly takes the lead.

"All right, Thunder, we're winning!" declares Derek as he lifts his hands.

Derek teases his friends back in Gibeon, gesturing through the screen.

Tommy and Chuck drive their cars aggressively, feeling upset that Derek has taken the lead. They glare at the video screen and see Derek teasing them, causing their ears to burn with anger.

DEREK'S RIDE

Some of the kids behind them high-five each other as they see Derek take control of the race.

"That's not fair!" mutters Chuck as he jerks the steering wheel of his car to avoid and on-coming truck. "Come on, Tommy, we can't let him win!"

"He's not going to 'win'!" grunts Tommy, grinding his teeth together, hoping this will make his car go faster. "See, he's lost on that road up above!"

Tommy and Chuck rock back and forth in their seats as they maneuver their cars through the streets of the virtual city. The crowd behind them goes crazy as they head for the straightaway.

"I hope Tommy 'wins,'" says Patricia, squeezing Peggy.

"I heard that!" exclaims Chuck jealously.

"We hope that you 'win,'" say Becky and Barbie, smiling.

Their comment makes the hair on the back of Chuck's head stand up. He slouches down in his seat and tries to ignore them.

"I think that they like you!" mutters Tommy.

"I don't know what you're talking about!" states Chuck as he blushes.

"Chuck's ... got ... a ... girlfriend! Chuck's ... got ... a ... girlfriend!" sings Tommy, teasing his friend.

Chuck lets go of the steering and grabs Tommy's shirt. The kids go wild, watching Chuck trying to choke Tommy for teasing him. Toby and Patricia back away from the machines, waiting for the two boys to spill out onto the floor.

"Get off me!" demands Tommy as he tries to drive his car. "Chuck ... you're going ... to make ... us ... lose!

"You're getting a steamroller!" threatens Chuck as he wrestles with Tommy. "Forget the race!"

"Fight, fight, fight!" shout several kids

"Look, Derek's stuck!" shouts Toby. "He's heading toward a dead end!"

Tommy and Chuck look at their screen to see what Toby is

talking about. Each one realizes that this is their opportunity to pull ahead of Derek and win the race. Chuck quickly lets go of Tommy's shirt and shoves him, hoping to throw him out of his seat. Tommy grabs hold of his steering wheel and catches his balance.

"You're going down!" says Tommy as he pounds the gas pedal and shifts gears.

Tommy's car accelerates forward.

"That's what you think!" says Chuck, hitting the Nitro Button. "See ya, sucker!"

The crowd huddles around Tommy and Chuck to get a better look at each video screen. The kids murmur about who they think will win the race. Some kids wonder if Derek will make it out of the game or live in there forever. The tension around the game grows thick as Tommy and Chuck grunt and moan, determined to win the race and rub it in each other's face.

The atmosphere inside the game is just as intense as Arnold's. The kids along the streets are cheering for their favorite racers. They whistle and hold up signs, waving at their favorite drivers. Derek and Thunder are quickly approaching the dead end of the bypass road that overlooks the highway. Derek turns around and sees Chuck's car shooting ahead like a rocket. Even through the game, Derek can sense Tommy and Chuck's desire to beat him.

"He hit the Nitro Button!" mutters Derek. "What are we going to do?!"

"Drive the car through the guard rails! We'll jump down to the highway and finish the race from there!" replies Thunder.

Derek's eyes grow enormous as he turns back to measure the height of the jump.

"*Excuse me?!*" asks Derek, quivering. "You mean … 'jump down' there?!"

"Turn the wheel to the left and I will handle the rest! Trust me!" replies Thunder.

DEREK'S RIDE

" *'Trust' you?!* I don't even know you!" mutters Derek with a crackle in his voice. "We'll be dead if…!"

"Hurry, we're running out of room! Just do it!" shouts Thunder.

Derek puts a death grip on the steering wheel and begins to pray.

"Please, God, don't let me die!" prays Derek, eyes squinted.

Derek braces himself and steers the car to the left. Thunder *crashes* through the guard rails; metal explodes from the impact.

" *Ahhhhhhhhhhhhhhhh!* " screams Derek as he flies through the air.

The spectators along the street look up in amazement as they watch Thunder and Derek coming down to finish the race. Many of the kids hold their breath, waiting to see what happens to Thunder when he slams onto the pavement.

"I hope that he makes it!" says one spectator.

"Awesome!" screams a boy. "Come on, Thunder!"

Chuck's car is approaching the point where Thunder and Derek are about to land. Tommy's car is close behind, as is another car. The four cars appear to be headed for certain disaster. Derek opens his eyes and notices Tommy and Chuck's cars directly in the path of Thunder. Another car exits the tunnel as well.

"Look out!" yells Derek, covering his face. "We're not going to make it!"

Thunder's chrome wheels spin through the air; there's no turning back.

All the kids in the arcade have their jaws dropped, waiting for the big crash. Some kids even have their faces covered, hoping that Derek and Thunder will be okay. Tommy realizes that the wreck is inevitable unless he backs off. He quickly down shifts his Florcei, slowing his car enough to let Derek and Chuck crash into each other.

I'm going to win! thinks Tommy, chuckling.

Chuck pushes the Nitro Button as if he's hammering a nail. Unfortunately, he used up all the Nitro Tank. Instead of becoming involved in the crash, he jams on his brakes.

"Ah, man! No fair!" screams Chuck. "Look out!"

His sudden step on the brakes catches another driver off guard. His decision causes a major car wreck between several cars.

"You idiot!" yells Chuck as his car spins out of control after being hit from behind. "Come on, stupid car! Drive!"

Patricia is holding onto Toby as they lean over Tommy and Chuck's backs. They're fidgeting and biting their lips, waiting for the race to be over.

Derek and Thunder are six feet above the street. The racing fans have cleared this area, expecting a fiery crash to light up the street.

"Ahhhhhhh!" screams Derek as he lands on the pavement with Thunder.

Thunder bounces off the street and lands on its two left wheels. Miraculously, he continues driving on his side with Derek high in the air.

"Thuuuunnnndddeeeerrrr!" screams Derek, driving the tilted car. "I can't drive like this!"

Tommy's Florcei passes Thunder and approaches the dark tunnel before the finish line. Chuck passes Derek, as well, and closes in on Tommy. On-coming trucks and ambulances cut off Tommy and Chuck's cars, almost causing the two cars to crash. Derek and Thunder swerve to miss a large pothole, sending Thunder back on all four tires; now he's ready to take names and win. Derek, sweating, shakes off the near-death experience, panting like a dog. The crowd along the streets are cheering and waving signs.

"Gun it, Derek!" screams Thunder.

Derek grinds his teeth and floors the gas pedal, positioning

Thunder to win the race. Tommy's car enters the dark tunnel first. Chuck's Tarri and Thunder enter the tunnel neck-in-neck. A fourth car creeps up on Chuck and Derek out of nowhere.

Jeffrey and several of Toby's friends are mocking the way that Tommy and Chuck are driving their cars in the seat of the game. Toby shakes his head and stares at the video screen.

"Where did *he* come from?!" demands Chuck. "I didn't see that car in the race!"

"You guys are done!" brags Tommy. "You'd better forget him and watch me, Chucky!"

The four cars jockey for position in the dark tunnel. Tommy is ahead by a few car lengths. Tires screech as the drivers maneuver their cars and try to maintain their speeds.

"Move to the left, Tommy!" screams a little boy.

"Come on, Derek!" shouts Toby.

"Hey, what about me?!" asks Chuck, frustrated. "Why does everybody root for Tommy and Derek? … Did you guys forget about my belly flop?!"

"*Hurry, Chuck, hurry!*" scream Becky and Barbie.

"There you are, Chucky!" teases Tommy. "Are you happy, now?!"

As the cars make it to the final turn in the tunnel, Tommy's Florcei skids as it slows down to make the turn. Thunder and the fourth car do the same.

"*Steamroller!*" declares Chuck as he guns it.

Chuck's Tarri goes barreling into the other three cars, sending them spinning out of control. The tunnel fills with smoke from burning tires spinning at high speeds. Lights flash off the walls of the tunnel as each driver tries to regain control of his car.

"*Chuck!*" yells Tommy. "Look what you did!"

The cars finally settle down at the straightaway of the tunnel. Tommy, Chuck and Derek shoot ahead of the fourth car as they race for the finish line. The three boys are racing neck-in-neck, about a car length ahead of the fourth car.

Tommy and Chuck are rocking back and forth in their games as if that's going to make their cars go faster. Patricia and Toby are jumping up and down, watching the boys head toward the finish line. Kids in the arcade are screaming like wild monkeys, cheering for their favorite drivers.

"Come on, Tommy!" scream several kids. "Drive faster, you're almost there!"

"Go, Chuck!" shout several other kids.

"Come on, Derek!" scream several more kids.

"Move, Thunder, move!" shout another group of kids.

The arcade is in pandemonium as the boys get closer to the finish line. One girl covers her eyes, overwhelmed by the suspense. Patricia squeezes Peggy, wishing that they all could win.

"Tell me who wins," says a girl.

"Punch it!" yells a little boy. "Come on, Chunk! I mean, Chuck! Sorry!"

The kids behind Tommy and Chuck begin to move like the waves in the sea, watching the starter girl get closer and closer. Chuck's appetite has reached an "all-time-high" due to the excitement. His stomach tells him that he can't go another minute without a bite of his candy bar. He reaches into his pocket for a delicious treat.

"*Noooooooooooo!*" screams Tommy as he watches Chuck's Tarri swerve to the left. "Grab the steering wheel you idiot!"

"Chuck!" screams Toby.

Chuck's untimely decision to eat causes Tommy, Derek and himself to crash into each other. All three cars, once again, spin out of control and fill the screen with smoke. Out of the smoke emerges the fourth car racing toward the finish line, unchallenged. The driver wisely backed off from the three aggressive drivers.

"That other guy's going to win!" declares a little boy.

The entire arcade watches the *mystery car* cross the finish line in first place. The starter girl waves the checkered flag, signaling that the race is over. Tommy shakes his head and reaches over, smacking Chuck.

"Nice move, Chuck!" states Tommy as he jumps out of his game.

"Ouch!" yelps Chuck, lowering his head. "I didn't do it on purpose!"

Chuck turns around and sees all the kids staring at him, making him feel as ashamed as if he passed gas.

"Sorry, everyone!" says Chuck as he steps out of his seat.

"*Help, help!!!!*" screams the starter girl from the game.

The crowd surrounding Tommy and Chuck turn their eyes back to the video screens. They see the starter girl jumping up and down, pointing toward a burning building. The spectators of the race all join together and look up at the tall skyscraper. Smoke quickly fills the sky as the fire burns out of control. Toby, Tommy, Chuck and Patricia step up to the screen and see Derek and Thunder pulling next to the starter girl.

Derek, with a sudden burst of adrenaline, jumps out of Thunder and rushes over to the starter girl. The crowd converges onto the street where the two are standing.

"Are you okay?! What happened?!" asks Derek.

"It's … it's Ginger! She's … she's in the building!" replies the starter girl, begining to hyperventilate.

Derek puts his hand on her arm to show her that he's there for her. Thunder senses that something's seriously wrong with the starter girl and drives up to the crowd.

"What's going on with the 'building'?" asks Thunder.

"I'm sorry, what's your name?" asks Derek.

"Lucy," replies the starter girl, in tears.

DEREK'S RIDE

"'Lucy's' friend, 'Ginger,' is stuck in the burning 'building'!" explains Derek as he steps next to Thunder.

"Hop in!" says Thunder, revving his engine.

"*Excuse me?!* What do you mean, 'hop in'?!" asks Derek nervously.

"We're going to save the day! Isn't that what you always dreamed about? Saving someone's life?" asks Thunder.

Derek has a vision of the hero's welcome given to him by Matilda at the electric parade back in Gibeon. He's filled with confidence as the vision ends.

"She'll be fine!" says Derek as he jumps into Thunder.

The crowd rushes over to Derek and Thunder.

"Thank you," says Lucy as she gives Derek her favorite scarf. "You're too brave. Please be careful!"

Derek puts it into his pocket and throws the car into first. Thunder peels out in circles, creating a large cloud of smoke. The spectators cheer for Derek and Thunder, giving them the encouragement they need to risk their lives. Girls put their hands over their hearts, waiting for their hero to save the day. Derek lets go of the brake and Thunder races off toward the burning building, leaving a trail of burnt rubber.

Back in the arcade, Chuck is eating popcorn by the handful as he watches his best friend and Thunder try to rescue Ginger and her friends. Tommy's mouth drops to the floor as he watches the two of them racing toward the burning building. Patricia squeezes Peggy and closes her eyes. Now it's not a matter of Derek coming out of the game, it's a matter of life and death.

"Derek hates fire!" states Chuck with popcorn flying out of his mouth. "Is there any way that we can help him?! Let me in there!"

"Be careful, Derek!" shouts Tommy at the screen.

"I can't watch this!" exclaims Patricia, peeking at the screen.

DEREK'S RIDE

"He's in good hands with Thunder," says Toby, watching his new friends worry about Derek. "You guys have nothing to worry about...."

"How do you know?!" asks Chuck, starting to freak-out. "You're not there!"

"Yeah, that's a fire Derek's heading into!" says Tommy, defending Chuck's anxiety.

"If anyone can help, it's Thunder!" says Toby confidently.

"Look, they're at the building!" shouts a little boy.

The crowd in the arcade turns and sees Derek and Thunder parked across the street from the building that's on fire. There are several fire trucks trying to put out the fire from different locations. Helicopters fly over the building, dropping water to help extinguish the flames. Ambulances race through the streets, sounding their sirens, getting into position to assist anyone caught in the fire. This game has captivated Tommy and the others; they remain speechless as they fear for Derek's life.

Derek and Thunder wait for the screaming ambulances to pass by before they make a move. Derek watches the crisis with eyes wide open, psyching himself up for the task at hand. Several firemen signal for Derek to move Thunder so that they can hook up their hoses to the fire hydrant located on the street corner.

"All right, Derek, let's do it!" says Thunder, revving his engine.

Derek looks around and waves to his friends back in Gibeon, letting them know that he loves them. He shakes his head and grips the steering wheel.

Please don't ever forget about me, thinks Derek, as tears begin to flow down his face.

"Look, there are a few people flagging from the roof!" screams one bystander.

Derek and Thunder look up and see Ginger and her friends

waving for help from the rooftop of the building. Derek notices that the helicopters have stopped flying overhead. He realizes that they've gone back to the lake to refill their water tanks.

"They'll never make it back in time!" states Derek. "We have to act now!"

"Punch it and head to the parking garage across the street!" instructs Thunder.

Derek shifts down and punches the gas pedal, sending Thunder screeching across the street.

"Then what?!" asks Derek as his head jerks.

"We'll head to the roof and jump to their building," replies Thunder.

"*Excuse me?!*" asks Derek, glancing up to see how high the jump will be.

Derek and Thunder enter the parking garage and zoom up the entrance ramp. Derek shifts gears aggressively, adjusting to the sharp curves. Round and round they go, screeching their tires against the concrete, trying not to lose control. Time is ticking for Ginger and her friends. Derek looks out the sides of the parking garage and sees Thunder elevating over the adjoining buildings.

"Please, God, don't let anything bad happen to me! I promise that I'll be good when I go home!" prays Derek desperately.

Derek and Thunder finally make it to the ramp that leads to the roof.

"Hey, that's the car that beat us!" mutters Derek.

Derek drives Thunder right in front of the mystery car and comes to a screeching halt. Thunder and the mystery car glare into each other's headlights; neither one makes a move. They act like two dogs meeting in the park, checking each other out from a distance. Obviously, there's a history between Thunder and the mystery car.

"What's wrong, Thunder?" asks Derek, sensing tension.

"This guy is everywhere!" replies Thunder, revving his engine.

DEREK'S RIDE

"What do you want to do?" asks Derek.

"I don't know. Let's see what he does first," replies Thunder.

Derek looks over at Ginger and her friends. The fire has made it up to the roof. The kids run over toward the edge of the building, trying to escape the raging flames and intense heat.

"Help us, please! Somebody, help us!!!!" scream the kids.

"We don't have time to waste!" says Derek. "If we're going to jump, let's do it now!"

The mystery car revs his engine and flashes its lights at Thunder. Derek and Thunder are blinded by the light.

Tommy, Chuck and Patricia are huddled together as they watch Derek on the roof of the parking garage. They, too, are blinded by the mystery car's extra bright headlights. The kids turn away from the video screens, trying to adjust their eyes. Patricia and Chuck have tears in their eyes, waiting for Derek to risk his life for Ginger and her friends.

"What's up with that other car?" asks Jeffrey. "How did he get on the roof first?"

"I don't know," replies Toby, covering his eyes from the brightness of the screen.

"What if he doesn't make it?" asks a boy.

"Don't say that!" replies Chuck, turning around abruptly. "You have to think positive!"

The boy shrinks down, realizing Chuck's passion for his best friend.

"We need to say a prayer!" says Patricia with a shaky voice.

"Good idea!" declares Tommy.

"Who's going to 'say' it?" asks Chuck, interrupting.

The kids look at each other, dumbfounded. No one wants to take the initiative to lead the prayer. There's too much riding on this one; Tommy and his friends are scared they might say the wrong thing. Little do they know how insignificant the words can be. It's

DEREK'S RIDE

their hearts that count, and the spirit within them prays on their behalf. Tommy takes a deep breath and looks at Chuck.

"*I* don't know what to 'say!' I always get in trouble at church!" mutters Chuck, looking toward the ceiling.

"Don't look at me!" mutters Tommy as Toby motions for him to say it.

"I'll 'say' it!" exclaims Patricia, pulling Peggy close to her heart and bowing her head.

All the kids in the arcade bow their heads, following Patricia's lead.

"God, please protect Derek and bring him safely back to us," prays Patricia nervously.

The room is silent enough to hear a pin drop. Tommy peeks up and looks at Patricia. She senses Tommy's eyes on her and slowly opens her eyes as well.

"Amen," whispers Tommy, smiling.

Patricia smiles at her friend for helping her close the prayer. They bow their heads back down and close their eyes.

"'Amen,'" says Patricia.

"What?! Where are we?!" asks Chuck, shaking his head and blinking his eyes.

The kids laugh at Chuck's remarks and gestures. They watch him try to snap out of the trance placed on him during the prayer. The crowd then turns their attention back to the video screens.

"What's that car doing there?!" demands Chuck, watching the light fade.

"I don't know," replies Tommy, confused.

"He's the guy who beat us!" states Chuck as he walks up to the screen. "I wish that he was here now. I'd give him a steamroller!"

"That 'car' has always shown up when you least expect it," says Toby.

"Is it a good 'car' or a bad 'car'?" asks Patricia fearfully.

258

DEREK'S RIDE

"I don't know," replies Toby.

"Some say that 'car' always wins the race," says a little boy as he breaks through the crowd. "His engine has more power that all the other cars combined."

"Yeah, no one can beat him when he races," says another boy.

"Do you think he's there to help or hurt Derek?" asks Tommy worriedly.

"I can't imagine why else he'd be up there if he isn't going to 'help' Derek with the rescue," replies Toby, trying to sound encouraging.

"I hope that you're right," says Chuck.

"I think they're going to jump!" shouts a little boy.

Inside the game, the mystery car slowly pulls forward and turns to the right of Derek and Thunder. The driver's side of the mystery car is facing Derek. Derek tries to see who's driving the car, but the dark tinted windows make it impossible. Thunder revs his engine, trying to intimidate his adversary ... or is he?

Oh boy, here we go! thinks Derek, as his heart pounds like a drum.

The mystery car's window rolls down, slightly, as the car comes to a complete stop. Derek clutches the steering wheel, ready to speed off.

"Have no fear. The battle is mine, not yours. Your good intentions will be rewarded and I will deliver them. Tie this rope to your car. It will be used as a rescue line to shimmy the kids over to safety," says a voice from the car.

Derek has a sense of déjà vu, reliving the time that Tommy read from Orin's scroll.

"Who are you?" asks Derek, squinting to see the face behind the voice.

"A friend," replies the voice.

DEREK'S RIDE

"Do you know who that is?" whispers Derek.

"No. No one has ever met him. I've ...," whispers Thunder. The conversation is broken up by a giant explosion. Derek, Thunder and the mystery car turn to face the building across the street. Ginger and her friends are jumping up and down as the fire flares up around the roof. Without hesitation, the mystery car revs its engine and spins its wheels. Smoke rises up from the car as it prepares for launch.

Tommy and the crowd in Arnold's watch the video screen as the mystery car prepares to jump. A large cloud of smoke covers the entire rooftop of the parking garage. Derek, Thunder and the mystery car can't be seen through the smoke. Patricia holds Peggy close and closes her eyes, anticipating Derek and Thunder to jump.

"Come on, Thunder, you can do it!" screams a little boy.

"'You can do it, Thunder'!" mutters Toby under his breath. "Please bring Derek back safely."

"I can't take it!" says Chuck as he paces in front of the game. "Is there any way that we can get into the game to help him?! *Somebody, answer me!*"

"It's the mystery car!" shouts Tommy as he jumps into the air. "Derek and Thunder aren't jumping!"

"Goooooooo!" bellows Chuck, crushing his soda.

"Yeaahhh!" scream several kids.

Tommy and the others follow the mystery car as it flies through the air toward Ginger and her friends. They watch in slow motion, hoping that the car will make the jump. Tommy grabs onto Toby. He holds his breath as the car sails high above the ground with its tires spinning. Becky and Barbie hold onto Chuck, fearful that the mystery car won't make the jump. Chuck realizes that girls are touching him and wishes that the car would land on him instead, putting him out of his misery.

I'm definitely getting cooties! thinks Chuck, standing frozen in one place.

DEREK'S RIDE

"He's not going to make it!" states one little boy as he ducks his head, waiting for an explosion.

"No, he's 'going to make it!' Look!" screams another boy, pointing at the video screen.

The mystery car barely lands on the edge of the building and bounces several times before coming to a stop on the building's roof. It continues to drive through the smoke and fire heading toward Ginger. Ginger and her friends rush over to the mystery car, welcoming their hero.

The arcade breaks out in a thunderous roar as the kids watch Ginger and her friends jumping into the basket. Tommy and his friends hug each other and jump for joy.

"They're going to be saved!" cries a little girl.

"All right, mystery car!" calls Toby as he's hugged by his friends. "Way to go, Derek!"

"Look at them go!" shouts a little boy, pointing.

The video screen shows Ginger and her friends being hoisted high above the sky, heading toward Derek and Thunder. Derek is standing next to Thunder and pulling the rope that holds the basket. His adrenaline has given him the strength of twelve boys.

"Go, Derek, go!!!" screams Chuck, jumping up and down with a mouthful of cookies. "Look at him! He's a hero! Do you guys have a newspaper that will take our picture?! Never mind!"

Becky and Barbie smile at Chuck, watching him cheer for his friend.

"Yeah, Derek!" exclaims Tommy, clapping his hands. "You're the man!"

"Look at our friend 'go'!" whispers Patricia to Peggy.

The kids continue to watch with excitement as Ginger and her friends make it to the top of the parking garage safely. Derek grabs hold of them and helps them out of the basket. Ginger and her friends hug and thank Derek for saving their lives. Ginger gives Thunder a kiss; he sounds his horn. The celebration is short-lived by a giant explosion on the roof of the burning building.

"*Noooooooo!*" scream Tommy and Toby.

The kids in Arnold's watch in horror as rescue helicopters fly over the building and dump their tanks of water. It appears that the mystery car was consumed in the explosion.

"Do you think the mystery car is okay?!" asks Chuck, shocked.

"After all he's done, I hope so," replies Patricia, saddened.

"Look! Derek is waving at us that they're 'okay'!" says one boy, pointing to the left of the screen.

"I want my friend back!" states Chuck impatiently. "How do we get Derek out of there?!"

"Yeah, Toby, when does 'Derek' leave the game?" asks Tommy.

"I don't know. That's up to Thunder," replies Toby, feeling pressure to give them a definite answer. "The last time that Thunder...."

"Wait! They're driving back down the parking garage!" yells Frank.

Derek, Thunder, Ginger and her two friends speed down the parking garage for their reunion with Lucy. Derek can't help but think about what had happened to the mystery car. Thoughts of who was in the car and what was said have Derek preoccupied.

"We can't thank you enough for saving our lives," says Ginger, shaken up.

"What did you say?" asks Derek, dazed as he drives Thunder.

"Are you okay?" asks Ginger.

"I'm thinking about the other car that came to your rescue. I'm also thinking about the possibility of us not making it back alive if he wasn't with us. Who was that?" asks Derek as they shoot out of the parking garage.

The heroes are met with a thunderous roar of cheers and

thanksgiving as Lucy and the citizens of Metropolis welcome back Derek and Thunder from their rescue mission. Derek turns the wheel and skids Thunder next to Lucy, reuniting her and Ginger. Ginger jumps out of the car and the two girls embrace. Tears flow out of their eyes, both realizing how close they were to losing their best friend. Derek and Thunder watch with big smiles, knowing that they helped save several lives.

"Great job, my friend," says Derek.

"You too, Derek," says Thunder. "Your friends will be proud. Heck, the city of Gibeon will be proud!"

Lucy lets go of Ginger and heads over to Derek and Thunder. She wants to personally thank them for rescuing her friends. Derek sees her heading over with one of those mushy smiles.

Oh no! thinks Derek, as he begins to blush.

Derek backs up against Thunder as Lucy closes in, wanting to thank her hero. Thunder begins to chuckle, watching Derek squirm.

"Thank you, Derek," says Lucy as she throws her arms around him. "I've never met someone so brave! You should be on TV!"

"You're welcome," mutters Derek, trying to pull away from her hug. "It's okay, really!"

"I don't know how I'll ever repay you for risking your life for my friend," says Lucy passionately.

"Don't worry ... it was nothing!" mutters Derek as he breaks away.

Ginger comes up from behind to thank Derek as well.

"Ahhhhh!" screams Derek as he backs into Ginger's hug. "What's going on with all the hugs?! C-h-u-c-k!"

"Thank you, Derek," says Ginger, hugging Derek like a stuffed animal. "We're showing you our appreciation, that's all."

"You're welcome!" grunts Derek as he breaks out of her

grasp. "All right, enough thanks! You're welcome! Do I have to spell it for you?!"

Thunder decides that Derek has had enough attention and can't take much more of the girls' affection. The crowd begins to close in, wanting to show their appreciation to Derek as well.

"Come on, Derek, it's time to get back to your friends," says Thunder. "Girls, we have to go."

"Okay, let's go!" exclaims Derek, eyes lighting up from Thunder's saving grace.

"No stay! *Pleeeeaaaasssseeee,*" beg Lucy and Ginger.

"Sorry, I must 'get back to my friends.' We have to go home soon, as well," says Derek as he jumps back into Thunder. "Hasta la vista, baby!"

As the crowd draws closer to Thunder, Derek revs the engine, scaring everyone away. Ginger and her friends scatter, knowing that Thunder is ready to exit the game.

"Bye, everybody!" shouts Derek, waving to the crowd.

The crowd backs away and cheers for their hero, watching the cloud of smoke emerging from Thunder's spinning wheels. The city street is consumed by Thunder's smoke.

A giant cloud of smoke appears in front of Street Speed III, similar to the one Tommy and the others see on the video screens. It's in the same spot that Thunder came to pick up Derek. Chuck, Patricia and Toby back away from the smoke as they wait for the arrival of Derek and Thunder.

"*He's coming, he's coming!!!!*" declares Chuck, pacing back and forth, looking for Derek through the cloud of smoke. "Come on, hurry!"

"Settle down, Chuck," says Tommy, coughing.

"You 'settle down'!" mutters Chuck as he crushes a candy bar. "I need to see my buddy!"

DEREK'S RIDE

"Yea, Derek's safe!" states Patricia, shaking Peggy up and down.

The roar of Thunder's engine drowns out any other sound in the arcade. All eyes are focused on the cloud of smoke as the kids look for Derek and Thunder. Tommy and the others let out a giant cheer, welcoming home their heroes. The smoke dissipates. The kids in the arcade see Derek sitting high on the driver's seat, waving to the children of Gibeon. Tommy and the others throw up their hands and salute their friend.

"Hail, Derek!" shouts a little boy. "Derek for mayor!"

"Long, live, 'Derek'!" calls another boy.

"'Derek!' 'Derek!' 'Derek'!" chants the crowd as Derek jumps out of Thunder.

Tommy and his friends practically tackle Derek.

"Chuck, I can't breathe!" mumbles Derek as his face turns red. "Okay, Chuck, you can let go now!"

"Derek, I missed you!" says Chuck, letting go of his bear hug. "Fine ... leave!"

"You saved the day!" exclaims Tommy as he rubs his friend's head. "You're a true hero! Wait until everyone back home hears about this one!"

Derek is now engulfed with affection and congratulations from his friends and the kids of Gibeon.

"*Ewww,* you probably have cooties from those girls that hugged you!" mutters Chuck as he brushes himself off. "I saw you in there! I think that you liked it!"

"What are 'cooties'?" asks Toby, reaching his hand out to Derek.

"Don't mind him. He's immature," says Patricia as she walks up to hug her friend.

"You get them from touching girls," replies Chuck, still wiping himself clean.

"There's no such thing as 'cooties,' you dummy!" states Tommy, shaking his head.

265

DEREK'S RIDE

The reunion ceases as the crowd notices Toby's facial expression as he stares at Derek. Tommy and his friends notice Toby staring at a tear in Derek's pajama pants where his pocket once was. They begin to think about the *unthinkable* while Derek absorbs the attention from a few kids.

"Everyone, please step back!" yells Tommy. "This is serious!"

Oh no! thinks Chuck, as he looks around the floor.

"What's wrong with you, Tommy?" asks Derek, confused.

"Where's the blue lightbulb, Derek?!" asks Chuck, pointing to the hole in his pocket. "You lost it, didn't you?! I knew it!"

"Ohhhhhhhhhhhhh!" moans the crowd as they stare at the rip in Derek's pants.

Derek reaches his hand into one pocket.

"Three tokens and no 'blue lightbulb'!" mutters Tommy as he examines Derek's hand. "Someone call Matilda! We need her help!"

"Check the other one!" says Chuck, bracing for bad news.

"We're never going home!" whispers Patricia to Peggy.

"You lost it, didn't you?!" asks Chuck as Derek reaches into his pocket.

The room becomes silent.

"*Noooooooooo!*" bellows Derek with his fingers peeking out the hole.

Tommy, Chuck and Patricia bow their heads, realizing that Derek lost the blue lightbulb. A spirit of frustration washes over their bodies, weakening them, realizing their ticket back home was lost over a stupid video game.

"What do we do now?" whimpers Chuck, imagining never eating his mom's fresh-baked, chocolate chip cookies again. "Does this mean that we *live* in Gibeon?"

"We're never going home, are we?" asks Patricia as she lowers Peggy to her side. "We need to go and get Mindy and Bucky!"

DEREK'S RIDE

"Hmhmhmhmhm!" coughs Thunder.

Derek and his friends turn and see Thunder moping as well. Derek walks up to Thunder with his head hung low, disappointed and ready to puke. The thought of him being responsible for his friends never leaving Gibeon is too much. The celebration has turned into a nightmare.

"What's up, Thunder?" asks Derek. "I went from being brother hero to brother zero!"

"There's a map for you in the glove box," replies Thunder. "Climb in, Derek."

"Oh, great! What are we going to do with a stupid 'map'?!" asks Tommy, pacing back and forth.

"What do I need a 'map' for?" asks Derek as he reaches for the glove box. "Unless it tells us how to get home, it will be of ... *THE LIGHTBULB!*" declares Derek as he raises it high into the air.

Thunder smiles and revs his engine. Tommy and his friends rush over to Thunder to show their appreciation. The weight of the world has been lifted from their shoulders. Thoughts of home replace their anxiety and visions of living in Gibeon forever.

"You dropped it during the race. I figured that you'd need this later," says Thunder as he gets smothered.

"Thank you, Thunder! You're our hero!" shout Tommy and Chuck.

The entire arcade celebrates as the blue lightbulb comes to life in Derek's hand. The music and light show is spectacular. Images of Mayor Messa and Matilda appear in the light, waving at their special guests. Even Thunder joins in as the kids dance around Arnold's and lift Derek on their shoulders. Derek is carted around the arcade, high above the crowd, unsuspecting of the *new arrival* that'll make his adventure look like a walk in the park.

CHAPTER SIX

THE HUNT FOR TAMMY

Tina's house is bustling with Bobbie, Tammy and Tina continuing to organize their plot for the evening. Bobbie has just returned from spying on Derek and his friends and has reported his findings to the girls. The tension is mounting as visions of this evening's mayhem appear in their imaginations. The three kids are standing in Tina's kitchen, hovering over her kitchen table. They are reviewing several maps of the city which Bobbie stole from Mayor Messa's office.

"Were you able to get the Tobit from the Mayor's office?" asks Tina as she turns the page to one of the maps.

"Not yet," replies Bobbie as he closes his bag.

"Do you think you'll have a problem getting it?" asks Tina while Tammy looks over the maps.

"What's this?" asks Tammy, pointing.

"It's the fire station," replies Bobbie.

"It's so big," says Tammy as she runs her finger over the map. "Can we…?"

"What about the Tobit?" asks Tina. "And Tammy, we need to focus!"

"Calm down, Tina, I'll get it," replies Bobbie as he makes a mark on a map.

"Sorry. You know that Jonathan and Mable won't be able to return to the city unless you get that book," states Tina as she folds up one of the maps. "Igor needs that book as well."

"I know … don't worry. I plan on getting it after I leave here," says Bobbie with a grin of reassurance.

"I don't know about you two, but I've got butterflies in my stomach," says Tammy.

"What do you mean by that?" asks Tina, dumbfounded.

"It's another way of saying that I'm nervous or excited," replies Tammy as she pulls out her wrestling mask. *"We're talking about a possible war!"*

"What's that for?" asks Bobbie, making a mark on another map.

"It's a wrestling mask. I wear it when I'm excited and getting ready to do something crazy," replies Tammy as Bobbie shakes his head.

"We need to bring Harry, Jason, Freddie, and Freddie's two sisters into this, you know," says Tina, realizing that Jonathan's dream of revenge is about to unfold.

"That's your responsibility," states Bobbie. "Did you make enough tarts?"

"We made enough for a whole block," replies Tina as she pulls one out of the basket and spins it in her hand.

"Can I have another one of those?" asks Tammy as she

watches it dance in Tina's hand. "They're *soooo* good and I like the way I feel after…."

"No!" say Tina and Bobbie.

"Sorry for asking!" mutters Tammy.

"We need all of them for tonight," says Tina as she puts the tart back into the basket. "Besides, if you go back to Zevon Forest without your friends … you'll be sweeping the swamp floor for the rest of your life."

"Okay, okay, I won't touch them!" declares Tammy, shivering at that thought.

"Take out six tarts for her friends and put away the others for later," instructs Bobbie as he makes his final mark on the map.

Bobbie looks at his watch and realizes that he has to get back to the mayor's office. Tina sees that he's ready to leave, again, and grabs the basket of tarts. She pulls the six out for Tammy to bring to her friends. Tammy grabs a smaller basket from Tina and begins to place the tarts into the basket.

"These smell better than any snack back home," says Tammy. "Are you sure that…?"

"Don't even think about it!" states Bobbie.

"Okay, okay! Take it easy!" says Tammy as she closes the top of the basket. "Gosh!"

"You, two, finish mapping out our meeting places for tonight. We have to be organized if this plan is going to work. I have to get back to the Mayor's office. I'll see you guys later. Good luck!" says Bobbie, rushing out the door.

Tammy puts down the basket and walks back to the kitchen table to get her assignment.

"This is Ephesus' Book Store. This is where we'll meet Jonathan and Mable …," says Tina, pointing to one of the marks.

"This is *really* happening, isn't it?" asks Tammy, interrupting, realizing it's time to get serious.

"Yes, it is," replies Tina as she makes another mark on the map. "From there we'll head down to Sirach's Deli and meet Harry and his crew."

"What about Matilda? What about Mount Chrome? How are we going to get past them?" asks Tammy, concerned.

"We've gotten this far without problems, haven't we? Jonathan and Igor will take care of them. You worry about your friends and the parade, and we'll worry about the rest," replies Tina with an evil grin.

"Fine! How long do I have until we meet you at 'Ephesus' Book Store'?" asks Tammy.

"We'll send an Ibex after you …," replies Tina, smiling at Tammy's perplexed look.

"What's an 'Ibex'?" asks Tammy, interrupting.

"It's a goat," replies Tina, chuckling.

"Oh. How will it know who we are?" asks Tammy.

"You sure do like to ask a lot of questions, don't you?" asks Tina.

"Sorry. I just want to make sure that we don't mess up the plan," replies Tammy, throwing up her hands.

"It will find you, don't worry. Just give your friends the tarts and head to the park," says Tina as she points to Eden's Park on the map.

"No problem," says Tammy, nodding. "This is going to be awesome! Total chaos!"

"You'd better get going, we're running out of time," says Tina, looking at her watch.

Tammy grabs her basket and heads out for her friends.

Mindy is looking back up the aisle, checking to see if Bucky is coming back from his visit to the restroom. Kids cringe in their seats from the sound of slurping sodas; the slurping orchestra could agitate a deaf person. Jack and Kris look back to see what's taking Bucky so long.

"He's going to miss the ending!" whispers Kris.

"I know," whispers Mindy as she shakes her head.

"Should I go see where he is?" whispers Jack.

"Shhhhhhhhhhh!" signal two kids as they turn around.

"Sorry," whispers Mindy.

The kids' attention is quickly turned back to the movie screen as the bear lets out a giant roar. The bear is following Ben through the thick, mountainous shrubbery. Ben is several hundred yards ahead of the bear. Several kids want to shout at the movie screen and encourage Ben, but restrain their tongues.

"*Daaaddd! Mooommm!*" shouts Ben as he climbs higher, looking back to make sure that the bear isn't behind him.

The calls for his parents echo through the mountains.

Ben finally makes it to a dirt road that runs through the mountain. His adrenaline kicks in as the bear lets out another roar that sends chills down his back.

"Let's see ... which way back to the ranger's office?" asks Ben to himself, looking in both directions.

Ben looks up, searching for the sun. Covering his eyes, he decides to head in that direction. It's getting late and Ben doesn't have much time before it gets dark.

Down at the ranger's office, Mrs. Hopkins and Lucy sit weeping; hope is fading fast. They're consoled by one of the ranger's secretaries. Mrs. Hopkins looks at the wall and notices all7 the family pictures taken from the park. She immediately wails out in agony, thinking about never seeing her son again.

"I can't believe he's gone!" cries Mrs. Hopkins.

"He's not 'gone.' We'll find him, I promise," whispers the secretary as she hugs Mrs. Hopkins.

At that moment, the office door flings open. Mr. Hopkins

and one of the rangers rush into the office with Ben's backpack. Mrs. Hopkins immediately jumps to her feet and looks for Ben.

"*Where is he?! Where is he?!*" asks Mrs. Hopkins hysterically.

"We haven't found him yet, but one of the rangers thought they heard a scream from on top of the mountain!" replies Mr. Hopkins, out of breath.

Mrs. Hopkins's eyes light up as a sense of hope washes over her body. Her sanity is restored at the thought that her son was screaming for help. She quickly grabs her bag and her daughter, ready to search for her son.

"We need to get up there!" declares Mrs. Hopkins. "He's all alone and probably terrified!"

"We're waiting for a helicopter to bring us there. It would take too long for us to hike it," states Mr. Hopkins.

"How soon will the 'helicopter' be here?!" asks Mrs. Hopkins worriedly.

"It should be here within the next five to fifteen minutes," replies the park ranger.

He gives Mrs. Hopkins a smile of reassurance that all will be well for her son. Mr. Hopkins grabs his wife and daughter and sits back down, waiting for the arrival of the helicopter. They console one another, hanging onto each other's hope for Ben.

Ben is running toward an old abandoned car. It sits at the end of the road that he chose to follow. He slows down, raises his arms and tries to catch his breath; the hike has been grueling. Knowing that there's nowhere else to go, he must make a decision; time is running out.

"Great! What am I going to do now?" asks Ben, panting as he walks up to the car.

He shakes his head as he examines the car; the tires are flat and rust has set in from the rain. Ben reaches for the driver's side door and yanks it open. The sound of rust breaking is definitely an indication that this car is going nowhere. He carefully looks inside the car and sees nothing that will help him in his predicament.

This pile of junk is useless! thinks Ben, as he climbs in.

Ben checks the glove box, then under the seats, desperately searching for anything that will help him. As he comes up from under the seat, he glances at the rear-view mirror and sees the bear walking toward the car.

"Oh no, it's the bear!" mutters Ben, covering his mouth as he shuts the door.

Ben reaches over and locks all the doors. He then lowers himself in the seat, trying to hide from the bear. Ben's heart begins to race as he waits for the bear to find him.

Bucky is now walking back to his seat, struggling to see exactly where the others are sitting. The dark theater makes it difficult for Bucky to locate his friends. All he can see are bulging eyes glaring at the movie screen.

"I know it's around here somewhere," mumbles Bucky.

Bucky almost trips over a kid's foot that's hanging out in the aisle.

Mindy and the others watch the movie in suspense, waiting for the bear to attack Ben in the car. Jack and Kris hold each other tight, as if the bear is coming after them. Bucky enters the row behind Mindy and the others by accident.

"Excuse me, pardon me, excuse me," whispers Bucky as he climbs over several kids, heading to the middle of the row.

Bucky sits down and realizes that he's in the wrong row. He reaches over to let his friends know that he's back.

"Ahhhhhh, the bear!" screams Mindy just when Bucky puts his hand on her shoulder.

"Where, where?!" scream Jack and Kris, startled as Mindy jumps out of her seat.

"Shhhhhhhhhh!" signal several kids.

"Sorry," whisper Mindy, Jack, Kris and Bucky.

THE HUNT FOR TAMMY

Bucky climbs over the seat to join his friends for the end of the movie.

Across town, Bobbie is standing before Mayor Messa and Matilda, waiting to receive instructions for his part in tonight's parade. Matilda is going over last minute counsel from the Tobit. Bobbie stares intently while Matilda turns the pages. He fantasizes about having the Tobit in his possession. Matilda and Mayor Messa have no idea where he'd been earlier in the day. His report to them was methodically put together, fooling even the elect. Matilda stares at a page. It reads:

RAPHAEL'S INSTRUCTIONS

As you burn the fish's heart and liver,
the smoke will chase away evil.
All good will be restored.

Matilda signals to Mayor Messa that she has it memorized. He then turns to another page. It reads:

EXHORTATION

Give thanks to Mount Chrome for everything!
Let everyone know of the great things
that he has done for you!
Proclaim to all what is rightfully his!

Matilda smiles at Mayor Messa, signaling that she's done memorizing the two pages he has set before her. The Tobit is the source of power given by Mount Chrome that will enable Matilda to handle what is about to happen to her beautiful city.

THE HUNT FOR TAMMY

Back in Zevon Forest, Jonathan, Mable and Igor are watching Mayor Messa, Matilda and Bobbie through the red cloud of smoke over the fire. Igor has several leaves from the Targola plant wrapped around his arms to heal the flesh wounds from his sorcery.

"It makes my skin crawl when they read from the Tobit," mutters Jonathan as he signals for one of his cronies. "What are they doing now?"

"Matilda is leaving his office," replies Mable. "Bobbie is signaling that everything's under control."

"What is it, master?" asks a boy, rushing next to the fire.

"How is Igor's potion doing? Is it ready yet?" asks Jonathan, looking back into the red cloud of smoke.

"Almost, my lord," replies the boy. "It should...."

"'Almost?!' That is unacceptable!" mutters Jonathan. "Igor!"

Igor pulls out a bag from his pocket and dips his walking stick in it.

"No! No! *Noooooo!*" screams the boy, bracing to be turned into some kind of rodent.

Mayor Messa and Bobbie are standing at the window, looking down on the city. Gibeon is lively; some citizens finish last-minute shopping while others prepare for the parade. The mayor is pleased watching colorful banners and signs being completed on his streets. Bobbie shakes off his trance from Jonathan and peeks back at the Tobit.

"This will be the greatest night in Gibeon history," states Mayor Messa as he takes a deep breath. "My guests may never want to return when I get through with them."

"You are brilliant, Mayor. No one in all of Gibeon can compare to you. I mean, next to Mount Chrome, no one can compare to you," says Bobbie as he grins away from the mayor.

THE HUNT FOR TAMMY

Mayor Messa walks back to the table, pleased by Bobbie's remark.

"Bobbie, please take this to Rachel for her to put away. Then meet me downstairs in the conference room," insists Mayor Messa, handing the Tobit to Bobbie.

Bobbie's heart begins to pound as Mayor Messa hands him the Tobit. He can't believe it's this easy. A lump develops in his throat as he envisions the celebration taking place in the wicked swamp. Mayor Messa has no idea to whom he's handing the sacred book of Gibeon. Evil has been masked ... once again.

"Yes, Mayor, right away!" says Bobbie, smiling.

Bobbie takes hold of the Tobit and heads out the door. His hands begin to shake as a vision of the pages needed is given to him by Jonathan and Igor. As Bobbie walks down the hall, he turns back to make sure that the mayor isn't following him. With the mayor not in sight, Bobbie quickly ducks into a closet.

"Okay, where's the book of Exodus?" mumbles Bobbie, thumbing through the Tobit.

Bobbie's hunt for Exodus leads him to page sixty-eight. Taking a deep breath, he carefully rips out a few pages and puts them into his pocket.

"Great! That will get Jonathan back into the city. Now I need the book of Colossians," mumbles Bobbie as he continues looking through the book.

Bobbie stops when he hears a noise down the hall. He hears people murmuring and footsteps walking his way.

This can't be happening! I must hurry! thinks Bobbie, rushing through the book.

Bobbie finds Colossians on page three-hundred and nine. He quickly tears out several pages and stuffs them into his pocket. Bobbie stands frozen, waiting for someone to find him in the closet with the Tobit. Sweat begins to run down the sides of his forehead. The footsteps stop outside the door.

THE HUNT FOR TAMMY

Just hand them the book and run! thinks Bobbie, nervously.

Whoever is outside the door continues walking, not knowing that Bobbie is in the closet.

Back at Mollie's Movie Theater, Mindy and her friends are watching Ben being terrorized by the bear. The kids in the theater watch in horror as the bear rocks the vehicle back and forth, trying to gain entry into the abandoned car.

"Run, Ben, run!" whispers one little boy.

"Leave him alone!" whispers a little girl.

"Help me! Somebody, help me!" screams Ben as he crouches away from the bear.

The rocking of the car has moved it closer to the edge of the mountain. The weight of the bear is about to send Ben on a ride that he'll never forget; if he makes it.

"Get away!" screams Ben desperately. *"Heeeeeeelp!"*

With one last roar, the bear pushes the car over the cliff. It rolls down the hill, picking up speed as it races down the steep incline.

"Ahhhhhhhhhh!" screams Ben, looking out of the windshield and seeing on-coming trees.

Ben quickly grabs the steering wheel and begins to steer the car. He barely maneuvers the car around the on-coming trees and bushes. The car bounces up and down as it jumps over bumps in the terrain of the mountain. Ben is tossed around as if he's riding a mechanical bull.

"Ahhhhhhh!" screams Ben, holding on for dear life.

The old car plows through bushes and tall grass, heading toward the bottom of the mountain. Parts of the car fly off as it travels down the rough terrain. Nothing in its path can withstand the force of the car. Tall, skinny trees snap like toothpicks as Ben braces for death.

THE HUNT FOR TAMMY

Ben's family has made it to the landing pad, waiting for the helicopter. They embrace as they hear the sound of the helicopter in the distance. One of the ranger's assistants notices something coming down the side of the mountain, heading their way.

"Look, it's a boulder!" shouts the assistant.

The group unknowingly watches Ben traveling down the mountain in the old abandoned car. What a sight! The sound of trees and twigs snapping gets closer and closer. Ben's parents realize that they're in a direct line with the barreling object.

"Everyone, stand back!" instructs the park ranger, pulling Ben's family aside.

The group moves out of harm's way and watches the "boulder" crashing through the edge of the woods.

"It's a car!" declares one assistant.

"What the heck is going on?!" asks the park ranger.

"*It's Ben!*" declares Mr. Hopkins. "He's driving the car!"

"'Ben,' be careful!" shouts Mrs. Hopkins as she jumps up and down.

"Yea, it's 'Ben'!" screams Lucy.

The group moves out of Ben's way as he drives into the lake. Mr. Hopkins and the park ranger immediately go after Ben. The remainder of the group follows them to rescue Ben; the adventure isn't over. Mr. Hopkins is the first one to dive into the lake, swimming frantically toward the sinking car.

"Dad, Dad!" screams Ben as water begins to fill up the car. "Help me, Dad! *I don't want to drown!*"

Mr. Hopkins reaches the car and motions for Ben to back up. Ben backs away from the driver's side window and his father kicks it in. Ben quickly exits the car just as it sinks to the murky bottom.

"Yea! We have 'Ben' back!" exclaims Lucy. "Mom, he's all right!"

Mrs. Hopkins holds her daughter and watches with tears as Ben and his father are reunited.

THE HUNT FOR TAMMY

The kids in the movie theater burst out in cheers for Ben and his family, watching the family reunion. Several kids high-five each other as girls wipe away tears. Watching Mrs. Hopkins and Lucy smothering Ben with love is overwhelming. The lights in the theater turn on and the credits begin to roll on the movie screen.

"That was such a good movie," says Mindy, choked up.

"I can't believe he made it," says Jack, shaking his head as he stands up.

"That was definitely one of the best endings that I've ever seen," says Bucky as he collects the trash from around his seat. "I wonder how the others are doing."

"I bet they didn't have as much fun as we did," replies Mindy, walking up the aisle.

Mindy, Bucky and their two new buddies head over to Arnold's Arcade to check on Derek and the rest of the gang. Each kid reflects on the movie as they exit the theater.

Derek is still wallowing in the glory from his adventure in Street Speed III. He's surrounded by the kids of Gibeon; some kids asking for his autograph while others are asking him questions. Thunder sits patiently next to Derek, smiling at his friend's moment of fame. He chuckles to himself, listening to Derek exaggerate about what really had happened on their adventure.

"I climbed on the rope to meet the kids! We were halfway over the city, inching our way across with our bare hands! I had one of Ginger's friends holding onto me the entire time!" explains Derek.

"Wow! You weren't scared?" asks Ricky.

"Nope!" replies Derek, sticking out his chest.

"What about the mystery car?" asks a little girl.

"I insisted that we go over and grab the kids, but he beat us there," replies Derek boastfully.

Thunder decides that he's had enough of Derek's fibbing and revs his engine.

"Ahhhhhh!" screams Derek as he leaps into the air.

The kids laugh at Derek.

"Why did you do that?!" asks Derek, putting his hand over his pounding heart.

"Ahhh!" screams Chuck as he turns and notices Becky and Barbie staring at him.

"Do you want some candy?" asks Barbie, smiling.

Chuck is now caught in a pickle. He must decide whether or not it's worth the risk of touching these girls in exchange for candy. Tommy sees Chuck struggling with this decision and pokes Chuck's side.

"Ahhh!" mutters Chuck, jumping away from Tommy. "What do you want?!"

"Just take the 'candy,'" replies Tommy, watching Barbie's eyes beaming at Chuck.

"Tommy! Chuck! Derek! Patricia!" scream Mindy and Bucky as they run through the arcade to be reunited with their friends.

Tommy and Chuck turn around and see their friends returning from Mollie's Movie Theater. Chuck grabs the candy from Barbie like a thief in the night and darts off to be with his friends.

"Mindy! Bucky!" exclaims Patricia, as if she hasn't seen her friends in years.

"How was the movie? Was it scary?" asks Chuck with a mouthful of candy.

It almost sounds as if Chuck is drowning while he eats the candy.

"It was great! Wow! It had one of the best endings ever!" replies Bucky, noticing Thunder. "Where did that car come from?!"

"How did it get in here?" asks Mindy, breaking away from Tommy's hug.

"He came 'here' through Derek ...," replies Patricia.

"'Derek?' How did Derek get a race car inside the arcade?" ask Mindy, interrupting.

The crowd clears a path for Derek, treating him as if he's a prince.

"What's *that* all about?" asks Bucky.

"Don't ask. We'd be here all day explaining," replies Tommy with a smirk on his face.

"Hey guys, do you like the car?" asks Derek, smiling. "Pretty cool, huh?!"

"Yeah, it's cool. But tell us how it got in 'here,'" insists Bucky. "I didn't see an entrance big enough for a car."

"I saw this game called Street Speed III. For some reason, I knew there was something different about the game. I could hear it calling me, in my head. I played it by myself and won," explains Derek as Chuck and Tommy roll their eyes. *"What?* I did win, you idiots! Anyway, I sneezed louder than I ever have in my life. Out of the sneeze came Thunder."

"You woke up a race car by a 'sneeze'?!" asks Bucky, shaking his head. "I don't believe...."

"That's right," states Thunder. "Derek's telling the truth about this one."

Mindy and Bucky jump back, startled that the car can talk. They carefully push Tommy and Chuck closer to get a better look. Patricia giggles, seeing her friends scared of Thunder.

"Even I wasn't scared of Thunder," whispers Patricia to Peggy.

"I'm so proud of you," whispers Peggy.

"Who are you talking to?" asks Toby.

"Myself," replies Patricia, smiling.

Bucky walks from behind Chuck, his human shield, to examine Thunder a little closer. Thunder smiles at Bucky, watching his facial expressions change as he checks him out. Bucky peeks into the car and sees a shiny stick shift and leather steering wheel.

"Do you like what you see?" asks Thunder as he winks at Derek.

"This is the *coolest* thing I've ever 'seen'!" declares Bucky with his mouth open.

"Tell them about your adventure when you and Thunder went into the game," suggests Toby.

"You 'went into the game?!' What was it like?!" asks Bucky, turning toward Derek. "Did you hear that, Mindy?!"

"Yeah ... weren't you scared?" asks Mindy as she walks up to Thunder.

"No way! You know how much I love racing games. This was a dream come true!" replies Derek, running his hand down Thunder's hood.

"Tell them about the last race," suggests Toby, nodding his head, watching Mindy and Bucky's eyes light up.

Chuck, however, lowers his head when Tommy turns and gives him a disgusted look. Becky and Barbie realize Chuck feels bad for ruining the race. They walk up to their hero and want to show him their support.

"Ahhhh!" yelps Chuck, turning and seeing the girls face to face.

"This is for you," says Becky as she extends out her hand.

ЄwwwW! thinks Chuck, as he carefully grabs the bag, making sure that there's no contact.

"What about the 'race'?!" asks Bucky. "Tell us what happened!"

"I got to 'race' against Tommy and Chuck. I also got to meet the people in the video game. They're real, too!" replies Derek, all lit up. "I even drove Thunder on two wheels!"

"*Coooool!*" mutters Bucky as he looks toward the video screens.

"Who won?" asks Mindy as she gets closer to Thunder.

"The mystery car!" replies Tommy, shaking his head at Chuck.

"Where's the 'mystery car'?" asks Bucky, staring at the screen.

"He got destroyed in the fire," replies Derek as he walks over to the game.

"What 'fire?' There was a 'fire' in the game?" asks Bucky.

"After the race, Lucy flagged us down to help Ginger and her friends get off a burning roof ...," replies Derek.

"Who's 'Lucy'?" asks Mindy, confused.

Thunder realizes that this conversation could take some time. To save Derek from a long-winded explanation, he decides to rev his engine. Thunder knows that this will get the kids' attention. The roar of the engine sends everyone jumping, including Derek. Derek and his friends quickly gather around Thunder, speculating that something's about to happen.

"What is it, Thunder?" asks Derek. "Did I do something wrong?"

"No," replies Thunder. "I have to go. The racers in Street Speed III need me."

"*Noooooooo!*" cry all the kids in the arcade.

"Can't we go for a ride first?" asks Tommy, imagining himself behind the wheel.

"Yeah, *pleeaassee!* We never get to do anything like this at home," pleads Chuck as he imagines himself winning the next race. "I'll give you a donut!"

Chuck double-checks to make sure that he has enough donuts to last him for a while.

"Sorry kids, one ride only," replies Thunder.

"Come on, Thunder, just 'one.' Please!" pleads Bucky as he envisions the crowd cheering him on as he crosses the finish line.

"Toby, would you explain to them why there's only one ride per adventure," mutters Thunder, backing away from the gang.

"Sure, Thunder. The rules of Gibeon only allow our guests to go on one adventure per game. There are many adventures in Gibeon and Derek was the lucky one to hit this adventure. Remember, these are the rules set by Mayor Messa, not me. And if any of you decides to disobey the rules … there are severe consequences," explains Toby.

The gang doesn't like the tone of Toby's voice.

"Tommy! Mindy! Bucky! Chuck!" yells Tammy, pushing her way through the crowd. "Coming through … can you move, please?! Hey guys, it's me!"

Several kids become agitated by Tammy's rudeness, watching her as she clings to the basket of strawberry tarts.

"Tammy!" shout Derek and his friends.

"Where have you been?" asks Chuck, realizing that she'd missed the entire show. "I forgot that you were even here!"

Derek and the others embrace and high-five each other. It seems like an eternity since Derek and his friends have been together. Tammy sees Thunder and becomes intrigued. She's suddenly overcome by a wicked sensation, as if Jonathan is placing some kind of spell on her. Tammy hears a voice in her head telling her to jump into the car.

"Cool! Let's go for a ride!" exclaims Tammy as she leaps into Thunder. "Hey, everyone, look at me!"

"*Noooooooo!*" scream her friends.

Thunder revs up his engine and squeals his wheels in circles. Tammy has made a grave mistake by disobeying the rules of Gibeon. Derek and his friends watch helplessly as the smoke from Thunder's exhaust pipe builds up, covering the entire room. The gang holds onto each other, listening to Thunder's engine stop. The smoke dissipates; no Tammy, no Thunder.

"Where did they go?!" asks Derek, looking at Thunder's track marks. "Oh no, Toby! What do we do now?!"

"Is she going to be *okay?!* Please tell us that everything's going to be all right!" pleads Mindy as she grabs onto Tommy's arm.

"Why did 'she' do that?" asks a little boy.

"Tammy's not one to listen too well," replies Bucky, fearful for his friend.

"This isn't good," says a somber Toby.

"Why do you say that?!" asks Chuck, worried that he may never see Tammy again.

"What's going to happen to her for breaking the rule?!" asks Tommy frantically.

"I don't know. No one has ever broken this 'rule,'" replies Toby worriedly.

"You've got to be kidding!" states Chuck as he squeezes a bag of chips. "See, that's what happens when you don't stay together! Matilda warned us of this, you know!"

"We're the only guests in the history of Gibeon to break a 'rule' like this?!" asks Mindy, throwing her hands into the air.

"Yup," replies Toby, shaking his head.

"Now what?!" asks Bucky, panicking.

"We'll just have to wait and see," replies Toby as he motions for Jeffrey.

"We don't have time to 'wait!' Can't we call Matilda or something?!" asks Derek.

"Matilda's busy getting things ready for your parade this evening," replies Toby.

"'Parade?!' Who wants to see a 'parade' when our friend is missing?! We have to find her!" declares Derek, feeling responsible for Tammy's disappearance.

"All right, guys, let's start looking!" suggests Tommy.

Tommy gathers his friends together to search for Tammy. The gang walks through the spot where their friend took off with Thunder. Derek follows the direction of Thunder's tire marks. Chuck walks over to Street Speed III and waits. A sense of fear washes over his body as he glares at the video screen. Tommy and the others continue to check the different video games to see if they can spot Tammy and Thunder.

THE HUNT FOR TAMMY

Unbeknownst to Derek and his friends, Tammy and Thunder have ventured into a game called Troas. Troas is a fighting game; its settings are located somewhere in Asia. It's a game that requires extreme skill, focus and knowledge. No one has ever been able to beat the ultimate warrior and rescue the princess from the evil Emperor.

The city streets are busy with young people going to and from work. The roar of Thunder's engine can be heard by the people in the game, moments before he appears. The people walking in the streets back off as a cloud of smoke appears, signaling the arrival of Thunder and Tammy. A young male, Asian gang member type, walks up to the smoke unafraid of what it might bring. He crouches down in a karate-type stance, ready to attack whatever it is that has invaded his turf. The smoke dissipates.

"Whoooooooooooooa!" mutters Tammy as they appear before the crowd.

The male's friends join in and surround Tammy and Thunder. They move in a circle around Thunder, waiting for Tammy to make the first move. Tammy immediately throws on her mask, hoping to intimidate the crowd.

"This is where you get off!" says Thunder as he opens his door and tosses her out.

Tammy tumbles to the floor and quickly gets up. She holds her hands in front of her, ready to defend herself from an attack.

This isn't good! thinks Tammy, as butterflies begin to churn up in her stomach.

"Who are you?!" demands one girl wearing a warrior-type headband.

"My name is Tammy. Where am I?" replies Tammy, frightened.

"Silence!" screams the young male who first approached the car.

Tammy jumps, knowing that she's no match for the seven

people surrounding her. She immediately drops her hands and takes off her mask as a sign of surrender. The young male senses that Tammy is willing to give in and do as he commands.

"We need to go to Soto's Palace at once!" states the young male.

"Who's 'Soto'?" asks Tammy timidly.

The young male points up to a mountain where there's a giant palace siting on the mountainside. The sky above Mount Tugi appears red and the moon is shining through several passing clouds. Tammy becomes numb as she stares at the eerie palace, knowing that she's in trouble.

"Come!" insists the young male, signaling.

Tammy reluctantly walks up to the young male. She's quickly apprehended and led to an awaiting vehicle. The car door opens and a large man with giant hands jumps out to let Tammy in.

I have to make a run for it! thinks Tammy, as she looks toward an alley.

Without hesitation, Tammy slams her foot on the large man's toes, crushing them. He jumps up in pain; she aggravated an old injury.

"Ahhhhhhhhhh!" screams the man, hobbling around.

Sensing that the young male would try to knock her out from behind, she ducks. The young male misses his target and punches the large man square in the jaw. The blow breaks the young male's hand and sends the large man crashing to the floor.

"Get her!" yells the driver as he watches Tammy running for the alley.

Tammy darts through the alley, fearful for her life. There are several gang members pulling out weapons as they chase her. Tammy throws down garbage cans and clotheslines as she runs, trying to knock her pursuers off track.

"You'll never get away!" screams one boy.

"We'll get you sooner or later!" declares a girl, trying to scare her into giving up.

THE HUNT FOR TAMMY

Tammy notices a broken window in the basement of a building and quickly ducks through it. The darkness of the alley allows her to go in unnoticed. The group of thugs runs right by her, still thinking that she's ahead of them. Tammy waits in the darkness, panting like a dog. The sounds of her friends' voices in her head give her strength.

"How am I going to get back?" mutters Tammy quietly.

"'Get back' where?" asks a mysterious voice from the darkness.

"Ahhh!" screams Tammy, quickly covering her mouth.

Tammy glares into the darkness, scared; trying to figure out whom in the world would be living in an old abandoned building. She cautiously looks through the darkness, searching for the origin of the voice. An old, wise-man appears out of the darkness. His long, white beard and half-closed eyes give him a look of wisdom beyond his years. Tammy steps back, scared from the sight of this Asian stranger.

"Don't be frightened. I won't hurt you," says the man with a raspy voice.

"Who are you?" whispers Tammy as she looks up at the broken window, making sure that none of her followers have found her.

"My name is Chen," he replies humbly.

A sense of peace washes over Tammy as a wind blows through the dark basement. It's as if Chen has some kind of mystical power.

"My name is …," whispers Tammy.

"Tammy," says Chen, smiling.

"How did you know?!" asks Tammy, spooked.

"I 'know' much about you," replies Chen as he closes his eyes.

Their conversation is broken up by running footsteps as another wave of people go looking for Tammy. Chen signals for Tammy to follow him into the darkness.

"She'll never make it out alive!" declares the young male as he catches up to the others.

Tammy realizes that she has no choice but to trust Chen. She takes a deep breath and follows his lead, walking cautiously through the darkness of the basement.

Derek and his friends are combing the arcade, checking every video game to see where Thunder might have taken Tammy. Several kids stand patiently before the games, waiting for Tammy and Thunder to appear. Toby has a search team on the other side of the arcade helping out as well. "Tammy!" echoes throughout the arcade as the kids search for the gang's lost friend.

"Thunder!" calls Toby, stopping in front of the Fighting Section of the arcade. "Where are…?"

Toby's mouth drops as he stares at the blank video screen of a game called Troas. The two Troas machines that are next to it are showing would-be-players how to play the game. He looks back and forth, realizing that something's not right.

"I think I found her!" shouts Toby as he walks up to the game. "Guys, they're in here!"

Derek and his friends break through the crowd and rush up behind Toby, trying to get a closer look at the game.

"Troas? That game is broken!" mutters Chuck as he shakes his head, disappointed. "Come on, we have to keep looking!"

"How do you know that she's in there?" asks Derek. "The 'game' isn't on."

"There's nothing happening. We should see them by now if they're in there. I agree with Chuck, 'we have to keep looking'!" states Tommy as he turns to check another game.

"No wait! I'm telling you that they're in there! Look at how the other two games are on and this one is not. And it's still plugged in!" exclaims Toby, showing everyone the plug to the game.

Derek and Chuck run up to the machine and start shaking it.

THE HUNT FOR TAMMY

"Tammy! Thunder! Come on, stupid game!" mutters Derek, banging his hand on the game. "We're sorry, Thunder!"

"Is anybody in there?! Tammy, answer us!" demands Chuck as he nudges the game with his body.

"Hey, guys, easy! You might break it and we may never get a chance to see Tammy again!" says Tommy.

"Somebody do something! Our friend might be 'in there'!" pleads Mindy as she looks around for help.

Derek and Chuck give up and walk away.

"Look! It's on!" declares Bucky.

"What do we do next?" asks Patricia.

"Tammy, we're here!" screams Derek with his face to the game. "Come on, Thunder! Answer me, it's Derek!"

The children of Gibeon gather around Troas. They know that Derek and his friends will have their hands full trying to rescue Tammy from this game. Toby and Chuck join Derek next to the game. They watch the video screen intently.

The screen shows two warriors fighting each other in an arena. The arena is surrounded by old Asian architecture. The half-destroyed ruins around the fighting area create a coliseum-type atmosphere. The mystical sky has an orangered glow with a fog setting in, which makes it difficult for the fighters to see each other at times.

"Cool!" says one boy, watching the two warriors slash their samurai swords through the air.

"How are we going to find her?" asks Bucky nervously. "What if she's thrown into one of those matches?"

"Wow, it seems so real!" states Tommy, staring at the screen.

"This is one of our most graphic games," says Toby, backing away as he formulates a plan. "Don't worry, Bucky, we'll get 'her' out."

"This 'game' looks like Dragons & Swords!" says Derek, recalling his dream.

THE HUNT FOR TAMMY

"Are you sure that she's in there?" asks Mindy, squinting. "I don't see her anywhere!"

She cringes, watching the fighters knock each other to the ground.

"I'm pretty sure. There's no way that this game should be off with the plug still in. It's one of our most popular games," replies Toby, nodding his head.

The kids are startled by the sound of Thunder's roaring engine; it sounds different. Derek and the others scatter, not knowing which direction the noise is coming from. Once again, the arcade is overwhelmed with smoke that changes colors. Derek and his friends creep up to the intense cloud, hoping to see Tammy.

"Tammy?! Tammy?! Are you there, Tammy?!" shout Derek and his friends as they try to see through the thick smoke.

An image appears as the smoke dissipates.

"*It's 'Tammy!' It's 'Tammy'!*" declares Chuck, jumping up and down. "She's back!"

Derek and Tommy run through the thinning smoke to welcome back Tammy. Mindy and Patricia hug each other, glad that the ordeal is over. Bucky wipes his forehead, relieved that the hunt for Tammy has ended.

"Ahhhhh!" scream Derek and Tommy, realizing that the figure before them is a boy rather than Tammy.

"What's wrong?!" asks Chuck as he watches Derek and Tommy run from Thunder. "I'm out of here!"

"Who are you?" asks Toby, stepping closer to see what's going on.

"My name is Lee," replies the young male from the video game.

Lee jumps out of the car and rubs his broken hand; the one that he used to hit the large man in the face when Tammy ducked. He glares at Derek and his friends with a look that could kill an elephant. The gang huddles together, trying to get a better look at Lee and show him that they're in this together. Lee assumes his position, ready to strike.

"Where's Tammy?!" asks Tommy as he takes the lead. "What did you do with her?"

"Yeah, 'where' is our friend?!" asks Bucky from behind Chuck.

"Get out from behind me, Bucky!" growls Chuck.

"Your 'friend' is busy with us. If you want her, come and get her," challenges Lee.

"How do we 'get her'?" asks Derek, stepping forward.

Toby and Jeffrey cautiously circle Lee, trying to intimidate him. Lee suddenly crosses his hands quickly, which sends the boys running.

"You must play the game and find her. You must also defeat the ultimate warrior ... which no one has done. Or, one of you can come back with me and find her," replies Lee with an eerie grin.

"No one's going alone! How about we all go?" asks Tommy, sweating.

Derek and his friends step back from Tommy, intimidated by Lee's evil presence. Tommy turns and sees that his friends aren't cooperating.

"Fine! I'll 'go' with Lee and find Tammy *myself!*" mutters Tommy, perturbed.

"Well, you have a feisty spirit. I respect that. So be it!" says Lee as he motions for Tommy to get into the car.

"Thunder, can't you do something?!" pleads Derek.

"Sorry, my friend. Rules are rules. One ride only," replies Thunder.

"*But* she didn't know! Please, Thunder, don't make Tommy go into that game!" pleads Mindy. "We can't lose two friends!"

"I'm sorry, kids, but I have a higher power to answer to," says Thunder as he revs his engine, ready to return back into Troas.

"No, wait!" exclaims Toby, breaking through Derek and his friends.

"'Wait' for what?" asks Tommy.

Toby walks up to Tommy while the arcade watches in suspense. Derek and his friends whisper among themselves. Lee rubs his hands, still ready to fight.

"I say that we *play* the game. You're a swordsman like me … and together I believe that we can win Tammy back!" replies Toby as he stares at Lee.

The crowd reacts to Toby's suggestion.

"I like his idea better, Tommy," says Chuck, trying to protect his friend from certain disaster. "Those warriors are too much!"

"Yeah, Tommy, you play a mean game of Tek Fighter II back home," says Derek, shaking his head. "Besides, you don't stand a chance with those guys! They'll use you like a fighting stick!"

"You can do it!" screams a boy from the crowd.

The kids in the arcade burst out in cheers for Tommy and Toby. Several kids begin to chant Tommy and Toby's names. Lee spins around, making sure that no one's going to jump him from behind. The momentum has shifted toward Tommy and his friends.

"*Silence!*" yells Lee as he crouches down in a fighting position.

The crowd cringes at Lee's command. Lee moves around Thunder like a crab, ready to strike should anyone try something foolish. His training keeps Lee alert at all times, especially when he's outnumbered.

"What's it going to be, Tommy?" asks Lee with a sinister look.

"Come, Tommy, let's play," coaxes Toby as he reaches out his hand.

Tommy stares at Toby's hand and then glances back at Thunder, thinking about Tammy on the other side. He turns back toward his friends and sees them eagerly waiting for his answer. Chuck and Derek are nodding their heads for Tommy to shake Toby's hand and play the game. Mindy and Patricia are praying and Bucky gives his buddy a thumb up.

"You're on!" declares Tommy, shaking Toby's hand. "We'll 'play the game'!"

"*Yeeeeeeeaaaaaaaa!*" scream Tommy's friends excitedly.

All the kids in the arcade join their celebration, to Lee's dismay.

"Fine! Let it be done as you wish! But I warn you ... no one has *beaten* the Spirit!" says Lee as he climbs back into Thunder.

The kids react harshly to Lee's threat.

"The 'Spirit?' What's the 'Spirit'?" asks Chuck with a gaping mouth.

Chuck and Derek turn back toward the game.

"What kind of warrior is he?" asks Tommy, second-guessing his decision.

"Don't let him intimidate you!" replies Toby, dodging the question. "We can take him!"

"I'll see you soon," says Lee.

Thunder revs up his engine and drowns out the noise in the arcade. Once again, the kids retreat from the giant cloud of smoke coming from Thunder's exhaust pipe. Tommy and Toby try to get one last look at Lee before he leaves. Mindy slowly walks up to Troas, yearning to see Tammy.

"I hope you're all right, Tammy," whimpers Mindy as she touches the screen.

"I know that she's 'all right.' Are you kidding? She's probably got someone in a choke hold or something!" says Chuck as he puts his hand on Mindy's shoulder.

"Yeah ... I bet everyone ran when she put on her mask," adds Patricia, cracking a smile.

"He's gone!" shouts a little boy.

Mindy, Chuck and Patricia turn around and see the smoke disappearing. They quickly turn back toward the video game, hoping to see Lee and Thunder appear on the screen. Tommy and the others rush over to the game, hoping to see some sign of Tammy. The kids of Gibeon have their attention focused on Tommy and Toby. The two boys mentally prepare themselves to do battle with the fighters and warriors of Troas. Tommy sighs, knowing that Tammy's life is at stake.

Inside the game, Tammy and Chen are walking through some dark, underground tunnel, trying to elude Lee and his people. Rats and other rodents scamper through the water-soaked tunnel as the two quietly move along. Tammy ducks under large spiderwebs that line the tunnel's ceiling.

"Ewww!" mutters Tammy quietly as she brushes off a sticky web from her head.

Chen turns and chuckles, watching Tammy wrestling with the web. The torch in Chen's hand barely lights up the tunnel. They have a hard time seeing as they continue trudging through the tunnel.

"Are you sure that you know the way?" whispers Tammy as she shakes off the thought of a rat touching her.

"Yes. Be quiet or they will find us," whispers Chen, humbly smiling.

Chen stops abruptly and signals for Tammy to be silent. He leans his head to the side, trying to listen to something that he senses above the tunnel. Tammy looks toward the ceiling and notices a small drainage cover that leads to the street. The sound of a car stopping causes Tammy's heart to pound.

"All right, my friend, you've served your purpose," says Lee as he opens the door.

Lee's voice echoes down into the tunnel. The sound of Thunder's door closing as Lee jumps out sends chills down Tammy's back. Chen nods his head; his suspicion is correct. Thunder, once again, revs his engine and heads back to his home in Street Speed III.

How am I going to get home now?! thinks Tammy, as she hears the sound of Thunder's engine disappear.

Chen and Tammy remain motionless until they hear Lee running away.

"That was the guy who was chasing me, wasn't it?" asks Tammy, hoping that Chen will say, "No."

"Yes, it was. His name is Lee. We must hurry. He will be back," replies Chen.

"Who is he?" asks Tammy, checking to make sure that there are no rats around her feet.

"Lee is the leader of a local gang. He's also an enemy of Soto and his warriors," replies Chen as he motions for her to move forward.

"Oh, great! Who's this 'Soto'?" asks Tammy, realizing that this is becoming her worst nightmare.

Suddenly, several voices mumbling can be heard from behind. It's a group of men heading in the same direction as Chen and Tammy.

"Come! We must move quickly!" whispers Chen, motioning for Tammy to follow him.

Tammy turns around and sees a torch light flickering around the dark tunnel. The group of men gains on Tammy and Chen. They, too, are trudging their way through the dark tunnel, trying not to fall and get bitten by a rodent.

"They have to be in here somewhere!" says one man. "We can't let Lee down!"

Chen and Tammy see a smaller tunnel branching off to the right.

"Hold this," says Chen, handing Tammy the torch.

"What are you doing?" asks Tammy, making sure that she doesn't drop the torch.

"I'm ripping part of my garment. I will place it on the wall, pointing them to the larger tunnel. That should throw them off," replies Chen, smiling.

Chen grabs the torch back and signals for Tammy to follow him down the smaller tunnel.

Tommy and Toby are now standing in front of Troas, ready to begin their *hunt* for Tammy. Derek and his friends step up behind the boys, prepared to scream and yell. Several kids argue with each other about who will win. The mood in the arcade has drastically changed. Everyone's serious; the breath of death dances around Arnold's.

"I hope they can do it," whispers one boy.

"Of course 'they can do it'!" mutters Chuck as he steps in the boy's face. "Cat got your tongue?! ... That's what I thought!"

"Calm down, Chuck!" insists Bucky, grabbing his friend.

"You 'calm down'!" mutters Chuck as he stuffs his face with potato chips.

"We all need to 'calm down,'" suggests Mindy, trying to keep the peace between her friends.

Mindy signals to Patricia that they should pray for their friends. The two girls bow their heads and offer a prayer for Tommy and Toby.

"What are they doing?" whispers a little girl.

"They're praying. I saw them do it in the deli earlier," replies a little boy.

"Let's get this started!" exclaims Tommy as he cracks his knuckles. "Hold on, Tammy, here we come!"

Toby reaches down and deposits several tokens into Troas. The video screen lights up and Toby makes the selection for two players to play the game. The next screen displays the different fighters that Tommy and Toby can choose.

"Pick Jet!" shouts a boy from the crowd.

"No, 'pick' Ken!" screams another boy.

Tommy and Toby turn around and signal for the crowd to be

silent. Watching the screen intently, they carefully scroll through the different fighters. They are as follows:

Li   Tun   Jet   Des   Ken   Pai   Zito   Do

Tommy moves his joystick and picks Zito. Zito is a masked fighter built like a piece of steel. There's not an ounce of fat on him. His tall, muscular body gives him an advantage over many of the warriors. His weapons of choice are the fighting stick and numbchucks.

"Great 'pick,' Tommy," states Toby as he continues to scroll through the choices.

Toby finally stops his joystick on Jet. Jet is a stocky fighter built like an army tank. He has supernatural strength that can overpower several warriors at once. His weapons of choice are the samurai sword and fighting pole.

The next screen shows Tommy and Toby the different warriors that they'll be up against. They are as follows:

Hagar   Goliath   Rush   Krul   Viper   Pagan   Worm   Serpent
Beast   Dar   Hawk   Ape   Spirit

Hagar looks like a giant troll with large, bulky muscles. His favorite weapon is the battering shield, capable of knocking-out fighters and warriors in an instant. Goliath is an extra-large warrior with giant hands and arms. He doesn't use weapons while he fights. It's his pure, brutal strength that forces his opponents into submission. Rush is a lean, martial arts expert that uses his hands and feet with lightning speed. His favorite weapon to use is the samurai sword.

"These guys look pretty tough!" states Tommy as sweat begins to form on his forehead.

"They're not that 'tough,'" says Toby confidently, trying to ease his partner's nerves.

Tommy and Toby continue to watch the video screen. Krul is a bald-headed warrior with a black beard and thick, black mustache. He almost looks like a pirate. He's covered with tattoos symbolizing his greatest victories. His favorite weapons are the samurai sword and the fighting stick. The Viper is half-man and half-snake. His weapon is his tail and quick hands. Pagan is a short, stocky warrior who looks like a monk. He's an excellent warrior. His favorite weapons are his mind and a fighting club. The Worm is a tall, skinny warrior with extra-long arms. His lanky body makes it difficult for his opponents to knock him out. The Worm's favorite weapons are the hurling sticks and tri-chucks.

"We have to beat all of them to win?" asks Tommy, shaking his head.

"Don't worry, we can do it," replies Toby, nodding his head. "You have to remain confident, Tommy."

"They're going down!" declares Chuck with chewed up cookies flying out of his mouth. "You're the man, Tommy! ... You, too, Toby!"

Chuck quickly looks away, noticing Becky and Barbie gazing up at him.

Appearing on the screen is the Serpent; he's half-man, half-lizard. This warrior's favorite weapons are his tail, hard scales and fighting stick. Next is the Beast; he's a four-armed warrior built like a demon. His large, hairy appearance often intimidates opponents into submission. He can use all the weapons at the same time. Next is Dar; he's a warrior that looks like a Viking. He loves to use his large fighting club. Next is Hawk; he's another masked, muscular warrior whose favorite weapons are his wrestling moves. He pins his opponents into submission. Next is Ape; he's half-man and half-gorilla, mostly gorilla. His large teeth and red eyes could scare the dead. Ape's favorite weapons are the shield and his raw strength. Finally, there's the Spirit. The Spirit is the only undefeated warrior of the group, as Lee mentioned before. His large body is made up of a mass of energy that can paralyze any opponent. The Spirit can rip off parts of his body and use them as weapons to destroy an opponent from a good distance. Many fighters and even foreign warriors have tried to defeat the Spirit, to no avail.

"*Greeeaaattt!*" mutters Tommy as he reads about the Spirit on the screen.

"How are you guys going to beat the Spirit?" asks Derek, shaking his head.

Chuck lowers his head and puts down the cookie that he was eating. Mindy lifts up her head from prayer and notices Chuck. She knows that something's serious because Chuck has stopped eating.

"What is it, Chuck?" asks Mindy hesitantly.

"It's the 'Spirit.' No one has defeated it! And now Tommy and Toby are getting ready to lose Tammy forever," replies Chuck, thinking about the loss of his friend.

"Hey! What kind of *attitude* is that?!" shouts a little boy.

Chuck immediately lifts his head, searching for the face behind the voice.

"He's right, Chuck! We have to stay positive!" insists Mindy.

"Have you played this game before?" asks Tommy.

"I 'play' it all the time," replies Toby.

"And? What about the 'Spirit?' Have you ever faced him?" asks Tommy anxiously.

"Remember, I'm the fencing champion of Gibeon. I've faced him many times and I'm not too shabby playing Troas," replies Toby.

"But 'not too shabby' doesn't bring Tammy home … *does it?!*" asks Chuck sarcastically.

"Easy, Chuck!" insists Tommy, trying to calm his friend. "What about the 'Spirit?' What makes you think that we can defeat the 'Spirit' this time?" he asks as he regains his composure.

"My instinct tells me that you're pretty good at this type of game. I've never had anyone to play with me that was good.

Besides, going into the game yourself wasn't a better option than playing the game together," replies Toby as he stretches his fingers.

"He's got a point, Tommy," says Bucky.

Tommy turns around and sees his friends nodding their heads. They support Toby's comment and his decision to play the game. His confidence and courage is lifted, seeing the desperation of his friends wanting Tammy back. He turns to Toby.

"All right, my friend, let's do this!" says Tommy, shaking his hand.

They turn back to the video screen and get ready for the first match.

Tammy and Chen are out of Tommy and Toby's view, running from Lee's hoodlums. They've made it to the outskirts of the city, only to be narrowed in for a certain capture. Chen stops and faces the on-coming hoodlums. He folds his hands and begins to meditate, preparing for battle. A strong wind blows, indicating Chen's readiness to fight.

"What are you doing?!" asks Tammy as she turns back, noticing Chen stopped. "There's too many of them!"

"Go!" insists Chen, ready for war.

Tammy runs back toward Chen and stops, realizing Lee's men are too close. Lee signals for his followers to step it up and make sure that they don't get away this time. The large man is limping as fast as he can, seeking revenge on Tammy for stepping on his foot.

"Come on! You can't take them! Let's get out of here!" mutters Tammy as she looks for a place to hide.

"Be not afraid. Go my child," says Chen as he pulls Tammy near. "*Marana tha!*"

Tammy is overwhelmed with a strange sensation as if Chen put her in a trance. She turns and sees a path in the woods and makes a dash for it. Chen resumes his position of meditation while Lee and the others surround him.

THE HUNT FOR TAMMY

"Get the girl!" commands Lee.

Chen summons a lightning storm full of hail and heavy rain, sending the men retreating back to Lee. His hoodlums become scared, acknowledging that Chen has some kind of supernatural powers. The sky lights up as Chen remains meditating.

"You're no match for us, old man!" declares Lee, wiping the flooding rain away from his face. "This storm doesn't scare me! Get him!"

Lee and his hoodlums circle around Chen, getting ready to attack. Tammy peeks back one last time, and then enters the woods. She stops in her tracks as she envisions Chen's death.

"Pssstt, come here," whispers a voice.

"Ahhh!" yelps Tammy as she turns toward a path in the woods.

A little Asian boy appears from the darkness. He looks to be about the same age as Tammy and her friends. His comforting smile eases Tammy's racing heart.

"Come, quickly," says the boy, signaling as he steps back into the woods.

Tammy turns back, again, and sees her savior preparing for battle. Knowing that she doesn't have a choice, she follows the little boy. He rushes through the dense woods, peeking back every now and then, making sure that Tammy is keeping up.

"What is your name?" asks Tammy, trying not to lose her breath.

"Pong," replies the boy, smiling.

Pong pulls away, signaling for Tammy to hurry. He wants to make sure that Lee and his hoodlums aren't able to catch them.

Lee signals to one of his men to make the first move on Chen. The man yells out a warrior-type grunt as he charges. Chen smoothly moves to the side and the man goes crashing to the floor. Another man charges Chen and attempts to tackle him. Chen leans to the side and trips the man, sending him sailing through the air and into his counterpart. Lee finally decides to take over. He rubs his broken hand and crouches down to fight.

"All right, old man, prepare to die," says Lee as he moves his hands across his body. "When I get through with you … you'll be begging for mercy!"

"My name is Chen … not 'old man'!" mutters Chen, frustrated, as he raises his leg and moves it to the side.

Lee's hoodlums watch with anticipation as the two get ready to fight. The rain has now become so heavy that it's blinding Lee and his hoodlums.

"What about the girl?!" screams a girl.

"Don't worry about her! She won't get far!" replies Lee as he closes in on Chen.

"*Hiyaaaaaaaaaaaaaaaaa!*" screams Lee as he chops his way toward Chen.

Chen throws up his hands and blocks Lee's attack. The two fighters move in circles as Chen fends off Lee. Both fighters let out grunts and groans as they punch and kick. Lee spins and misses Chen's head by inches. He begins to tire, frustrated that Chen is so quick.

"Help me!" mutters Lee, catching his breath.

A muscular girl runs into the circle, somersaulting her way toward Chen. Chen slouches down with his hands raised in front of him, ready for the attack. The girl lunges forward with her foot extended, intending to kick Chen in the chest.

"*Diiiiiiiiiiiiiiiiii!*" screams the girl as she sails through the air toward Chen.

Chen moves to the side and kicks the girl off course. Chen's kick sends the girl crashing to the floor in agony.

"You had enough?!" grunts Chen as he assumes his meditative position.

The storm silences as Chen inhales.

"Not yet old man! Let's see how you will do with this!" says Lee as he pulls out a knife.

"My name is Chen, not 'old man'!" grunts Chen, waving Lee over. "Huh!"

As Lee and his hoodlums close in, the group is overcome with an overwhelming sense of fear. The large man with the broken toe stares in shock. His eyes bulge out as he looks at Chen.

"Run!" yells Lee as he drops the knife and retreats toward the city.

A ball of energy, like fire, flies into Chen, sending him crippled to the ground. He shakes uncontrollably, paralyzed by the Spirit's power.

Sitting on top of a rock is Pong, waiting for Tammy to catch up. He smiles and shakes his head, watching her struggling up the hillside. With arms folded over his knees, Pong nods his head for her to rest.

"You're too fast for me!" mutters Tammy, buckling over.

"You must be 'fast' out here or else," says Pong, smiling.

"How come you always smile when you talk?" asks Tammy.

"*Happy!*" states Pong, grinning even bigger.

"How come you're all alone? Where's your family?" asks Tammy as she checks around to make sure that Lee and his hoodlums haven't found their spot.

"Soto has them," replies Pong as he looks to the ground.

Tammy senses that she just hit a sore spot in Pong's life. She walks up to comfort Pong as he plays in the dirt with a stick. Tammy extends out her hand as a gesture of friendship.

"Ahhhhhh!" screams Tammy as Pong flips her on her back.

"You, too, slow," mutters Pong, resuming his position on the rock.

"What is *wrong* with you?!" groans Tammy as she helps herself up off the ground.

"I trust nobody. My father told me this when he hid me from Soto," replies Pong.

THE HUNT FOR TAMMY

"Who is this 'Soto' I keep hearing about?" asks Tammy as she continues to pick the sticks out of her hair.

"He's the warlord of Kabit," replies Pong as he peeks over Tammy's head.

Tammy's hair stood up on the back of her neck when she heard Pong say, "Warlord." The conversation is interrupted by the sound of a loud gong ringing out from the mountainside.

"What is that?" asks Tammy as she looks to see where it's coming from.

"There's a new fighter," replies Pong. "Come, we must go," says Pong, heading down a path.

"'New fighter?' Where are we going? Why won't you answer me?!" asks Tammy as she follows Pong like a puppy dog.

Tommy and Toby are standing before the game, ready to begin their first match. Tommy's Zito and Toby's Jet are warming up in a fighting arena that's set in the hills. The backdrop of the video screen is beautiful. The sky is a yellowish-red with a sliver of the moon peeking through the clouds. Spectators are lining up to sit on the broken stone fixtures that surround the arena. This match appears to be taking place in a lost city in the Asian mountains.

"Are you ready?" asks Toby, glancing down at the buttons of the game.

"'Ready'!" declares Tommy.

"You can do it!" screams a little boy from the packed arcade.

Hagar and Goliath enter the screen from the left, ready to fight Zito and Jet. The four fighters circle the ring, pounding their fists, waiting for the gong to sound. Each fighter stares intently into his opponent's eyes, trying to instill fear before the match. A bald stumpy man wearing a robe walks up to the gong to start the fight. Hagar, Goliath, Jet and Zito position themselves to grab their weapons of choice as soon as the gong sounds.

Tommy and Toby hold their joysticks, tight, and examine the buttons on the game one last time. Tommy makes sure that he knows which button is for kicking, which button is for punching, and which button is for blocking. He also examines the chart that surrounds the joystick; it explains to a player how to jump, duck, kneel and spin.

"Come on, Tommy!" shouts Chuck as he paces back and forth, crushing the piece of cake in his hand. "I believe in you! Yeeeeeaaaaahhhhhh!"

"You can do it, Toby!" shouts a boy. "Take Goliath out!"

"I can't take the pressure," says Bucky, walking away.

The kids in Arnold's settle down as they watch the Master of Ceremonies raising the baton to hit the gong. It's as if the man is moving in slow motion, swinging his arm to strike the gong. Zito and Jet take off toward the weapons table to grab their favorite weapons. Zito quickly places a set of numb-chucks in his belt and grabs a fighting stick. Immediately, he's greeted with a punch to the back of the head from Hagar. The blow sends Zito tumbling across the floor, but only for a moment.

"Get up, Zito!" scream Chuck and Derek. "Tommy, do something!"

Zito rises to his feet with his fighting stick, ready to take down Hagar.

Jet and Goliath are exchanging blows, each one blocking the other's offensive. Toby craftily maneuvers Jet, ducking and dodging Goliath's giant roundhouses. He takes a swing at Jet and misses. Jet quickly rushes in and head-butts Goliath in the mid-section.

"Yeah, Toby!" shouts Derek, hitting Chuck.

"Hey!" says Chuck as he rubs his head. "Come here! You want to wrestle?!"

Goliath buckles over from the devastating shot to the abdomen. Jet grabs his fighting pole and clobbers Goliath over the head, knocking him out cold. The screen reads "K.O." Toby quickly maneuvers Jet to help Zito. Zito is losing a grappling match with Hagar. Hagar senses something behind him and turns to see what it is. He's greeted with a splintering blow from Jet's fighting club; it knocks him out instantly. Zito and Jet celebrate with a victory hug as the screen reads "K.O." The man strikes the gong, indicating that the first stage of battle is over.

Tommy and Toby leap up and high-five each other as they celebrate their victory. Several kids are whistling and screaming, showing their support for the boys. Mindy and Patricia jump up and down, relieved that the first fight is over. Max and Tucker hug Toby for saving Tommy's Zito from a certain defeat. Derek turns to high-five Chuck and spills his drink instead.

"Derek!" yells Chuck as he looks down. "Now look at my pajamas!"

The kids laugh at Chuck.

"Sorry, dude!" says Derek, chuckling behind Chuck's back. "Here, you want to get me back ... spill some on me."

"*There's Tammy!*" shouts Bucky, pointing at the video screen.

All eyes shift toward the video screen. The celebration ceases as the gang sees Tammy and Pong sitting in the stands, getting ready to watch the next match. Tommy and the others stare at the screen, watching Tammy and Pong trying to remain inconspicuous, careful not to get noticed by Soto.

"'Tammy!' Over here, 'Tammy'!" shout her friends from the arcade.

"She can't see or hear us," says Toby as he prepares for the next match.

Derek and his friends become frustrated and settle down. They move closer to the game, hoping to get a better look at Tammy and Pong.

Tammy starts to fidget as Rush and Krul enter the fighting arena. The stage for this match is located in a circular fighting area that's raised above a moat of water. The temporary bridge is removed after Zito and Jet enter to fight. There are large, predator-type birds circling the fighting area, looking for something to eat. The sky has turned to haze. There's a deep orange sun beginning to set through the mountaintops.

Pong cautiously looks around the old outdoor stadium. He searches the crowd for any signs of Soto's people while Tammy takes in the fight. Tammy realizes how serious Pong has become and settles into her seat.

"Your friends are playing the game," whispers Pong.

"How do you know?" whispers Tammy as she peeks toward her left.

"I feel it," replies Pong, glancing over at some commotion in the stands.

"I'm here! I'm here!" shouts Tammy as she jumps up and waves recklessly. "Tommy, I'm right...!"

"Sit down and be quiet! You're *going* to get us captured!" mumbles Pong, pulling Tammy back down in her seat.

Soto's protégé, Tret, noticed Tammy's outburst from his seat in the Parlor. He summons several of Soto's bodyguards.

"Bring them to me!" demands Tret as he scratches his chin.

Tret's ghouls rush out of the Parlor to apprehend Tammy and Pong.

Outside the game, Derek and the others are going ballistic behind Tommy and Toby. They saw Tammy signaling to them; this has given them hope. Tommy tries not to lose focus and feed off of his friends' excitement.

Don't lose your cool. It's not over yet, thinks Tommy, as he anticipates the next match.

"She sees us!" exclaims Bucky as he knocks Peggy out of Patricia's hand. "Sorry!"

"Take it easy, Bucky! Tammy can't 'see us.' She only knows that we 'see' her," explains Mindy, picking up Peggy for Patricia.

THE HUNT FOR TAMMY

"You can do it!" screams a little boy.

"Everyone, be quiet!" insists Derek. "The match is about to start and Tommy and Toby need to concentrate!"

The kids refocus on the screen and see the Master of Ceremonies approaching the gong. He grabs the baton and raises it, signaling that the match is about to begin. The four fighters circle each other, waiting to grab their favorite weapons from the weapons table. Each fighter uses his tactic to instill fear and doubt in the other fighters.

The crowd around the fighting arena cheers for their favorite fighter, waiting for the gong to sound. They're starting to grow impatient with the Master of Ceremonies. Because Tammy knows that her friends are watching every move she makes from outside the game, she glances toward the sky every now and then, hoping that they see her face.

"Knock him out, Krul!" yells a man.

Krul looks toward the section where the man is sitting, then toward the sky, fist raised.

"*Yeaaaaah!*" bellows Krul in a barbaric tone.

"What's our next move?" asks Tammy.

"Wait, patiently," replies Pong as he canvasses the area for Soto's men.

"'Wait' for what? We need to make a move!" states Tammy, throwing her arms around as if she's about to wrestle with Krul.

"We can't 'make a move,'" says Pong as he calms Tammy down. "I need to find someone first."

The Master of Ceremonies swings the baton and strikes the gong. Zito and Jet take off toward the weapons table, taking their eyes off their opponents; big mistake. Rush catches up to Jet before he can reach his weapon and knocks him to the ground. Immediately, Rush takes advantage of Jet's position and starts pounding him with a barrage of punches to the back of his head.

311

THE HUNT FOR TAMMY

The crowd goes crazy, watching Jet getting destroyed. Tammy has a hard time controlling herself; frustrated that she can't jump up and give them a piece of her mind.

"Zito! Help me!" yells Jet as he starts to lose consciousness.

Zito turns from the weapons table and sees his partner being defeated. He quickly grabs his fighting stick and numb-chucks and heads back to help Jet. Krul has other plans for Zito and knocks him back. The blow from Krul's fighting stick sends Zito flying into the air. Zito tumbles to the ground, slowly gets up, and shakes off the "cobwebs" in his head.

"Finish him!" screams a man. "Nail him to the ground!"

Zito retaliates by using his fighting stick, knocking Krul to his knees. Without another moment to waste, Zito throws his fighting stick in the direction of Rush. Rush continues to pound on Jet, unaware of the approaching fighting stick.

"Look out!" shouts a boy.

Bam! The fighting stick slams into Rush's forehead as he looks up.

"All right, get him!" screams Tammy, leaping from her seat.

"Sit down!" insists Pong as he pulls Tammy back into her seat. "You must listen!

"Sorry!" says Tammy. "I get excited when I watch wrestling and full-contact sports!"

The crowd is now on its feet, watching the four fighters *battle* for their lives. Each fighter is exchanging blows and jumping high into the air, trying to knockout the other one. The battle is intense. Weapons smashing against each other can be heard throughout the arena. Zito and Jet grunt and moan, becoming bloodied from the fierce fighting.

Tommy and Toby are kicking their feet while they play the game. They act as if they're fighting in the ring themselves. They're pounding the buttons on the video game, desperately trying to win their match. The crowd around them is rowdy; yelling, screaming and whistling. It's loud enough around Tommy and Toby to make a person deaf. Chuck and Derek are fidgeting as they watch the match. Their voices are hoarse from all the cheering.

"Come on, Tommy!" mutters Chuck, spilling his drink. "Tammy needs you! Kick him!"

"Show them who's the boss, Toby!" shouts Derek as he dodges Chuck's mess.

"I can't watch," says Patricia to Peggy.

"Come on, guys!" screams Bucky, feeding into the energy of the arcade. "Jump, 'Toby,' jump ... now punch him!"

Tommy raises his hands into the air. Zito has knocked Krul to the floor once again.

"Finish him, 'Tommy'!" screams a little boy. "Somersault on top of him!"

Tommy quickly moves Zito over toward Krul to finish him. He uses his numb-chucks and gives Krul shots to the head and body. The kids in the arcade go wild, watching the blow to the side of Krul's head that knocks him out.

"You did it, you did it!" screams Mindy as she turns to make sure that no one saw her act like one of the boys.

"Come help me!" mutters Toby, pounding the game and fighting off Rush's attack. "Get up!"

Tommy quickly sends Zito over to where Jet and Rush are fighting. The two fighters have made it to the edge of the arena. Both are flirting with the possibility of falling into the moat. As Zito approaches to help, Rush grabs Jet and drags him over the edge and into the water. The two fighters find themselves underwater contending with many foreign creatures. Large snakes with big teeth swim through the water, smelling their next meal. A large, prehistoric-looking piranha takes a bite at Jet's leg and misses.

"What's that?!" asks Derek, noticing an alligator-type creature heading their way.

THE HUNT FOR TAMMY

"Get Jet out, Tommy! Hurry, help him!" shouts Chuck, crunching his potato chips like there's no tomorrow. "Look at that thing!"

Tommy moves Zito over to the ledge and stretches his fighting stick toward Jet. Rush sees the monstrous alligator-type creature getting closer and tries to stop Jet from reaching the stick. The creature opens its large mouth, hoping to make a meal out of both Rush and Jet.

"Hurry!" scream several kids.

Jet swims to the stick and grabs hold of it. As Zito pulls Jet up, Rush grabs Jet's leg and pulls him back under. Jet tries to kick Rush, but to no avail. If Rush is going to perish by the alligator-type creature, so will Jet.

"Look out!" scream Chuck and Derek.

Zito didn't finish off Krul like he thought he did. Krul is charging Zito like a raging bull with nothing to lose. He's looking to knock him into the moat with the others, regardless of what happens to him. As Krul leaps for Zito, Zito moves slightly right, sending Krul flying into moat. Jet lets go of the fighting stick and moves out of Krul's path. Krul lands on top of Rush, knocking loose his hold on Jet. Jet quickly grabs onto Zito's fighting stick and is pulled out of the moat.

"*Yeeeeaaaaaaaaaa!*" scream all the kids in Arnold's.

The arcade erupts in clapping and whistling as the kids watch Rush and Krul battle the monstrous alligator-type creature.

The gong sounds and Zito and Jet are announced the winners of the match. Tret's ghouls are moving through the stands heading toward an unsuspecting Tammy and Pong. The crowd cheering blinds them to what is about to happen. Tammy examines the food being eaten in the row ahead of them.

"*Ewww!* What's that?" asks Tammy, quivering.

She watches a boy swallow something very slimy.

"That's Pau," replies Pong, smiling, watching Tammy's face turn pale.

"*Gotcha!*" screams one of Tret's ghouls as he grabs Tammy.

"Ahhhh! Pong!" screams Tammy as she tries to get away.

The crowd backs off. They know better than to get in the way of Soto's men. Pong is quickly apprehended by two large men. Tammy and Pong are pushed through the crowd and shuffled toward the Parlor.

Tommy and his friends stare at the video screen, shocked. Mindy holds Patricia, comforting her, as Chuck drops his donut to the floor. The kids in the arcade become silent and stare at the screen, mouths dropped.

"They've got Tammy!" declares Derek, pointing. "What are we going to do now?!"

"Where are they taking her?" asks Mindy, terrified. "Now she's gone! Toby, *do* something!"

"Can't you go after them?!" asks Derek, clinching his fist as if he's going to jump into the game and save Tammy.

"We have to complete the game. That's the only way to get 'Tammy' back," replies Toby, cracking his knuckles for the next match.

"Don't worry. We're going to get 'her,'" says Tommy, nodding his head while hiding his true feelings.

The gang glares at the screen and tries to locate Tammy and Pong through the rowdy spectators; no luck. They watch as a group of men murmur about Soto's men dragging Tammy and Pong away. Bucky hugs Patricia, trying to comfort her worrying heart. Chuck and Derek see the next screen light up. It shows Tommy and Toby's next opponents. Both get charged up for their friends to do battle.

"Get them, Tommy! Come on, Toby, you can do it!" growls Derek.

"Smash them!" yells Chuck as he crushes a cupcake in his hand. "No more games, 'Tommy!' Take it to the hole!"

THE HUNT FOR TAMMY

"I *love* it when he does that," says Becky to Barbie.

Tommy's friends move closer to the game and settle down. They watch Zito and Jet preparing to fight in the bottom of a volcano. The video screen shows molten rock bubbling up from the fiery pits that line the volcano floor. Hot steam rises out of several mini-volcanoes, singeing the fighters as they pass by the percolating pits. The spectators settle on top of rocks and ledges located around the volcano. People cheer for Viper and Pagan as they enter through a dark cave.

"Go Viper!" shout several boys.

"Rip his head off!" screams a man cheering for Pagan.

Derek and Chuck can't believe the graphics of this game. The four fighters face off in the arena, waiting for the gong to sound. The volcano floor begins to rumble, indicating that the volcano is awake. Each fighter carefully watches the ground, making sure that they don't step into a lava pocket. Viper takes a cheap swing at Zito, using his tail. The crowd *hisses* at Viper's attempt to strike Zito before the gong.

Toby maneuvers Jet close to Zito, covering each other's blind spot. Pagan is sitting Indian style on a rock, meditating.

"What's up with him?" asks Tommy, moving Zito around Jet.

"He uses his mind to fight," replies Toby as he sends Jet kicking in the air to intimidate Viper.

Mindy canvasses the video screen to see if she can see Tammy.

Meanwhile, Tammy and Pong are standing in the Parlor, facing Tret as he paces. His ghouls stand close behind the kids, making sure that they don't try anything stupid. The two of them are terrified; Pong envisions himself working in a factory for the rest of his life. One of his men shoves Tammy forward so that Tret can get a better look at his new guest.

THE HUNT FOR TAMMY

"Hey!" yelps Tammy, stumbling.

"Leave her alone!" insists Pong.

"Be quiet!" demands one of Tret's men as he smacks Pong on the back of the head.

"What is your name, little girl?" asks Tret, smirking.

He walks around Tammy with his hands behind his back.

"My 'name' is Tammy. Who are you?" asks Tammy, overcome by the presence of evil.

The sound of the door knocking grabs everyone's attention. Tret braces himself and signals for one of his men to answer it. The man pulls out a fighting stick and walks over to the door. He's prepared in case it's one of Tret's enemies. Tret has many enemies who want to take over as Soto's protégé. Tret's men have been trained well and will die for their boss.

"Who is it?" asks the man, ready to strike.

"Yamato!" replies a voice.

Tret's men quickly line up in formation behind Pong and Tammy. Pong's eyes grow wide, realizing who's on the other side of the door. Tret humbly walks up to the door and opens it; he knows better than to let his men answer this one. Several large men walk through the door and examine the room. Some men carry knives while others carry fighting sticks, ready to clean house. Not a sound is made while they check the room.

"Soto, Sir!" says Tret as he bows before his boss.

Soto, a large man who looks like he could be a sumo-wrestler, walks through the door and sees Tammy and Pong. Tret's men bow before Soto as he walks into the room. No one makes eye contact until he speaks. He's wearing a beautiful, silk, red robe that catches Tammy's eye.

"So, this is the girl that Lee's people were talking about. Too bad he lost her," says Soto as he checks out Tammy.

Tammy begins to sweat, feeling as if she's going to pass out. The presence of this giant Asian man looking down on her is overwhelming. Pong swallows hard, knowing what Soto is capable of doing. All eyes are focused on Soto and Tammy.

"What is her name?" asks Soto.

"Tammy, Sir," replies Tret as he straightens himself up.

"Bring her to my Palace at once," says Soto, stroking her head.

"What do you want with me?" asks Tammy as she begins to cry.

"Don't be afraid. I'm not going to hurt you," replies Soto as he hands her a silk handkerchief.

"Take me instead! Let 'her' go!" demands Pong like a barking dog.

Soto smoothly walks over to Pong with a look of death on his face. Pong shivers as Soto stands over him. The room becomes silent as everyone waits for Soto's words. Not many people survive after raising their voices at Soto, let alone look at him. Pong shrinks down as Soto leans closer and breaths down his neck.

"You are coming with me. Now I have your entire family," says Soto, grinning.

"What about the two fighters, Sir?" asks Tret respectfully.

Soto walks up to a large window on the opposite side of the room. He watches Zito, Jet, Viper and Pagan battling each other. Yamato walks over to the window also.

"Should we send the Spirit now, Sir?" whispers Yamato.

"No. Let them have their fun. The 'Spirit' can wait," replies Soto.

Pong shivers from hearing Yamato's whisper. Soto turns to face Tret and the others.

"Walk these two over to the Pit. I want you to introduce them to the 'Spirit,'" says Soto.

"Yes, Soto, Sir, right away!" says Tret, signaling for his men to follow Soto's orders.

THE HUNT FOR TAMMY

The men clear a path for Soto to exit the Parlor and head back to his Palace. Tret's men follow closely behind.

Down in the Pit, several warriors are battling with the Spirit. These warriors are used by Soto as a tune-up for the Spirit's upcoming fights. Usually, the Spirit fights three to five warriors at a time. The Spirit looks like a giant mass of energy shaped like a warrior. He's as tall as any other warrior and has a body that's indescribable. There are bright lights and energy moving very rapidly within the frame of the Spirit's body. The warriors in the Pit try to take the Spirit down with several types of weapons.

"Take his legs!" shouts one warrior as he swings his fighting stick toward the Spirit's head. "Hurry, use your club!"

Without looking back, the Spirit blocks the fighting stick, breaking it in two. The warrior then tries to sweep the Spirit's legs, but is paralyzed by a ball of energy taken from the Spirit's body. Several warriors back away, watching the fighter squirm on the ground in agony. They also prepare themselves for the Spirit to strike again. He can tear off any part of his body and throw it at them, sending them to the same fate as their friend on the floor. Most of the shields used in the game are unable to block these fiery masses of the Spirit's body.

"Ahhhhhhhh!" screams a large warrior as he charges the Spirit.

The Spirit spins around and throws another piece of his body at the warrior. The warrior is knocked off his feet as the ball explodes on impact.

"He's amazing!" declares a new trainer.

"The Spirit is undefeated. No warrior can match his power!" states one of Soto's men.

The two trainers turn and see Tret with his men. They're bringing Tammy and Pong into the Pit. The trainers immediately leave their seats to greet Soto's protégé.

"Tret, Sir. What can we do for you?" asks one of the trainers as they bow before Tret.

"We are here to show the Spirit to our new guests. Bring them up close and let them see his awesome power," replies Tret as he signals for Tammy and Pong.

"Isn't this Bet's little boy?" asks the one trainer, looking at Pong.

"Yes, he is. He will be reunited with his family in the factory," replies Tret with an evil smile.

"Momma! Papa! What have you *done* with them?!" screams Pong as tears flow from his eyes.

"Ahhhhhh!" screams one warrior as he's tossed across the Pit by the Spirit.

Tammy and Pong quickly turn and see the Spirit fighting off several warriors. Chills travel down their bodies as they watch in awe. One of the Spirit's trainers grabs Tammy and Pong and leads them to the edge of the fighting arena. The Spirit senses their presence and holds up his hand, stopping all warriors from fighting. His fiery eyes glow as he looks intently at Soto's newest guests.

"Help! Somebody, help me!" cries Tammy fearfully as the Spirit walks their way. "Please let me go!"

"There's no one to 'help' you, little girl," says one of Tret's men.

"Wait until the two new fighters get here! They'll defeat the 'Spirit'!" threatens Pong.

Tret and his men laugh at Pong's foolishness. The laughter ceases as the Spirit walks over to the edge of the fighting arena. Tret and his men back away and bow down before the Spirit. They have a great deal of fear and respect for the ultimate warrior. The Spirit breathes heavily as he checks out Tammy and Pong. His x-ray vision looks into their souls, making sure that neither one of them is a threat.

The Spirit lets out an eerie roar as he lifts his hands high into the air. This is his way of letting everyone know how powerful he is. His body illuminates multiple colors in different directions, blinding everyone that looks. The entire group shrinks down with fear; the Spirit's groan can be heard throughout the mountain region. Birds fly out from the trees, fearful as well. Animals scamper for a place to hide, knowing exactly where that sound came from. The Spirit quickly resumes his match and finishes his show of power.

"Your 'fighters' don't stand a chance," says Tret as he watches the Spirit defeat the remaining warriors. "Bring these two to Soto!"

"Yes, Sir, right away!" say two of his men.

The men grab hold of Tammy and Pong and lead them to Soto's Palace.

Tommy and Toby have just beaten Worm and the Serpent; two outstanding fighters. The boys dance around the arcade and celebrate with several kids, knowing that they're closer to rescuing Tammy. Unfortunately, they have no idea what's happening inside the game; their mood might be different. Derek and Chuck punch each other in the arm as Max, Robert and Jill cheer for Tommy and Toby. The kids of Gibeon are going crazy throughout Arnold's. They eagerly wait for Tommy and Toby to start the fifth stage of the game.

Bucky is passing out sodas to his friends; the cheering and yelling have made them thirsty. Becky and Barbie are following him with snacks. Mindy hands Tommy a towel to dry the sweat from his forehead. By the looks of his messy hair and sweat, Tommy looks as if he was in the game, fighting the warriors himself.

"Thanks, Mindy," says Tommy, smiling. "This game is tougher than I thought!"

"Easy, Chuck! Not so hard!" mutters Toby, cringing from Chuck's deep massage.

Chuck looks like a boxing trainer, trying to loosen up Toby for the next match.

"Sorry Toby! Just trying to make sure you're ready," states Chuck as he smacks his gum and backs off. "*Ahhhh!*" screams Chuck as he backs into Becky and Barbie.

They're holding up a piece of chocolate cake for their sweetheart. Chuck cringes at the thought of having to take another thing from them, knowing that they have a crush on him.

Well, all right, thinks Chuck, quickly grabbing the cake without touching either girl.

"I wonder how Tammy's doing," says Patricia as she approaches the video screen to look for her friend. "We're fighting for you, Tammy."

The crowd settles down and joins Patricia next to the game. Tommy and the others scan the video screen, looking for Tammy and Pong. All they can see are people gathering for the next fight. Chuck and Derek shake their heads, frustrated, wondering what's happening to their friend. Tammy is nowhere to be found. They watch the Beast and Dar moving into the next arena, ready to do battle with Zito and Jet. The spectators in the game go crazy, watching the Beast and Dar warming up.

"That warrior looks tough!" declares Chuck, pointing at the Beast. "I bet he could wipe out three fighters!"

"Chuck! Whose side are you on?!" asks Tommy as he turns and gives his friend a nasty look.

"Sorry, Tommy, I'm on your 'side'!" replies Chuck, shrinking his head back like a turtle.

Tommy and Toby assume their positions behind the game. The boys crack their knuckles and prepare to fight against the Beast and Dar.

The match takes place in an open arena located at the edge of a dark wicked forest. The forest leads up to Soto's palace. There are several ferocious lions chained to trees at the edge of the fighting arena. They leap at the fighters as they pass by, hoping to catch some dinner. Each fighter carefully circles the arena, making sure that they don't get too close to the lions. The Master of Ceremonies walks up to the large gong. It's strung up between two large trees. He grabs the baton, looks at the fighters, and swings it at the gong. "*Gooonnnggg!*" The fighters rush toward the weapons table.

Chuck grabs hold of Jeffrey, Bucky covers his eyes, and Becky and Barbie grab onto Derek. Several kids cheer and pound their fists, ready for Tommy and Toby to wage war. The girls' hearts pound as the fifth stage of the game has begun.

"Hurry, Tommy, hurry!" shouts Derek as watches the Beast closing in on Zito. "Look out!"

The Beast takes a giant leap forward and knocks Zito and Jet to the ground before they reach the weapons table. The fighters tumble across the dirt floor.

"Get up!" scream several kids.

Chuck paces back and forth nervously.

"'Look out'!" screams Bucky as he covers his face.

Dar swings his mighty fighting club at Jet and Zito as they try to get up. The swing could take out an entire army. Toby quickly maneuvers Jet to duck under the on-coming club. Tommy isn't so lucky. The club *nails* Zito square in the chest, sending him flying across the arena floor once again.

"Roooaaarrr!" growls a lion, lunging toward an injured Zito.

"Get away, Tommy!" mutters Mindy, jumping.

"Oh no!" screams a little boy.

The lion's paw rips some flesh from Zito's shoulder as he moves away from the tree. Zito falls to the floor in agony. The Beast comes charging at Zito to finish him off.

"Tommy, watch out for the Beast!" screams Derek as he punches the air. "Try to take his legs out!"

"Come on, Tommy!" groans Toby. "Crouch to the ground!"

Zito stands up, dazed from all the action. He finds himself without a weapon to fight a charging Beast. Zito looks around helplessly.

"Lead him to the lion!" screams a little boy behind Chuck.

THE HUNT FOR TAMMY

"Good idea!" exclaims Tommy.

Tommy quickly maneuvers Zito back toward the tree. The lion lunges at Zito several times, seeking to finish what he started on his shoulder. The smell of blood has the lion pacing back and forth, barring his teeth.

"*Raaaaaaaaaaaaaaa!*" bellows the Beast as he approaches a wounded Zito.

The Beast leaps forward to grab Zito, but Zito ducks out of the way. The spectators cheer as the Beast sails next to the tree where the lion is chained. Zito wastes no time and limps toward the weapons table.

"Eeeek!" squeals the lion as the Beast knocks him out.

Zito turns and sees the Beast in a state of rage, heading his way. With the Beast approaching, Jet sends Dar to the floor and heads over to help his friend.

"*Noooooooo!*" wails Jet as he watches the Beast knockout Zito with a barrage of hits to the head.

The Beast backs away from Zito and raises his hands, victorious.

The kids in Arnold's stand before the Troas video game with their mouths wide open. Several kids hold onto one another as if they're at a funeral. They watch the red "K.O." light flash on and off on the screen over Zito's lifeless body. Tommy releases his death grip of the joystick and backs away from the game.

"Now what?!" asks Derek as tears begin to form in his eyes. "Does this mean that the hunt for Tammy is over?"

"You can't win alone, can you?!" asks Chuck, watching the Beast celebrate his victory.

"Tommy hurry! Put two tokens into the game! You can still play!" states Toby, shuffling through his pockets, looking for two tokens.

THE HUNT FOR TAMMY

The video screen reads:

TO CONTINUE TO PLAY
INSERT 2 TOKENS
10 ... 9 ... 8 ... 7 ...

Derek and his friends check their pockets for two tokens. The race is on to find Tommy what he needs to continue playing the game with Toby. It seems that the gang has used up all their tokens playing other games.

"Quick, somebody, do something!" shouts Derek as he watches the countdown reach five. "I'm out of 'tokens'!"

"We're running out of time!" declares Chuck, pulling out candy from his pockets.

As the gang watches their hope fade away, a boy reaches between several kids and inserts two tokens into the game.

"*Bobbie?!*" asks Toby, shaking his head.

"Hey, you're the kid I saw when we first got here!" says Tommy, resuming his position, ready to fight.

"Where did you come from?" asks Derek, patting Bobbie on the back.

"I've been busy with my Dad," replies Bobbie, lying through his teeth.

Several kids congratulate their new hero.

Word of Tammy getting sucked into the game spread throughout Gibeon like wild fire. Jonathan sent Bobbie over to Arnold's to make sure that his plans aren't going to be spoiled by a rotten girl. The kids refocus their attention on the video screen as the game prompts Tommy and Toby to get ready. Bobbie falls back into the crowd and observes the kids carefully.

Inside the game, Zito and Jet are regrouping in the center of the fighting circle. Each one checks to make sure that his weapons are ready for battle. The Beast and Dar circle around their adversaries. The crowd is out of control, watching their favorite warriors prepare to shed blood. The lions practically break free from their chains, sensing weakness and smelling blood.

"All right, Zito, this is it! We must take them down!" states Jet as he twirls his fighting pole.

"No prisoners!" exclaims Zito, eyeing the Beast.

The Master of Ceremonies walks up to the gong and strikes it with the giant baton. The fighters rush toward the center of the fighting arena with their weapons drawn. Jet and Dar connect with their fighting clubs and knock each other to the ground. Dar shakes off the dirt and leaps onto Jet. The two fighters wrestle on the dirt floor and head toward a hungry lion. Jet reaches deep within his soul, mustering up the strength to throw Dar off him.

"*Raaaaaa!*" growls Dar as he sails through the air.

Jet quickly heads for his fighting club and pursues Dar. Dar crashes to the ground and is welcomed by a blow from Jet's club. He struggles to get up. Jet positions himself for the knockout.

"This is for the girl!" declares Jet, wiping the dirt from his face.

He crouches down and waits until Dar looks his way. With a powerful kick, Dar is knocked unconscious. The crowd cheers for Jet's victory as a lion breaks free from its chain. Jet positions himself to fight the lion with his samurai sword. He wields the sword around his body, grunting and screaming. The lion stops short of Jet, yielding to the shiny blade of the sword that slices before his eyes.

On the other side of the fighting arena, Zito is blocking the Beast's attack. The Beast is using numb-chucks and a samurai sword simultaneously. Zito's quick hands block each and every blow from the Beast. His offensive moves are pushing Zito back toward a raging lion.

"Jet! Come help me!" yells Zito.

The Beast turns and prepares to defend himself against Jet.

THE HUNT FOR TAMMY

Zito seizes the opportunity and hits the Beast in the mid-section. The blow knocks the wind out of the Beast, sending him to his knees and his weapons to the floor. Zito wastes no time and hits the Beast across the face and over the head. His bluff pays off; the Beast falls face down in the dirt.

"You did it! You knocked-out the Beast!" exclaims Jet as he rushes over to Zito.

The two embrace and celebrate their victories.

Yamato is leading Tammy and Pong through Soto's garden. The two kids observe Soto's slaves tending to his exotic greenery. There are men, women, and children trimming Bonsai trees and planting flowers thoughout the garden. No one dares to look at Tammy and Pong as they pass by, fearful of punishment.

"What are they going to do with us?" whispers Tammy as she glances up at the guard tower.

"We will work here," replies Pong, looking for his family.

"Silence!" demands one of Soto's men.

Tammy and Pong are shoved forward. Pong tries to catch Tammy as she trips over his foot and stumbles to the ground.

"Hey!" mutters Pong, defending Tammy.

"I'm okay, Pong.... *Chen!*" yells Tammy, lunging forward.

She's quickly apprehended by one of Soto's men.

Chen quietly continues his chore of trimming a Bonsai tree. He knows better than to make a scene. Chen nods his head, motioning at Tammy to keep moving forward. She sees his subtle smile and keeps walking. Tammy is touched by Chen's spirit, giving her a boost of confidence and courage.

Soto walks to his window and sees his new guests arriving. He knows how valuable Tammy is for his organization. Soto's rival gangs are trying to outbid one another to have her.

"Bring her up here," insists Soto to one of his men.

"Yes, Soto, Sir!" says the man as he heads for the garden.

THE HUNT FOR TAMMY

Dun, a messanager with a stocky build, enters the door and humbles himself before Soto. Everyone knows the price they'll pay for not acknowledging Soto as Emperor. Soto senses the man's presence and turns from the window.

"Soto, Sir …," says Dun, bowing his head.

"I know … they're winning," says Soto, grinning.

Dun quickly raises his head, surprised by Soto's calm reaction to Zito and Jet. Soto motions for a servant to bring him his afternoon tea. A petite Asian woman and a man bring the two men a tray of tea.

"Thank you, you may go," says Soto as he grabs his cup and motions for Dun to grab one as well.

"But, Soto, Sir, they're coming after you. Are you not worried?" asks Dun as he sips his tea.

Soto finishes his tea and walks across the room to another window. Dun places his cup on the table and follows Soto. The two men stare at the Pit and watch the Spirit as he defeats the last of his sparring warriors.

"Do you forget who I have working for me?" asks Soto, smiling.

"No, Soto, Sir," replies Dun. "But it's been so long since fighters have made it this far."

"Enough!" demands Soto as he turns toward Dun.

Dun immediately bows before Soto, expecting to be destroyed. No one questions or doubts Soto and his ways. Many men have lost their lives for such foolishness; some for less. Soto has control over the entire mountain region because of his reputation and power.

"I'm sorry, Soto, Sir! Please forgive me!" pleads Dun.

"The Spirit has *never* been defeated! He will crush Zito and Jet with no problem. I will end this madness now!" declares Soto, signaling for some of his men to join the two next to the window.

"Yes, Soto, Sir!" says a man, bowing.

"Tell the Spirit it's time," says Soto, rubbing his hands.

"What about Hawk and Ape?" asks the man.

"The Spirit will crush them too!" replies Soto as he turns back toward the window. "And bring the girl to me."

"Yes, Soto, Sir, as you command," says Dun, rushing out of the room.

Soto signals for everyone to leave. He's not taking any chances and wants to make sure that Tammy is by his side. She's the prize, and the reason why Zito and Jet are fighting. Soto has always used people as leverage to get what he wants. Since coming into power, many families in his region have been victims of kidnappings and extortions.

Back in the arcade, Derek and Chuck are rubbing Tommy and Toby's shoulders, getting them ready for their next match. Tommy glances over at Toby with a look of relief, thinking that Bobbie is on their side. Bobbie blends in well with the other kids, discussing the importance of the next match. He glances at Tommy and squeezes out a fake smile, giving him a thumb up to show his support.

"Hawk is so cool," whispers one boy.

"What?!" asks Chuck, frowning at the boy. "Are you crazy?!"

The boy cowers back, sorry that he even opened his mouth. Mindy and Patricia huddle together, trying not to let the pressure get to them. Bucky is helping Becky and Barbie pass out more snacks and drinks. Their hospitality helps ease the thick tension among the kids.

"How are these next two warriors?" asks Tommy, shrugging his shoulders.

"They're tough … real tough," replies Toby, shaking his head.

"Don't worry, 'Tommy' … Zito and Jet are 'tougher'!" declares Chuck as he notices Tommy getting nervous. "Come on, brother! Gut check! Don't make me show you mine!"

"Yeah, Tommy, you're fighting with the best 'warriors'!" states Derek, shaking his head at Chuck's attempt to break the tension. "Chuck! Put your pajama shirt down!"

The kids in the arcade settle down, watching the video screen prompt Zito and Jet to head to their next fighting arena. Mindy and Patricia drop their heads in prayer as Bucky crosses his fingers.

"Here we go!" says Toby, gripping his joystick.

The kids huddle close to the video screen to watch Zito and Jet.

Zito and Jet walk into a dark cave on the side of a mountain. It's barely lit up by several large torches. There are people standing along the tunnel waiting for the fighters to enter the arena. Some hostile spectators *hiss* and *boo* at Zito and Jet while others *cheer* them on. A light smoke fills the air from several burning fires within the cave.

"All right, my friend, no holding back!" says Jet as he smashes his hand with Zito's for good luck.

"'No holding back'!" declares Zito, nodding his head.

The two fighters finally enter into a large cavern. Inside the cavern is an enormous indoor stadium packed with screaming fight fans. Zito and Jet glare at the crowd and feed into the excitement, using this as a motivator for their match. Torches that line the stadium seats flare up, creating a blinding light. Jet notices large bats and strange creatures on the cavern ceiling, waiting for their dinner.

"This place is out of control!" states Zito, watching some kind of wicked animal trying to get out of its cage. It looks like a prehistoric wolf. "Imagine having that beast as a pet! *Yeeeeeaaaaahhhhhh!*"

"Just the way I like it!" declares Jet, taking in a deep breath. "Bring 'em on!"

"Look!" says Zito as he points at Soto and Tammy.

THE HUNT FOR TAMMY

Soto, his bodyguards and Tammy are sitting in a special section carved out of the mountain. It overlooks the entire cave. Soto waves to his people from a magnificent throne as his bodyguards stand next to him, eyeing the crowd for would-be threats. Tammy is seated in front of him, observing the crowd as well. She's terrified. The crowd begins to chant Soto's name; he basks in his glory. The noise level rises.

"That must be the girl!" shouts Jet, glancing up at Soto's section.

"How are we going to get her?!" asks Zito, watching his partner's back.

The conversation is interrupted by the *roar* of the crowd; Hawk and Ape exit another tunnel and make their way toward the center of the cavern. The crowd is awestruck by Hawk's size and evil eyes that pierce through the holes in his mask. Jet focuses on Ape's impressive body. Ape takes notice and lets out an eerie roar, beating his chest. The sound of his chest pounding can be heard throughout the cavern.

"You're going down!" yells Hawk, raising his arms and glaring at Zito and Jet.

"Bring it on!" screams Jet, watching Ape slouch down and shuffle across the floor.

The crowd breaks out into a chant, "Hawk! Hawk! Hawk! Hawk!" Zito and Jet sense that the crowd wants to see them finished in this round, once and for all.

"I'll take Ape!" shouts Jet as his heart pounds uncontrollably.

"No problem, the Hawk is mine!" shouts Zito over the noise of the crowd.

The fighters eyeball the weapons table as the Master of Ceremonies takes his position. He takes his place on a large platform overlooking the fighting arena. The Master of Ceremonies glances up at Soto, seeking his approval to begin the fight. Soto raises his cup and signals for the gong. "Gong! Gong! Gong!" sounds the gong as the man hits it with the baton.

"*Arrrrrrrrrrrrrrrrr!*" scream Zito and Jet as they rush toward the weapons table.

Ape grabs Hawk and tosses him toward the weapons table. Hawk sails through the air like a missile and reaches the table first. He quickly grabs a fighting stick and grabs a shield for Ape.

"Catch!" screams Hawk as he tosses the shield back to Ape.

Hawk turns back to the table and is blasted by a flying body-shot from Zito.

"Two can play at that game!" says Jet, brushing his hands clean from tossing Zito.

Zito immediately starts kicking and punching Hawk, trying to knock him out early. Hawk rolls away from the attack. Regaining consciousness, he charges Zito and wrestles him to the cavern floor, fighting for a submission. Zito kicks himself up from his hind legs, only to be met with a strike from Hawk's fighting stick. Zito is temporarily dazed by the strike to his face. He staggers off toward a fire pit.

The kids in the arcade are going ballistic watching Toby maneuvering Jet to take on Hawk. Toby is smashing the punch and kick buttons as he moves his joystick forward.

"You can do it!" screams a little boy. "Kick his legs!"

"Get him, Toby! Knock his lights out!" yells Derek as he knocks a box of popcorn out of Chuck's hands. "Smash the Ape!"

"Hey, watch it!" mutters Chuck as he reaches down to pick up the box.

"Ohhhhhh!" moan several kids.

Chuck rises up and stares at the video screen. He sees Jet striking Ape with several right hands to the side of the head. Tommy almost kicks Toby off balance as he duels with Hawk.

"Tommy, watch your feet!" screams Toby, shifting back and forth.

"Sorry!" says Tommy. "I can't help it! This is how I play!"

"It's Tammy!" shouts Bucky, pointing to the top right of the screen.

Mindy and Patricia open their eyes and see Tammy standing before Soto.

"*It's her, it's her!*" declare Derek and Chuck as they jump up and down.

The gang rushes close to Tommy and Toby to get a better look at their friend. Many kids in the arcade feel Tommy and his friends' pain. They see how much they miss Tammy and fear for her life. Chuck looks around to see if he can find something to get her attention.

"'Tammy!' 'Tammy!' We're here!" screams Derek, waving his hand back and forth.

"She can't see you, remember?" asks Toby, concentrating on the game.

"Please get her back!" pleads Mindy, tears watering from her eyes.

"We need 'her'!" declares Patricia as she squeezes Peggy. "We're counting on you, Tommy."

Bucky walks up to Mindy and hands her a napkin for her eyes. The kids of Gibeon love the fact that Tommy and his friends care about each other and look out for one another, in spite of their teasing and horseplay.

"Kick him!" screams a little boy. "Use your weapons!"

The attention, once again, shifts to the fight as the action intensifies.

Zito and Hawk are fighting a defensive fight. Each fighter masterfully blocks the other's offensive strategy. Hawk reaches within his soul and marches forward, twirling his fighting stick, ready to end the nonsense. Zito does back flips and somersaults to avoid Hawk's attack.

"Get him!" yells a man from the crowd. "Jump on him!" "Come on, Zito, don't let him win!" screams a girl.

Back and forth the two fighters exchange blows to the body. Neither one can get a clear shot for a knockout.

Meanwhile, Ape and Jet are locked up in a grappling move. Each one has an arm around their opponent's neck and the other arm is clinging to their shoulder. They battle in circles, pulling each other to and fro. Ape's height advantage is cancelled out by Jet's supernatural strength. Ape bellows out a cry, wondering how Jet can be winning.

"Don't let him win, Ape!" screams a man from the crowd. "Pop his ears!"

"Get his legs, Jet!" yells another man.

Jet wrestles Ape next to a standing pool of fire. The mini-volcano is shooting flames into the air every few seconds. Jet grabs Ape's hands and presses him to his knees. Jet's strength has finally taken its toll on Ape as he pulls him toward the fire.

"Yeeaahh! Finish him!" scream several fans.

"Come on, Ape! You can do it! Crush Jet!" shouts a man as he leans over a railing, swinging his fist.

"You're going down, Ape!" grunts Jet as sweat pours out of his body.

"NO ... I'M ... NOT!" grunts Ape, lifting his hands back up with a sudden burst of strength. "It's ... you ... that's ... 'going' ... 'down'!"

The crowd is standing on its feet, cheering for their favorite fighters. Some spectators get impatient, realizing that the fighters aren't even close to being knocked-out. Soto signals at a man that's standing next to the Master of Ceremonies. He reaches over and strikes a small gong. The gong's sound goes unnoticed over the roar of the crowd. The man quickly disappears through a tunnel on the side of the platform.

"Watch this," says Soto, grinning.

At that moment, the cavern begins to shake as if there's a

mini-earthquake. People stare at one another, wondering why the ground is trembling. Many spectators cover their heads as they watch parts of the cavern ceiling falling to the ground. The crowd is perplexed, trying to figure out how the fighters could cause the mountain to shake with such great force.

"Look over there!" shouts a man as he points to the other side of the cave.

The spectators shift their attention to a wall that's collapsing and forming a new tunnel. Out of the falling rocks and dirt emerges the Spirit. His lights and energy beam throughout the cavern. The Spirit displays his power in a mighty way. The tremors settle down as the Spirit raises his hands high into the air, looking to end Zito and Jet's quest for Tammy.

"Spirit! Spirit! Spirit!" chants the crowd as he heads toward the fighters.

Zito, Jet, Hawk and Ape step away from each other as they watch the Spirit approaching. Hawk and Ape walk up to their ally.

"Soto must have sent you," says Hawk as he reaches out his hand.

The Spirit quickly swipes his mighty arm across his body and strikes Hawk square in the chest. The blow sends Hawk *sailing* across the cavern as if he's a child. Ape quickly grabs a samurai sword and tosses it at the Spirit. The Spirit pulls off a piece of his shoulder and slings it at the flying sword. The ball of energy destroys the samurai sword in midair, causing the crowd to roar. Spectators are blinded by the Spirit's ball of fire.

"What's going on?!" asks Zito, watching the Spirit go after Ape.

"I don't know, but I have a feeling we're next!" replies Jet as he picks up his fighting stick.

"How are we going to defeat that?!" asks Zito as he readies himself with his numb-chucks and fighting stick.

"I don't know, but everything has a weakness. We must find its weakness!" replies Jet, turning back to see Ape retreating from the Spirit.

Ape grabs a fighting club off the weapons table to defend himself.

"Why are you doing this?!!!" grunts Ape as he tries to block the Spirit's attack.

Ape grabs a shield from the floor and fights off the barrage of blows from the Spirit. The Spirit remains silent, pressing Ape back toward a lava pit. Zito and Jet watch in awe as the Spirit's body begins to circulate and glow more intensely, indicating that something big is about to happen.

"*Noooooooo!*" bellows Ape as the Spirit rises into the air and expands in size.

Ape crouches to the ground and covers himself. The Spirit descends and administers a mighty *blow* with both arms to the head. Ape is knocked-out cold. The crowd belts out a thunderous cheer and stands on its feet. Jet and Zito are totally confused and fearful for their lives.

Soto smiles at the Spirit and raises his cup, pleased with his ultimate warrior. Tammy turns and sees the Spirit glaring at her as if she's next. Soto's men sit Tammy down in her seat, preparing her to watch the end of her rescuers' lives.

"I just want to go home!" cries Tammy as the two men back away.

"This *is* your 'home,'" says Soto as he motions to the Master of Ceremonies.

Soto's men watch in awe as the Spirit walks around the center of the arena, waiting for the gong to sound. Zito and Jet huddle together, trying to figure out their strategy.

Tommy and Toby are wiping off the sweat from their hands, preparing for their match against the Spirit. Derek and Chuck pace back and forth nervously. They still can't believe the Spirit destroyed Hawk and Ape.

"No one has beaten the Spirit?" asks Chuck with potato chips flying out of his mouth.

"Not yet. But don't worry. We've made it this far! Now's not the time to get negative!" replies Toby as he focuses on the video screen.

"Toby, look at me. Tammy is like our sister. She needs us. Please tell me we can beat the 'Spirit'!" pleads Tommy as his friends close in for support.

"Look, I can't guarantee anything. All I know is that we have to fight better than before if we stand a chance. We've done great so far, so I don't see why we can't defeat him," says Toby convincingly.

Mindy grabs Patricia and pulls her to the side, between two video games.

"We have to pray!" insists Mindy, glancing around to make sure that no one's looking.

"Okay, but what do we 'pray' for?" asks Patricia as her heart races.

"We have to pray for the solution to defeat the Spirit. Everyone has a weakness. We need to pray for the Spirit's weakness," replies Mindy, folding her hands.

Mindy and Patricia bow their heads and begin to pray for Tommy and Toby. Patricia begins to cry, sensing hopelessness in her prayer. Mindy squeezes her eyes tightly as she asks God for the answer. Their prayer seems like an eternity.

"Hey, look, they're praying again!" says one little boy, pointing.

"Maybe we should do the same," suggests his friend.

"Do you know what to do?" asks the little boy.

"No, but just copy what they 'do,'" replies his friend.

The two little boys bow their heads and fold their hands like Mindy and Patricia. Patricia senses their presence and peeks, noticing their effort. Her mouth drops, overcome by emotion.

"Mindy!" whispers Patricia, keeping her eyes on the boys.

Mindy opens her eyes and sees Patricia pointing at the two

little boys. Mindy is overwhelmed with a sense of love and com-passion, watching the boys pray.

"That's it! I have the solution!" screams Mindy.

"What is 'it'?!" asks Patricia as she jumps, startled from Mindy's sudden outburst.

The boys raise their heads, startled as well.

"Zito and Jet must *humble* themselves in front of the Spirit! That's his weakness!" replies Mindy. "Come on, Patricia!"

The girls rush over to share their revelation with Tommy and Toby. Mindy stops and kisses the two little boys on their cheeks.

"Yuck!" mutters the first boy, wiping his cheek.

"Thank you," says his friend, smiling.

"Tommy! Toby! I've got it!" screams Mindy as she push-es her way through the crowd. "Please … let me through!"

"Mindy, what is it?!" asks Tommy, motioning for the kids to move out of her way.

Chuck and Derek grab Mindy's hand and bring her next to Tommy and Toby. Bucky breaks through the crowd, enlightened by the sense of hope that's written all over Mindy's face. Tommy real-izes that Patricia can't get through and motions for a large boy to help her.

"'What is it, Mindy'?" asks Toby, making sure that the match isn't starting.

"The Spirit's weakness is humility!" declares Mindy as she tries to catch her breath. "Don't fight him! Bow in front of him!"

"'Humility?!' What's that got to do with fighting?!" asks Chuck, frowning.

"I say you go for it! Fight the 'Spirit' with every weapon on the table!" says Derek, clenching his fists.

"Yeah, if you 'bow' before the 'Spirit' … he's going to destroy you!" says Bucky, gulping. "Then we'll never get Tammy back!"

Tommy and Toby scratch their chins and shake their heads. At this point, anything is worth trying. Especially since Toby has never beaten the Spirit. Watching the way that the Spirit destroyed Hawk and Ape has silenced their fighting spirits. Neither Tommy nor Toby wants to show the crowd signs of weakness and crush all hope.

"I think that we should try to fight the 'Spirit' first, and then submit if that doesn't work," suggests Toby as he glances at the video screen.

"Good idea! If we 'fight' cautiously, we can look for another weakness. If not, then we drop our weapons," says Tommy, turning toward Mindy.

"What if he crushes you first? Then we'll lose Tammy forever!" states Mindy worriedly. "I'm telling you … it's the only chance you've got!"

"If we circle the Spirit and let him fight us, then we stand a chance to find a weakness. Have faith, Mindy. We've gotten this far," says Toby as he puts his hand on Mindy's shoulder.

"Look, I prayed about this," states Mindy. "And the answer I got was to humble yourselves before the Spirit. God won't steer you wrong. Won't you at least consider it?"

"Look! The match is about to begin!" declares Chuck as popcorn flies out of his cup.

Toby and Tommy turn back to the video screen and grab hold of their joysticks. Each boy is ready to pound the kick, punch and block buttons. Their hearts pound rapidly, nervous about the game of their lives. The arcade becomes silent as the kids watch their two heroes getting ready to battle against the almighty Spirit. All eyes are focused on the screen as they watch the Master of Ceremonies holding the baton high in the air.

Soto lifts his glass in the direction of the Master of Ceremonies. The crowd silences as Soto's people wait for his command to strike the gong. The Spirit glares at Soto's section, waiting for his glass to drop. Fire begins to shoot out of the lava pools around the Spirit. The tension in the cavern is intense.

THE HUNT FOR TAMMY

Jet and Zito position themselves to rush the weapons table. Their strategy is to grab as many weapons as they can carry and be prepared for war. The fighters intend to launch an assault on the Spirit like never before. Their hearts pound like a tribal drum, knowing that this is the fight of their lives. Tammy's life is at stake and the gang is depending on them to defeat the Spirit.

"This is it, my friend. Fight with caution," says Zito as he glances at Soto.

"Focus on finding his weakness. Remember, wait for him to attack," suggests Jet as he rubs his hands with dirt.

They touch each other's hand as a sign of good luck and strength. Jet's intense eyes pierce through Zito.

"Let the match begin!" shouts Soto, dropping his glass.

Zito and Jet watch Soto's glass fall to his side in slow motion. "*Gooonnnggg!*" sounds throughout the cavern as the Master of Ceremonies strikes the gong. Zito and Jet take off running toward the weapons table. The crowd goes ballistic, chanting and cheering for their favorite fighters.

The Spirit stands still in the center of the cavern, waiting patiently for Zito and Jet. He has his arms folded over each other and his head bowed. The energy within the Spirit's body is moving rapidly, glowing like a fire. Beams of light and explosive sparks shoot from his body into the crowd and throughout the cavern. The spectators are practically blinded by the Spirit's laser light show.

Jet and Zito load up their weapons as they, too, are partially blinded from the Spirit. Their blood flows even faster as the vibration coming from the Spirit shocks their bodies. Waves of energy flow through the cavern.

"I'll grab the fighting club and numb-chucks and you grab the fighting ball and chain!" says Jet, making his final selections.

"What about the boomerang?!" asks Zito, double-checking to make sure that all his weapons are securely fastened to his belt.

"Grab it!" replies Jet as he lifts his fighting pole and club toward the Spirit.

"Better take a shield too!" shouts Zito, placing the boomerang in his belt.

The crowd rises to its feet with a thunderous roar, waiting for Zito and Jet to battle the Spirit. The two fighters head toward the center of the cavern to face their impending doom. Their faces resemble stone monuments as they focus on the Spirit. Zito is leading the way with a shield held in one hand and a fighting club in the other. Jet follows close behind, peeking around Zito with a fighting stick in his hand, ready to strike. In the background, Soto is glaring down at the fighting area as his bodyguards watch over Tammy. Soto's adrenaline rushes through his body as he anticipates the match to start. Several of his servants tend to his every need.

"Crush them, Spirit!" shouts a man from the crowd.

"End it!" screams another man.

"Come on, Jet! You can do it!" screams a man standing next to them.

The three men break-out into a fight over their favorite warriors. This fight then starts a giant brawl with the people next to them. The crowd around them backs away as arms swing wildly and bodies fly across several seats. Soto looks down on the crowd, disappointed. He hates to see his own people fighting. This incident will bring wrath and judgment upon all those involved. Many of them will probably end up working in one of his factories. He signals for his men to breakup the fight.

The Spirit rises from his meditation and sees Soto's men heading toward the brawl. He glances over and sees Jet and Zito cautiously approaching him, ready for war. Without looking, the Spirit breaks off a large piece of his body and tosses it at the brawl. Jet and Zito watch in awe as the ball of energy sails toward the unsuspecting fighters. The flaming missile lights up the cavern.

"Whoooooa!" mutters Jet as he waits for it to hit the crowd.

Soto's men see it coming and back away, rightfully so. The

illuminating ball of energy hits the fighting spectators and drops them to their knees, paralyzed. Shock waves travel throughout the stands, sending others to their knees as well. It's as if a small bomb went off. All eyes in the cavern turn back toward the Spirit.

"*Roooaaarrr!*" growls the Spirit, raising his arms high into the air.

Immediately, he pulls off another piece and throws it toward Jet and Zito.

"Incoming!" yells Jet as he grabs the back of Zito.

Jet ducks down behind Zito as he raises his shield, bracing for the ball of energy to hit them. Jet holds onto Zito, expecting to be destroyed. The crowd becomes still, waiting for the impact. Soto stands to his feet, anticipating Zito and Jet's demise. The ball's illumination intensifies as it approaches Zito's shield. With eyes closed tight and every muscle tensed up, Zito and Jet are hit. *BOOOOOM!!!!!* The impact sends Zito and Jet *flying* across the cavern in a sonic wave of light.

"Yeeeeaaaahhhh!" screams a man cheering for the Spirit.

"They've got to be dead!" says another man.

Each fighter tosses end over end, heading in different directions. Zito and Jet seem unconscious, flying through the air like rag dolls. Their weapons are tossed in every different direction as well.

Oh no! thinks Tammy, covering her mouth.

Her hope of rescue looks as if it's finished. She looks up at Soto and is repulsed by his evil smile. He motions for her to turn back around. Tammy and the screaming crowd watch as Zito and Jet tumble across the cavern floor. The Spirit seems to be motioning toward Tommy and Toby as he watches Zito and Jet. It's as if he's teasing the boys through the game.

Derek and Chuck squirm as they watch Zito and Jet come to a complete stop next to a lake of fire. Bucky and Mindy hold each other, eyes closed, waiting to hear the bad news. Patricia, Becky and Barbie lock arms as they wait for Tommy and Toby to react.

THE HUNT FOR TAMMY

"Get up! Come on, Jet! Toby, do something!" shouts a little boy.

Tommy and Toby stare at their energy bar at the top of the screen. The Spirit's strike has depleted ninety percent of their energy.

"We're not done!" declares Toby, celebrating. "We're still in the game!"

"Thank God!" states Tommy, wiping the sweat from his forehead. "Come on, Zito, get up!"

"Yeeeaaahhh!" scream Chuck and Derek as they jump up and down. "Hurry, Tommy, regroup!"

The two boys punch each other excitedly.

"Guys, quit it!" insists Tommy as he maneuvers Zito to get up.

Chuck and Derek settle down at Tommy's request. Toby maneuvers his joystick and raises Jet up off the cavern floor. The kids in the arcade go ballistic as they watch Jet staggering over to Zito on the video screen.

"No more fighting! You have to humble Zito and Jet before the Spirit," insists Mindy as she walks up to Tommy and Toby. "I told you ... it's your only chance."

"At this point, we don't have a choice. Our guys are so weak that his breath could knock them out," says Toby, nodding at Tommy.

Jeffrey, Derek and Chuck move forward to get a better look at the game.

Jet and Zito huddle together and brush off the dirt from their bodies. The crowd reacts with a thunderous roar as they watch the two fighters formulate a plan of action. The fight fans are amazed that Zito and Jet can still walk after what the Spirit did to them. Zito glances at the crowd and sees blurred images; he's still dazed and confused. The volts of electricity that went through his body could've lit up one of Soto's factories. Zito then looks into Jet's eyes.

"Are you okay?" asks Jet, holding out his hand.

"Yeah, and you?" asks Zito as he touches Jet's hand much slower than before.

"Spirit! Spirit! Spirit!" chants the crowd.

The Spirit surveys the crowd, making sure that there's no more trouble. He then focuses on Soto's section, seeking instruction from his superior. Soto signals for the Spirit to end the match. The Spirit nods at Soto then resumes his meditative position, facing Zito and Jet. His body expands in size. The energy field within his body lights up more intensely as well. From the looks of it, there's a buildup of force that could destroy the mountain. An intense *humming noise* silences the crowd.

"Let's walk to the Spirit and humble ourselves," says Jet, eyes glowing in the Spirit's light. "We don't have a choice ... we're at his mercy."

"Let's do it!" says Zito, throwing his boomerang to the floor.

Zito and Jet release all their weapons and walk side by side toward the Spirit. Their hearts pound with each step, knowing that they're defenseless. Thoughts of death race through their heads. Zito begins to second-guess their humble offering. The spectators shake their heads in disbelief as they watch Zito and Jet walk to the center of the cavern. The crowd reacts *harshly* to their cowardice.

"Are they crazy?!" asks one man as he throws up his hands. "They must fight until the end!"

"They must have a death wish!" replies his friend. "Pick up your weapons, you cowards!"

"How can they fight with no weapons?" asks a man, over-hearing the two men's conversation.

"They can't! The Spirit will most certainly destroy Zito and Jet!" replies the first man as he turns back to the row above. "I think...."

"Look! What are they doing?!" asks his friend.

The two men turn and see Zito and Jet bowed down before

the Spirit. Both fighters are prostrated, with their hands to their sides and their heads facing the ground. The Spirit senses their presence and lifts from his meditation. He slowly walks toward Zito and Jet. His *thunderous* footsteps can be heard throughout the cavern. Rocks from the cavern ceiling and walls begin to fall as the Spirit approaches the fighters.

"Finish them!" shouts a man from the crowd. "Fry them with your power!"

The Spirit turns his head toward the section of the stadium where the man had called out. His fiery eyes send chills through the entire crowd. The man's buddies immediately back away, acting as if they don't know him. The spectators are silenced, anticipating another piece of the Spirit to be hurled their way.

"*Be humble, be humble!*" whispers Zito, nervously.

"I'll do the talking," whispers Jet, trembling.

The Spirit glares down on the two fighters. Zito and Jet are overwhelmed with fear as the Spirit's breathing intensifies. Images of lightning and fire race through their minds.

"I can't take it anymore! The pressure's too much!" whispers Zito.

"Oh, great, Spirit … we humble ourselves before thee. Have pity on us. We have come in peace," says Jet as he holds out his hand with his eyes shut tightly.

The crowd becomes silent, waiting for the Spirit to destroy them. All eyes are on the Spirit as he ponders Jet's surrender. The delay bewilders everyone. Many people in the crowd look at Soto for an explanation. Soto's stone face confuses them. He waits patiently for the Spirit to end this nonsense.

"What are they doing?" whispers a man. "Are they insane?"

"It looks like they're giving up," replies his friend.

"They can't 'give up!' Nobody gives up!" whispers the man.

Soto raises his cup toward the Spirit, indicating it's time to finish Zito and Jet. His men raise their cups as well, toasting Soto for his royalty. The crowd braces for an explosion to rock the cavern. Tammy bows her head, anticipating the Spirit's final move.

"*Finish them!*" shouts Soto, lowering his cup.

The crowd lets out a tremendous *roar*, supporting Soto's command. The Spirit turns back to Jet and Zito and stares at their attempt to surrender. He focuses on Jet's hand shaking in front of him. Zito and Jet's humility overwhelms the Spirit with a sense of compassion that he's never felt before. No warrior or fighter has ever bowed before him. He's always had to bow before Soto and listen to his commands.

"*Roooaaarrrrrrrrrrrrrrr!*" groans the Spirit as he raises his head and hands toward the cavern ceiling.

The entire cavern shakes.

Jet and Zito tremble with fear, anticipating the Spirit sending them into the next millennium. The Spirit transfigures into a magnificent white ball of energy. His body expands and lights up with white, yellow, and blue lights. The lights dance around the cavern, blinding much of the crowd, including Soto and his men.

"You have proven to be good adversaries. No warrior has ever humbled himself as you. I know you've come for the girl. Let it be done as you wish," says the Spirit.

Zito and Jet slowly open their eyes through the blinding light. They're in total shock. Neither one wants to move too quickly. For years they've watched the Spirit destroy many warriors and fighters, some never returning to the ring.

"Great Spirit, what about Soto and his army?" asks Jet, covering his eyes.

"You take the girl to Chen. I will take care of 'Soto' and his men," replies the Spirit as his light fades out. "Hurry … 'Soto' will summon his 'army'."

Soto realizes that something has gone drastically wrong. He immediately slams down his cup, frustrated, and motions for Tret.

THE HUNT FOR TAMMY

Steam rises from Soto's large head; he feels betrayed.

"Bring me my troops, now!" demands Soto, reaching for Tammy.

Soto's men signal for his army. A man located at the top of the stadium blows an *ancient horn*. The sound of the horn echoes throughout the cavern, making everyone's skin crawl. The spectators look toward a tunnel at the opposite side of the fighting arena.

"Ouch! Take it easy!" yelps Tammy as Soto rushes her back to his Parlor.

The crowd waits patiently for the real battle to begin.

Chen is busy trimming a Bonsai tree under the watchful eye of Soto's men. He looks toward the sky and listens to the sound of the horn blasting out from the mountain. Chen sees several of Soto's men running toward the guard station. After a brief discussion, Tonga, the main guard, blows a whistle and flags his men to head into the cavern.

"Back to work!" demands a patrol.

Chen and his fellow workers resume their positions, careful not to upset the guards. Chen is suddenly overwhelmed by the Spirit. Riki, a guard, notices Chen going into a trance and grabs his fighting stick in case Chen rebels.

"Meet the girl in the tunnel," says the Spirit in Chen's head.

Chen snaps out of the trance and jumps to his feet. Riki positions his fighting stick to strike Chen. Chen lifts his leg, ready to snap-kick Riki. Two other guards notice the commotion and head Chen's way. They want to make sure that none of the prisoners escape.

"Yaaaaaaa!" screams Riki as he swings his fighting stick.

Chen blocks the stick and kicks Riki in the mid-section. The blow sends him flying into one of the Bonsai bushes. A little girl giggles to her mother as she watches Riki struggling to get out of the bush.

"Run!" screams Chen as he prepares for an attack.

The prisoners take off running for the woods. Chen circles around and crouches low to the ground, preparing to take on the other two guards. The garden breaks out into chaos as many of the prisoners take advantage of the lack of guards. Some prisoners stay behind and seek revenge on their captors.

The Spirit, Jet and Zito are huddled together in the center of the cavern, surrounded by Soto's army. Guards continue to pour into the cavern, prepared for an "all-out-war." The stands begin to empty; many spectators fear for their lives. They know that the battle will have many casualties. Several fans look back to catch one last glimpse of the Spirit, Jet and Zito.

"Hail, Soto!" declares a man, deciding to wait it out.

"Down with the Spirit! Destroy Jet! Kill Zito!" yells another man.

Soto's massive army holds its position around the three warriors. His guards are equipped with shields, helmets, swords, fighting sticks and many other weapons. The sea of green uniforms is overwhelming compared to the Spirit, Jet and Zito. Soto's army cautiously moves in for the kill.

"What's the plan?!" asks Jet, clutching Zito.

"I will handle them! You grab the girl!" replies the Spirit.

"*Attack!!!!!*" shouts the army leader.

"*Ahhhhhhhhhhhhhhhhh!*" scream the men in the army as they converge on the Spirit, Jet and Zito.

The spectators that have stayed behind prepare for the bloodshed.

Soto's army rushes forward with their weapons drawn; they approach from every different direction. The Spirit stretches himself over Jet and Zito like an igloo, creating a shield of protection against the army's attack. Soto's men attack the Spirit from the air and strike him with brutal ground force. Fighting clubs and sticks strike against the Spirit with enough force to dismember any warrior. Waves of arrows dissolve as they hit the Spirit's body. Nothing seems to penetrate his energy field. The army leader signals for the second wave of attack. Men charge the Spirit and begin to stab him with their swords.

"Ahhhhhh!" screams a fighter, thrown into the air by the Spirit.

"My arm! I can't feel my arm!" screams another fighter as he pulls out his paralyzed arm from the Spirit.

"Pull back!" shouts the army leader.

Soto's army retreats from the Spirit, realizing that they need a different strategy. He quickly regains his original form, gloating in his power. The army leader signals for his fire-starters to catapult their bombs from the outer parts of the fighting arena. Soto's army backs away even farther, making sure they're not caught in the upcoming firestorm.

"Get ready to get the girl!" says the Spirit as he surveys the crowd.

"'Ready' when you are!" shouts Jet over the rowdy crowd.

The Spirit pulls off a large piece of his back and hurls it toward Soto's section. The ball of energy *explodes* on impact and leaves his men paralyzed on the floor in agony.

"Go!" yells the Spirit, watching the army leader signal for the firestorm.

Soto's army launches giant fireballs from all sides of the cavern. The cavern lights up as a second wave of firebombs is launched.

"Ready ... now!" shouts a lieutenant as he drops his arm.

Balls of fire *sail* through the cavern, heading toward the center of the fighting arena. Jet and Zito cover their heads as they run through Soto's paralyzed men. The Spirit folds his arms and meditates as the blazing fire descends in his direction.

"Yeeeaaahhh!" shouts the army leader.

Soto's army crouches low to the ground and the men hold

their shields over their heads. Jet and Zito stop on the steps of the stadium and look back toward the Spirit. They watch in awe as the firestorm rains on the center of the fighting arena. A giant *explosion* lights up the cavern as several large fireballs make contact with the Spirit. Soto's men pull back even farther; the heat is too intense.

"*Spirit!*" screams Jet, edging back to help him.

"Come on! We must get the girl!" yells Zito, holding back Jet from running to the cavern floor.

Zito and Jet cover their eyes as another explosion rocks the cavern.

Tommy and Toby are still being mobbed for defeating the Spirit. Kids are rubbing their heads and slapping them five, treating them like celebrities. Chuck, once again, finds himself swarmed by Becky and Barbie. They're trying to offer him some weird candy to celebrate. Becky is even teasing him, reaching out her hand to touch him. Mindy and Patricia hug the two little boys that prayed with them.

"I said it was nothing!" states one of the boys, trying to pull away from Mindy. "It's okay, really! Hug him!"

"Thank you," says his friend as his face turns beet-red.

"What's next, Toby?" asks Tommy as he shakes a little boy's hand. "Thank you for the support!"

Chuck snatches the candy from Barbie and runs off like a squirrel going to eat his nut.

"After the Spirit comes the Emperor's Palace. The winners of the game have a chance to rescue the princess. I've never been to this level, so we'll have to wait and see," replies Toby, waving at his friends.

"'Princess?!' You mean to tell me that Tammy is a 'princess'?!" mumbles Chuck with a mouthful of cake. "I think I'm going to be sick!"

"How cool is that?" asks Mindy, shaking her head at Chuck.

THE HUNT FOR TAMMY

"Tammy's no 'princess!' She's too tough to be a 'princess'!" states Derek as he puts his arm around Chuck. "Give me some of that!"

Chuck pulls away from Derek, but is quickly thwarted by his admirers. Bucky laughs, envisioning Tammy in a princess outfit with her wrestling mask on. Tommy and Toby take their positions at the game and get ready to meet the Emperor. It's a good thing that they're oblivious to what's happening inside the game; it'd be too much for the kids to handle. Derek and his friends huddle next to Tommy and Toby as the game continues.

Meanwhile, Soto and his men are dragging Tammy through a dark tunnel. The musty smell of the tunnel turns Tammy's stomach as she heads toward Soto's Palace. Soto glances back every now and then making sure that no one's following them. Tammy, realizing that her chances of getting out of the game are fading, tries to break away from Soto's grip. Her fear that she'll never see her friends again gives her an adrenaline rush.

"Help! Somebody, help me!" screams Tammy as she stumbles and tries to maintain her footing. "Get off me!"

"Quiet! There's no one to 'help' you!" says Soto as he sees Jet and Zito appear out of the darkness. "Take care of them!" he says to his guards.

Soto's men stop and Tammy and Soto press forward. Jet and Zito slow down as they prepare to fight a dozen or so men holding fighting sticks, ready for war. The men position themselves around Jet and Zito, creating a moving wall.

"This is it, Zito! It's now or never!" states Jet, raising his hands. "Are you guys sure you want this to happen? Why don't you do the right thing and give us the girl."

"Use this!" says Zito as he hands Jet a fighting club. "Now you 'guys' are in big trouble!"

"Who are you to tell us what to do?! We are here to fight until the death!" exclaims a guard.

"Get them!" shouts another guard.

Soto's men attack Jet and Zito with everything they have. Jet and Zito position themselves against each other, fighting off Soto's men. The two fighters' arms and hands move like lightning as they defend themselves. The sounds of fighting sticks connecting with Jet's fighting club echo throughout the tunnel. One man has his fighting stick taken away by Zito.

"That's it! You guys are going down!" declares Zito as he begins to attack the men.

"Attack!" yells Jet, blocking several strikes with his fighting club.

Zito twirls his fighting stick, knocking several of Soto's men's weapons from their hands. Jet immediately takes advantage of the opportunity and knocks them out. The other men realize that they're next and drop their weapons.

"No more! We surrender!" shout the men as they bow before Jet and Zito.

"So that's what it felt like when we did that to the Spirit," says Zito, smiling.

Jet and Zito leave the men behind and head toward Soto's Palace

Soto, hearing Zito and Jet approaching, realizes that he's not going to make it to his Palace. Tammy's heart begins to pound; her hopes of a rescue have been restored. Soto stops running and looks toward a black hole in the wall of the tunnel.

"If I can't have you, neither will your friends!" says Soto as he catches his breath.

"What are you going to *do* with me?!" asks Tammy as she looks toward the dark hole.

"I will send you to the trolls and rumlins. No one will ever be able to find you then!" replies Soto, wrestling Tammy toward the hole.

"No! Please, somebody help!" screams Tammy as she tries to bite Soto. "Help! Ouch!"

THE HUNT FOR TAMMY

Soto drags Tammy to the opening in the wall. Fighting with Soto, she looks down the dark tunnel leading to the world of trolls and rumlins. Soto notices Jet and Zito getting closer and hurries to get Tammy into a position to throw her down the tunnel.

"No, please! I'll do anything!" pleads Tammy as Soto pushes her head toward the opening. "Someone, *help me!*"

"No wait! We have something in exchange for the girl!" shouts Jet, stopping short of Soto and Tammy.

"If I can't have her, neither shall you!" mutters Soto. "She will be banished to the underworld forever!"

Jet and Zito know exactly what Soto is talking about. They've heard many legends and myths about the underground world that exists under the mountain. Only one person has made it back alive from the land of trolls and rumlins, centuries ago. That person was placed under a curse and became a troll, over time.

"I don't need anything! You have nothing of value to me!" says Soto with Tammy pressed against the opening of the tunnel.

Tammy continues to fight Soto, to no avail.

"There must be something we can offer you for the girl!" says Zito with his hand extended as a peace offering.

"Please, let us serve you for her release!" pleads Jet, thinking about a way to snatch Tammy.

"You will never make it out of here alive!" declares Zito as he tries to use a threat to change Soto's mind.

"I have no life! The Spirit was my life," says Soto, saddened. "Now, I am ready to lose my life!"

Soto readies himself to face the wrath of Jet and Zito.

"No, stop!" pleads Tammy with her head leaning in the tunnel. "*Don't let go of me!*"

Jet and Zito back away from Soto.

"Ah!" yelps Soto as he gets kicked in the head.

Chen backs away, ready to strike Soto again. His stealth training, along with Jet and Zito's cooperation, allowed Chen to sneak up on Soto from the opposite side of the tunnel. The blow knocks Soto semi-unconscious.

"Help me! We're falling!" screams Tammy as Soto falls into tunnel, still holding onto her. *"Noooo!"*

Jet and Zito leap forward and grab Tammy's legs.

"Hold on, Tammy! Quick, Soto's weight is dragging her! Grab Zito's fighting club!" says Jet.

"Hurry, she's slipping!" states Zito.

Chen grabs Zito's fighting club and clobbers Soto over the head.

"Ahhhhhhhhhhhhhhhhhh!" screams Soto as he heads toward the world of the trolls and rumlins.

Tammy and her rescuers watch Soto disappearing into the darkness. Zito and Jet pull Tammy out of the tunnel. She quickly turns and hugs Chen.

"My child, are you okay?" asks Chen, hugging Tammy.

"Yes, I am, Chen! I can't believe I almost ended up down there! Am I glad to see you!" says Tammy with tears in her eyes. *"You saved my life!"*

"So, you're 'Chen,'" says Jet as he bows before Chen.

"Oh no! We must bow before the Spirit only," says Chen, smiling.

"The 'Spirit!' What happened to the 'Spirit'?!" asks Zito, turning around.

"He instructed me to meet you here. He's fighting Soto's army," replies Chen.

"Did you see him?" asks Jet, smiling at Tammy.

"No. He spoke to me in my mind," replies Chen.

"What do we do next?" asks Jet.

"I must take her back to the city," replies Chen.

"Not 'the city!' What about those *people* who tried to capture me?!" asks Tammy as she backs away from Chen. "We don't want to fight that gang alone! Let's take these guys!"

"Don't worry about Lee and his thugs. The Spirit said he would meet us there. Come, we must go at once," replies Chen.

"What if the 'Spirit' is dead?" asks Jet. "The fire in the cavern was so intense!"

"The Spirit will never die. You, two, are great fighters. He has instructed me to tell you that you are to oversee the new Palace," replies Chen, nodding his head goodbye.

"Thank you, Jet. Thank you, Zito. I want you to know that I have a wrestling mask, too," says Tammy, pulling out her wrestling mask.

Zito grabs hold of it and smiles. He starts unfastening his mask, wanting to give it to Tammy as a souvenir.

"*No!* I can't see your face!" states Tammy as she grabs hers back. "Back home that's a sign of weakness."

"Okay, I will remain faceless," says Zito, chuckling.

"Be careful. We need you in the 'new Palace,'" says Jet as he shakes Chen's hand.

"Don't worry. My people 'need' me too. I will return," says Chen, nodding his head.

Chen and Tammy rush down the tunnel to exit the mountain.

Lee and his band of hoodlums are hanging out, still recovering from their run in with Chen. Looking to take out their frustrations, they wait patiently for their next victim. Residents of the city rush to their cars as they exit stores, hoping not to be noticed by Lee or his thugs.

"Get off!" screams one woman as she fights with a boy over her purse. "I told you … let go!"

Lee's hoodlums laugh as they watch the woman win back her purse and run away. Lee notices a man and a woman carrying a brand new TV out of a store. He slides off the back of a car and waves for his gang to join him.

That would look great in my place! thinks Lee, as he heads their way.

THE HUNT FOR TAMMY

The couple notices Lee and several of his men following them.

"Hurry, dear!" says the man to his wife. "Don't look back!" he mutters as they quickly push their shopping cart toward their parked car.

"Get them!" shouts Lee, waving along his thugs.

He stops to make sure that no one else will get in their way.

"Ah! Please, leave us alone!" screams the woman as two thugs pull her away from her husband and go through her purse. "Please, somebody, help!"

Several bystanders take off running.

Chen and Tammy hear the woman's cries as they return to the city through the alley where Tammy was chased by Lee and his gang.

"Hurry, we must help!" says Chen, speeding forward.

Oh no, not another fight! thinks Tammy, as she follows Chen.

Chen and Tammy emerge from the alley.

"It's the old man! Get him!" screams a man as he lets go of the purse. "You will pay for our wounds!"

"*My name is Chen!*" he mutters, positioning himself to fight.

"You won't win this time, 'old man'!" says Lee as he nods his head to the side.

Ogden, a giant bodyguard, pushes his way through Lee's gang to take out Chen. Lee hired this massive warrior to protect him from such an occasion. The man is bigger than any warrior in Soto's arsenal. He cracks his knuckles, prepared to destroy Chen. Lee glares at Tammy, visualizing the price that Soto would pay for her. What he doesn't realize is that Soto is no longer around to pay him.

"Prepare to die, little man!" declares Ogden.

Chen is no match for Ogden. Tammy throws on her

THE HUNT FOR TAMMY

wrestling mask and takes cover from the upcoming beating. Ogden bends a crow bar as if it's a paper clip. Chen prepares himself for the first strike.

"Look, it's the Spirit!" shouts one of Lee's hoodlums as he points to the sky.

The entire group looks toward the sky and watches the Spirit descending upon them from the clouds. The sky lights up from the Spirit's illuminating body. His eyes of fire pierce all those who can see him. Different shades of light bounce off the buildings as the Spirit prepares to land on the city street.

"Run for your life!" shouts a man as he runs toward the dark alley.

Lee's men abandon him and run for cover as well. None of them want a repeat of their last encounter with the Spirit. Chen humbles himself to the ground and waits upon the Spirit. Tammy realizes that she'd better do the same thing if she expects to see her friends again. This is a first for Tammy. The Spirit glares at Ogden with his fiery eyes.

"You're on your own!" states Ogden as he runs away.

The husband and wife drop to their knees as they watch the Spirit getting closer to the ground. Lee is overpowered by the Spirit and falls into a trance. Several bystanders fall to the ground in fear of the Spirit.

"I'm sorry!" shouts Lee as he falls to his knees. "Have mercy on me!"

The Spirit lands in front of Chen and Tammy. The clouds dissolve and Lee passes out from fright. Tammy tries to peek, but quickly shuts her eyes. The Spirit's energy is overwhelming and paralyzes everyone that's present.

"Well done, Chen. You were obedient, and for this you will be rewarded," says the Spirit.

"Thank you, oh, great, Spirit," says Chen as he holds up his hand.

"Are you ready to go home, Tammy?" asks the Spirit.

Tammy raises her head timidly, realizing that she's going back to Gibeon.

"Yes, I am, Mr. 'Spirit,'" replies Tammy, feeling as though she's going to pass out.

The Spirit chuckles; no one's ever called him, "Mr. Spirit." Chen, Tammy, and the husband and wife rise as the Spirit raises his arms. The Spirit lights up the street, prepared to send Tammy back to her friends. He grabs a piece of his side and throws it to the street. *BOOM!!!* The giant explosion is blinding. Out of the smoke appears the mystery car from Street Speed III.

"This is so cool!" mumbles Tammy, watching the black car shine through the smoke.

"Wait until the kids hear about this," whispers the man to his wife.

Tammy and the others are startled, watching the driver's widow roll down slightly. Images of strange faces appear in Tammy's imagination.

"Do not be afraid! You are safe with me," says a voice from the mystery car.

"Go Tammy, and be with your friends. Your adventure is over," says the Spirit as the car door opens.

Tammy turns to Chen and becomes teary-eyed. Thoughts of what might've happened to her had she not met him race through her head. She walks over and gives him a giant hug.

"Thank you, Chen, for everything. I will never forget you," says Tammy, smiling toward the Spirit.

"You're welcome, my child. Now go, before I start to miss you," says Chen as he strokes her head.

Tammy walks up to the Spirit, trembling and full of fear. The Spirit senses her humble, thankful heart and lowers to one knee.

"Thank you, Spirit. Will I ever see you again?" asks Tammy, shaking.

"You're welcome, my daughter. We will meet again in the sky ... 'now go,'" replies the Spirit as he blows her in the direction of the mystery car.

Daughter?' thinks Tammy, as she gets into the car.

The car door shuts and the mystery car revs its engine. It spins its wheels and creates a giant cloud of smoke, sending him and Tammy back to Arnold's. Chen, the husband and the wife wave goodbye to Tammy and watch her disappear. Chen says his goodbye to the couple and heads back to Soto's village on the wings of the Spirit.

CHAPTER SEVEN

THE PARADE

Tommy and his friends are jumping for joy as they watch Tammy disappear on the video screen. Arnold's explodes with kids whistling and cheering, waiting for her arrival. The pressure is off, thinking Tammy is in good hands with Thunder. Little do the kids know that Thunder is on his next adventure without Tammy.

Tommy and Toby smile at one another as they are engulfed in a sea of kids. Hands of all types grope the two boys as the kids congratulate their heroes. Mindy and Patricia smile and shake their heads, knowing that it's the girls who are the real heroes. Chuck is stuffing his face with cookies given to him by Becky and Barbie. He has finally realized that they don't have cooties and it's safe for

THE PARADE

him to make contact with his two little admirers. The kids' cheering is interrupted by the roar of an engine.

"Look out, here comes Thunder!" shouts one boy as a cloud of smoke appears in front of the game.

"She's here, she's here!" yells Bucky as he raises his hands in victory. "All right, 'Thunder'!"

Tommy and the others rush to the outskirts of the smoke.

"Come on, 'Thunder'!" shouts Derek. "See, I told you he could do it!"

Jeffrey pats Chuck on the back as he chokes on a cookie.

The kids gawk, watching an image of a car appearing in the thick smoke. Tommy and the others break out in a thunderous roar, waiting for Tammy to appear. Derek and Tommy inch closer to see their friend as the smoke dissipates.

"It's not Thunder, it's the mystery car!" declares Derek as he pulls back.

"How's that possible?!" asks Tommy, shocked. "He was destroyed in the fire!"

"Mumbarknkgna!" mumbles Chuck with a mouthful of cookies.

"What? Chuck, quit talking with your mouth full!" says Tommy as he shakes his head. "Come on, spit it out!"

"Sorry! Maybe it's not Tammy in there. Maybe it's a warrior!" states Chuck as he hides behind Toby.

"What?!" cry out several kids as they jump back in fear.

"Everyone, stay back!" commands Toby, waving his hands. "Any sign of a 'warrior' and everybody run!"

Derek and Tommy move away from the smoke, waiting for the door to open.

Mindy and Patricia hold onto Bucky in case it's a warrior. They'd be better off fighting the warrior themselves than to have Bucky fight for them. All the kids in the arcade are ready to run in case Chuck is right.

THE PARADE

"I'm back, guys! Mindy! Tommy! Derek! Where are you?!" yells Tammy as she emerges from the driver's side door.

"*Yeeeaaa!*" scream the kids as they rush to welcome back their friend.

"Tammy, we missed you! Come here!" says Mindy, pushing her way up to her friend. "Thank God you're still alive! For awhile it didn't look like you were going to make it!"

"Are you okay?" asks Tommy as he gives Tammy a hug. "Guys, give her some room!"

"What was it like in there?" ask Derek as he fights off the other kids. "Did you see the Beast up close?!"

"I'm okay, I'm okay!" replies Tammy as she motions for everyone to back away.

"Guys, let her have 'some room'!" demands Toby as he waits to hear her story. "If you want to hear what happened, back off!"

The kids back away and stare at Tammy like she's a movie star. Several kids examine her, checking to see if she brought anything back from her trip. Tammy's emergence out of the video game has several boys bewildered. One minute she was real, the next minute she was digital, now she's real. Tammy gloats, taking in all of the attention and clears her throat.

"Everyone be quiet, she's about to speak!" shouts a girl.

"Well, it was *terrifying* when I first got 'there.' There was a gang that I had to fight off immediately! Luckily, my wrestling moves were too much for them to handle. They didn't stand a chance!" explains Tammy as she pulls out her wrestling mask.

"You fought off an entire 'gang'?!" asks one boy.

"How many people were there?!" asks a little girl as she breaks through the crowd.

"I don't know, maybe twenty or thirty. It happened so fast, I couldn't keep track," replies Tammy, lying through her teeth. "You don't have time to count when your hands are moving so quickly!" says Tammy as she puts on her mask and shows them her moves.

"'You fought off' that many people?!" asks Chuck as he attacks a sandwich. "Tell us more!"

"Yup! It was like I got supernatural strength when I arrived in the game. I think I became a warrior!" replies Tammy, puffing out her chest.

"Then what happened? What was the Spirit like?" asks Toby anxiously.

"What about Zito and Jet? What happened to them?!" asks Tommy as his heart begins to race.

"The 'Spirit' was the coolest! He kicked butt over everyone. As far as 'Zito' and 'Jet' ... I helped them defeat Emperor Soto!" replies Tammy as she notices Tina moving through the crowd.

"'Emperor Soto?' Tell us more about 'Emperor Soto'!" insists Derek, aware of Tina's presence as well.

"Let's just say Soto will never be the same," brags Tammy, suddenly touched by Tina's presence.

She makes eye contact with Tammy inconspicuously. Tina then places a spell on Tammy before she has a chance to cause anymore trouble. Tammy hears Jonathan's voice in her head telling her, *The fun is over. Finish your task. I have what I need.*" Tammy takes off her wrestling mask and shakes off the trance.

"Wait! What about the battle with 'Soto?' How did you make it back to the city?" asks Tommy, grabbing Tammy's arm.

"Guys, I'm tired. I'll tell you more after I eat something," replies Tammy as she walks away from the mystery car. "Come on, Chuck. Let's go battle some hamburgers!"

The mystery car's driver's side window rolls down slightly. Several kids scamper, thinking that something bad is about to happen. Derek cautiously walks up to the car.

"Derek, my friend, don't forget to bring the blue lightbulb to

THE PARADE

tonight's parade," says a voice from the mystery car. "You shall be rewarded in its due season."

"Who said that?!" asks Chuck, positioning himself to take someone down. "Derek, be careful!"

"It's the car, you dummy!" replies Derek.

"The 'blue lightbulb!' We forgot ...," states Tommy.

"Don't worry, I have it right here," says Derek as he shows it to the crowd.

The lightbulb seems to breathe in Derek's hand. A tornado of blue and green light illuminates from the blue lightbulb, making its way to the ceiling. Streaks of white light shoot out from Derek's hand and bounce off several kids' faces. The kids are mesmerized by the kaleidoscope of color and placed under a trance. Tommy and Derek shake off visions of the Spirit and groove to the music.

Matilda's song plays throughout the arcade as well, making the children drowsy. Some kids dance to the beat while others gaze into the light. Tommy and his friends are in a trance as they watch Matilda synchronize her gift with the blue lightbulb. Tina pulls Tammy aside while the others are distracted by Derek's electric orchestra of light.

"We're wasting time! Meet me at the deli with your friends. And don't forget the tarts," says Tina.

"'The tarts!' Where are 'the tarts'?!" asks Tammy, looking around the arcade frantically.

"They're over there in the corner. See? Get them before they're all gone!" mutters Tina, pushing Tammy forward.

"Chuck, get away from there!" shouts Tammy. "Don't even think about it!"

If there's one thing that could break Chuck's trance, it's food. He quickly closes the basket of tarts.

"What?!" asks Chuck as he shrugs his shoulders. "I should

steamroller the both of them!" mutters Chuck as he puts the basket back where he found it.

Tina and Tammy walk over to meet Chuck next to the Swamp Catchers game.

"I swear I didn't eat any!" declares Chuck, waiting to be smacked.

"That's okay, Chuck, they're for you and your friends," says Tina with an evil grin.

"They're for *me?!*" asks Chuck, licking his chops. "Can I have…?"

"No, Chuck! And they're for all of us!" replies Tammy, knowing that Chuck would eat the whole basket if they let him. "Hey, the music is stopping. I think we'd better go see what's going on," suggests Tammy as she winks at Tina.

Derek watches as the light disappears in his hand; the show has come to an end. Tommy and the others notice Tammy, Tina and Chuck walking their way. Something doesn't sit right with Tommy as he stares into Tina's eyes. Chuck waves at his friends with the basket in his hand. A person might think that Chuck had found a pot of gold by the smile on his face. Tina fidgets as she sees Mindy approaching.

"What is it, Chuck?" asks Mindy as she glances at Tina. "What's in the basket?"

"Yeah, Chuck, what did you find now?" asks Derek as he takes a whiff of the sweet smelling tarts.

"Tammy and Tina made some delicious strawberry tarts for us," replies Chuck as he winks at Tammy. "She said that Matilda told her to make them."

"That was nice, Tammy. Thank you, Tina," says Patricia as she gets a whiff of the delicious tarts.

"I'm starved! Can we have one now?" asks Derek as he reaches for the basket.

"Matilda also said that we have to meet her at the deli. We'll eat the tarts there," replies Tina, pushing Derek's hand away. "Good things come to those who wait."

"That's right! We still get to go to the parade, too. With all the excitement I forgot!" says Tommy as he puts his hand on his head. "Don't forget guys, we're the Grand Marshals for the parade." Derek clears his throat. "I'm sorry. And Derek is the Master of Ceremonies."

The gang takes a moment to visualize what the parade might be like. Tommy imagines himself starting the fireworks show and being surrounded by a large group of kids. Derek sees himself on one of the floats as a king, sitting on a throne and waving at his people. Chuck sees himself catching all the candy in his mouth that would be thrown from the floats. Patricia sees herself marching with a bunch of dolls and waving to the citizens of Gibeon.

"Guys, we have to go!" states Tina, waking them from their temporary fantasies. "We don't want to keep Jo … I mean Matilda waiting, do we? Matilda says that she has plans for you, plans so great that you may never want to leave Gibeon."

"'Never leave Gibeon?!' It would have to be something great for me to stay here. I really like this place, but …," says Chuck.

"Guys, we have to go! This conversation is over," says Tina as she heads toward the exit.

Tina motions for Derek and his friends to follow her to the deli.

"There's something not right with Tina," whispers Mindy. "I have a *weird* feeling."

"What do you mean by that? She made us tarts. I like her and so do the others," whispers Patricia, pulling Mindy along.

"Hey, Toby, want to join us at the deli?" asks Tommy, almost forgetting who helped him get his friend back to Gibeon. "Come on, it will be a blast!"

"I can't. I have to check in with my Mom and Dad. I'll

meet you guys before the parade starts," replies Toby as he waves goodbye to his new friends. "We'll save it for the parade!"

"Thank you for everything, my friend. I'm sure glad that I met you in my dream," says Derek as he shakes Toby's hand. "I feel like I've known you forever. If it was up to me, I'd stay here forever! *Gibeon rocks!*"

"I know what you mean, Derek. I feel like you're my brother. Sometimes you meet someone and connect with them right away. Those are the types of friendships that you want to hold on to. Now get going, you're going to be late. As far as the parade, you guys haven't seen anything yet!" says Toby with a smirk.

"'Anything yet'?!" asks Derek worriedly.

"What's that supposed to mean? I'm ready to go home now. This adventure has worn me out," says Bucky as he shakes his head. "If there's any more action, I'll die!"

"Don't worry, guys, it's all good! I'll catch-up with you at the Mayor's office," says Toby as he heads home.

"Don't mind him, he's just excited about what Mayor Messa has planned for you guys," says Tina as she motions for the gang to move along. "Now come on, we're going to be late. We're on a schedule."

"I definitely have to eat something before the parade," says Tommy, smelling the basket of tarts. "I have a great feeling about tonight!"

Chuck is trailing close behind Tammy like a puppy dog, hoping one of the tarts pops out of the basket. He pretends to grab the basket from Tammy and take off like a bandit.

"Chuck! Leave Tammy alone!" yells Derek, sneaking up on his buddy.

"Ah, it's the Spirit! Real funny, Derek!" mutters Chuck as he backs away from the basket. "You want a piece of this?!" asks Chuck as he flexes. "Ouch!" he yelps, thinking that he popped a blood vessel.

Tina makes her way to the front of Arnold's. She checks her

watch, knowing that they're pressed for time to see Jonathan. Frustrated, Tina waves the gang along to head out onto the street. Thoughts of disappointing Jonathan make her skin crawl. The children of Gibeon wave goodbye as Derek and his friends walk toward the exit. The kids have giant smiles on their faces as Toby's friends try to touch them before they leave the arcade. The gang embraces their celebrity status in Gibeon. Chuck, the last one to leave the arcade, blushes as he sees Becky and Barbie blow him a kiss. He immediately sprints out the door.

In the alley around the corner from Arnold's Arcade, between Donald's Deli and Big Horn Shoe Store, Bobbie, Harry, Jason and Freddie are having a meeting. While the gang was playing and watching movies, Bobbie was busy with Jonathan and Mable devising a plan for Harry and his counterparts. Bobbie peeks over toward the street as the boys discuss Jonathan's instructions. Each kid has an adrenaline rush strong enough to run through a building.

"Now, Jason, repeat your assignment from Jonathan," insists Bobbie sternly.

"I'm to keep my mouth shut," mutters Jason as he looks at the ground.

Harry and Freddie poke each other and laugh at their friend.

"*Quiet!* This is serious business! Harry, what about you?" demands Bobbie.

"I'm supposed to tell Derek and his friends about my Dad and Mayor Messa," replies Harry, standing at attention.

"And?" asks Bobbie as he wiggles his fingers.

"Oh yeah, I'm supposed to break out the strawberry tarts," replies Harry, sweating.

"Good! And you? What's your part?" asks Bobbie as he slowly marches up to Freddie.

"I have to tell them about the Rhodes Award given to me by Mayor Messa from last year's parade," replies Freddie nervously.

"Good! We're all squared away. Oh no! What are *they* doing here?! I guess we're not going to meet at the fire station. That means we go to Plan B, we eat the tarts here," says Bobbie as he sees Tina at the entrance of the alley. "All right, guys, show time!"

Tina notices Bobbie and the others in the alley and begins to panic. Thoughts of Jonathan's plan being ruined by this unexpected meeting run through her head. She quickly gathers her thoughts and her composure. Jonathan speaks to Tina in her mind, reminding her of Plan B.

"Oh, look, it's Bobbie," states Tina as she stops the gang.

Tommy turns and sees Bobbie and the others huddled together in the dark alley. Their mischievous spirits strike Tommy in the heart. Tommy immediately breaks away from the gang and runs toward the group of hoodlums. He's making sure that Bobbie doesn't slip away before he can interrogate him. Chuck, Bucky and Derek take off running as well. Mindy, Patricia, Tammy and Tina take their time walking down the alley.

"Hey wait! Bobbie, don't go anywhere!" yells Tommy. "I need to talk to you!"

"Slow down!" requests Chuck, falling behind.

"Remember, don't say anything. I'll handle this," says Bobbie, stepping forward. "I will signal to you guys when you are to speak…. Hey, Tommy, what's up?"

Tommy screeches to a halt in front of Bobbie and tries to catch his breath. Bucky and Derek stop behind their friend, waiting to see why they were rushing. They're confused at their friend's sudden interest in Bobbie. Chuck, however, can't come to a complete stop and crashes into Derek and Bucky.

"Ouch!" screams Derek as he nearly falls to the ground. "What's wrong with you?"

"Chuck, you idiot!" shouts Bucky as he stumbles into Jason. "Sorry, it was his fault."

"Why do you keep hiding from us?" asks Tommy, inspecting Bobbie and his crew. "One minute we see you, and then the next minute you're gone!"

"I'm not 'hiding' from anybody," replies Bobbie. "Tina, would you explain, please!"

"Yes, you do! The minute we arrived in Gibeon, you took off!" states Tommy as he notices the basket next to Harry's feet. "What's up with all the baskets?"

"Hi, Bobbie, what's the problem?" asks Tina as she walks in between Tommy and Bobbie.

"Hi, Tina. Please tell them that I'm not 'hiding' from anyone," replies Bobbie.

"Relax, Tommy. Bobbie's dad is very close with Mayor Messa. He runs errands for his dad and the Mayor all day," explains Tina convincingly. "Can you guys keep a secret?"

Tommy and his friends look at each other.

"Sure!" replies the gang, smiling.

"Bobbie is a *spy* for the Mayor," says Tina.

"What? A 'spy?!' No way!" declares Derek as he steps forward.

"Yes, it's true. That's why I act the way that I do. I watch the city for the Mayor … undercover," says Bobbie, prompted by Jonathan in his head.

"Oh man, we're going 'undercover'?!" asks Chuck.

"No, Chuck, you're not. This is my job. I'm sorry that I made you guys feel uncomfortable but, ever since Jonathan, Mayor Messa isn't taking any chances," explains Bobbie as he winks at Tina.

"Who are they?" asks Derek, sensing that something's not right.

"This is Freddie, Jason and Harry," replies Bobbie, pointing. "Take it easy, Derek."

Bobbie nods at his friends.

"Hi, everyone, welcome to Gibeon," say Freddie and Harry.

The boys look at Bobbie for approval.

THE PARADE

"Do you guys want to know what the Mayor has prepared for you tonight?" asks Bobbie, smiling. "Come on, think about it! Let your imaginations run wild."

The tone of Bobbie's voice shifts Derek and his friends' attention back to the parade. It's no longer important who Bobbie is or why he's been so elusive. Everyone now wants to know how their adventure will end. The mental images of the parade dance around Derek's friends' heads.

Mindy sees herself holding a giant hose and shooting bubbles over the jubilant crowd. Bucky sees himself tossing Chocolate Covered Ants to the screaming kids. Chuck smiles as he envisions himself alone on a float, masquerading as a pirate. Actually, the gang smiles as they envision Chuck as a float.

"You know what's going to happen 'tonight'?" asks Chuck as he wipes the chocolate from the side of his mouth.

"He 'knows' everything," replies Tina, grinning. "If your dad were best friends with Mayor Messa, don't you think you'd 'know' everything too?"

"Go ahead, Harry, tell them," insists Bobbie as he motions for Harry to step forward.

"My Dad is responsible for the fireworks show. He and Mayor Messa have been best friends since they were kids. I overheard my parents talking at lunch about tonight's show and it's going to be incredible," says Harry dramatically.

All eyes are now on Harry.

"Man, I can't wait! We haven't seen a good 'fireworks show' in years!" says Bucky.

"Tell us more!" demands Derek.

"Yeah! Can we get near the spot where they light the 'fireworks'?" asks Chuck.

"I don't want to ruin the surprise, but all I can tell you is that one of you will get to start the fireworks," replies Harry, smiling.

Derek and his friends' eyes light up.

THE PARADE

"What? Who is it?!" ask Chuck, Tommy and Derek as they push each other.

"What about the floats? Are there any animals in the parade?" asks Mindy.

Bobbie winks at Freddie.

"There are plenty of animals and the 'floats' are mechanical. I'm sure we have 'floats' that you haven't ever seen before," replies Freddie, joining the conversation.

"'Mechanical?' What do you mean by that?" asks Mindy, glancing at Tina as if she's mechanical.

"That's right, mechanical. They're operated by a remote control. My float won the Rhodes Award last year. We built a float that had a ride for the kids. Kids enjoyed swinging around the float as they cruised down Main Street," replies Freddie, smiling.

Bucky and Derek stare at Freddie and envision a ride that spins like a merry-go-round. Tommy visualizes himself on a moving swing and Chuck sees himself on an ice cream truck. Derek accidentally smacks Chuck on the side of the head as he swings Bucky around.

"Hey, watch it!" yelps Chuck, rubbing his head. "You'd better run!"

"What's wrong with him?" asks Patricia as she notices Jason's strange behavior.

"Don't mind him, he's shy," replies Bobbie.

Jason nods at the gang, confirming Bobbie's reply.

"Hey, you have a basket too!" states Chuck, pointing. "If I see another basket ... okay, I'll calm down!"

"That's right. Tina and your friend Tammy made some tarts for us as well," says Harry as he picks up the basket.

Now Harry is talking Chuck's language. He hands Chuck the basket, watching him salivating like a dog. Chuck grabs the basket and opens it, releasing the sweet smelling aroma of the strawberry tarts. Tommy bends down to get a better whiff as the smell dances around the kids' noses. Bucky and Derek jockey for position to get the first tart.

"Why don't we all have one now?" suggests Harry as he pulls out a tart.

Chuck's eyes pop out of his head. The strawberry tart in Harry's hand seems surreal. Its sugar-coated top glistens, almost blinding Tommy and his friends. Mindy has even lost her focus on Tina for a bite of a delicious tart.

"Good idea! Here, take 'one'!" says Chuck as he helps himself to Harry's basket. "'One' for you, 'one' for me ... 'one' for you and *two* for me!"

Harry moves out of the way as Chuck passes them out to his friends. Bobbie, Jason, Freddie and Harry watch the strawberry tarts get dispersed; their plan unfolds perfectly. Leave it up to Chuck to make the plan run smoothly.

"Let's celebrate the parade early!" says Tammy as she passes her basket to Bobbie. "Here, join us!"

Bobbie gives her the eye, pleased with Tammy's obedience.

"Here, guys, take one. We can't let our new friends celebrate alone," says Bobbie as he opens the basket.

The entire group of kids has a strawberry tart in his or her hand. Patricia and Mindy compare their tarts, seeing which one is bigger. Chuck glances over to make sure he's not getting gypped. Derek and Bucky chuckle as they watch Chuck move his head back and forth, examining everyone's tart.

"To the 'parade'!" exclaims Tina, lifting her strawberry tart.

"'To the parade'!" exclaim Tommy and his friends as they lift theirs for a toast.

All the kids bite into their strawberry tarts at the same time. The group is immediately put into a trance and find themselves in the middle of a giant, tornado-type spin. The tornado of light is more intense than Tammy's previous trips to Zevon Forest. Its colors change from orange to red to yellow to green in an instant. Debris is tossed around the alley as the group gets ready to journey to Zevon Forest. The kids clench their fists, scared, as they're lifted into the air.

Jonathan, Mable and Igor appear in the tornado, waving at Derek and his friends. The gang gets dizzy as they watch several wicked creatures from the swamp try to take a bite at them. One giant Gorl snaps its large mouth at Patricia. Derek and his friends scream as they watch what feels like a horror movie unfold before their eyes. Bobbie and his cronies' wicked laughs send chills throughout Tommy and Tammy's bodies.

Images of the gang's past appear in the tornado as well. Tammy and Derek see themselves hurting Jimmy and Frankie. Tommy, Bucky and Chuck see themselves stealing from their parents while Mindy and Patricia see their worst nightmares resurface.

As the tornado of light ends and the kids come out of their trances, Derek and the others find themselves standing before Jonathan and Mable in Zevon Forest. The wicked swamp that surrounds them is *alive*. Groaning and screeching cries ring throughout the dark forest as the outcasts of Gibeon prepare themselves for revenge on Mayor Messa. The kids see torches moving throughout the darkness of the forest. Derek and his friends are surprised that the presence of evil is somewhat inviting. Each one shakes off his or her trip to the wicked forest.

Jonathan is standing before a raging fire with the torn pages of the Tobit in his hand. He grinds his teeth as he senses his day of redemption at hand. Jonathan's wicked army preparing for battle is seen in the flames of the fire. Derek and his friends move closer to the fire and observe several kids harnessing giant, bear-like creatures while others load rocks into bags. The kids remain silent, waiting for Jonathan to speak as they watch him move around the fire.

Derek and his friends have been transformed back into their old, rotten selves; the same rotten selves that toilet-papered Old Man Jones' house and started the giant food fight at Franklin

Thomas School. As a matter of fact, Jonathan has given the gang an extra dose of wickedness. There's no way he's going to miss this opportunity to use pawns as great as these. The images in the fire disappear.

"Who are you?" asks Tommy as he walks in front of his friends.

"My name is Jonathan. I'm the ruler of Zevon Forest. Welcome, my friends," replies Jonathan with an evil smirk.

"'Zevon' who?" asks Derek as he glares into the dark forest.

"You're in Zevon Forest. This is my home, or should I say, soon to be ex-home," replies Jonathan, shaking Bobbie's hand. "Hello, my old friend, welcome to the party."

Tommy and his friends duck when a large raven flies over their heads. The darkness of the forest feeds into the darkness of their souls. Eating the forbidden fruit may have been the greatest *mistake* of their lives. The presence of evil is manifesting in Derek and his friends' bodies. Each kid watches their friends transfigure before their eyes.

"How do you two know each other?" asks Tommy as he stares at the papers in Jonathan's hand.

"Let's just say we're old friends. In case you're wondering what I have in my hand, this is my ticket back to Gibeon. These papers will also help us ruin Mayor Messa's parade and give *me* the power to rule Gibeon," replies Jonathan as he examines Tommy and his friends. "What you saw in the fire are our preparations to attack the city…."

"'Ruin the parade?!' We finally get to 'ruin a parade?' All right!" exclaims Derek excitedly.

"Forget the 'parade!' We get to 'attack the city!' Are we talking full combat?! If so, I'm ready!" declares Tammy as she pulls out her wrestling mask. "It sounds like you're planning a war."

"What kind of 'power' are you talking about?" asks Chuck as he finishes his tart.

THE PARADE

"The same power as Matilda and Mount Chrome have," replies Jonathan as he rolls up the papers in his hand. "With their powers I will be unstoppable. Mayor Messa will bow at my feet!"

Tommy and his friends see Jonathan's wicked expression and know that tonight isn't a joke. The thought of having the same power as Matilda is overwhelming to the gang. In the wrong hands it could mean anarchy and chaos beyond measure. It makes the kids' hair stand on end, feeling the presence of evil lurking. Mable and Bobbie watch Jonathan pacing around the group, unrolling the papers in his hand once again. Jonathan mumbles to himself as he contemplates what the page he's reading means. His murmuring and wicked laughter have Tommy and the others on edge.

"Did you know about all this?" asks Tommy.

"Yup! This is where I was while you guys were playing," replies Tammy as she twirls her wrestling mask in her hand. "This adventure will make what happened at Arnold's look like a walk in the park!"

"What was in those tarts?" asks Mindy, trying to shake the "cobwebs" out of her head.

"The forbidden strawberries were in the 'tarts.' Tammy and I prepared them for you so that we could help Jonathan seek revenge for what Mayor Messa did to him and Mable. We couldn't carry this out without your help," explains Tina as she moves next to Jonathan.

Derek and his friends stare at each other, confused yet curious. Thoughts of what the night might have in store for them dance around their heads. A fog begins to set in as tension flows through the bones of each and every kid present around the fire. The cool swamp mist penetrates the gang, firing up their wicked spirits.

"How are *we* going to 'help'?" asks Bucky, reaching for Jonathan's bag of magic. "Hey, this reminds me of Jamie's bag! What is…?"

"I don't think so! Igor, come here!" shouts Jonathan as he jumps in front of Bucky.

Bucky pulls back his hand, waiting for Jonathan to strike him. Tommy and Derek rush to Bucky's aid to defend their friend. Jonathan's spell has given them a spirit of boldness in the midst of the impending doom.

Chuck glances over toward the swamp and sees Igor appearing out of the darkness. His mouth drops in fear as he watches Igor limping his way. Mindy huddles next to Patricia as Igor's appearance becomes apparent to all by the light of the fire. Bucky and Derek gag as they realize that blood is oozing from Igor's bandages. Never has the gang witnessed the manifestation of such evil sorcery. Igor's spirit rushes through each kid, sending shock waves down their bodies.

"What is *that?!*" asks Tommy, stepping in front of his friends. "He looks like a monster! Why is he bleeding?"

"I think I'm going to be sick!" mutters Patricia, covering her mouth.

Chuck backs away as Igor walks up to the fire.

"Everyone, this is Igor. I'm sorry that I snapped at you, Bucky. This 'bag' can be very dangerous if used by the wrong person. Igor, show them what our plans are," says Jonathan as he steps away from the fire.

Igor grunts and pulls out a knife. Once again, he cuts off a piece of his flesh and throws it into the fire. Derek and his friends gag and seem to shrink as Igor *cries out* in pain. Tammy, Mindy and Patricia step away from the fire, ready to pass out. Igor's flesh wounds glisten in the light of the fire. A large, red cloud of smoke rises above the fire. Images begin to appear in the smoke as it changes different shades of red. The boys regain their composure and realize that this is the coolest thing they've ever seen. Tommy and Derek inch their way closer to the fire.

"This is what I need you to do when the parade starts," says Jonathan.

THE PARADE

"*Cool!* I can't believe we're in this cloud!" states Derek as he leans toward the fire. "It's like we're watching a movie!"

"*Silence!* Let me finish. You'll receive the remote to start the fireworks show and that will throw off the Mayor. These are your positions, and these are the places that we shall meet. That is Ephesus' Book Store. As you can see there will be *mass destruction* and *total chaos*. Derek, remember this spot. I'll need you to distract his men as I head to the Altar Room. In there, I'll receive the power to rule Gibeon," explains Jonathan as his face transfigures, almost like a demon.

The kids back away from the fire as the cloud of smoke disappears. Chills travel up their legs as the presence of evil overwhelms them. Tammy tries to look back into the fire for more details about the night. Bucky and Patricia shake their heads, trying to accept the fact that this isn't a dream.

Mable brings over a map of the city that she stole before her expulsion from Gibeon. Jonathan lays out the map on the floor next to the fire. Tommy and his friends gather around the map, waiting to hear Jonathan's plans. Chuck and Derek smile at one another as they visualize the destruction Jonathan will bring upon Gibeon.

"All right, guys, pay attention. This is Hank's Hamburgers …," says Jonathan, pointing to the map.

"Hey, we ate there today!" states Chuck as his stomach growls.

Tina and Bobbie shake their heads, disappointed.

"This isn't about eating! This is where I will meet you when the band moves onto Main Street. From here, we will carry out the diversion," says Jonathan, looking at Freddie, Jason and Harry.

"'Diversion?!' What's a 'diversion'?" asks Chuck anxiously.

Jonathan gets up and slowly walks over to Chuck, frustrated by his interruption.

"Could somebody give this kid some food to shut him up?!" asks Jonathan, staring into Chuck's eyes.

"I don't need 'food!' I'll be quiet!" says Chuck as he shrinks back.

"Good! Now the diversion ...," says Jonathan as he glances back at Chuck, "...is the plan for Freddie, Jason and Harry to distract Mayor Messa and his security force. They'll create trouble and draw attention to themselves. This will be your opportunity to help me make it to the Altar Room. Mayor Messa's men will be busy apprehending Freddie, Jason and Harry while you guys destroy the parade. When I give the signal, my army will charge out of Zevon Forest and deal Gibeon its worst nightmare!" declares Jonathan as he takes a deep breath. "Igor, return to the swamp and finish preparing my army."

The kids around Jonathan's camp clear a path as Igor retreats to the swamp.

"That's *awesome!* That's what happened to us back home. Mayor Duncan, the mayor of Hummel County, had a taskforce that tried to catch us ruining his parade. As his men apprehended us, Jimmy, Frankie and Tosha had free reign to destroy the parade. They did everything we would've done and got away with no problems," says Tommy, beginning to fall into Jonathan's evil ways.

"We need supplies! Rope, marbles, knives, horns, shaving cream, umm ...," says Derek frantically.

"Enough! I know what you guys are capable of doing!" says Jonathan.

"How do you 'know' what we can do? We just met you," says Derek as he walks next to Tommy.

Jonathan sprinkles some dust from his bag over the fire. The cloud of red smoke appears over the fire once again. Tammy nudges Mindy, shocked at what she sees. Tommy and the boys move closer as several images appear before their eyes.

"Hey, that was the Hummel County Parade two years ago! Look, there's Derek tying a rope to a float! And there's Tammy putting grease on the street!" declares Chuck, shocked.

THE PARADE

Tommy and Derek stare with mouths wide open.

"That's right. I've had my eyes on you kids for some time," says Jonathan, grinning. "I knew you kids would be perfect for this task. You want *Story Time* ... here is your Story Time!"

The kids are gripped with fear.

"Look, the float is crashing into the lamppost!" yells Bucky.

Jonathan waves his walking stick over the fire and the cloud disappears.

"See ... you guys have no idea who you're dealing with. Igor's sorcery is more powerful than you can comprehend. Don't make me use it on you ... now pay attention," says Jonathan with a sinister tone.

"What are 'marbles?' And who's 'shaving cream'?" asks Bobbie as he looks at Jonathan.

Derek and his friends chuckle at Bobbie's questions. Jonathan and Tina don't find it amusing that their friend has no idea what Derek is talking about. Tommy senses Jonathan's anger and motions for his friends to settle down.

"Sorry Jonathan! 'Marbles' is a game that we play and 'shaving cream' is what our Dads use to shave their faces," replies Tommy, trying to keep the peace.

"We have a game called tracks. We use these to play the game. Can this be used to ruin the parade?" asks Freddie as he pulls out a giant marble.

"Holy cow, it's a giant marble!" states Derek as he shoves Chuck.

The gang walks over to examine the baseball-sized marble in Freddie's hand. Derek smiles at Tommy as he visualizes the damage that could be done with one of these marbles. Chuck takes hold of it and moves it around his hand. After all, he's the strongest of the group and will be the only one to wreak havoc with Jonathan's tracks. Chuck pulls it close to his body as Derek tries to touch it. Patricia and Mindy are saddened that Freddie, Harry and Jason will be the ones to take the fall.

"What's going to happen to them?" asks Mindy, turning back to Jonathan.

"Freddie, Jason and Harry will be cast out of Gibeon. The parade is a sacred ceremony for the people of Gibeon. Mount Chrome descends upon the city to be with his people. Mayor Messa has zero tolerance for anyone who disrupts the parade," explains Jonathan as he walks behind Jason and Freddie.

"What about 'Mount Chrome?' Aren't you afraid of his power?" asks Derek as chills shoot through his spine.

"Yeah! There's something about that mountain! I could feel it when we were standing on the dam with Matilda. What will happen to us if we get caught?" asks Tommy, concerned.

"You will be sent to the forest too," replies Jonathan with both arms around his buddies.

"Don't worry about a thing. Jonathan has the secrets to the Tobit that will enable us to enter back into the city," says Tina, noticing the kids' anxiety building.

"That's right. I also have in my hand the scriptures that will give me the power to overthrow Mayor Messa and control all of Gibeon," says Jonathan as he lifts up the papers toward the sky. "Here … enough of the foolishness!"

Jonathan throws some dust from his bag over Derek and his friends. Tina and the others watch as the gang is overcome by a numbness that silences their tongues. Wickedness permeates their bodies as the dust disappears. Jonathan's spell causes Derek and his friends to focus their attention on the Tobit. He unrolls the torn sheets and signals for everyone to gather around the fire. The sounds of the forest cease as Jonathan prepares to read from the Tobit.

"This is the page that will allow us to enter into Gibeon," says Jonathan. "Enough of the talking. Get closer and meditate on the words on this page."

Freddie, Jason, Tina and Harry bow before Jonathan, knowing that he'll be the ruler of Gibeon soon. Chuck and Derek can't decide if they should bow as well. Jonathan clears his throat as the others peek over his shoulders. The page reads:

JOURNEY TO GIBEON

Catch a Tigris Fish.
Cut open the fish and take from it the following:
Heart, Liver, Tail and Gall.
Burn them immediately.
The smoke from the four will send you on your way.

Tommy and his friends step back, cringing from the idea of cutting open a fish and pulling out its heart, liver, tail and gall. Mindy and Patricia shake their heads in disgust. Tammy shakes off the thought of touching fish guts.

"Do we have to watch you cut the fish?" asks Mindy, bracing for the answer.

"No. We'll handle that," replies Jonathan, chuckling.

"What about me?" asks Bucky, beginning to feel queasy.

"You have to help too. You can help with the fire," replies Jonathan, grinning. "Igor will prepare several potions and brews before we leave Zevon Forest. All of them are necessary to fight whatever Mayor Messa and Mount Chrome have in store for us."

"It's okay Bucky, I'll be with you," says Tommy as he walks over to comfort his friend. "Think about the time that we fought those bullies over Mrs. Hamper's dog...."

"Cool, we get to see fish guts and stuff!" says Chuck as he rubs his hands.

"What's wrong with you? I bet you'd eat them if you could," says Derek, disgusted.

"*Eww,* that's gross!" declares Chuck as he shoves Derek.

"Enough! We're wasting time!" says Jonathan with beady

eyes. "Now pay attention, there's more! I need to find the page that will protect us from Matilda's powers."

Chuck and Derek straighten up and focus on Jonathan's hands. Jonathan continues to flip through the torn pages. His face lights up as he finds the page. He motions for everyone to get closer and remain silent. It reads:

SIGHT RETURNED

Save some of the Tigris Fish Gall.
Smear it on your eyes.
Sight will be restored.

"We could go blind?!" asks Tammy as she backs away from Jonathan.

"Matilda can use her light to 'blind' those who are disobedient or disruptive. She's never used it on anyone, but we know it exists," replies Tina.

"How do you 'know'?" asks Tommy as he motions for everyone to settle down.

"Before Mable and I were cast out of Gibeon, I used to be very close to Mayor Messa and Matilda. I used to visit them regularly in his office with his son, Richard. We were best friends. One day I overheard Mayor Messa's secretary talking on the phone to her neighbor about Matilda's power to thwart disobedient and disruptive people. And, that she'd use this power should Gibeon come under any kind of attack," explains Jonathan, walking around the gang.

"What do you mean, 'come under attack'?" asks Tommy. "This place is too much fun and too peaceful for it to have a war. We didn't meet any bad people when we were in the city," says Tommy, confused. "Who in the world would 'attack' a place like this?" he asks as he looks around the evil swamp. "Never mind!"

"Wherever there's good, there's evil lurking. We were cre-

THE PARADE

ated good and look at us now," says Jonathan as he points at his cronies. "It's been like that since the beginning of time."

A wicked breeze passes through the forest. Tommy can see the evil in Jonathan and his friends' eyes, glowing in the light of the fire. Derek and his friends are overwhelmed with Jonathan's power and the tainted tarts. Even though this adventure has taken the gang to a whole new level of wickedness, they can't help but waiver in their decision to participate. Jonathan senses that the gang needs another dose of his magic as he notices Bucky and Derek murmuring to one another.

"*Harat, Te, Kecha!*" chants Jonathan as he waves his walking stick.

A medieval gong rings throughout the forest. The deep sound of the gong startles several wicked birds and causes them to fly back to their homes. Tommy and his friends close their eyes as a *wave* of reddish-yellow light passes through Jonathan's camp, traveling out from the swamp. Another wicked breeze follows the wave, causing Derek, Tammy, Tommy and Chuck to open their eyes. Flashes of the kids' teachers scolding them churn within them a fire for revenge. Each kid watches a window of his or her life appear in midair.

"Look at Old Man Jones! I told you he was the one who ratted on us!" states Derek. "Come on, Mindy, look! There's Randy teasing you in front of his friends."

"Hey, there's Principal Barnes making us scrub the floors!" declares Chuck. "That's it! No more Mr. Nice Guy!"

"Well then, what are we waiting for? Let's do this thing!" says Tommy as the wave of light disappears.

Derek and the others get charged up from Tommy's attitude. Bucky and Derek high-five each other as Tammy throws on her wrestling mask. They all want to get revenge for the times they've gotten into trouble, and they're ready to get going. Chuck mistakenly bites into a piece of wood, thinking that it's food.

"Yuck!" screams Chuck, spitting.

"Here, take this!" insists Jonathan as he hands him another tart. "*Botak, Re!*"

"So what's next?" asks Derek as he shakes his head at Chuck.

Several evil kids from the dark forest wander into the light of Jonathan's camp.

"I need to find the scripture that tells me about Matilda's powers. I also need to find the scripture that takes her powers away," replies Jonathan as he continues thumbing through the torn pages. "Excellent work Bobbie! You brought me everything I needed. You shall be rewarded."

"What about us? How *do* we get home after you get what you want?" asks Mindy as she sets down a log.

The rest of the gang shifts their attention to Jonathan's face. With all the excitement and drama of the day, everyone has forgotten about going home. Between the great movie Mindy and Bucky watched and Derek and Tammy's adventures in Arnold's Arcade, who could think about home? Jonathan calmly looks up to address Mindy's question.

"Matilda will tell you how to get 'home.' You kids are great actors. I've seen it in the smoke. When you see her, you must act as if nothing happened to you. I'm sure she'll rush you back 'home' when she sees the danger at hand," replies Jonathan, lying through his teeth.

Mable and Tina smile at one another, knowing very well that Jonathan is using Derek and his friends as pawns. The *only* thing on Jonathan's mind is revenge and ruling Gibeon. He could care less about what happens to the gang, even if Derek and his friends perish.

Chuck and Derek peer over at the evil forest as an owl lets out a wicked screech. Tommy stares into the darkness and sees a set of beady eyes glaring back at him. The fog begins to thicken, a sign that Igor is strengthening the army.

THE PARADE

"What if Matilda finds out we've been with you? She'd never send us 'home.' We'd be stuck here with you!" says Bucky, moving closer to Tommy for protection. "I don't know…."

"*Silence!* I told you not to worry! Besides, once I have the power of Mount Chrome, nothing will be impossible. I'll make sure you get 'home' myself. I just need you to do your thing with the parade so that I can do my thing in the Mayor's office," says Jonathan as he locates the page. "Everyone come back to the fire and pay attention. This is the pinnacle of my quest for power!"

Jonathan signals for Tina to move closer to read the page with him. Tommy and his friends realize that this is the page that will end Mayor Messa's rule of Gibeon. An eerie sense of destruction passes through their heads as they watch Jonathan's face transfigure into a tyrant. The page reads:

THE ALTAR

Inside the Altar sits the Golden Chalice.
Within the Chalice is the Drink of Life.
Through it, there is power for eternity.
Anyone who drinks of the cup,
shall inherit the land.

The gang steps back from Jonathan as they watch him grow supernaturally. Jonathan almost turns into a monster before their eyes; his hair grows all over his body and his face elongates. Derek and Chuck huddle close to Mindy and Patricia, trying to keep them from vomiting as they watch Jonathan's skin changing colors. Tommy grabs onto Tammy and Bucky and shuffles them away from Jonathan. The gang is gripped with terror, not knowing if Jonathan will turn on them and cast them out into the swamp.

"How would *you* like to drink from the cup? You, too, could have supernatural powers and could be like Mount Chrome," says

Jonathan as the flames from the fire shoot up. "You could return home with this power. No longer will the bullies in your neighborhood have power over you. You'll be able to perform magic anytime, anywhere."

Derek and his friends snap out of their fears. The thought of drinking from the cup has given them a new meaning for their trip to Gibeon. Delusional thoughts of grandeur about having the same power as Mount Chrome race through their heads. They can't decide whether or not to use these powers in Gibeon or back home.

Derek and his friends envision themselves as rulers of Gibeon. Tommy sees himself dressed like a prince as the kids of Gibeon wait on him, hand and foot.

"Ah," sighs Tommy, smiling.

Jonathan walks over to the fire.

Derek visualizes himself riding down the street in Thunder as the kids of Gibeon salute their king. Even his friends are having to wave at him from the street.

That's what I'm talking about! thinks Derek, as he shakes his head.

Tina and Mable join Jonathan at the fire.

Tammy sees herself dressed like her favorite wrestler, standing before the city on the balcony of a castle. The crowd is chanting, "TAMMY! TAMMY! TAMMY!"

Cool! thinks Tammy, with a smile.

Chuck visualizes himself dressed like a medieval king and eating a giant turkey. Kids are bringing him all kinds of snacks and treats as he sits on his throne. His two admirers from Arnold's are fanning him while he eats.

Yum! That would be nice! thinks Chuck, licking his chops.

"Guys, snap out of it!" demands Jonathan. "That's enough with the dreams. Come here!"

Mable walks over with some of the things that Derek had

requested. She lays them in front of the fire for Jonathan to distribute. Tommy and his friends march over to Jonathan and examine Mable's pile of stuff. The gang doesn't recognize any of the items laid before them. They look at one another, dumbfounded, trying to figure out what Mable has brought them.

"What's that?" asks Chuck as he points to the left of the pile.

"That's a Mulder," replies Jonathan as he picks it up.

"A who?" asks Chuck.

"A Mulder!" replies Jonathan, moving it in front of the fire. "See how you can shine a light off it?"

"That's not a 'Mulder,' that's a mirror!" states Chuck as he shakes his head.

Tommy and the others back away from the pile.

"Ahh!" screams Chuck as he turns and sees Jonathan standing inches away from his face.

"If you can't keep your mouth shut, I'll shut it for you!" says Jonathan with glowing, red eyes.

"I can keep my 'mouth shut!' You don't need to 'shut' it for me! Ain't that right ...," says Chuck nervously.

"Silence!" demands Jonathan.

Chuck retreats behind Tommy and Derek.

"Don't bring your trouble around here!" whispers Derek, keeping his eyes on Jonathan.

"Yeah, Chuck, settle down. You're going to get us hurt," whispers Tommy.

"Tommy, take this Mulder and use it to blind the band. There's enough light on Main Street to blind the city. Derek you take the rope and Tammy you take the Slurge," says Jonathan as he passes out the items.

"What exactly is a 'Slurge'?" asks Tammy as she mulls over the heavy bag.

"Slurge is wet dirt. You'll throw it at the floats and that will cause them to short-circuit," replies Jonathan, looking over the remaining items.

Chuck timidly moves toward Jonathan to see what he has for him. Jonathan quickly glances up at Chuck, sending him two steps back from the fire.

"Here, take this!" grunts Jonathan as he lifts a heavy bag. "I saw the way you were handling it before. *No mercy!*"

"Wow! This is for me?!" asks Chuck as he takes the heavy bag. He immediately takes out one of the giant marbles and shows it to his friends. "Whoa! I could smash a giant window with this!"

"What about them?" asks Tammy, looking at Mindy and Patricia.

"You girls will be given tungals once you get into the city," replies Jonathan as he steps away from the fire.

"What's a 'tungal'?" ask Mindy and Patricia.

"It's a small device that washes buildings and large objects. The soap that comes out from the machine can be overwhelming," replies Jonathan with an evil grin.

"Cool!" says Tammy as she pictures the streets full of soap.

"Guys, we need to get going to the deli before Matilda beats us there," says Tina, looking at her watch. "We're not late, but we need to hurry."

"Mable, take Rupert and the others to Igor. Report to me on his progress and bring him this. He'll need my bag for the trolls and fruggers. Everyone else return to the fire. This scripture is most important in case there's a problem. This passage will strengthen you and deliver you in time of weakness," says Jonathan as he pulls out another torn page from the Tobit.

He signals for several wicked kids to join them at the fire.

"Good luck to you! I'll see you on the other side!" states Mable as she disappears into the darkness of the swamp. "*Hail Jonathan!*"

"Guys, this will help you to be strong in the presence of

Matilda or Mayor Messa. I'll use another dose of Igor's magic to build up your strength. But this is the true source of power," says Jonathan as he holds the page up to the light. The page reads:

THE SHEPHERD

Along the right path do you guide me,
for your namesake.
As I walk through the valley of death,
no fear of harm is what I feel,
as I know you're at my side.
Your staff and rod give me courage.

Derek and his friends are placed under a temporary trance as the words from the Tobit come alive in their bodies. The kids are filled with supernatural strength and confidence to walk in the presence of Matilda and Mayor Messa. Each kid nods at one another, signaling their readiness to head back into Gibeon.

Jonathan is using all means to *trick* these kids into getting what he wants. He thinks that by using Mount Chrome's words, he can manipulate Derek and his friends. A lack of knowledge on their part places them in the hands of the root of all evil. A strong gust of wind blows through the forest as Jonathan raises his hands toward the dark sky. Jonathan glances over and sees Igor standing at the edge of the swamp. He has a torch raised to the sky and a small dragon at his feet. The two connect in the spirit; the time has come.

"*Eeeeeeeeeeeeeeek!*" screeches Igor as he takes off into the darkness.

Igor's cry wakes Tommy and the others from their trance. Jonathan and Tina watch as the kids come back to life. His camp rejoices as they watch their fearless leader prepare for war. Tammy and Bucky stare at Jonathan as he sprinkles some of his dust over a small fire. Tommy and the others shake their heads as goose bumps cover their bodies.

"I've never felt like this before!" says Derek as he takes a deep breath. "I feel like I could take on five or six kids at once!"

"What did you do?" asks Chuck as he flexes. "My arms feel like they're growing! Hey, even Mindy and Patricia look tougher! Sorry!"

"I'm glad to see that Igor's sorcery is working. Now go and make me proud. Remember, vengeance is mine!" says Jonathan, raising his hand toward Tommy and his friends. "*Vadoo, Makem, Tobat!*"

Jonathan is caught up in a whirlwind of light and disappears. His camp is lit up with lightning that sends everyone to the ground. A strong gust of wind blows through the forest, bringing with it several evil spirits that dance around the fire. The *medieval gong* sounds and Jonathan's magic comes to an end. Tina and the others slowly rise up and brush off the dirt. Once again, Jonathan has left Derek and his friends a present they'll never forget.

As the wickedness of Zevon Forest is mounting, the streets of Gibeon are coming alive. Many residents have taken their kids out early to enjoy the festive mood. Mr. and Mrs. Dunkerst are grabbing last minute snacks for their kids from an assortment of vendors. No one wants to hear little Johnny or little Bertha complain that they didn't get a snack while they watch the other kids "going to town" on their candy. Unique dogs roam the streets looking for a child to play with or a ball to catch.

Samantha, a small girl with lots of freckles and strawberry hair, stops and listens to the music playing from the outdoor cafés. She watches intently as waiters and waitresses dance around the sidewalk and serve their guests. The citizens of Gibeon have no idea what's about to hit them. Several kids are standing in front of

THE PARADE

Viper's, swapping tales of what had happened at Arnold's Arcade earlier in the day.

"There was this kid who ate everything at the café. I think his name was Chunk," says one little girl.

"What about the girl who beat up everyone in the Troas game? I heard that she beat up the Mayor, too," says a little boy.

"That was nothing compared to Thunder!" adds another boy. "Derek said that he jumped over three buildings to reach the burning building!"

The three children continue gossiping.

Several people gaze at the floats that have made it to the street early. Tutter Jofin argues with his neighbor about who's got the best float. Several boys and girls walk up to the Casey's Animals float. Mr. Casey has outdone himself this year. The purple drapes around the bottom of the float shine from the streetlights. There's a water fountain in the middle of the float for his exotic birds to bathe. His birds cry out as the water shoots into the air every few seconds. Mr. Casey, somewhat plump with a perpetual smile of kindness, is standing next to the float, making sure there's plenty of food for his animals.

"Are you going to have a Lungar this year, Mr. Casey?" asks a little girl.

"Yes, dear, a real big one," replies Mr. Casey as he hands her a piece of candy.

"Thank you, Mr. Casey. We love your float," says the girl's father. "Personally, I think it's the best one out here."

"Well thank you, sir. Wait until it gets dark. My animals will look spectacular on the stage as they show off for the crowd," says Mr. Casey, smiling.

"Hey, Mom, look!" says the little girl, pointing across the street.

Mr. Casey and the girl's family turn and see some of the band members heading down the alley for a last minute rehearsal. Their silver uniforms shine as though they're wearing suits of armor. Timmy and Jerome pound on their electronic drum sets, giving the crowd a little taste of what tonight will sound like. The two boys can play a mean tune for kids their age. At thirteen and fifteen, they're good enough to be playing with the adults. A girl runs her fingers up and down the keyboard of a portable synthesizer. By the looks of this group, the band will be rocking Gibeon into the fourth dimension.

"Can I hit the drum?!" cries a little boy as he runs up to the band.

"Sure. Be careful," replies Jerome as he lowers himself down and hands the boy his drumstick. "Okay, little buddy, not too hard."

"BAM! BAM! BAM!" blasts the drum as the boy pounds it with the drumstick.

"That's enough, sweetheart, give Mommy the drumstick," says his mother as she takes it away. "Here. Sorry about that, he gets a little carried away."

"That's okay. I did the same thing when I was his age," says Jerome, smiling.

"Hey, guys, look. It's Bobbie, Freddie and Jason," says Timmy, pointing across the street. "What's wrong with them? Jason looks paranoid."

"I wonder where they're going," says one of the girls. "They look like they're trying to hide something."

"I heard Freddie's sister say that her brother is up to no good," says Jerome, twirling his drumstick.

"Forget him, what about that Bobbie?" asks another boy. "He gives me the creeps."

"What do you mean by that?" asks one girl.

"He's always sneaking around the city. No one really knows him except the Mayor and Matilda. He's got that 'horse look' to him. You know, the look someone has when they look at you sideways ... like this," replies the boy as he tilts his head.

THE PARADE

"Okay, kids, break it up! Time for rehearsal," says Mr. Jackson as he walks up the alley.

"Yes, Sir!" respond the band members as they get back into formation.

Mr. Jackson marches them toward the rehearsal. The kids glance back one last time at Bobbie and his crew as they disappear into the crowd. Timmy and Jerome sense that something's not right, but can't put their fingers on it. They turn back to follow them, but the sound of music echoing down the alley redirects their attention to the rehearsal. Mr. Jackson motions for everyone to hurry and catch-up with the others. The boys don't realize how close they were to foiling Jonathan's plans had they walked across the street.

Down at the end of the street stands Mayor Messa, his son Richard and Matilda. They're marveling at the surprise float for Derek and his friends. Richard and his friends have been customizing this float all day. Richard gloats with his friends at a job well done. Derek's float has more lights than any other float in the parade. It resembles the very thing that brought the gang to Gibeon.

"Great job, son! These kids will be impressed," says Mayor Messa as he walks around the float. "You even have a sleth!"

"Thanks, Dad. The girls can use the sleth in case it gets cold. If you think you're impressed now, watch this," says Richard as he grabs a remote control.

Richard smiles at Matilda as he pushes one of the buttons. Mayor Messa and Matilda break out in giant smiles as they watch part of the gang's float light up. The lights flash around the outer part of a giant screen that sits at the end of the float, almost like cars going around a race track. Mayor Messa chuckles as he sees THANKS DEREK blinking on the center of the screen. The bright blue sign for Derek stands out over the multicolored lightbulbs that surround the sign. Richard sees how impressed his father is and pushes another button on the remote. The sign now flashes the following:

TOMMY ... TAMMY ... CHUCK ... MINDY ... BUCKY ... PATRICIA

"You have each kid's name programmed into the remote?" asks Matilda, glowing with excitement.

"Yup! These kids are going to explode when they see this! They can even jump up and down on it if they want to. We made the top layer extra-soft," replies Richard. "Show them, Tito."

"Whoopee! ... Anyone ... want ... to ... try ... it?!" asks Tito as he bounces around the top of Derek's float.

Mayor Messa rubs Richard's head, congratulating his son.

"These kids will want to stay here forever," says Mayor Messa as he looks under the float. "I think the children of Gibeon would like that, even with the incident at Arnold's. They have brought much joy and laughter to my people."

"I wonder where 'they' are now," says Richard as he shuts down the float.

"'They' should be at the deli. Speaking of which, I'd better be going," states Matilda. "I'll see you two later."

Matilda flies off and disappears.

"Hello, everyone, *wow!*" says Toby as he walks up gawking at Richard's masterpiece. "That's the coolest float I've ever seen! I wish I had one of those in my room!"

"Hey, Toby. How was your day with Derek and his friends?" asks Mayor Messa, extending his hand out.

"Fine, Sir. Those kids are something else. We almost lost Tammy in the Troas game," replies Toby, shaking his head. "But don't worry, everything worked out just fine."

"You 'almost lost Tammy?' How?" asks Richard as he lays the remote control back on the table.

THE PARADE

"Tammy didn't hear Thunder's warning about the rules when she came into the arcade. She saw Thunder and jumped into him after Derek finished his adventure. Then Thunder took off into the hardest game in Arnold's," replies Toby.

"You're lucky to get her back. Jacob Mitz is still in there somewhere," says Richard, shaking his head. "Dad, how come you didn't tell me about that?"

"Well, son, to be honest, it slipped my mind. Oh, look at the time. It's getting late! I need to meet Bobbie in my office in ten minutes. I'll see you kids after my meeting," says Mayor Messa as he rushes off toward his office.

The mayor doesn't have a clue about Bobbie's visitation to Zevon Forest and his changed heart. Mayor Messa will practically hand over Gibeon to Jonathan and his thugs if something drastic doesn't happen. It's been too long since his last contact with Mount Chrome. The mayor knows that Mount Chrome won't impose his will and reveal his wisdom and knowledge unless sought. Too bad the mayor has been more concerned about the well-being of his guests and has forgotten about his own citizens.

In the alley next to Donald's Deli, Tommy and his friends are brushing themselves off from their return from Zevon Forest. Tina checks to make sure no one saw them return back to Gibeon. The gang is bewildered and terrified by Jonathan and Igor's magic. The kids examine one another, making sure there's nothing suspicious about them that would give away Jonathan's plans. Each kid is reflecting on the visions given to him or her by Jonathan in the tornado of light. Jonathan made sure to instill tremendous *fear* into Tommy and his friends, making them think twice about opening their big mouths.

"Guys, we have to hurry and get in," states Tina, looking at her watch. "I don't want Matilda to get suspicious."

"Why can't we meet at Hank's?" asks Chuck. "I like their...."

"We're not 'meeting' there because Jonathan saw Hank's full of the Mayor's security force. We're going with Plan C," replies Tina.

"Does everyone remember what Jonathan told you?" asks Tommy.

"Yes!" replies the gang.

"Good, lets go," says Tina as she walks toward Donald's. "Now remember, stay close."

Tommy and the others stop behind Tina as she makes it to the street. She carefully peeks around the corner to make sure that Matilda doesn't see them exiting the alley. The gang's blood starts pumping as the kids grab onto one another, waiting to be ambushed.

"All right, guys, follow me," says Tina as she waves her arm. "We'll blend in with the crowd."

"Everyone stay close … and no one get lost!" says Tommy as he leads his friends onto the crowded street.

Tina and the gang walk through the bustling street and stop in front of Donald's Deli. Tommy and Derek think that they hear voices of children talking about them. Paranoia is setting in for many of the kids as the reality of the evening begins to wear them down. Tina senses their uneasiness and checks the street, making sure that no one's spying on them. As Tina opens the front door, the kids jump back toward the street. They're blinded by vivid blue and white lights shooting off the front glass of the deli.

"It's the Spirit!!!!" shouts Chuck, freezing in his tracks. "We didn't do anything!"

"Ahhhh!" scream Derek and the others as they cover their eyes.

"Kids, it's only me!" says Matilda, laughing. "You can open your eyes now."

The group quickly turns around, hearing Matilda's voice.

"Hi, Matilda, you scared us!" says Tommy, motioning for his friends to stand at attention. "You reminded us of the 'Spirit'."

THE PARADE

"We were just coming to see you," says Tina with a mischievous smile.

"Did you kids have fun today?" asks Matilda, signaling for everyone to get closer.

"We saw the best movie, ever! The kids were crying at the end when Ben was reunited with his family," replies Mindy as she pushes a nervous Patricia along.

"Our day was better! We raced Derek in Street Speed III and watched Tommy and Toby play Troas to rescue Tammy!" replies Chuck as he notices a cake through the window.

"Yeah, I heard about your last adventure. Toby told me everything," says Matilda indulgently as she shakes her head at Tammy.

"I didn't know, I swear! I'm sorry if I caused you any trouble," says Tammy, faking her true feelings.

"You should've seen Toby and Chuck in the dueling cage. Chuck took out half the city," says Derek, laughing.

Chuck frowns at Derek and clenches his fist.

"Well, it sounds like you kids had a great time. I'm sure you'll have plenty to talk about when you get home. Speaking of which, Derek ... do you still have the lightbulb?" asks Matilda seriously.

All eyes focus on Derek's pocket.

"Relax!" says Derek as he pulls out the blue lightbulb from his pocket. "See, it's right here! *Bla!*"

Derek holds up the blue lightbulb toward Matilda. Matilda waves her hands in front of it, causing it to breathe in Derek's hand. Derek is overwhelmed with a tingling sensation from his head to his toes as the blue lightbulb illuminates the street and shoots into the deli. Matilda waves her mini-staff toward Derek's hand which starts a beautiful melody.

Several kids run to the front window of Donald's Deli to watch Derek's show. Blue and green lights reflect off their heads as they watch the kids dancing in the streets.

"Where did she find these kids?" whispers a little boy.

"I don't know, but they're weird," whispers his friend.

"Hail, Derek!" shouts a kid who was at Arnold's earlier.

Matilda sees her children falling into a trance and decides to stop the show. Another wave of her hand quickly makes the light disappear. Derek snobbishly shakes his head toward his friends and puts the blue lightbulb back into his pocket. The children of Gibeon resume their hunt for a good spot to watch the parade. Tommy monitors his friends' behaviors, making sure they're holding up strong. The gang is given a dose of Igor's wickedness as a vision of the swamp flashes before their eyes. Jonathan is fighting from Zevon Forest to gain control over the kids after Matilda's distraction.

"All right, kids, time to enter the deli. And Chuck … try not to scare the kids," says Matilda, smiling. "Come now, your friends are waiting."

"*What?*" asks Chuck as he shoves Bucky. "I think she was talking about you!"

The kids in Donald's Deli stop eating and applaud their special guests as Derek and his friends enter behind Matilda. A large group of kids surrounds Chuck, waiting to see what he orders. Derek and the others take their seats at a special table and smile at their adoring fans. The gang is overwhelmed with joy and love as several kids bring them gifts. The battle within is raging as thoughts of destroying their city and revealing Jonathan's plans plague Derek and his friends.

"How are we going to get home, Matilda?" asks Derek as he sits in his chair.

The deli becomes silent. Tommy and his friends notice that all eyes are on them. Derek motions to his friends to remain silent as he hears Igor's voice in his head telling him to be strong. Matilda senses that something's wrong with the gang as she notices several kids fidgeting in their chairs.

THE PARADE

"You'll find your way back 'home' in the parade," replies Matilda as her eyes peer over the table.

"But *how* will we know?" asks Derek, confused. "What if we miss our chance to go 'home'?"

Matilda lands on Derek's table. Tommy, Chuck, Derek, and Tammy remain still as Matilda tries to sniff out trouble. Bucky and Patricia force out a smile, trying to reassure Matilda that they're okay. Matilda flies in front of Mindy, only to be overwhelmed with a sense of déjà vu. Matilda has a flashback of her encounter with Mindy in her room. The music from the Gratchin plays in Matilda's head as she glares at the flickering light.

"This one!" says Matilda with piercing eyes.

Derek, Tammy and Tommy become paralyzed. The thought of Mindy revealing their plans is overwhelming. The kids glance at one another, dumbfounded as to what to do next.

"'This one,' what?" asks Derek with a crackling voice.

"It's her faith that will get you 'home,'" replies Matilda, smiling.

"Everyone, *look!*" screams a boy.

Derek and his friends glance over in the direction where the boy is pointing. They rush to the storefront window and see a raging fire in the middle of the street. The giant flame changes colors and has several images come to life in the fire. Matilda is disturbed as she watches the citizens of Gibeon rushing back into their homes and stores. A few brave boys walk cautiously around the fire, trying to figure out where the images are coming from. Derek and his friends feel the presence of evil through the window.

Matilda rushes out the front door and notices the crowd backing away from the center of the street. Derek and the others pour out of Donald's and gawk at the red cloud of smoke that appears from the fire.

"Who's that?! *Ewww!*" mutters a little boy as he covers his mouth.

"It's a monster! Look at his face, it's contorted!" states a boy, looking away.

"That's Igor," replies Matilda as she motions for everyone to stay away.

"Who's 'Igor'?" asks Tommy, playing dumb.

"Igor is a sorcerer. He lives in Zevon Forest with Jonathan," replies Matilda.

"Your time is coming, Matilda!" warns Igor in a wicked tone. "Jonathan will have his day! Ha, ha, ha, ha!"

"Yeah, Matilda! You *will* perish with the rest of Gibeon!" says a wicked troll from the cloud of smoke.

The crowd gawks as they watch several wicked trolls holding up their torches and celebrating around Igor.

"I have prepared an army to avenge Jonathan! You will never escape his wrath!" threatens Igor as the cloud of smoke disappears.

A wicked wind whips through the street and extinguishes the fire.

The people of Gibeon are gripped with fear as chills travel down their spines. Igor's words and visions have filled the citizens of Gibeon with a feeling of hopelessness. Kids hold onto each other as if Igor is going to appear in their city. The people of Gibeon knew this day was coming, but no one ever talked about it. Tina rejoices silently as she envisions the upcoming war. Derek and his friends feed into the fear of several children, knowing what Jonathan has planned for Gibeon.

Igor, Jonathan and Mable are huddled around a large fire, watching Matilda try to calm down her people from Igor's mystical appearance. As the smoke fades over the fire, one of Jonathan's servants brings him a large bag. In it, are the ingredients for Igor's magic potion that will allow everyone in Zevon Forest to enter into Gibeon. A group of wicked kids backs away as the stench turns their stomachs. Several disfigured kids from Igor's army watch closely as their master walks away from the fire.

"We have the heart, liver, tail and gall. What's next?" asks Jonathan as he quickly closes the bag.

"Bring me the page," replies Igor as he stirs a large kettle over a separate fire.

Jonathan hands him the torn page from the Tobit.

"The smoke from the four will send you on your way," mumbles Igor as he finishes reading the page. "As you go, I will finish creating our army. From my blood shall arise a *Trengasor,* the greatest of all creatures. I will ride the Trengasor into the city. With my blood, I will also create an army of Migota Dragons and Vultars. Your warriors shall ride these into battle. The rest is a surprise."

Mable shakes with fear as she holds onto Jonathan for protection. The kids surrounding the camp tremble from Igor's sorcery. His words and tone have silenced even Jonathan. Many of Jonathan's henchmen shake as they envision Igor's blood dripping onto the fire.

"Here you are, my friend," says Jonathan as he nervously hands Igor the bag.

Jonathan quickly pulls back as he notices a worm coming out of Igor's nose.

A gust of wind blows through the dark forest. Jonathan's camp is *overwhelmed* by the presence of evil; spirits from their past fly by in a wave of orange light. The wicked spirits do a war dance as a medieval gong rings throughout the swamp.

Matilda is reassuring some of the city leaders that everything's under control. If they feel the least bit threatened, the night will be cancelled. Many of them have flashbacks of Jonathan's battle with Mayor Messa's army. Several men and women murmur their opinions about the night. Matilda flies back over to Derek and his friends.

THE PARADE

"What did 'Igor' mean by, 'it's your time'?" asks Derek, winking at Tommy.

The members of the gang secretly look at one another.

Matilda realizes that the parade will be ruined and that anarchy will take place if she doesn't do something immediately. Matilda grows in size and lights up the street.

"Citizens of Gibeon, listen up! Igor has *no* power over Mount Chrome! Our Great Mountain shall destroy Jonathan and his cronies along with Igor and all their wickedness!" shouts Matilda.

The people of Gibeon humble themselves to the ground in the name of Mount Chrome. Several older kids shake their heads at the thought of a battle. The presence of their Great Mountain is felt as Matilda sprays a mist over her people. Tommy and his friends take a knee, knowing what's happening out in the swamp. Chuck and Derek wink at one another and hold back their laughter. The thought of getting caught arouses their mischievous spirits.

Matilda rises above the street and prepares herself for her people. She spins in the air and sings the Song of Gibeon. Her angelic ballad places the people under her power. Several kids stand up and raise their hands toward Matilda as she sings. They rejoice and are eased by Matilda's show. The street becomes a wave of moving arms that flow with the sound of the music. Matilda turns into a revolving strobe light as blue, yellow, purple and white lights dance off the buildings.

"I'm starting to change. My body is becoming numb," says Tammy.

"We *must* fight it!" whispers Tommy to Derek, locking hands.

"I don't know how much more of this I can take," mutters Chuck as his hands shake.

Derek and his friends lock hands, complying with Jonathan's command.

THE PARADE

"I feel weird!" whispers Bucky.

"I'm starting to feel dizzy," whispers Patricia, almost losing grip of Peggy.

"Everyone repeat *'THE SHEPHERD!'* That will fight off Matilda's trance!" says Tommy as he lowers himself to the ground. They all bow their heads and turn away from Matilda's light.

As I walk through the valley of death, no fear or harm is what I feel, as I know you're at my side, think Tommy, Bucky, Derek and Mindy, clenching each other's hand.

Your staff and rod give me courage, think Tammy, Chuck and Patricia.

Jonathan's presence is felt in their meditation. Matilda has no idea what's happening below as she wails out the end of the song. The streets of Gibeon are packed with people dancing and rejoicing for Mount Chrome. Slowly, Matilda's light show fades away and the children fall to the ground. Matilda ends the song and flies onto Derek's shoulder. The presence of Igor and his threats have been removed from the hearts of Matilda's people. Unfortunately, Derek and his friends are no longer her people.

"I must return to Mayor Messa's office to make final preparations for the parade. I expect to see you in front of Walley's Ice Cream in one hour. Don't be late!" says Matilda as she flies away.

"Yes, Matilda!" shouts the gang.

Tina glares at Derek and his friends.

"I'm glad she's gone. I don't know how much more I could've handled the pressure," states Chuck as he notices a boy eating ice cream. "Can I have some?"

"Me, too! It's as if she knows we've seen Jonathan and is playing games with us," says Tammy, pulling out her mask.

"Settle down. She has no clue what's going on. I felt your energy when you were meditating on the scripture," says Tina convincingly. "Don't underestimate Jonathan and Igor's power."

"When are we getting the rest of our stuff? And what about

our meeting with Bobbie?" asks Tommy as he hits the back of Chuck's head for eating the kid's entire ice cream.

"Ouch! What?!" yelps Chuck as he rubs his head.

"Be patient everyone. Bobbie is with the Mayor by now and doing his thing. Let's have something to eat. You guys are going to need the energy. Besides, this may be your last meal in Gibeon," says Tina with an evil grin.

"Last one in is a rotten egg!" screams Chuck as he races back into Donald's.

Derek and the others rush off to catch their friend.

Mable watches from a dark alley across the street and makes a mental note of all that just happened. Igor's spell-breaking potion with the Tigris Fish has worked and Zevon Forest is bleeding into Gibeon. She disappears into the darkness to report back to Jonathan.

Bobbie, Mayor Messa, and a few of his assistants are down at the mayor's office. The atmosphere is intense as Bobbie walks around the conference table with a handful of pictures and papers. Mayor Messa is shaking his head back and forth in disbelief.

"How could this happen?!" asks Mayor Messa, taking possession of one of the photographs. "This ranks up there with Jonathan's demise!"

"I *told* you about these kids a long time ago. Don't worry, we have them right where we want them," says Bobbie as he hands the mayor some more photos.

"So, this is who hit Tooth & Nail Hardware! How could Freddie and Jason do this to me? And Harry?!" asks Mayor Messa, disgusted. "Their parents will be devastated!"

Mayor Messa's mouth drops as he looks at a picture of Freddie carrying an ax.

"Your men are on them. They won't get away with this!" declares Bobbie, trying to comfort the mayor. "I told you that you could trust me."

"But he won the Rhodes Award last year! What's he planning to do with that ax?" asks Mayor Messa.

"'He's planning' to chop one of your trees down and let it crash onto one of the floats," replies Bobbie seriously.

"What's this?!" demands Mayor Messa, looking at another photo.

"It's Harry, organizing nails to blow out the tires of your floats," replies Bobbie as he laughs inside. "We must organize your security force and bring them to justice! This is the only threat that my team has uncovered."

Bobbie revels over how worked up Mayor Messa is getting from Jonathan's diversion.

"That's it! You must see my security force at once and tell them what you know! We need to catch them before it's too late!" says Mayor Messa as he slams the photos onto the table and rises to his feet. "Use all means necessary to end this plot!"

"Yes, Sir, right away!" says Bobbie as he gathers the scattered photos off the table.

"Oh, Bobbie … great job! I always knew I could 'trust' you," says Mayor Messa as he heads toward his office to meet with Matilda. "I will let Matilda know what's going on."

"Thank you, Sir, I won't let you down!" says Bobbie with an evil grin.

He watches as Mayor Messa leaves with the keys to the Altar Room. Bobbie's mind races as he devises a plan to steal them from the mayor. For now, Jonathan's diversion is working. He knows how Mayor Messa will focus all his energy on Harry and the others. Bobbie snaps out of his contemplation as the door to the conference room swings open.

"Mayor Messa sent us! He said that you have knowledge of a plot to ruin his parade!" states Officer Trent as he enters the room, followed by several security guards.

"Yes, I do. Give me a minute to gather my notes," says Bobbie as he shuffles through some papers.

Officers Garber, Holtz and Mackel take seats at the conference table. The others gather around and discuss what they'll need to beef up security and protect the city of Gibeon from any attack. Officers Trent and Holtz are muscleheads with matching crew cuts and dark sunglasses. They've been waiting for something like this to happen for a long time. The mayor's security force calls them, "Adrenaline junkies." Officer Mackel, a people pleaser, pulls out several maps and starts plotting their line of defense.

"Do you think we'll need to call Mayor Messa's army?" asks one guard.

"We are instructed to have them on standby," replies Officer Trent.

All right genius, think! What can I tell them that will help Jonathan make it to the Altar Room? thinks Bobbie, as he paces around the room.

"Do you have any idea where these kids are now?" asks Officer Trent anxiously. "Guys, contact Zone One and Three and put them on alert!"

"I don't know 'where' they're at now, but I have a very good idea 'where' they'll be when the parade starts," replies Bobbie as he walks to the window, looking at his notes. "Tell your men to wait by Sirach's Deli."

Bobbie looks down on the busy street and sees Jonathan dressed in a disguise, standing by a mailbox. He's wearing a hooded jacket that only lets his beady eyes peek through the darkness of the hood. Bobbie can feel Jonathan's spirit piercing through his soul as Jonathan glances up at the mayor's window. Making sure that no one will see him, Jonathan partially reveals his evil face, letting Bobbie know that he's waiting.

"Okay, our men will be at 'Sirach's.' Where else should I position my men?" asks Officer Trent as he stands up to approach Bobbie.

"Those locations will work for now," replies Bobbie, walk-

THE PARADE

ing away from the window. "I have to talk to Freddie's sister first. She always knows how to find him. I'm going there now to find out where Freddie's going to be when the parade starts. I'll meet you at Gelf's Golf in thirty minutes. Then we can make our final plans to end this wickedness."

"Are these the suspects?" asks a security guard as he grabs hold of the photos.

"Yes, they are," replies Bobbie. "It's despicable that these kids would betray the Mayor!"

"Okay, men, get a good look at these 'kids!' We must apprehend these suspects!" says Officer Trent as he passes the photos around.

Bobbie glances at his watch.

"Shouldn't we show these photos to the others? That way they can be on the lookout for these kids while they're on the streets," says one security guard as he examines a picture of Freddie.

"Good idea, Johnson! Bobbie, we'll see you at Gelf's!" says Officer Trent as he rushes the others out the door. "Bobbie, you know how to contact me. Let me know if anything changes!"

Bobbie nods his head and watches the mayor's men leave the office. He heads back to the window to look for Jonathan. Once again, he spots him through the crowd, hanging out by one of the lampposts. Jonathan's careful not to stay in one spot for too long. He sees his buddy in the window and waves subtlety. Bobbie points to Icona Ink and motions for Jonathan to meet him there in fifteen minutes. Jonathan nods his head and disappears into the crowd.

Matilda is sitting in Mayor Messa's office going over his meeting with Bobbie. She's shaking her head in disbelief about his report of what Bobbie has uncovered. Visions of the boys' sabotage flash through her head as she watches the mayor pacing around his office. Her thoughts about Derek and his friends have disappeared with this new threat.

THE PARADE

"These kids could do *serious* damage to our city! They must be stopped at once!" declares Mayor Messa, pounding his pencil onto his desk.

"Does security know about this?" asks Matilda, trying to make sense of Freddie, Jason and Harry's odd behaviors.

"I just sent them to the conference room to meet with ...," replies Mayor Messa as a knock sounds on the door. "Who is it?"

"It's Bobbie!" replies Bobbie from the hallway.

"Come in.... We were just talking about you. Come here, son," says Mayor Messa as he waves Bobbie over to his desk.

Bobbie is careful not to make eye contact with Matilda. Mayor Messa stands up to congratulate Bobbie for spoiling Freddie, Jason and Harry's plot to ruin his parade. The *game* of cat and mouse is on between Bobbie and Matilda. Matilda senses that something is different, but is thrown off by his great deed. She knows the magnitude of destruction that could've taken place had Bobbie not come forth with his discovery. Bobbie feels a clash within his soul from Matilda's presence.

"Great job, Bobbie," says Matilda as she watches Bobbie shake Mayor Messa's hand. "Is there anything else that we need to be aware of?" she asks as she tries to look into his eyes.

"Turning in these kids was nothing. Even though some of them are my friends, I had to do it. It's the least I can do for this great city. I would do *anything* for you and Mayor Messa," replies Bobbie, glancing over at Matilda. "There's nothing 'else' to worry about."

"'It was nothing?' This is bigger than you can imagine. You're a hero! This could earn you a key to the city! In fact, why don't you take my keys to Flo and have her make you a replica of the Altar Room key. This way you can get a head start for tonight's ceremony," says Mayor Messa as he hands Bobbie his giant set of keys.

Bobbie watches as if the keys are coming to him in slow motion.

THE PARADE

"Yes, Sir, right away!" says Bobbie, staring at the keys in his hand.

He's shocked at how easy it was to obtain the key.

"Matilda, please check on the band while I check on the progress of my security force," says Mayor Messa as he picks up some papers from his desk.

Bobbie notices the Tobit on the corner of the mayor's desk. His stomach drops, waiting for the mayor to pick it up.

Please don't find the missing pages! thinks Bobbie.

"Yes, Mayor Messa, right away," says Matilda as she flies out of the room.

"And Bobbie, you'd better get going, too," says Mayor Messa.

Matilda glances back at Bobbie before she exits the room.

I'd better visit Mount Chrome. **Something's not right,** thinks Matilda, as she waves goodbye to Bobbie.

"Bye, Matilda! Give my best to Charlie!" mutters Bobbie, watching Matilda disappear. *Good. That will keep her busy,* thinks Bobbie, as he heads toward another door.

The stage is set for a war to end all wars. Matilda is off to see Mount Chrome as Bobbie hurries to see Jonathan with the key to the Altar Room. Mount Chrome, the source of *all* power and goodness in Gibeon, has been watching this epic story unfold. Igor's army is rising up from the depths of the swamp and his wicked sorcery is something not many will be able to withstand. Things are happening in Zevon Forest that only the dead could handle. Mount Chrome has been preparing his own army for the ages to come. Derek and his friends have no idea what they agreed to when they decided to come to Gibeon.

The Gibeon band is tuning up their instruments, preparing for the big goodbye celebration for Derek and his friends. It's not your typical method of tuning since the band is electronic.

THE PARADE

Drummers walk around with their paper-thin drum boards, striking the surfaces with a drumstick in one hand, and adjusting the bass levels with their other hand. Several band members nod their heads to the beat as the band jams a warmup tune. Girls tease each other about the boys, trying to decide who's the cutest. The boys, of course, take advantage of the attention and show off.

Trumpet players hold a long, flute-looking device that lights up when it's held above a player's chest. There are different colored keys on the top that play different notes. Several players line up and wait for their cue. One boy plays a soothing melody to impress the girls. His friends nudge each other as they notice the girls melting to his melody.

"Right there!" says a girl, smiling. "The music is perfect!"

"?#@?*&??%#@!!*&%?#?*@?!???*&%$@#+?!" blasts out of Hector's tuba.

"*Hector!*" scream several band members, putting their hands over their ears and making disgusted faces.

"I've heard better sounds come from my dog!" says Jackie jokingly.

"Sorry, I'll fix it!" mutters Hector as he fumbles with his instrument.

"Check out my new cymbal," insists a boy.

"Cool! Do you know how to use that?" asks his friend as he examines the plate-looking device.

"*Clinggggggggg!*" rings out from the cymbal as the boy strikes the other side.

"Ahhhh! I'm deaf!" yells his friend as he holds his ears to stop the ringing.

Hector notices that the boy is laughing at his friend. Like a cat on the prowl, he sneaks up behind "Mr. Cymbal" and hits a note on his tuba.

"?#@?*&??%@!!&%?#?*@?!???*&%$@#+?!" blasts out of Hector's tuba.

THE PARADE

"Ahhhhhhh!" screams the boy as he leaps into the air, grabbing his ears.

"All right, kids, settle down! Mayor Messa will go crazy if he sees the way you're acting! Is this any way to show our special guests how we behave in Gibeon?" asks Mr. Jackson. "Now line up so that we can begin our rehearsal," instructs Mr. Jackson as he fixes his hat.

"Yes, Sir!" bark several band members.

The kids make fun of Mr. Jackson's long, bushy mustache and large feet. He almost looks like a clown. Mr. Jackson steps on a ladder so that the entire band will be able to hear him speak. The band members pick up their instruments and head toward their leader. The joking ceases as Mr. Jackson raises his hands.

"You guys need to be ready before Matilda gets here. We can't let her or her guests down with a sloppy performance. No one wants to be responsible for messing up this celebration, do they Mr. Korah?" asks Mr. Jackson as he bends down to face Joseph Korah.

"No, Sir!" replies Joseph, standing at attention.

"That goes for you too, Mr. Toms!" exclaims Mr. Jackson, noticing David Toms giggling with his friends.

"Sorry, Sir!" says David as he wipes the smirk off his face, standing at attention.

"Good! Now take your positions and let's hear what you've got!" says Mr. Jackson as he blows his whistle.

He grabs his silver conductor's stick and holds it in the air. The band members scurry to grab their instruments and file into position. The kids look like a sea of silver as they line up, ready to crank out a tune. Each member stares ahead, appearing like a statue, waiting for their leader to drop his stick. The pressure heightens as Matilda appears behind Mr. Jackson. She decided to make a quick stop before visiting Mount Chrome.

Oh no, don't screw up! thinks a drummer, as he begins to sweat.

THE PARADE

Jelly bean, jelly bean! thinks a heavy-set, tuba player, trying not to crack under the pressure of Matilda's watchful eyes.

"A one and a two and a ...," says Mr. Jackson as he swings his conductor's stick back and forth.

The band breaks out into a symphonic-type melody. Several bystanders move to the beat, indicating their approval of the music. The area behind Arnold's Arcade lights up from the band's instruments as the sun begins to set. Matilda begins to groove as the smooth melody lifts into the sky. Strange birds fly onto the rooftops of the adjoining buildings to listen to the band play "Song of Nature."

"Great tune! Derek and his friends will be pleased," whispers Matilda into Mr. Jackson's ear.

"Oh yeah, watch this," says Mr. Jackson, leaning forward and whipping his hand across his body.

Mr. Jackson holds both hands in the air, signaling for the band to stop. His band members swallow hard in the dead silence, anticipating which song he'll select. Jerome and Timmy smile at one another as goose bumps run down their arms. Mr. Jackson pushes a button on the conductor's stick which lights up the top. A deep orange light shining from his conductor's stick illuminates the entire alley.

"A ONE AND A TWO AND A...!" shouts Mr. Jackson as he swings the lit conductor's stick back and forth.

The band breaks out into a *funky beat,* something like what might be heard at a college football game. The sound of the drums and tubas overshadows the rest of the instruments. A few parents dance to the beat; the music reminding them of their school days. The entire band dances in place with their instruments as if they're at a dance club. Matilda smiles, watching the area behind Arnold's come to life. People even dance in their windows, high above the street. Little Jessica and Tony jump up and down as their parents try to groove to the beat as well.

"Now we're talking!" states Ronald as he swings his trombone back and forth.

The band shuffles around in formation to create a giant star.

"That's awesome!" declares Matilda as her eyes grow, impressed with what Mr. Jackson has put together for Derek and his friends. "This is most impressive, Mr. Jackson! The Mayor will be pleased."

Matilda looks into the distance and sees that Mount Chrome is active. The change of colors in the heavy cloud indicates that her presence is requested. She waves to the band and heads toward her master. Thoughts race through her head of what Mount Chrome knows and why he's calling her. Matilda is about to get news that will extinguish her gleaming light.

The streets of Gibeon are now packed with its residents searching for a better spot to watch the electric parade. Children are fidgeting behind the ropes as they wait for their favorite floats to enter the streets. People are bobbing their heads to the beat of the band, unsuspecting of the impending war. It's written in the Tobit that no one but Mount Chrome would know the time, day and moment of his return to Gibeon.

Main Street looks like the Las Vegas Strip, with its colored lights that blink on and off throughout the city. Children have all kinds of glow sticks and funky flashlights, playing with one another on the sidewalks. The futuristic city of Gibeon is transformed by the setting sun.

"Look at little Timmy," says a mother, smiling while her son dances.

Several members of Mayor Messa's security force start to motion for people to get off the streets.

"Look at the moon, Mommy," says one little girl, pointing at the sky.

Several families glance up toward the sky. It's been a long

THE PARADE

time since the citizens of Gibeon have seen a full moon. The crowd gawks as they watch the discolored moon changing colors. An occasional white cloud passes by the orange moon, creating a shadow over the city. There's even an eerie haze around it that changes everyone's mood.

Usually, a full moon means that the vibe of Gibeon will be festive and friendly, but not so on this particular night. It's as if Jonathan and Igor's sorcery is *seeping* into the city through the night air. The people can't explain the sudden feeling of uneasiness that falls upon them as they look up into the sky. In spite of the impending doom and mood swings, the atmosphere in Gibeon is rocking.

"All right, people, clear the streets! The parade's about to begin!" shouts one security guard as he canvasses the crowd for Freddie, Jason and Harry.

"Craig, I need you right away!" yells another security guard from across the street.

Craig rushes over to his counterpart.

"They've spotted Freddie and Harry walking toward Fannie's Fishery," says the security guard as he places his two-way radio back into its holster.

"Where's the third?" asks Craig, watching a kid dash across the street.

"They're trying to locate him now," replies the security guard.

"Good. There's no way we're going to let anything happen to the Mayor's parade! Not as long as we're on duty!" states Craig as he puffs out his chest.

"That's right! This town is safe with us out here!" says the security guard, slapping his partner's hand in a high-five.

The security guard's two-way radio beeps.

"Come quick! We've located the third suspect! He's around the corner from you guys!" says a voice coming out of the two-way radio.

THE PARADE

"All right, Craig, got to go! You stay here! Derek and his friends should be here any minute," says the security guard as he takes off down the street to go after Jason.

"Go get 'em, Stan!" shouts Craig as he takes his position back on the street.

The two guards have no idea what's brewing out in Zevon Forest. All they know is that some kids are trying to ruin their parade. The entire army of Gibeon will be crying for the mountains to fall on them when Jonathan *unleashes* his fury through Igor.

Mount Chrome is lit up magnificently from the full moon. The orange light from the moon overshadows the mountainside, creating ideal feeding conditions for the animals. Strange animals resembling large anteaters graze on the mountain foliage, just under the clouds. The heavy white cloud creates a perfect border for the animals to travel around the mountain. Several birds fly up to the mountain, landing on unique looking trees. A soft grumbling echoes down the mountainside, as if Mount Chrome is speaking to his animals.

The animals scatter from Matilda's light as she heads up the mountain and lands on her sacred stone. Matilda humbles herself before Mount Chrome, sensing that this could be the conversation that she has dreaded her entire life. Lightning shoots through the heavy cloud as Mount Chrome acknowledges Matilda's presence. The cloud descends upon her.

"Yes, Mount Chrome, how may I serve thee?" asks Matilda, trembling.

"My good and faithful, Matilda, the time has come. I know that you have sensed the presence of evil in Bobbie and your guests. There's an army birthing at the hands of Igor and his sorcery. He's organizing his beasts and warriors to overthrow Gibeon. Jonathan had Bobbie steal pages from the Tobit under the Mayor's nose. He's using *my* words to trick many," explains Mount Chrome.

THE PARADE

"But how is this so, your Excellence?" asks Matilda, lowering her head.

"Jonathan is the father of all lies. His heart is most deceitful and desperately wicked. Who really knows how bad the heart is? From it flow evil thoughts, deception and murder. But take courage, my daughter. Wars must happen, but I have *final* authority over all. He has no power over me," replies Mount Chrome.

A gust of wind blows down the mountain as the sound of thunder grips Matilda with fear.

"What shall I do?" asks Matilda as she lifts up from the stone.

"You shall bring to me the Roga Stones. From them I shall raise up an army to defeat Igor and all his wickedness. Jonathan wants war, then war I shall give him! Go and bring me the Mayor's army. And don't forget the stones," replies Mount Chrome as the heavy cloud ascends.

"Yes, Master. As you command," says Matilda humbly.

Matilda belts out a melody, singing praises to Mount Chrome.

The animals slowly creep back up the mountain as Matilda gives Mount Chrome a show of thanksgiving. Her light show and music are spectacular. Matilda's peace is restored and her courage is built up as Mount Chrome overwhelms her with his Spirit. All life on the mountain gazes at Matilda as she prepares for war.

Derek and his friends are standing before Tina, going through the bags that hold the supplies they'll use to ruin the parade and help Jonathan achieve his goal. Chuck gawks as he raises one of the giant marbles out of his bag. Mindy and Patricia show each other their tungals and horns that they'll use to disrupt the band. Tommy shakes his head as he envisions using the Mulder. Wickedness bounces off Derek and his friends as the effects of Igor's magic continue to manifest in the kids.

THE PARADE

"Hey! Ewww!" mutters Derek as he wipes off a small piece of Slurge from the side of his face.

Tammy elbows Bucky, proud of her aim.

"Guys, save it for the parade! We have to meet Matilda in twenty minutes and we still have to see Jonathan first," says Tina as she checks her watch.

"Hail, Derek!" calls a boy as he walks to the parade with his family.

Tina and the gang are startled by the boy's proclamation.

"Wave, Derek!" mumbles Tina, smiling.

Derek waves and is overwhelmed with fear.

"Guys, it's Toby! What do we do?!" asks Derek frantically.

"Let me handle this. You guys head to Hank's. I'll catch-up with you there," replies Tina, relaxed.

"Guys, look at this group! … Come on, we'll blend in with them," says Tommy as he grabs Mindy by the hand. "No one get lost! We can't let this fall apart now; we're too close to Jonathan's return."

One by one, Tommy and his friends disappear into the next passing group.

The gang finds themselves being tossed around a group of kids dressed like futuristic clowns. They're wearing jumpsuits with unusual colors and have obnoxious accessories. Chuck tries to squeeze a clown's giant purple nose, but is met with a smack on the hand. Derek and his friends gawk at the clowns' creepy faces. Many of them have strobe lights in their hands to enhance the visual affects of the parade. The sea of clowns is perfect for Tommy and his friends to move through the city.

"What?" asks Chuck as a boy mimes, 'Hello,' to him. "Just say it!"

"This is so cool! What kind of clown do you think he is?" asks Derek as he checks out the kid's painted face.

The gang walks through the street undetected as Tina makes

her way to converse with Toby. Each kid surveys the crowd, looking for their new fearless leader, Jonathan. Flashes of light send chills down Mindy and Bucky's spines as they wait to be discovered. Tammy motions for them to relax as she catches a set of beads.

Derek and his friends' eyes light up as they turn and see the city of Gibeon in its entire splendor. The music from the band eases their tension as they watch kids dancing on the sidewalks. There are laser-lights and flashing lightbulbs exploding before their eyes. No one really knows if they're going to survive the night, but it's too late to turn back now.

"Well, guys, this is it!" states Tommy, smiling to the crowd.

"Are we *really* going to go through with this?" asks Bucky as he waves to a fan.

"Yes, now drop it! We're finally going to ruin a parade and make up for lost time!" replies Derek as he notices Toby on the move. "Guys, hurry, there's Toby!"

Toby muscles his way through the crowd, searching for Derek and his friends. Tina quickly reacts, noticing Derek and the others exposed. She sees the nervousness on Patricia, Mindy and Bucky's faces. Without her to do the talking, one of the kids might crack under pressure and reveal Jonathan's plans. Tina puts away the torn pages of the Tobit and rushes over to Toby.

"Hey, Toby, where are you off to?" asks Tina, grabbing his arm.

"I'm looking for Derek and his friends. Matilda's waiting for them to go over last minute instructions for the parade. Have you seen them?" asks Toby as he looks down at her hand.

Toby looks up at Tina and stares into the eyes of a demon.

"No, I haven't 'seen them.' I was hoping that you could tell me where they are," replies Tina as she cringes from Toby's piercing stare.

THE PARADE

"What's wrong with you? Something's not right," says Toby, watching Tina's face change color. "Come here!"

"Nothing's 'wrong' with me! ... Let go! ... Get away from me!" mutters Tina.

"You're lying! You've seen Jonathan! Give me that!" demands Toby as he grabs her bag.

Tina and Toby play tug-of-war over the bag. The grunting and moaning of the two struggling to take possession of the bag attracts a large crowd. Tina and Toby are surrounded by kids feeding into the action. Several girls back away as the battle intensifies.

"Fight! Fight! Get him!" screams a little boy as he breaks away from his mother.

"Leave the girl alone!" shouts a little girl.

"Get her, Toby!" yells another boy. "Don't let her take that from you!"

Toby and Tina fly backward as the bag rips in half. The contents of the bag go flying into the air as Toby and Tina tumble onto the street. The crowd moves in closer, wanting to see what Tina has in her bag. She quickly jumps to her feet and scurries to collect her things.

"What's this?! That's a page from the Tobit!" screams Toby, pointing. "Where did you get this?!"

Tina pushes several kids out of the way and takes off running into the crowd.

"Somebody, stop her!" yells Toby as he quickly picks up the torn pages of the Tobit. "Don't let her get away! She's a *traitor!*"

People yell at Tina as she fights her way through the crowd. Igor doses her with supernatural powers that allow her to bully her way down the street. Toby stuffs his pockets with the torn pages and takes off running. As Tina approaches an opening in the crowd, she turns back and sees Toby tripping over a kid's wagon.

That will stop him! thinks Tina, as she takes off the other way.

"Not so fast, Tina!" declares Richard as he catches her in his arms.

"Ah! Were did you come from?! Let me go!" threatens Tina, panting. "I'm *warning* you … get … your … hands … off … of … me!"

Tina tries to break away from Richard's hold. Mount Chrome dosed Richard with supernatural powers as well. His powers supersede Igor and Jonathan's powers combined.

"I watched the whole thing from across the street. You're not going anywhere, so relax! Let's see what this is all about," says Richard as he waits for Toby to catch-up.

Tina gives up her fight and lowers her head. She knows her part in Jonathan's plot to overthrow Gibeon is finished. Tina hears Igor's voice telling her not to say a word. She shivers at the thought that Igor is watching them. A vision of her tied to a tree in the swamp, surrounded by wicked creatures is given to her as insurance for Tina to keep her mouth shut.

Toby slows down to rub his sore knee and catch his breath. He pulls out the torn pages of the Tobit and holds them up for Richard to see. Toby's blood rages as he realizes that Tina is part of something bigger than Harry's plans.

"Is that what I think it is?!" asks Richard, focusing on Toby's hand.

Tina remains silent as she recites ***"THE SHEPHERD"*** in her head.

The crowd following Toby applauds for their heroes, realizing the two boys have uncovered something horrible. Joshua, a medium-built boy with dark hair, recognizes the torn pages of the Tobit and shares his revelation with his friends. Several families overhear their conversation and decide it's time to go home.

"Thank you, Richard. I think there's more trouble out there. I need to find Derek and his friends. Here, I'm sure your father will want these back. I'd better go and see your father's security force.

THE PARADE

I have a bad feeling that something horrible is about to happen. I'm getting this feeling we're about to see signs and wonders never seen since the beginning of time," says Toby, glaring into Tina's eyes.

Tina remains cold as ice.

"You have a lot of explaining to do to my Father! Whatever your plans are, they will cease at once! My Father will call upon Mount Chrome and seek out all wickedness! Now let's go!" says Richard as he pulls Tina by the arm.

Jeffrey breaks through the crowd and grabs Tina's other arm.

"Thanks, Jeffrey," says Richard as he watches Toby disappear.

"No problem, Richard. We have to hurry, something's happening in Zevon Forest. The people who live on the outskirts of the city said that they saw a *wicked glow* coming from the forest," says Jeffrey as a sense of uneasiness locks his knees.

Richard stops.

"Did they see anything else? Does my Dad know about this?" asks Richard nervously.

Tina silently rejoices.

"They saw several large, wicked birds flying over the forest. One man said they looked like scavengers, big enough to eat a small boy. One boy said he heard a lot of *groaning* and *wailing* coming from the swamp. That kid isn't coming to the parade tonight. As far as your dad, I just heard about this ten minutes ago," replies Jeffrey.

"Are the flood lights still lighting up the perimeter?!" asks Richard as his heart begins to race.

"As far as I know, they still are," replies Jeffrey, digging into Tina's arm.

"Come on, we don't have any time to waste! We must warn my Dad!" states Richard as he pulls on Tina.

Down the street in front of Ted's Turtles is Jonathan, inconspicuously standing next to a large sign and watching the crowd having fun. The *rage* inside him amplifies as children zip by, giggling and laughing. He recalls the times when he used to live in Gibeon and partake in the parade. Flashes of his childhood bring tears to his eyes, yet give him the edge to complete the task at hand. The voices of Jonathan's family crying out for him drive him to madness. Jonathan looks away, realizing that several kids have noticed his evil eyes peeking out of his hood. Their bodies are overwhelmed with a cold sensation that makes their hair stand up.

"What's wrong with him?!" whispers one boy to his friend as he licks his ice cream cone.

"He must be sick! Keep walking!" whispers his friend as he speeds up.

"Pssst! Turn around," whispers Bobbie as he breaks through the crowd and creeps up to Jonathan.

Bobbie feels as though he could pass out as Igor's curse travels through his body. His hand begins to tremble and shake as he reaches into his pocket. Cold sweat begins to slowly drip down the sides of his head as he realizes what's about to happen. Jonathan surveys the area and slowly turns around. In true undercover form, Bobbie hands Jonathan the key to the Altar Room. The handoff sends chills through Bobbie's body, as if a part of Jonathan attached itself to Bobbie's soul.

"Vengeance is mine!" mumbles Jonathan as he places the key into his pocket.

Without another word, Jonathan disappears into the crowd. Bobbie shakes off his encounter with Jonathan and quickly checks the streets to make sure no one saw the handoff. He forces out a smile as Terone, Jackie and Samuel pass by. The pressure is mounting up for Bobbie, knowing that he's in over his head. With little time to contemplate his position, Igor appears on the sign overlooking the street. Bobbie is the only one who can see him. From the sign, Igor uses his blood to zap Bobbie with a red light that strengthens him.

Bobbie comes out of his trance and ducks into Ted's to lay low for awhile. With new confidence and Igor's watchful eyes, Bobbie pulls out some notes from the Tobit and plays out his part for the evening. He even visualizes himself as Jonathan's protégé once Jonathan takes control of Gibeon. Bobbie peeks out the front glass window and observes the people incognito.

"May I help you, son?" asks the shopkeeper.

"Ah! No thanks, I'm just looking," replies Bobbie, startled. He immediately pretends to be browsing for a pet.

"Okay, just let me know if there's anything you need," says the shopkeeper as he walks back to his counter. "In case you were wondering, we're having a sale on Gromins. Their pink shells and large horns are unique, you know."

Bobbie watches the shopkeeper return to the register. He browses the turtles in the window, glancing at the street from inside of Ted's. As Bobbie looks down the street, he sees Matilda with Derek and his friends. The flashes from cameras blind the spectators; many people snap pictures of the gang. Derek and his friends feel they deserve an award for their outstanding performances. The veil is pulled over Matilda, Mayor Messa and the citizens' eyes as the kids remain vigilant not to blow their covers. At least that's what they think. They have no idea where Matilda has been. Bobbie peers back toward the register, making sure that the shopkeeper doesn't catch on to his spying.

Matilda brings Derek and his friends to a well-decorated cabana, standing high above the street. Red, blue and green lights flash along the sides of the gang's special bungalow. Matilda keeps glancing back at their bags as she gets closer to the steps of the cabana. In Tammy's bag is a bit of Igor's flesh to mask their wickedness. It's so powerful that even the elect shall be fooled before the night is over. Matilda's instructions are to get Derek and his friends situated and then report to the mayor what Mount Chrome has revealed to her. Her focus is shifted toward the crowd, thinking that she sees Freddie, Jason and Harry.

"Watch your step," says Matilda as she corrals the gang up into the cabana.

"Wow! Look at all these people!" says Bucky as he looks down on the crowded street. *"We're famous!"*

"Hi! Cheeeeeze!" says Chuck with his teeth flaring as a boy takes his picture.

"I can't believe I'm the Master of Ceremonies. This is too much!" says Derek, waving to the crowd. "We love you!"

"Here Derek, you're going to need this to start the parade," says Matilda.

"Cool. What do I do with 'this'?" asks Derek as he examines the snail-looking whistle. "You're going to have to show me how to use this thing. Get away, Chuck, it's not food!"

"When I give you the signal, you'll blow into that small hole on the side. This will tell everyone that the parade is starting," replies Matilda as she sees one of the mayor's security guards motioning for her. "You kids stay right here. I have something important to take care of."

"How come Derek gets to blow it?!" asks Chuck, trying to take it away. "Whatever!"

Matilda stops.

"Derek gets to 'blow it' because this is *his* adventure. Don't worry, Chuck, *you'll have your turn one day.* Kids, I have to go. The Mayor is waiting for me. I'll be back shortly," replies Matilda as she flies off toward a group of security guards.

Tommy shuts the cabana door.

"That was a close one! Did you see her looking at our bags? She knows something, I feel it," says Tammy as she lays her heavy bag of Slurge on the floor.

THE PARADE

"If 'she knew something,' why didn't she ask us what was in the bags?" asks Bucky as he opens his.

"I bet it's the diversion! She was looking down the street on the entire walk here. I caught her observing the crowd as if she were looking for Freddie and the others. It's working!" replies Tommy as he makes sure that Matilda is gone.

Derek peeks over Tommy's shoulder.

"That's right, look!" says Derek, pointing.

Chuck and Mindy rush to the cabana window.

"Look at them go! Those security guards are after Freddie, Harry and Jason! This is it guys!" states Chuck as he grabs a giant marble out of his bag.

"Put that thing away! We need to see Jonathan and the others first," says Tommy as he lowers Chuck's hand.

"Hey, where's Tina?" asks Mindy, scanning the crowd.

"Yeah, aren't we supposed to wait for her?" asks Derek.

"That's right! We have to '*wait* for her'!" replies Tammy, sticking up for her new friend. "No one's going anywhere!"

"All right, we'll 'wait' ten minutes. After that we're on our own. Agreed?" asks Tommy as he puts his hand out in the middle of his friends. "Come on, Tammy!"

"'*Agreed*'!" say Tommy and his friends as they do their secret handshake.

Derek opens the cabana door, not wanting to seem suspicious. Anxiety is building in the kids' heads as thoughts of ruining the parade on their own play through their minds. Images of Igor's army appear before their eyes, reminding them of the upcoming battle. Chuck tells Derek that he's ready, even though Patricia and Bucky argue over Tammy. Tommy and Mindy wave to their admiring fans as a large group from Arnold's makes their way through the crowd.

"I sure hope Tina's okay," says Derek out the corner of his mouth as he catches some beads. "She's going to miss all the fun."

THE PARADE

The citizens of Gibeon have no idea who they're cheering for as they gather around the cabana. Kids continue to whistle and wave to Derek and his friends, waiting for them to start the parade.

Mayor Messa is preparing to leave his office and join his people. Thoughts of Freddie, Jason and Harry brew in his mind as he gathers his keys and the remote for Henry Fire Starter off his desk. He turns toward the window, thinking that he hears something strange coming from his city. The mayor is fuming as he visualizes his people being tormented by evil. He shuffles papers around his desk while he fumbles to make sure that he has everything.

"What the heck?!" asks Mayor Messa as Richard and Jeffrey burst through the door, restraining Tina between them. "Son, what is it?!"

"Dad, you're not going to believe this! Look at what Tina had!" replies Richard as he puts the torn pages of the Tobit on his desk. "Toby discovered this!"

Mayor Messa's eyes bulge out as he leans under the light and sees that his most sacred book has been pillaged. Chills run down his arms at the thought of blasphemy. The mayor lifts from his desk and gets in Tina's face.

"Where did you *get* these?!" demands Mayor Messa with the torn pages in his hand.

Tina recites *"THE SHEPHERD"* under her breath and remains silent. Jonathan and Igor have instilled supernatural fear into her that not even Mayor Messa could break. The silence irritates the mayor as he glares into her wicked eyes. Jeffrey grabs onto Tina's arm even harder, trying to get her to speak. Tina closes her eyes and focuses on Jonathan.

"Want to play silent with me, do you?" asks Mayor Messa as he tosses his keys to Richard. "Son, go and bring me the Tobit!"

"Yes, Dad!" says Richard, heading for the door.

Mayor Messa grabs Tina and sits her down in front of his desk. Two security officers rush into the mayor's office as Richard exits.

"Good! You guys watch her while I talk to Jeffrey," says Mayor Messa as he signals to Jeffrey.

"Yes, Sir!" say the security officers as they grab hold of Tina.

Jeffrey releases Tina and heads to the corner of the mayor's office to speak with him in private. Tina begins to feel the pressure as the two officers glare into her eyes. She glances over and sees Mayor Messa and Jeffrey whispering in secret as they stare back at her. A sense of loneliness overwhelms Tina as thoughts of Derek and his friends race through her head. A sudden vision of Jonathan quickly ends her self-pity. She knows that Igor's curses are worse than the mayor's punishment for her wicked deeds.

"What are you going to do?" whispers Jeffrey as he shakes his head, trying to intimidate Tina.

"I'm 'going' to wait until Richard brings me the Tobit. There's a scripture entitled, *'WATER FROM THE ROCK'* that I will use on her," replies Mayor Messa.

"Here it is, Dad!" states Richard as he rushes into the office.

"Thank you, son," says Mayor Messa, rubbing his son's head. "We're going to get to the bottom of this whether you like it or not!"

"She deserves Zevon Forest, Mr. Mayor! Better yet, she deserves the Abyss! No one has made it back from there!" states a guard, trying to get Tina to speak.

Mayor Messa, Richard and Jeffrey slowly walk toward his desk. The three stare intently at Tina, shaking their heads. Richard and Jeffrey use breathing tactics to break Tina's silence. Richard slowly lays the Tobit in front of his father and backs away from his desk. He notices Tina fidgeting in her seat as if she's in the electric chair. Tina's palms get clammy as Richard, Jeffrey and the security officers glare into her eyes. The tension in the office thickens as Mayor Messa thumbs through the Tobit.

"Where's *'THE SHEPHERD'* ... and *'THE ALTAR'?!"* demands the mayor as his face turns red.

"Answer him!" demands Jeffrey.

NO HARM OR FEAR IS WHAT I FEEL! NO HARM OR FEAR IS WHAT I FEEL! NO HARM OR FEAR IS WHAT I FEEL! thinks Tina, gripping the chair.

"That's it! If you don't want to tell me, I'll drag it out of you!" warns Mayor Messa as he flips through the pages of the Tobit.

He finds what he's looking for. The page reads:

WATER FROM THE ROCK

Go with your people to the rock.
Bring the elders of Gibeon.
I will be in your presence.
Strike the rock with your staff.
Water will flow from the rock.

Mayor Messa slowly walks from behind his desk with the Tobit wide open. Jeffrey and Richard follow close behind. Tina's eyes bulge out as the pressure mounts.

"Grab my staff, son," instructs Mayor Messa, focusing on Tina. "It's behind the painting of Mount Chrome."

"Yes, Dad!" says Richard as he heads to the corner of his father's office.

Tina seems to shrink in her seat, repeating the scripture even faster in her head. The two security guards grab hold of Tina even harder, making sure she can't get away. Tina watches helplessly as Richard makes his way toward his father with the golden staff. She swallows nervously as images of the Abyss flash before her eyes. Richard smirks at Tina as he hands his father his golden staff, a gift from Mount Chrome.

"Go with your people to the rock! Bring the elders of Gibeon! I will be in your presence! Strike the rock with your staff! Water will flow from the rock!" recites Mayor Messa as he gently places the tip of his golden staff on Tina's foot.

Tina's foot lights up the mayor's office. Beams of light shoot from the spot where the golden staff is touching her foot. Tina rocks in her chair as vibrations travel through her body. Her body glows as if she had swallowed all the lights in Gibeon. Suddenly, the booming voice of Mount Chrome fills the room.

"So it shall be with my word. It will never return back void, but shall do Thy will. It will achieve what I have spoken, now and forever," says Mount Chrome.

Mayor Messa, Richard, Jeffrey and the security guards humble themselves to the ground. The presence of Mount Chrome is overwhelming and the room becomes cold as ice. Tina can't believe that she hears the voice of Mount Chrome in the mayor's office. She begins to cry uncontrollably as the blinding light continues to shoot out of her body.

"I'm sorry, I'm sorry! Please forgive me!" screams Tina as she shakes in her seat.

Mayor Messa pulls back the golden staff and the light disappears. Jeffrey, Richard and the mayor step back to give Tina room to breathe. They can see that she's distraught and on the verge of hyperventilating. Mayor Messa hears the voice of Mount Chrome in his head.

"Is there something you would like to tell me now?" asks Mayor Messa in a loving, fatherly voice.

"It's … it's Jonathan!" cries Tina as she lowers her head.

"'*Jonathan*'?!" ask Jeffrey, Richard and the mayor.

Before another question can be asked, the interrogation is broken up by the thunderous boom of fireworks. All eyes shift toward the mayor's window overlooking the city. Mayor Messa, Jeffrey and Richard immediately rush to the window to see what's going on. The sky over Gibeon is illuminated by rockets that sail through the air. Purple and white flowers appear over the city as the fireworks explode.

"Who gave the orders for the fireworks to begin?! No one can do that but *me!* How did the parade start without me?!" demands Mayor Messa frantically.

He reaches into his pocket for the Henry Fire Starter remote. As Mayor Messa pulls out the remote from his pocket, his eyes bulge out of his head. His hands begin to shake as he realizes that someone switched remotes.

"Who could have done this?! This is a travesty!" declares Mayor Messa, trying to retrace his steps from this afternoon.

"Where's Matilda?!" asks Richard as he feeds into his dad's state of panic.

"It's Derek and his friends. They're planning to ruin your parade," says Tina, sobbing.

"'Planning to ruin my parade?!' They're 'ruining' it already! Who knows what's going on in my streets! We need to get down there right away! You can tell me the rest of Jonathan's plans on the way!" states Mayor Messa emotionally.

"Grab her!" says Richard as he helps his dad gather his things. "You're going to pay for this, Tina!"

The two security guards lift Tina from her seat and the group rushes out of the mayor's office to thwart Derek and his friends' plans to ruin the parade. Tina begins her confession about Jonathan's plot to overthrow Gibeon and the impending war with Igor's army. Igor is watching from Zevon Forest as Tina divulges what had happened earlier in the day. He darts from the fire to finish building his army and warn the others about Tina. *The battle between good and evil is coming to a head.*

Derek and his friends are blending in with the rowdy crowd as Henry Fire Starter is going ballistic. Derek is having a blast, continuing to press Mayor Messa's remote control. The entire parade has stopped to watch the magnificent fireworks show in the sky. The skies of Gibeon light up with every color imaginable. There are red, blue, green, yellow, pink, white and orange trails of light falling from the sky. Several giant explosions startle some of the little kids.

"I thought we'd see this at the end of the parade," says one man to his wife.

"I'm scared, Mommy," says their daughter.

"Don't worry, sweetheart, Daddy and Mommy are here to protect you," says the mother as she picks up her daughter.

"I'm going to have to complain about this to the Mayor, tomorrow!" states the father.

"Hey, watch it!" mutters their son as he gets trampled by Chuck.

"Sorry!" says Chuck as he moves by with his bag of giant marbles.

The gang is positioning themselves to attack the parade. The fireworks show has everyone looking to the sky, giving them the freedom to move about with little attention. Chuck settles in behind a giant statue of one of the founders of Gibeon.

"Hey, aren't you the kid who tackled my friends in Arnold's?" asks one boy.

"Yeah, now beat it!" snarls Chuck.

What's his problem?! thinks the boy, stomping away from Chuck.

Chuck makes sure there are no other distractions. He readies himself to release the wave of giant marbles onto the street. Images of Frankie and Jimmy ruining the Hummel County Parade bring a smile to his face. Chuck glances across the street and sees Mindy and Patricia giving him the thumbs up. The girls blend in perfectly with other kids.

The sounds of whistling and popping fireworks hold everyone's attention. Mindy and Patricia look toward the sky and watch the spectacular fireworks show as well. A little girl smiles at Patricia then glances back toward the sky. How terrible it is that the children of Gibeon have befriended a group of rotten kids about to destroy their beautiful city.

"Wow, look at that!" says Mindy, pointing at a giant blue and green explosion. "It looks like an animal."

"We've never seen anything like this back home," says Patricia as her eyes follows the falling flames.

I wonder what's keeping Tammy, thinks Mindy.

Mindy looks back down and sees Matilda with Mayor Messa's security force. They're corralling Freddie, Jason and Harry toward the mayor's office. The citizens of Gibeon move aside for the mayor's security force, giving them room to do their job. The boys resemble a chain gang heading off to prison. Freddie, Jason and Harry look up, making sure that all the attention is on them. Harry even struggles with two guards, creating even more attention for himself. Matilda has no idea that it was Bobbie who stole the mayor's remote control for Henry Fire Starter and gave it to Derek. As the group passes by, Mindy motions for Chuck to keep still.

"Look down at your shoes!" mumbles Mindy as she grabs Patricia.

"Why, what's wrong?" asks Patricia as Mindy pulls her away from the street.

"Matilda is heading this way," mutters Mindy out the side of her mouth.

The girls hide their faces until Matilda is out of sight.

"I'm here guys!" declares Tammy as she drops the heavy bag of Slurge on the ground.

"Ahhhhh! Where have you been?!" asks Mindy, picking up her horn.

"I was looking for Tina, but I couldn't find her anywhere," replies Tammy, noticing Chuck hiding across the street. "Have you seen her?"

THE PARADE

"No," replies Mindy as she watches Matilda disappear into the crowd. "I'm starting to get worried. What if she's in trouble?"

"'She's' too smart to get into 'trouble.' I bet 'she's' with Mable and Jonathan," replies Tammy.

"Look, there's Bucky!" says Patricia, pointing to the center of the street.

The girls' mouths drop as they see Bucky strolling down Main Street dressed like a clown. Mable knocked-out one of the performers and stole his outfit and gave it to Bucky to wear. He waves to Chuck and the girls as he horses around with the other clowns. His friends can't believe their eyes. It's as if Bucky had been a circus clown his whole life.

"Guys, I'll be right back," says Bucky, throwing a set of beads to the crowd.

He heads toward Mindy and Patricia. Bucky reaches into his pocket and grabs some candy to pass out. The crowd revels in Bucky's kookiness as he stumbles around the street, throwing candy to several kids. Bucky is having the time of his life.

"Here girls, candy for everyone!" says Bucky, chuckling.

"Stop it, Bucky, you're not a clown!" exclaims Tammy as she grabs the candy and smiles at the crowd.

"Where's Tommy?" asks Mindy as she smiles to the onlookers.

"There's a large group of clowns coming before the band. He's in with them," replies Bucky as he throws candy into the crowd.

"What about Derek? Where's he?" asks Tammy as she throws her candy to a set of twin girls.

"'He's' on one of the floats," replies Bucky as he runs out of candy. "Sorry! Here, take these!"

"That lucky brat! Why does he get to ride a 'float'?!" asks Tammy.

"He's the Master of Ceremonies, that's why. Look, I have to go. We'll meet down the street," replies Bucky as he sees the other two clowns waving him back.

THE PARADE

"Since Tina's not around, we'll meet by the fountain instead of Hank's. Remember, the fountain is where Matilda said we'd go home," says Mindy as she turns toward her friends.

Bucky runs off to join the other clowns as the city lights illuminate the streets. The citizens of Gibeon cheer for the clowns as they play with each other, walking down the street. From the looks of the party, a person wouldn't know that trouble is around the corner. Tammy and the girls smile at several bystanders, waiting patiently and listening for the band.

"Hey, look, there's Bobbie!" states Patricia as she points across the street.

Bobbie is slowly making his way toward Chuck. His observation from Ted's Turtles has paid off. Bobbie has calculated the number and positioning of the mayor's security force. His mental notes will come in handy for the rest of their plans.

"Pssst! Chuck!" whispers Bobbie, noticing the girls across the street.

"Ah, you scared me!" mutters Chuck as he fumbles with a giant marble in his hand.

"Where's Tina?" asks Bobbie as he signals to the girls.

"I don't know. I thought she was with you.... Oh, the band!" says Chuck, pushing Bobbie aside. "This is it, Bobbie … *total destruction!*"

Chuck steps onto the street and estimates his release of the marbles.

The city explodes into song and dance as the music from the band echoes between the buildings. A group of clowns heads down the street, throwing candy and toys into the crowd. Close behind is the all powerful Gibeon Electric Band marching in perfect formation. Their instruments light up the streets even more as their groovy beat peaks the kids' excitement. The gang has their work cut out for them as they try not to get caught up in all the festivities.

"I'm going to look for Tina. You guys get ready to do your

thing," says Bobbie as he pats Chuck on the back. "Remember, Igor is watching."

Bobbie gives Tammy and the girls a thumb up and disappears into the crowd.

Tommy takes the lead and shepherds the clowns down Main Street. His clown outfit is deep purple with huge white ruffles. Tommy is also a natural when it comes to becoming a clown. It's hard to believe that he could take part in Jonathan's war after seeing the children of Gibeon treat his friends like heroes. He turns around and sees the band jamming, oblivious to the danger that awaits them. The other clowns are dancing around the street as Tammy prowls along the curb. Tommy signals to his friends for the attack to begin.

Okay, here it goes! thinks Tommy, as he pulls out a horn from his pocket.

Tommy blows the horn and runs ahead of the other clowns. That's the signal Chuck and the girls have been waiting for. The horn, which was stolen by Bobbie from the mayor's security force, is louder than the band. The sound of the horn echoes between the buildings, reaching Bucky and Derek's ears.

"*Yee-ha!*" screams Chuck as he releases the wave of marbles onto the street, before he quickly disappears into the crowd.

The giant marbles head toward the unsuspecting clowns and the band. The streets of Gibeon have become a bowling alley as the first marbles hit and take out several clowns. The crowd reacts as they watch the clowns *flying* into the air. The citizens of Gibeon have no idea that Chuck caused the ruckus, and think that it's part of their act. The next wave of marbles takes out several band members. The band's jamming beat turns into a junkyard folly as instruments fly into the air. The spectators plug their ears from the screeching noises of the band's instruments. Anarchy is about to unfold.

"Look, Mommy, they're silly!" says one little girl.

THE PARADE

"Ahhh!" scream several clowns and band members as they land on their backs.

Tommy grabs his knees, laughing.

The *chaos* on Main Street has the citizens of Gibeon on the edge of the street, trying to get a better look at the action. Mindy and Patricia take advantage of the leaning crowd. They slowly creep up to the curb and make sure no one is watching them. "HONK!!!!!!!!!" blasts out of Mindy and Patricia's horns. The people of Gibeon rush onto the street. They scamper around and look as if they're being attacked by aliens. Mindy and Patricia pull out their tungals and begin to flood the streets with soap. People run out of the high pockets of soap screaming, drenched in white suds. Parents wipe the soap from their kids' eyes as they scamper for cover.

"Run for your life!" screams one boy as he grabs his younger sister.

"It's the *Gooligans!* They're here!" shouts another boy.

"Ahhh!" screams one woman as she looks frantically for her daughter in the sea of people.

The clowns and the crowd continue to trip over the giant marbles and slip on the soapy streets and sidewalks. The first phase of Jonathan's plan is working. Mindy, Patricia and Tammy disappear into the chaos and prepare themselves for phase two.

Many people from down the street rush over to see what's happening. Main Street is in a state of pandemonium. Mr. and Mrs. Jasper grab their children and run home, wondering what's happening to their peaceful city. Tammy slinks through the bustling crowd and makes her way to the curb. She begins throwing the Slurge by the handful at the floats. The floats immediately short-circuit, sending giant sparks bouncing off the buildings. Peoples' faces light up as the floats catch on fire. Parents grab their children and run for cover.

THE PARADE

Further on down the street, Mayor Messa and his security force are exiting the mayor's building. The whistling sounds of fireworks and short-circuiting floats grab their attention. The group stands in shock, watching people running for their lives as smoke rises from Main Street. Richard and Jeffrey's mouths drop as they watch buildings catch on fire. The mayor's worst nightmare is coming true as he feels the presence of Jonathan. He's been haunted with dreams and visions ever since the day he banished Jonathan and his followers to Zevon Forest.

"What the heck?! Somebody *do* something! Sound the alarm!" bellows Mayor Messa, panicking. "Look at my city!"

His top security officer runs inside the building and pulls an alarm lever.

The emergency alarm sounds throughout Gibeon like a war siren. The citizens of Gibeon look toward the sky and are gripped with fear. This is the siren they thought they'd never hear in their lifetime. Families look out of their high-rise apartment windows, trying to figure out what to do next.

Security officers file out from the mayor's building in all directions. Richard grabs Tina and follows his father onto the street. His heart is burning as he feels his father's pain. Jeffrey grabs hold of Tina's other arm and digs into it, resenting her for being part of this mass chaos.

"We're right behind you, Dad!" shouts Richard as he signals for the others to follow.

Meanwhile, Jonathan is watching the chaos from the safety of several thick bushes across the street. He waits patiently for the mayor's security force to empty the building. His eyes grow in the darkness of his hood as he sees his revenge unfolding. Jonathan's breathing speeds up as he visualizes his entrance into the Altar Room. He zeroes in on a side door of the mayor's building.

With the majority of the mayor's security force gone,

THE PARADE

Jonathan makes his way across the street. He cautiously moves through the crowd unnoticed, and catches the door as the last security guard exits. Jonathan glances back toward the street, making sure that no one sees him.

"The Golden Chalice is *mine!*" exclaims Jonathan as he enters the building.

The door shuts and the hunt is on. Jonathan creeps down the hall heading toward the elevators. The flashing lights in the building create shadows that startle Jonathan. His blood is pumping as he lowers his hood and takes a deep breath. The voice of Igor telling him about his plans to exit Zevon Forest lights up his eyes. Jonathan's wicked face is transforming by the minute. If it keeps up, he'll be more grotesque than Igor.

The sound of running footsteps quickly squashes his moment of glory. Jonathan combs the long hallway in search of the elevators. After noticing the sign down to his right, he begins his trek toward the Altar Room. Jonathan tiptoes through the hallway in case someone decided to stay behind. He can hear his heart pounding as he smells victory at hand.

"I knew those kids were trouble!" says a security officer heading down one of the corridors of the building. "They'll *never* see the light of day once the Mayor gets through with them!"

The sound of many footsteps rushing through the corridor sends Jonathan into a panic. He grabs the first door that he sees and fights to turn the door handle; it's locked. Jonathan then shuffles around and checks several doors as the officers get closer. Finally, he finds an unlocked closet and ducks into it. His heartbeat echoes in the darkness as thoughts of being captured race through his mind. The footsteps stop just feet away from the closet door. Sweat drips from his eyebrow as he prepares himself for a confrontation. Jonathan sees the shadow of the officers stop in front of the closet.

"Come on, guys, we need to hurry! The Mayor needs us out there!" says one officer.

THE PARADE

That was close! thinks Jonathan, listening to the guards exiting the building.

Jonathan slowly opens the door and peeks out to see if there's anyone else coming. With a look to the left and a look to the right, he enters into the hallway to continue his walk toward the elevators. Flashes of Mayor Messa's demise dance around his head. Jonathan visualizes the mayor bringing him and Mable their lunch.

"Revenge is mine! I'll show these people never to mess with me again!" mumbles Jonathan. "They will kiss my hand and bend a knee at my command!"

Jonathan walks to the elevator and presses the button to go to the ninth floor.

"Jonathan," whispers a voice.

"Ah! How did you get in here?" whispers Jonathan as he positions himself to attack.

"I snuck into the building from other side," whispers Mable, backing away from Jonathan. "With all the commotion on the streets, it was easy."

"This is it! Our time has come!" says Jonathan.

The elevator door opens and the two get in. Jonathan pushes the button for the ninth floor and off they go. It looks as if all those years of patience and planning have paid off for Jonathan and Mable. He smiles at her as he watches each floor pass. Suddenly, Jonathan closes his eyes and grabs his head. Mable grabs his arm and begins to shake him.

"What's wrong?" asks Mable.

"Igor says that his army is in the swamp and preparing to come into the city. His sorcery is more wicked than planned. He has one last warrior to birth. Mayor Messa's army will be no match for Igor's creation," replies Jonathan as he snaps out of his trance. "The day of redemption is at hand!"

"I can see it now ... you're mighty throne in the Mayor's office. No one will ever tell us what to do again," says Mable.

THE PARADE

Mable smiles and nods her head as she envisions Igor's attack on the city. Jonathan and Mable stand quietly as they head to the ninth floor.

The full moon's brilliant light illuminates Mount Chrome and provides perfect visibility for several animals trying to find food. The heavy cloud at the top of the mountain glows with bolts of lightning flashing every few seconds. The cloud itself has a bright light that's almost blinding, indicating something's about to happen. Animals scurry down the mountain as the rumbling of thunder deepens.

Matilda and Mayor Messa are making their way up the mountain with his army. This meeting has been called according to Mount Chrome's command. The mayor left his city knowing that he has bigger problems to worry about. Matilda has given him glimpses of Zevon Forest through her light. She has gathered the Roga Stones for Mount Chrome to raise up his army to fight alongside Mayor Messa's army. All who are present are trembling with fear as they feel the mountain palpitate.

"We are here as you commanded, oh, Great Mountain," says Matilda as she flies to her sacred stone. "We need *you* to deliver us from evil … it has made its way into your great city."

Mayor Messa and the others stop a few yards from the heavy cloud as they watch it change colors. Mount Chrome's Spirit seeps into the flesh and bones of his people. He knows that it's by his strength alone that they'll be able to withstand Igor's sorcery. The cloud descends upon Matilda as she humbles herself. The mayor and his army bow down as well, knowing that Mount Chrome is about to speak.

"Hello, my children. You have done well to obey my commands. *Evil* like never before is coming to my city. Igor is raising up his final creature to lead his army into battle; the *Trengasor*. You must be aware of what you're up against. Here, see for yourselves," says Mount Chrome.

442

THE PARADE

The heavy cloud around the mountain begins to change colors and light up even brighter. Mayor Messa and his army back away and stand at attention. Their eyes grow wide as Igor's wickedness seeps into their bodies from the cloud. The soldiers in the mayor's army shake their heads as they witness evil being created in front of their eyes. Mayor Messa signals for everyone to settle down and pay attention. He knows that he can't show any signs of weakness or fear if he plans on leading his troops into battle. General Hofta, a stern-looking man, and his son walk up next to Mayor Messa and show their alliance.

In the cloud, they see Igor and his malicious army gathered around a large fire in the middle of the swamp. He has created an army full of wicked trolls, large, beast-like men, similar to cavemen, and large vulture-type birds called Vultars. These are the birds that some of the citizens reported to Jeffrey. There are wicked kids sitting on the backs of some of the birds, loading up rocks in their satchels. At the edge of the swamp are several disfigured giants, pounding their fighting clubs to the floor. The sounds of *grunting* and *hissing* come alive from the cloud as Igor walks up to the fire with a large knife.

"This is for our leader, Jonathan! Gibeon will never be the same! We shall *pour* out a fury like never before!" declares Igor as he signals for his helper.

A small, grunt-looking creature brings Igor his bag. Igor sprinkles some dust from the bag onto the fire, sending flames shooting into the sky. He then cuts his arm and holds it over the fire.

"*Arrrrrrrrrr!*" cries Igor as he lets the blood drip onto the fire.

Igor runs away as an explosion lights up the swamp. In the fire appears a large object forming; it's the Trengasor. The fire changes colors and the Trengasor lets out a ferocious roar. Igor's army backs away as he steps out of the fire. The Trengasor looks like a giant armadillo/dinosaur mix, with horns everywhere. It has large tusks and giant teeth protruding from its mouth. The Trengasor snarls at the army as Igor walks back to the fire.

"Listen up! Fear not! He's under my control! We are ready for war!" shouts Igor as he raises his walking stick toward the sky.

"*Yeeeeeaaaaaaaaaahhhhhhhh!*" scream the evil members of his army as they raise their weapons and torches.

The entire swamp glows with a fiery light that swirls around the forest.

"Mount up, army!" shouts Igor's officer with his club raised; he looks like a demon. "We shall fight until death! *Raaaaaaaaaaaaaaaaaa!*"

The vision in the heavy cloud disappears as Mount Chrome bathes his mountain in a soothing white light. Peals of lightning and thunder resume shooting across his heavy cloud. A cool mist falls from the sky and creates a numbing feeling for Mount Chrome's people.

"How are we to fight them, my Lord?" asks Mayor Messa, trembling. "We're no match for them."

"Evil such as Jonathan and Igor has been present since the foundation of the world. But have no fear. Do not lose heart at the sight of your enemies. The battle is mine, not yours. Stand firm and I will deliver you. Bring me the stones," says Mount Chrome.

An officer of Mayor Messa's army breaks through the crowd with a large bag. He places it before Matilda and humbly backs away. All eyes focus on the bag of Roga Stones as the soldiers wait to see their Great Mountain redeem them from Jonathan and Igor.

"Scatter the stones before me. Then you shall retreat to the base of the mountain. I will raise up an army like no other from these stones! Who is Igor, that my power shall crush and break *every* bone of his army. I will call you to myself when I am finished," says Mount Chrome.

"Army, pull back!" shouts the officer.

THE PARADE

Mayor Messa and his army head down the mountain.

Matilda sings a song of praise to Mount Chrome for his wondrous deeds. Her angelic ballad eases the racing hearts of Mayor Messa's army as they watch her green and yellow lights dancing around the heavy cloud. Her illuminating light touches the bag of Roga Stones. The golf ball-sized stones float out of the bag and scatter themselves in perfect sequence on the mountainside. Matilda's ballad can be heard throughout the mountain range as the heavy cloud descends upon the stones.

Mayor Messa and his army watch from the base of the mountain as the heavy cloud lights up. Flashes of yellow, gold and blue explode within the cloud. The soldiers cover their eyes as the light from Mount Chrome floods the valley. Chills penetrate their inner most parts as a wave of Mount Chrome's Spirit travels down the mountain.

"*It is finished!*" says Mount Chrome.

The soldiers open their eyes and see images in the heavy cloud rising up from the ground. Several of the mayor's men are tempted to leave, witnessing large objects coming to life before their eyes. A silhouette of a giant warrior with wings appears in the cloud. He lets out a cry that sends everyone to the floor. A silhouette of a large warrior with four arms appears at the bottom of the cloud. Silhouettes of smaller warriors pop up around the entire mountain. Some of the younger soldiers grab onto each other for support.

"Look, the forest is on fire!" shouts a boy.

Mayor Messa and his army turn their attention toward Zevon Forest. The group is *awestruck* as they watch a burning glow moving through the forest, heading toward the city of Gibeon. A mushroom of fire lights up the sky above Zevon Forest. Hazy smoke rises above the trees as Igor's army presses forward.

"Come, let us prepare for war!" declares Mount Chrome as Matilda's song comes to an end.

THE PARADE

Back on the streets of Gibeon is *pandemonium*, as the domino effect of the gang's antics spreads throughout the city. People are rushing to get their kids to safety as firefighters battle a fire created by Derek and his friends. Freddie grins at Jason and Harry as the three are held by the mayor's security force. Too bad they're not aware of the new army created by Mount Chrome. The citizens of Gibeon are oblivious to what's happening up on the mountain. Instead of peace and security, it's every man, woman and child for themselves as the citizens of Gibeon watch the destruction of their city.

"Where are Derek and his friends?! Bring them to me at once!" demands a lieutenant as he watches the last firework explode. "They'll pay for this severely!"

"Yes, Sir!" exclaim several security officers.

They take off running down the street.

"Those kids will never go home! They'll spend the rest of their lives cleaning this place up!" states the lieutenant, assessing the damage.

"Oh no!" exclaims Richard as he watches a large sign crashing onto the street. "Watch her! I need to help the others!"

Richard rushes toward the deli.

"Kelcher and Davidson! You guys head toward Lexington Street!" shouts the lieutenant as he glares at Tina.

Mindy and Patricia are running through the crowd to get closer to the Baker's float. This is one of the last floats not vandalized by the gang. Tracy Baker, the owner's daughter, is hysterical as she watches several people running in terror. As tears begin to fall from her eyes, she notices Mindy ready to use her tungal on her parent's float. The two girls make eye contact as Mindy prepares to pull the trigger. Tracy's hurting soul pierces through the spell placed on Mindy from the forbidden strawberries.

"Why are you *doing* this to us?" asks Tracy, fighting back the tears. "What have we ever done to you to make you act this way?"

THE PARADE

Tracy's emotions are too much for Mindy as she remains frozen with the tungal pointing up toward the float. She snaps out of her trance and notices all the chaos. It suddenly dawns on her that her friends are responsible for this mess. Guilt and shame wash over Mindy's body as she sees Tracy's crying eyes preparing to be tungaled.

"I'm so sorry! This isn't how we act! We ate some strawberries given to us by Tina and we met Jonathan. He's the reason why this is happening!" explains Mindy as she begins to cry.

Suddenly, Tracy covers herself from an attack by Patricia.

"No, wait! Put it down, Patricia!" demands Mindy as she grabs Patricia's hand. "Patricia, wake up, it's me, Mindy!"

Mindy stares into Patricia's dazed eyes. Her look is too much for Patricia to withstand as Mindy's spirit penetrates the curse of the strawberries. Patricia glances at the float and realizes what she was about to do. Tracy looks down and gives Patricia the same look that she gave Mindy. Once again, the spell from the forbidden strawberries is broken.

"Oh my gosh! What happened?!" asks Patricia as she snaps out of her trance.

"You guys ate the forbidden strawberries and were put under Jonathan's spell," replies Tracy as she sees Mayor Messa's security officers approaching.

"Who's 'Jonathan'?!" asks Patricia.

"There's no time to explain! You'd better run before they catch you!" replies Tracy, observing the officers breaking through the crowd.

"What about our friends?! How do we break their spells?!" asks Mindy, pulling Patricia away from the float. "Come on, Patricia! ... What do we do?!"

"Your faith will 'break their spells!' *Rebuke* the spirit of the fruit!" screams Tracy as she watches Mindy and Patricia disappear into the chaotic crowd.

THE PARADE

"Tracy, where did they go?!" asks one security officer as he catches his breath.

"I think they went that way!" replies Tracy, pointing in the wrong direction.

"Come on, we need to find them!" says another officer. "Hurry, men!"

"Wait, what's that?!" asks the first officer. "I thought that everyone was out of the building!"

The two officers look up at Mayor Messa's building and see that the lights are turned on in his office. An image walks across the large window facing Main Street. Jonathan and Mable have no idea that they're being watched by the security officers.

"I wonder if the Mayor went back to his office. We'd better go and check it out," says the second officer.

"You're right, forget the kids. We need to get back there!" says his counterpart. "I'll let the others know our plans!" says the officer as he pulls out his two-way radio.

The two officers take off running toward Mayor Messa's building. Tracy jumps off her float to help Mindy and her friends.

Mable is busy ransacking Mayor Messa's office, looking for a memento to take with her. In her search, she throws pictures against the wall and breaks fine vases; all in protest of what the mayor did to her and Jonathan. A wicked smile washes across her face as a sense of redemption flows through her mind.

"I can't wait until you bow before Jonathan!" states Mable as she looks at a cracked picture of the mayor and his family. "It's your turn to live in Zevon Forest!"

Mable finds a cool pocket flashlight in his top drawer. She turns it on and slices the blue light across the room as if she's sword fighting. Visions of the battle between Igor's army and Mayor Messa's army dance around her head.

I wonder what's happening down below, thinks Mable, as she heads toward the window.

THE PARADE

She sees several of the mayor's security officers racing toward the building.

"Jonathan, hurry, the Mayor's security force is coming!!!" screams Mable as she heads toward the Altar Room.

Jonathan is standing before the Altar Room, staring at the bright light that glows from under the door. This is the moment that he's been waiting for. Jonathan has had dreams and visions about this day for years. His daily meditation has been the only reason for living under the horrible conditions of Zevon Forest. Jonathan's body shakes as he glances down the hall, making sure that no one's coming to steal his moment.

He knows the story behind the Golden Chalice. Jonathan's parents told him when he was younger about Mount Chrome's child and that he was killed at a young age for no good reason. The essence of his body remains in the cup. Anyone who drinks of it will never die. In it is the power capable of destroying fortresses. No more swamp! No more bugs! No more forest! No more fruit! This and much more are what lie behind the door in the Altar Room. Jonathan takes a deep breath as he slowly puts the key into the door. His hand begins to tremble as sweat pours down the sides of his head.

"Come on, baby, almost there," whispers Jonathan as he unlocks the door.

Jonathan slowly swings open the door. He covers his eyes as the bright light shines off the golden Altar, directly in his face. Jonathan carefully inches his way toward the Altar, waving his hands in front of him. A burning vibration washes through Jonathan's body as he moves closer to the Altar. It's as if a force is pushing against him as he walks through the room.

How does anyone get to this thing? thinks Jonathan.

As he makes it within two feet of the Altar, the lights shut off. Jonathan gawks at its magnificence; the golden Altar lights up the room by itself. The Altar is solid gold and has two doors in front, decorated with precious stones. Jonathan squints as a supernatural light glows through the stones. It appears to be singing to Jonathan as it rests atop a large marble table. Jonathan falls to his knees before it.

"This is it! *I* will be the ruler of Gibeon! I will now have my throne in the recesses of the north and the people of Gibeon shall bow before me!" declares Jonathan with his hands raised toward the ceiling.

Jonathan slowly stands back up and walks to the table. He carefully opens the doors to grab the Golden Chalice.

"*What?!* Where is it?!" demands Jonathan as his world closes in.

The Altar is empty, no Golden Chalice.

"'It's' in a safe place!" says a voice from the corner of the room.

Jonathan swings around.

"*Toby!* How did you know that I would be here?!" asks Jonathan with his fists clenched. "Where's the Golden Chalice?!"

Jonathan slams the Altar's doors and cautiously heads toward Toby.

"Tina told us everything!" replies Toby as he moves out from the corner.

"'Tina!' Where is she?! What did you do with her?!" asks Jonathan with intense eyes. "You'll never make it out of here alive!"

"I'm ready to lay my life down for my brothers. Do with me what you have to, but I will never tell you anything," says Toby, noticing the evil emanating from Jonathan.

"Come on, old friend. Give me the cup. You, too, can share the power with me. With it, we'll have the authority over all of Gibeon," coaxes Jonathan as he inches closer.

"Never!" declares Toby, realizing that the fate of Gibeon is at stake.

THE PARADE

"*Roooaaarrr!*" bellows Jonathan as he charges Toby.

"For Gibeon! *Roooaaaarrrrr!*" grunts Toby as he charges Jonathan.

The two boys collide in the middle of the room, like two bucking rams. Jonathan grabs hold of Toby and pulls him to the ground. The boys moan and grunt as they wrestle around the Altar Room floor. Jonathan has nothing to lose by ending Toby's life. The thought of losing his opportunity to rule Gibeon and take revenge on Mayor Messa drives Jonathan insane. His appearance changes before Toby's eyes.

"I ...will ... destroy ... you!" mutters Jonathan as he chokes Toby.

"N-e-v-e-r!" gasps Toby, trying to break free.

The room begins to spin for Toby as he goes in and out of consciousness. Jonathan continues to apply pressure as Toby's body becomes limp. He's going to squeeze the Golden Chalice out of Toby if that's what it takes for him to find his power to rule Gibeon.

"Goodbye, old friend," says Jonathan, lifting Toby's lifeless arm.

Jonathan climbs off Toby and stands over his motionless body. He pushes Toby's leg with his foot, checking to make sure that he's finished. Jonathan feels somewhat vindicated for ending Toby's life after his lack of cooperation. Toby has an angelic look on his face that gives Jonathan the creeps. Jonathan glances at the empty Altar and becomes enraged.

"Those kids are going to pay for letting Tina get caught! They'll never go home!" states Jonathan as he pulls out another page of the Tobit from his pocket. "Come on, where's the scripture?! ... There!"

The page reads:

THE PARADE

THOUSAND-YEAR REIGN

With this key and heavy chain,
fire and sulfur shall be upon thee.
Grab hold of the dragon,
and be thrown into the Abyss.

Jonathan pulls out a key attached to a chain from his mystical bag. He holds them toward the sky, knowing that he must hurry to find Derek and his friends. The key and chain begin to glow in his hand as shock waves travel down his arms. Jonathan takes a deep breath as he considers his next move.

"If I must suffer, so shall they!" declares Jonathan in an eerie tone. "I will show them evil like never before! They'll be wailing and grinding their teeth, and crying out for the pain to end, but there shall be no relief!"

Jonathan puts the key and chain back into his bag and heads out the door.

As Jonathan rushes back toward the elevators, he hears footsteps heading his way. His stomach turns as he searches for a place to hide. Jonathan's thoughts of revenge are now on Derek and his friends. No one is going to end his quest to bring those kids to the Abyss. He quickly ducks down a stairwell and hears a struggle in the hallway.

"Let me go! You'll pay for this!" says a voice with the group. "Wait until Jonathan finds you! Igor!"

"Mable! Sorry, my friend," whispers Jonathan as he puts the bag into his pocket. "'Igor' should be here soon. They'll *all* perish in the Abyss!"

He darts down the stairs, heading toward the lobby. Jonathan shows his true colors, abandoning his best friend. There's no room for dead weight in his pursuit of power and revenge. His eyes glow with a reddish color as he makes his way toward the ground floor. The hunt is on to find Derek and his friends as Jonathan shuffles down the stairs, filled with evil.

The security officers make it around the corner with Mable held tight. They halt in their tracks; mortified at their discovery.

"What the heck?! This isn't good!" says one security officer as he sees the door to the Altar Room wide open. "Someone call for backup!"

The security officers slowly walk up to the door. Each officer has his fighting stick drawn, ready for battle. One officer waves everyone back as he peeks into the door. Tension mounts; the thought of vandalism to the most sacred place in Gibeon becomes a reality. Two guards grab hold of Mable, sensing that she's partially responsible.

"*Toby!*" screams the officer, noticing his lifeless form. "Grifen, call for a medic! *Noooooo!*"

The other officers rush to the entrance of the Altar Room. The group stares in shock at Toby's lifeless body. Even Mable becomes upset, watching the guards lower their heads in memory of Toby. The city of Gibeon will be in heavy mourning when they find out one of their sons is gone.

"Quick, go find the person or persons who did this!" demands the officer.

Several guards take off running.

"You'd better tell me everything you know or else!" demands the officer, grabbing hold of Mable.

"I'm sorry! I'll 'tell you everything,' I swear!" cries Mable as she looks away from the room.

The officer leads Mable and the guards toward Mayor Messa's office.

Jonathan is running down the final stairs before he reaches the lobby. His breath becomes louder as he focuses on his revenge for Derek and his friends. Pounding footsteps break up his moment of glory. He glances back up the stairs and sees security officers chasing him.

"Stop, right there!" shout two officers, trying to keep their balance.

"You can't escape!" yells another officer.

Jonathan rushes down the last steps and darts out the exit door. He finds himself in the lobby, but not alone.

"Wait! Stop! Get him!" screams Officer Jules.

Jonathan frantically looks for a direction to run. His heart races as a sense of desperation washes through his body. Jonathan notices a large crowd in front of one of the entrances to the building. The people are practically busting down the glass, seeking answers to the madness and chaos that has visited their city. Jonathan grabs hold of his mystical bag and makes a mad dash for the door.

"Someone, stop him!" yells Officer Jules as he chases Jonathan toward the door. Officer Jules' weight almost causes him to slip on the freshly polished floors. "Whoa! Don't let him get through those doors!"

Jonathan pushes his way though two security guards and bursts open the door. The citizens of Gibeon pile into the building, screaming and demanding to see the mayor. The guards are overwhelmed by Mayor Messa's people showing them their injuries and telling their horror stories of what's happening out on the streets. Officer Jules watches helplessly from the window as Jonathan disappears into the crowd. Jonathan glances back at him, smiling, and then vanishes. Officer Jules is shaken up by the evil look on Jonathan's face and knows that the trouble has only just begun.

Mayor Messa and Matilda are staring at Zevon Forest from the outskirts of the western side of Gibeon. Their stomachs churn from the fading sounds of the city's sirens heard in the background. There's an *eerie silence* coming from the dense woods that sends chills down Mayor Messa's spine as he mentally prepares for war. An occasional set of eyes peeks out of the darkness, but soon disappears. The city floodlights illuminate the giant field that separates Zevon Forest from the city. Several strange rodents scurry for a place to hide, sensing the danger looming.

Standing behind Mayor Messa and Matilda is Mount Chrome's army raised up from the Roga Stones. In the lead are Zito, Jet and the Spirit. Behind them are Hagar, Goliath, Rush, Krul, Viper, Pagan, Worm, Serpent, the Beast and Dar. Several hundred yards down is Hawk, the warrior who cried out from the heavy cloud. Mount Chrome has given him wings and a squadron of large hawks, big enough to carry the younger soldiers. This facet of the army will be used to fight Igor's army of wicked Vultars. This giant army of muscle, adrenaline and supernatural powers is focused on the dark forest. Each warrior stares straight forward, ready for war. Thoughts of what will appear from Zevon Forest flash before their eyes. Zito and Jet envision wicked creatures resembling giant bears rushing out from the darkness. Others see disfigured warriors and animals disappear before their eyes.

Mount Chrome has pulled these warriors out of the Troas game and given them a new heart to fight for Gibeon. Mount Chrome has also added new members to Mayor Messa's army. These new fighters have their own supernatural powers to fight the demonic forces of Igor's army. There are warriors and fighters of all sizes and ages, ready to fight until death. The entire army is equipped with bows and arrows, fighting clubs, fighting sticks, torches, rocks and shields of all sizes.

Everyone remains still as Matilda flies by this massive wall of force, braced for the upcoming battle. Mount Chrome's new army is lined up from one end of the city to the other. The eyes of all the warriors and fighters could scare the dead, and their hearts pound like drums. Not a word is spoken. Mount Chrome has prepared them for the attack and given his army glimpses of the wicked swamp. He's also prepared the hearts of his people back in the city. Mount Chrome has given them visions of Igor's wickedness and strengthened his children with courage. Matilda stops as she hears a *rumbling* in the distance, coming from Zevon Forest. Her acute hearing allows her to prepare the others.

"*They're coming!*" shouts Matilda as beams of red and yellow lights shoot from her body.

Her warning echoes throughout the field.

Mount Chrome's army readies itself for the attack. The soldiers can now hear the rumbling that Matilda heard. It sounds like a runaway freight train approaching; the sounds of warriors and creatures charging echo throughout the forest. Mayor Messa retreats behind his wall of warriors as he notices a reddish-orange glow rolling through the dense forest. A light smoke begins to seep out of the forest as well. The sounds of screaming creatures and beasts fade in and out of Zevon Forest as the ball of light draws near.

"Prepare yourselves! The time is here!" shouts Zito, assuming his stance.

Jet and the Spirit lower themselves to the ground.

Zevon Forest melts before Mount Chrome's army as a tremendous ball of fire *explodes* from the forest, blinding the soilders. Out of the fire comes Igor riding the giant Trengasor, leading his army toward the city. In his hand is the head of a rodent; he holds it up for everyone to see. The Trengasor lets out an eerie roar, attempting to intimidate his adversaries. Flying out of the fiery haze is the army of wicked Vultars. On their backs are trolls and warriors equipped to throw rocks and attack the city from the sky. Next are the cavemen-like warriors of all sizes, charging through the fire with looks that could kill the dead. Each one has a weapon that could take down a tree. They're followed by the Migota Dragons ridden by wicked trolls and kids yielding swords and fighting sticks. From one end of Zevon Forest to the other end, Igor's army races across the giant field to overthrow Gibeon.

"*ATTACK! RAAAAAAAAAA!*" bellows Igor as he throws the rodent's head back into the fire.

Igor watches Hawk and his squadron of hawks fly from the rooftops of several tall buildings. As he approaches the city, Igor sees the citizens of Gibeon turning off their lights and preparing for the upcoming bloodshed. The screeching noises of the large hawks can be heard throughout the lit field as their passengers prepare an aerial assault on Igor's army. The thunderous footsteps of the Trengasor slow down as Igor pulls his harness.

"Incoming! Take cover!" yells Igor as he lifts his shield.

His entire army stops and raises their shields.

Rocks and burning torches sail through the dark sky above the light. Hawk's offensive makes its way through the light below and crashes onto Igor's army. *BOOM!* Fiery explosions blanket the giant field as several of Igor's warriors catch on fire. They're immediately smothered and rolled through the field, extinguishing the flames. The rocks and torches pulverize many of his creatures and wicked trolls. The war is on! The sounds of Igor's army crying out in pain and agony are music to Mayor Messa's ears.

Mount Chrome's army seizes the opportunity to attack as Igor's warriors and beasts protect themselves from a second wave of rocks and burning torches.

"*ATTACK!*" shouts Zito as he waves his arm forward.

"*ARRRRRRRRRRRR!*" scream the warriors in Mount Chrome's army as they race toward Zevon Forest.

The field is full of Mount Chrome's screaming warriors and fighters, ready to defend Gibeon. With shields and weapons drawn, they position themselves for a collision with evil. Each warrior sees his life flash before his eyes as they run through the smoke-filled field. The ground rumbles as Mount Chrome's army tramples toward Igor and the Trengasor. The stage is set for a war never before seen. Members of Mayor Messa's army recall the tale of this day as they run through the field; it was taught to them when they were children. At the time, they were too young to understand that this must happen to fulfill all prophecy in the Tobit; *the end of evil*.

High above the giant field, the battle is taking place between Igor's wicked Vultars and Hawk's squadron. The soldiers and evil trolls on the backs of the Vultars are using everything that they have to fight the giant hawks, as well as launch an assault down below. Both sides fly in and out of the darkness above the lit field, looking to get an advantage. Vultars and hawks crash into each other after playing a serious game of chicken. The midair collision sends the birds and their passengers spiraling down toward the field.

Igor lifts from his defensive position and resumes his charge toward Gibeon. The sounds from above give him a new burst of adrenaline. He swallows some magic potion and spits fire toward his adversaries. Igor and the Trengasor tread through many battles, sometimes crushing their own army. Thoughts of Jonathan and the Golden Chalice race through Igor's mind. Unfortunately, He's unaware of Toby's heroic sacrifice.

Viking, Serpent and Dar battle with several wicked giants created by Igor's sorcery. Back and forth they swing their weapons, only to be blocked and swiped away. One particular Cyclops is giving Dar a hard time. The banging of fighting clubs against shields can be heard throughout the field. The action is fierce as sweat, blood and tears smear the entire battlefield. Flashes of the holocaust teachings enter into several of Mayor Messa's men as they regroup for their next battle.

Several fighters from Mount Chrome's army knock the wicked trolls off the backs of the Migota Dragons. His warriors quickly subdue their adversaries and lead them toward a holding cage where they will await the wrath of Mount Chrome. The fighting intensifies as each side battles for their leader. Unfortunately,

THE PARADE

Igor's army is being misled by false promises and manipulation. The Trengasor breaks through his army and tramples over several of Mount Chrome's fighters. The Spirit breaks through his army to meet Igor and the Trengasor head-on.

"*Ahhhhhhhhh!*" yells the Spirit as his body expands and lights up.

BOOM! Igor is thrown off the Trengasor as he collides with the Spirit. A large number of fighters from both sides are thrown to the ground as a wave of intense energy mushrooms across the field. The collision lights up the battlefield. Warriors from both sides struggle to regain consciousness.

Back in the city, Chuck continues to roll the giant marbles down the street. Igor's curse overwhelms Chuck with visions and feelings that would drive anyone insane. No one knows where the marbles are coming from, due to the pandemonium. Chuck rejoices in the destruction done at his hands. This has taken his mischief to a whole new level. Men, women and children fall to the ground, tripping over his evil deed. Chuck's sinister laugh is soon cut short by one of his own.

"*Chuck!* Stop that, right now!" screams Mindy as she tries to catch her breath.

"What's your problem?!" asks Chuck with a surprised look on his face. "Here, take one! You're going down, sucker!"

"Do what Tracy said!" says Patricia, hiding behind Mindy.

Chuck ignores the girls and readies himself to launch another marble.

"I *rebuke* the spirit of the fruit!" yells Mindy with her hands held in front of Chuck.

Chuck stops in mid-swing. He drops the marble to the ground as he snaps out of the spell, shaking his head. Mindy slowly drops her hands to her sides. She's prepared to rebuke the fruit again if necessary. Patricia opens her eyes and notices the change on Chuck's face.

THE PARADE

"What happened?! Why is everybody running?!" asks Chuck as he turns around.

"We ate the forbidden strawberries. Jonathan put us under a curse and we caused all this," explains Mindy, pointing down the street.

"'Strawberries?' When did we eat 'strawberries'?" asks Chuck as he rubs his head.

"I don't know, but we have to get the others and head to the fountain," replies Mindy, watching several security officers moving through the crowd.

"I guess I won't need these anymore," says Chuck as he drops the bag of giant marbles. "Where's Derek?"

"He's on a float. Come on, before he does more damage!" replies Mindy as she grabs hold of Patricia and drags her onto the crowded street.

Chuck follows the girls, checking back to make sure Mayor Messa's men aren't behind them. The three kids dodge in between people as they search for their friends.

"Hold up!" says Mindy. "There's Matilda!"

She motions for her friends to duck. There's no telling what Matilda might do to them for destroying the city of Gibeon. The kids' stomachs churn with fear at the thought of getting caught. Besides, the rest of their friends are still missing in action and need to be rescued before they get hurt. Mindy and the others slowly get up when they watch Matilda fly down the street.

"*Gotcha!* You kids are finished!" screams a security officer, grabbing hold of Patricia.

"Ah! Help, Mindy!" screams Patricia as she tries to break free.

"Leave her alone! Let her go!" screams Mindy as she tries to pull Patricia away.

"You kids are in big trouble! You'll never be able to leave

Gibeon!" mutters the security officer as he plays tug-of-war with Mindy. "Wait until...."

CLUNK!!!! Chuck knocks-out the security officer with a giant marble from the street. Mindy pulls Patricia to safety and quickly makes sure there are no other surprises.

"Great job, Chuck! Are you okay?" asks Mindy as she reaches out her hand.

"It was nothing!" says Chuck as he gives her five.

"I'm okay, but we'd better go," replies Patricia, checking on Peggy.

"Bucky, stop!!!" shouts Chuck, noticing that his friend is trying to light a firecracker.

Mindy rushes through the crowd.

"Hey, guys, isn't this great?!" asks Bucky as he lights the match.

"No, Bucky!" screams Mindy, swatting the match from his hand.

"What's your problem?! What happened to our plan?!" demands Bucky. "Come on, we have...."

Chuck and Patricia stop short of their friends.

"I *rebuke* the spirit of the fruit!" shouts Mindy with both hands in Bucky's face.

Bucky is paralyzed by Mindy's rebuke as he drops the firecracker in his hand. Chuck and Patricia gawk as Bucky's clown face transfigures into a happy clown face. They cautiously approach their friend to see if he's okay. Mindy holds tight.

"Bucky! It's Chuck, Mindy and Patricia! Snap out of it!" shouts Chuck as he snaps his fingers in front of Bucky's face.

"Why are you guys staring at me funny?" asks Bucky, shaking his head.

"We don't have time to explain! The Mayor's security force is after us. We have to find Tammy, Tommy and Derek!" replies Mindy.

THE PARADE

"*Whoopee!* Hey, everyone, look at me!" screams Tammy as she rides a giant Lungar through the street. "Charge!"

Mindy and the others turn around.

"Oh no, we have to stop her! Tammy, stop throwing the Slurge!" yells Mindy as she runs back and forth, trying to keep her eye on Tammy. "Come help me, guys!"

They watch in horror as the storefront lights short-circuit.

"How are we going to 'stop' that thing?!" asks Bucky while Patricia holds onto his arm.

"I got it! This should do it!" replies Chuck, picking up another giant marble.

"You can't hit that!" says Bucky.

"Oh yeah? Watch this!" says Chuck, hurling the giant marble across the street.

It's as if the giant marble is going in slow motion through the air. Mindy and the others follow the giant marble as it sails over the crowd. The girls close their eyes, hoping Chuck's throw will hit its target. Tammy and the giant Lungar are standing still as she prepares to toss a large Slurge ball at Larry's Lights. This is one of the largest stores in all of Gibeon. If Tammy is successful, she'll start a massive fire that will spread throughout the city. CLUNK!!!!! The giant marble hits the Lungar square in the head, knocking it to the floor.

"Ahhhhh!" screams Tammy as she falls to the ground.

"Yea, Chuck, you did it!" scream Bucky and Patricia as the three celebrate.

"Oh, there goes Mindy!" states Bucky.

"Let's go!" insists Chuck, rushing over to help his friend.

Bucky and Patricia follow close behind. Mindy and her friends fight through the crowd that's gathered around the fallen Lungar. Kids are careful not to get too close as the presence of evil makes their skin crawl. Tammy shakes off the dirt as several parents grab their kids.

"Who did that?!" asks Tammy, ready to fight.

THE PARADE

"Those are the kids that ruined our city!" shouts one boy.

"*Ooohhh!*" moans the crowd.

"Wait, I can explain! It was Jonathan!" declares Mindy as she breaks through to Tammy.

"*'Jonathan'?!*" asks the crowd, terrified.

"I saw him a few minutes ago and he asked me if I saw you guys," says a little boy as he breaks through the crowd.

"Stop right there! You're not going anywhere!" screams Mindy, noticing Tammy trying to sneak away.

"Yeah!" shouts Chuck as he prepares to be hit. "That's *enough*, Tammy!"

"What happened to you guys?! Never mind, I'm going to find Jonathan!" states Tammy as she turns to disappear into the crowd.

"I *rebuke* the spirit of the fruit!" screams Mindy as she charges Tammy.

Tammy drops to her knees and grabs her head. For some reason the curse has hit her harder than her friends. Chuck and Patricia hold onto each other, waiting for Mindy's cry to be heard. Tammy crawls on the ground in agony as the battle of good versus evil implodes within her body.

"Come on, Tammy, you can beat it!" screams Chuck.

"Please, 'Tammy,' come home!" pleads Patricia.

"I *rebuke* the spirit of the fruit!!!" screams Mindy over Tammy's body. "Leave her alone!"

Tammy goes into convulsions on the street floor. The second rebuke sends the curse flying out of her body and into the sky. Tammy falls to the floor exhausted. Her friends, fearing the worst, rush to her aid.

"Tammy, we love you!" shouts Patricia while Mindy tries to get her strength back.

"Tammy, it's Chuck! Snap out of it!" yells Chuck, snapping his fingers in front of her face.

THE PARADE

"*Yeeeaaa!*" screams the crowd as they watch Tammy get up off the street.

"What happened? Why is everyone staring at us?" asks Tammy, awakening from her curse.

"Stop! Hold it right there!" yells a security officer.

"Look! We're being attacked!" screams a man, pointing toward the sky.

The sudden noise of hawks and Vultars flying overhead disperses the crowd. The buzzing sounds of the birds' large wings drown out any other sound coming from the streets of Gibeon. Several families cringe as the screeching cries of birds fighting send chills down their bodies. Chuck and his friends rush under a storefront cabana as several rocks crash into the buildings and onto the street below. Lights blow out from several stores as Igor's soilders hit their targets. A hailstorm of rocks and fire fall from the sky, injuring several kids and their families.

"Run for your life!" screams a boy, running for cover.

Chuck and his friends watch in awe as Hawk's squadron battles with Igor's wicked creation.

"Hey, look, it's Hawk! He has wings!" shouts Tammy as she watches Hawk chase two fighters through the air. "Get them, Hawk!"

Hawk knocks the birds to the ground.

"'Look,' down there!" shouts a boy from the next storefront.

Chuck and his friends shift their attention down the street.

The battle from the field has now poured onto the streets of Gibeon. Pagan and Krul are battling several creatures and men from Igor's army. One giant caveman is swinging his fighting club and taking out several street lights. Pagan rushes in and grabs his legs. The two warriors wrestle around the street as the citizens of Gibeon watch from a distance. Gibeon is overwhelmed with evil as Igor's spirit blows through the city. His cries can be heard in the ear of every man, woman, and child.

THE PARADE

Several kids from the mayor's army are fighting with Igor's wicked kids. The sounds of screaming fighters and warriors rise above streets. Many of the side streets clear as people shut their windows, hiding from the intense fighting. Migota Dragons run through the streets, but are quickly picked up by Hawk's birds.

"Go and find your friends! Hurry! We can't hold them, forever!" says a boy as his friends block a group of security officers.

"We will end this madness! Jonathan will pay for this with a steamroller!" declares Chuck as he squishes a cupcake.

"Thank you! We'll never forget this!" says Mindy as she leads Tammy and the others through the crowd to look for Tommy and Derek.

"Where did they go?!" demands a lieutenant as he tries to go around the group of kids. "I demand that you tell me now!"

"They went that way!" says the boy, pointing in the wrong direction.

The security officers take off running through the crowd. Several kids chuckle as they watch them heading away from where the gang had run. They turn around and see their new friends try to cease Jonathan's evil curse and put an end to the destruction of the City of Lights.

Down the street stand Mayor Messa and part of his security force, watching the unthinkable. Worm, Dar and Goliath fight off several warriors from Igor's army in front of the mayor's building. The crowd cheers as Goliath bodyslams an eight-foot tall giant to the ground. Several parents cover their children's eyes as blood seeps from the evil giant's head. Two cavemen wield their fighting clubs and knockout five men from the mayor's army. Dar quickly swings himself around a lamppost and sails toward the cavemen. The mayor cringes as he hears the cries of his people during this war of the worlds. Hawk's squadron swoops down onto the streets and captures many trolls and creatures looking to destroy the city. Mayor Messa forces out a smile as several families cheer for Hawk.

THE PARADE

The mayor's security force has Tina, Freddie, Jason and Harry close at hand. Their parents are heading their way to hear Mayor Messa's punishment for their part in Jonathan's vengefulness. The kids know that they'll more than likely be exiled to Zevon Forest. Their hearts melt as guilt and shame wash over their bodies for agreeing to Jonathan's madness.

"Look at this place! Where's Jonathan?! Where's Matilda?! Where are those kids?! Someone, give me some answers, *now!*" demands the mayor as he wipes the sweat from his forehead.

"We have every man looking for 'Jonathan' and 'those kids,' Sir! They'll be brought to justice!" says an officer.

"Look, it's Johnson!" says one officer, pointing down the street.

Officer Johnson is running through the crowd, signaling for the mayor to stay put. Mayor Messa motions for people to clear a path for his man to get through.

"Mayor Messa! Mayor Messa! We're about to apprehend Derek and his friends!" exclaims Officer Johnson as he catches his breath.

"When?! Where?" asks Mayor Messa, panting. "Let's go and get them!"

"They're at the fountain and we're closing in!" replies Officer Johnson excitedly. "We should...."

"Well, what are we waiting for? Let's get to the 'fountain!' They're never going home! I want to see this first hand!" says Mayor Messa, rallying his troops. "These kids will pay severely for what they did to my city!"

"What should we do with the prisoners, Mr. Mayor?" asks one security officer.

"Bring them with us! I want the whole town to see who's responsible for this mess!" replies Mayor Messa. "I want them to feel the piercing eyes of my people, convicting them of their wrongs!"

"What about their parents? How will they know where to find us?" asks one of the officers holding Tina.

"You and Thompson stay behind and wait for 'their parents.' When they get here, bring them to the 'fountain' so that they can meet the whole cast of this heinous crime!" replies Mayor Messa.

"Yes, Sir!" say the officer and Officer Thompson.

"Wait, Mayor Messa! We've spotted Jonathan!" shouts a security officer, breaking through the crowd.

"Hold up, men! I need to hear this!" says Mayor Messa as he throws his hand up into the air.

"Let him through! Move it, move it!" screams one officer, pointing.

"All right, Jackson, where is he?!" asks Mayor Messa, fuming.

"He's heading toward the fountain, Mayor!" replies Officer Jackson, out of breath.

"They're all heading for the 'fountain!' We'll catch all of them at once! Wait, we need to call upon the power of Mount Chrome! What if Igor and his army have made it to that part of city? I've seen the evil of Jonathan's wrath out in the field! … Where's Matilda?" asks Mayor Messa as he looks toward the sky.

The crowd is startled by a sudden ball of light appearing over the street. The citizens of Gibeon back away as the light illuminates the area; its colors change from red to green to purple. Matilda appears in the light as the laser-light show intensifies. Her people rejoice as a mist sprays the crowd and eases their troubled hearts. Matilda's music and ballad send Igor's army running.

"Matilda, where are you? We need you!" declares Mayor Messa as he walks up to the ball of light.

"I'm with Mount Chrome. I've been watching you from his cloud," replies Matilda, glowing.

"Take courage, my children. The power7 of darkness shall

not overthrow the children of light. I will be with you shortly," says Mount Chrome through the ball of light.

The entire crowd drops to the street in fear. The presence of Mount Chrome is stronger than ever as his Spirit penetrates his people. Mr. and Mrs. Keltar cover their four kids as their bodies begin to tremble. A gust of wind blows through Main Street, putting out all the burning fires. The remainder of Igor's army retreats toward Zevon Forest as Mount Chrome flexes his muscles.

The ball of light and Matilda disappear as the wind settles. The crowd slowly rises to its feet. One by one, the citizens of Gibeon cheer for their mayor and Mount Chrome. They're given a new sense of hope after being visited by their Great Mountain. Mayor Messa is overwhelmed with emotion as the crowd erupts in applause.

Up on Mount Chrome, Matilda is choked up as she watches Mayor Messa lead Tina and the others toward the fountain. In the cloud she sees the multitudes come out from their homes and shops to encourage the mayor. The people in the streets separate as Mayor Messa and his troops make their way down Main Street. Matilda can feel the love and emotion of her people crying out for their mayor and Mount Chrome.

"You are most gracious, oh, Great Mountain," says Matilda from her stone. "We surrender all to you, Mount Chrome. Your faithfulness and saving power are beyond measure. Blessed are those whose strength is found in you."

"Take courage, my daughter. The new Gibeon will be even greater than the first. I will never abandon or forsake you or my children. Your trust in me has been pure and unwavering. For this you shall be rewarded," says Mount Chrome.

"What about Igor and Jonathan?" asks Matilda, fearfully.

The heavy cloud changes colors as peals of lightning and thunder shoot across the mountain. Matilda can see images of the giant field appear in the cloud. She sees a battlefield of bodies and creatures, near-death, spread out between Zevon Forest and the city of Gibeon. Smoldering fires are everywhere. Zito and Jet are walking through the field, gathering up what's left of Mount Chrome's army. The atmosphere is somber as the warriors on each side lick their wounds. A giant Cyclops carries several wicked trolls and cavemen toward the forest.

"The Trengasor is dead?!" asks Matilda excitedly.

"Yes, he is. The others will meet their fate, soon enough," replies Mount Chrome.

"What about all those little battles that are taking place in the city? The Mayor's men are losing. Wait … there come Dar and Goliath!" says Matilda.

"I will put an end to Jonathan and Igor's war soon. Now you must prepare yourself to return to the city," says Mount Chrome.

The heavy cloud lights up a magnificent shade of blue and descends upon Matilda.

Tommy and his friends are huddled together in front of the giant fountain. The fountain is taller than most buildings and has its own light and water show. The crowd around the gang is somewhat hostile as they survey the damage to their city. The citizens of Gibeon circle the fountain, enraged as falling debris continues to drop from the sky. Their hearts bleed for the mayor; he's done so much for his people over the years. Several parents rush their children away as they foresee the ensuing confrontation. A few bigger kids look for an opportunity to apprehend the gang, wanting to be heroes.

"It wasn't our fault! Let us explain!" pleads Tommy as he protects his friends.

"We didn't mean to do this to your city, we swear!" shouts Derek as he prepares for the worst. "Please … let us…."

"You destroyed our 'city!' Look at it! You'll pay for this!" shouts one father.

THE PARADE

"Mayor Messa won't let this go unpunished!" screams a boy, holding his fist in the air. "You'll be lucky to live in Zevon Forest!"

"Come on, Mindy! How do we *go* home?! We can't hold off this crowd much longer!" says Tommy out the side of his mouth. "Don't make us use our powers from Jonathan!" yells Tommy, bluffing.

The crowd backs away.

"Yeah, 'Mindy,' think, think!" says Chuck, shifting his body back and forth, trying to intimidate the kids that are getting closer. "Come on, guys, we don't have all day!"

Mindy slouches down between her friends and begins to pray.

"Lord, please help!" prays Mindy.

"*Jonathan!* He's here! Everybody run!" screams one boy as he points down the street. "He's turned into a monster!"

The entire crowd turns around.

Tommy and his friends are overwhelmed with fear as they feel Jonathan's presence. His spirit pierces their souls as his voice echoes in their heads. They can see Jonathan running through the crowd; he's disfigured and grotesque. The evil inside of him has been brewing for this moment as thoughts of ending the gang's lives drive him forward. The crowd disperses as Jonathan approaches the fountain. Several of Igor's henchmen file out from an alley and follow their leader.

"*He's coming, he's coming!* He has Igor with him now!" screams Tommy as he looks for a place to hide.

"What do we do?! He's going to bring us back to Zevon Forest!" states Derek, panicking.

"Somebody 'do' something, quick! Tommy! Tammy!" screams Bucky, grabbing onto Tammy.

"Look, it's the Mayor!" shouts a boy.

"Oh no, Mindy, what do we do now?! Hurry!" demands Tommy, shaking.

THE PARADE

Mindy stands up and is led to the opposite side of the street. As she looks down a long alley, she notices three floats waiting to be showcased. One in particular is shaped like a *giant bed*. It has multi-colored lights racing around its borders and a screen lighting up with different colors. It's the surprise float that was built for Derek. The buildings protected the three floats from Igor's attack on the city. Mindy is overwhelmed with tingles and goose bumps as flashes of the tunnel ride home appear before her eyes.

"Look! There's our ride home! Come on, hurry!" shouts Mindy, pointing.

"Wow! Look at that thing! That must be the surprise float that Matilda was talking about! Okay, let's go!" exclaims Derek, gawking.

"How could we have missed 'that'?!" asks Tommy as he gathers his friends.

"Guys, they're getting closer! I'll see you there!" says Chuck as he takes off running.

"All right, everybody, run!" shouts Tommy, leading his friends in the direction of the alley.

"*Aaaaaaaaaaaaaahhhhhhhhhhhh!!!!!!!!!*" screams the gang as they make a mad dash for the bed.

The crowd panics and clears a path for Derek and his friends.

"Where are those kids?!" demands Jonathan, panting like a rabid dog. "Igor, do something!"

"Ahhhh!" scream several kids as they see wicked Jonathan looking around for Tommy and his friends.

The crowd disperses; the presence of evil is overwhelming.

"What *business* have you here?!" asks one father as he grabs his son.

"None of your 'business,' old man!" replies Jonathan as Igor pulls a frog's leg out of his bag. "Igor can use that to reduce all of you to dust!"

THE PARADE

"*Oooohhhh!*" moans the crowd.

"That's right, move back! Someone had better cooperate with me, *now!*" demands Jonathan, looking desperately for the gang.

"They went that way! Now leave us alone!" screams a girl as she points toward the alley.

Jonathan wastes no time and rushes off after Tommy and his friends. His blood boils as images of the gang crying out from the wicked swamp flash through his mind. Jonathan's skin begins to change colors, symbolizing another dose of his wickedness being poured out upon the city. The groans of Tammy and Bucky in agony, sounding in Jonathan's head, bring him a temporary moment of pleasure.

The remainder of the crowd moves out of his way as he seeks revenge to drag them to the Abyss. Jonathan and his henchmen push aside all those who refuse to get out of the way. The crowd then turns back, watching some people get pushed out of the way by Mayor Messa's entourage.

"Where are Derek and his friends?! Where is Jonathan?!" demands Mayor Messa as he breaks through the crowd.

"Over there, Mr. Mayor!" scream several people.

Mayor Messa jumps on the fountain and looks down the street and sees Jonathan pursuing Tommy and his friends. He becomes enraged that the gang has discovered their way home. His only hope is that the kids don't figure out how to use the bed float before he gets there.

"People of Gibeon, pay close attention! I have a reward for anyone who can apprehend those kids! Leave Jonathan to me!" states Mayor Messa.

The crowd charges after Tommy and his friends. Everyone knows how generous the mayor is when it comes to gifts and rewards. The opportunity to serve Mayor Messa and bring the gang to justice motivates even the meekest of citizens. The smell of redemption drives the hunt for Tommy and his friends as several kids grab weapons to subdue the gang.

"Get them!" scream several kids as they run down the street.

"Come on, men, let's end this plunder!" screams Mayor Messa as he jumps down from the fountain.

"Wait! … Tina, Freddie, Jason!" scream their parents as they break through the crowd.

"*Mom! Dad!*" scream Tina, Freddie, Harry and Jason as they try to break away from the mayor's security officers. "Please let us go!"

The mayor motions for his men to hold back the kids' parents. The parents struggle to get through to their kids, but to no avail. Thoughts of punishment and the mayor's consequences bring tears to the mothers' eyes. Tina and Freddie's moms fall to their knees and cry out for mercy. Mayor Messa signals for several of his men to go after Tommy and the others.

"I want you to know that this hurts me more than it hurts you. They've done this injustice, not to me, but to Mount Chrome. Your children are guilty of sabotage and must be punished," says the mayor, pacing.

Tina and the others bow their heads as they hear Mayor Messa's charges. The parents begin to cry, knowing what stiff punishments are usually handed down for such a charge. They reach out to their children and are quickly subdued by the mayor's security force. Helplessness and agony wash through Tina, Freddie, Harry and Jason's parents as they become numb.

"This can't be! She's not that type of girl! Please have mercy, Mayor Messa!" cries Tina's father as he tries to push through security.

"Not my little Freddie!" cries his mother as her husband embraces her. "Honey, do something! He'll never make it out there in the forest!"

The crowd looks down on the kids as if they are the jury to

a murder trial. The sorrow weighs heavy on Tina and the others as they watch their parents *fighting* for their freedom. They begin to cry, feeling their family's pain and sense of loss.

"Take me instead!" screams Harry's father, fighting back his tears.

"Yeah, I'll take the punishment!" cries Jason's father as he holds his hysterical wife.

"The 'punishments' for their crimes will be handed down after I deal with Tommy, his friends, and Jonathan!" says Mayor Messa as he turns to join the pursuit.

Derek and his friends have managed to get the bed float out of the alley and onto the street. They continue to push it along, hoping that something will happen. With no signs of getting home, they stop the float and circle it like sharks. Tammy holds up her wrestling mask, warning everyone to stay back. Chuck snarls at several kids and holds up an empty bag of candy, bluffing that it contains Igor's magic powder.

Beams of light reflect off the shiny, silver sheets as the wind blows. It's the same eerie breeze that signifies Jonathan's presence. Chuck and Derek pull the purple sheets away from the bottom of the float, only to find a piece of wood a few inches from the street.

"How are we supposed to get under there?!" asks Chuck, panicking. "There's no room!"

"There's got to be an opening somewhere!" says Derek as he continues to lift the sheets.

"What about the back?!" asks Bucky, staring at the flashing bed.

Tammy and Tommy run to the back of the bed and lift the sheets.

"There's no space here, either! What do we do?!" asks Tammy as she begins to panic, watching the approaching crowd.

THE PARADE

"Come on, guys, hurry! We're *goners* if you don't make it work!"

"Let's get on the bed! Maybe we'll find what we're looking for up there!" suggests Tommy. "Maybe there's some kind of lever or button that we need to push! You get on first, Patricia!"

The gang helps each other get on to the bed. Tommy, Derek, and Bucky struggle to get Chuck up on to the float. The flashing lights are blinding. The pressure builds up as the gang searches for a clue as to how this bed is going to get them home. Bells and alarms blast from the float, driving Chuck and Tammy crazy. Tommy and Derek ward off several kids as they check behind some large pillows for their way home.

"Hurry, they're coming!" screams Patricia.

"The Mayor will take you kids down! You should just give up now!" shouts Gregory.

"Hurry guys, grab that hose! This should stop them!" screams his friend.

Derek and the others stop and look down the street.

Jonathan and his henchmen continue to throw giant marbles onto the street as they get closer to the float. Their grunting and growling send the crowd away as a fiery haze singes a group of kids. Several of his wicked trolls pick up pieces of the buildings and throw them into the air. Igor ignites smoke bombs made of toad's horns and tosses them down the street. Jonathan would rather die than let Derek and his friends return home. The blood in his eyes indicates his rage and determination to destroy the gang.

Mayor Messa and his security force are rushing up the street, jumping over the giant marbles. The people of Gibeon *cheer* for their mayor as he dodges the falling debris thrown by the trolls. Igor's smoke bombs blind them temporarily, giving Jonathan an advantage to reach Derek and the others first. The families of the accused follow close behind as the chase intensifies. Visions of Jonathan in the Abyss and Derek and his friends rebuilding the city flash before the mayor's eyes. Jonathan's cries for relief from the fiery pit bring a temporary moment of satisfaction to Mayor Messa's troubled heart.

Jonathan pulls out the key and chain from his mystical bag as he approaches the gang. He waves them in the air for Derek and the others to see. Jonathan's eyes glow with fire as he shoves several security officers out of the way. Igor's evil spells are strengthening Jonathan and the others. Igor's chanting sends chills down Derek and his friends' spines as the group closes in.

"You will be in the Abyss with me forever! No one will escape the *'THOUSAND-YEAR REIGN'!*" yells Jonathan as he breaks through the crowd.

"Look, the sky is falling!" shouts a man.

"It's Mount Chrome! Hail to our Mountain!" screams another man. "Our savior has come to visit his people!"

Everyone looks up toward the sky.

Time stands still as the heavy cloud of Mount Chrome descends upon the city of Gibeon. It falls from every direction and brings with it an illuminating light. The citizens of Gibeon fall to their knees and humble themselves to the floor as Mount Chrome makes his presence felt. An overwhelming sense of peace and love brings tears to his people's eyes as the right hand of Mount Chrome reaches through the cloud to touch his children. The Tully family peeks up and silently rejoices, knowing that the time has come to truly go home.

Zito, Jet and several other warriors stop running and fall to their knees as well. The entire city is gripped with fear and trembling as Mount Chrome's Spirit overshadows the city. A group of Igor's warriors quickly retreats toward Zevon Forest as Mount Chrome sends fire and heat through their bodies.

"You will *never* take me down!" declares Jonathan as he continues his quest for revenge. "Get out of my way!"

Seeing the cloud approaching rapidly, Mindy drops on the bed and begins to pray. Tommy and the others walk to the foot of the bed to receive their impending doom. They don't understand the falling cloud and watch Jonathan and Igor getting closer and closer. Tommy looks back up and begins to shake and tremble. Something tells him that this is the work of Mount Chrome, but the wicked cry of Igor breaks up his moment.

"This is it gang," says Tommy somberly. "I'm sorry that I failed you guys."

He embraces his friends and prepares for Jonathan's wrath. Mindy peeks up from her prayer and notices something weird about the bed.

"*That's it! That's it!*" screams Mindy, rushing to the headboard. "Derek, come here!"

"What's *'it'*?! What's wrong with you, Mindy?!" asks Tommy as he turns to join her.

Derek and his friends balance themselves and follow Tommy across the bed. The sudden movement in weight has the bed rocking. Chuck grabs Tammy and saves her from falling off. The gang dodges flying debris thrown at them by several wicked trolls. All eyes are focused on Mindy's finger as she points to a burnt out lightbulb. The kids' stomachs turn as a sense of hope washes over their bodies.

"Derek, where's the *blue lightbulb?!* The blue lightbulb will get us home!" says Mindy frantically as the clouds descend upon the buildings.

"Yeeeaaa, Mindy!" scream her friends as they jump up and down on the bed.

"Hurry, Derek, hurry!" screams Tommy, noticing Jonathan a few yards from the bed. "Come on, Igor's pulling something out of his bag! Chuck, throw it back at them!"

Derek reaches into his pocket to grab the blue lightbulb. His friends motion for him to check faster as they fight off several of Jonathan's trolls and cronies. Tammy pounds a pillow over a large troll's head and sends him toppling on top of his buddies. Derek's

hand fumbles around his pocket as he sees a few of Igor's follow-
ers approaching from the other side. Several large bullies converge
on the bed with sticks and rocks, ready to fight for the mayor.
"Where is it, Derek?! We need it now!" demands Chuck,
shaking.
"Come on, 'Derek!' Don't fail us now!" screams Tammy.
"Throw a pillow at them, Bucky!"
"Shut up, you guys! You're making me nervous!" yells
Derek as he checks the other pocket. "Come on, stupid lightbulb!"
The entire world is centered around Derek's other pocket.
His friends' mouths drop as they realize that the blue lightbulb is
gone. Each kid drops to their knees, saddened by the fact that
they're not going home. Mindy, Bucky and Patricia begin to cry as
images of Zevon Forest appear before their eyes. Mindy sees her-
self carrying a pot toward a fire, never to return home. The others
embrace as they prepare to be hit with one of Igor's curses.
"Here!" says a voice from next to the bed.
Mindy looks over and sees Tracy's hand extended up to the
top of the bed.
"The blue lightbulb!" screams Tommy as he jumps to his
feet.
"Where did you find it?" asks Mindy, grabbing it from
Tracy's hand.
"It was on the floor, now hurry!" replies Tracy as she steps
away from the bed.
Mindy rushes over and replaces the burnt out lightbulb with
Derek's blue lightbulb. A *giant explosion* of light illuminates the
entire street, sending people running for cover. The explosion sends
the wicked trolls and kids that are latching onto the bed, sailing
through the air. Jonathan covers his eyes, blinded by the spectacular light show. Greens, blues, aquas and reds shoot from the giant
cloud of smoke. Igor searches through the thick cloud of smoke,
looking for the gang. As the light show settles and the smoke clears,

THE PARADE

Jonathan and Igor open their eyes. The bed float is gone and Derek and his friends are journeying back home.

"*NOOOOOOOOO!*" bellows Jonathan as he looks toward the sky.

At that moment, Mount Chrome's cloud touches the street. His children are paralyzed by a sense of awe as the mountain's Spirit passes through their bodies. All the citizens of Gibeon and his army are caught up in the cloud and disappear. Jonathan, Igor, and his followers are frozen in their tracks as a strong gust of wind filled with light, blows through the streets.

Mount Chrome is lit up brilliantly and filled with his people and his army. His children are stacked up to the border of the heavy cloud, covering the entire mountain. Families embrace one another as they look down upon their smoldering city. Mount Chrome has restored sanity to his people as his Spirit continues to manifest within their bodies. Each man, woman and child has an everlasting spring dwelling within them that is preparing each one of them for Mount Chrome's promise.

The heavy cloud provides light for the people to see as Matilda makes her way toward her sacred stone. Peals of lightning and thunder shoot across the cloud as the mountain shakes. Chills travel down everyone's spine as a cool mist showers Mount Chrome's people. His children take a knee, knowing that their Great Mountain is about to speak. The mountain is covered with people of all ages paying homage to the one who has all power.

"Oh, Great Mountain, how may I serve thee? Your power and might have delivered us from the hands of the wicked one," says Matilda as she humbles herself.

"My children ... how I have longed for us to be together. You've been faithful in your perseverance through these evil times. *The gates of evil will never prevail over my Kingdom.* Here, let me show you what has been predestined before the foundation of the world," says Mount Chrome.

The heavy cloud descends upon Matilda.

The citizens of Gibeon retreat several yards down the mountain as the cloud changes colors. Mount Chrome's powers are felt around the entire mountain as he reveals his will. The people watch in awe as images from the giant field appear in the cloud. Several families gawk as they see Igor's army dragging the Trengasor toward Zevon Forest. Several wounded Vultars try to fly into the forest with their injured passengers close by. Eight giants carry the wounded into the barren woods. The spirit of defeat swirls around the giant field as bloodied warriors from Igor's army look for reprieve.

"*LOOK!*" shouts a troll.

The battered army turns back toward the city and sees a *giant wave* from Mount Chrome heading their way. The wave is roaring toward Zevon Forest and is made up of wind, light, and fire. In it, are Igor, Jonathan and the rest of the stragglers left in the city. Their wicked cries send the others hurrying into the forest. Mount Chrome's wave lifts the Trengasor and the rest of Igor's army, carrying them off deep into Zevon Forest. The giant field is swept clean of all evil and wickedness as the wave disappears.

Mount Chrome's people and children rise up and praise their Great Mountain. The roar of cheering can be heard throughout the mountain region. Mayor Messa and Jet embrace along with Mount Chrome's army, celebrating the demise of Jonathan and Igor. The citizens of Gibeon rejoice with their new army, created by Mount Chrome. Dar and Pagan are smothered with kids pulling on their legs. The Serpent and Krul are throwing giggling children up into the air. Their parents smile as the love of Mount Chrome overwhelms his people. Hundreds of children dance around with their parents as they witness evil being destroyed.

The mountain begins to rumble, sending everyone back on to the floor. The heavy cloud changes colors and now emits a purple-green light. The citizens of Gibeon cover their ears as a *thunderous roar* sounds from the top of Mount Chrome. Mount Chrome isn't finished with Igor and Jonathan.

A gigantic *ball of fire* lights up the sky as it lifts from the top of the mountain and heads toward Zevon Forest. The citizens of Gibeon raise their heads and watch it leave a trail of fire and smoke. From a distance it looks like a giant meteor. The raging ball of fire descends upon the middle of Zevon Forest. *BOOM!* It hits the wicked swamp and creates a giant explosion that lights up the entire region. Zevon Forest is changed into a lake of fire before everyone's eyes. The citizens of Gibeon are awestruck as they witness a true miracle. The lake of fire burns steadily with no signs of life. Matilda is shocked as she hears the wailing and gnashing of teeth of those destined to this eternal fire.

FLASH! The celebration is quickly ended as Mount Chrome lights up the entire region with his light. All life on the mountain drops to the floor, blinded as Mount Chrome fills his people with his unfailing love. Men, women and children tremble as an overwhelming sensation penetrates their bodies. They feel as though they're going through some kind of metamorphosis. The rumbling of the mountain settles to an eerie silence. No one wants to make a sound as they try to figure out what just happened. Everyone saw their entire life flash before their eyes, recounting both the good and bad times.

Slowly, the citizens of Gibeon open their eyes and rise to their feet. Matilda belts out an angelic ballad as the people see Mount Chrome's true light; the night has turned into day. Everyone is speechless as they try to figure out where they are; nothing looks the same. Mount Chrome's children are overwhelmed with a sense of peace and happiness like never before.

"Toby! Look everyone, it's Toby!" shouts Jeffrey.

All eyes focus on Toby walking up the mountain. The citizens of Gibeon let Toby walk through as he heads toward Matilda.

THE PARADE

He's smothered with love that's beyond measure. His friends and family cheer for their unsung hero.

"But we thought that you were dead!" says Mayor Messa.

"What happened?" asks Matilda as she flies off her stone.

"Before I entered the next life, I saw a vision. Mount Chrome gave me a vision of his Son. His Son told me, 'this is not to end in death, but is for the glory of my Father,'" replies Toby, gleaming with joy.

"My children ... what Toby has spoken is true," says Mount Chrome. "This is the promise that I made to your ancestors, a new Gibeon where my Kingdom will have no end."

Music from the city of Gibeon grabs everyone's attention. All the inhabitants of Mount Chrome look down on their new city; it's made of solid gold. The golden light bouncing off the tall buildings illuminates the valley as new birds fly over the city. Mount Chrome's children rejoice as they watch multiple rainbows forming over the city of Gibeon. Matilda leads the way as Mayor Messa brings his people down to their new home. Mount Chrome's joy is complete as he watches his people take possession of their inheritance.

As for Derek and his friends ... *they, too, have a surprise waiting for them.*

IJN PUBLISHING, INC.

What Lies Beneath The Bed
Pirates of The Sea ©

Tommy and his friends are returned from their journey to Gibeon, only to find themselves on the beach. It's there that Captain Nephren (Skeletal Pirates of the Nether World) encounters his nemesis; the gang. Tammy is touched by evil as she watches Captain Nephren disappear into thin air. That night, she has a nightmare about Captain Paul (Good Pirate) and the impending attack from his wicked brother, Captain Herod, and Captain Nephren.

Tammy explains the gang's *calling* at Bucky's tree fort. Tommy and his friends aren't ready to help Captain Paul return the Red, Green and Blue Orbs back to Cyrus, the King of Onibeus (Undersea Kingdom) and restore his Kingdom. Gabriel, Captain Paul's parrot, visits the gang and reveals to them the urgency to travel to the nether world and help restore Onibeus. With promises of treasure, power and fame, how could Tommy and his friends resists?

After many visions, dreams and nightmares, the gang has a sleepover at Tammy's house to travel through the nether world under her bed and help Captain Paul. Unfortunately, Captain Paul isn't there to meet Tammy and her friends as they land on his abandoned ship; her worst nightmare has come true. Tammy and her friends find themselves on three major adventures, lead by Gabriel: 1) Tuga's Island (Character from Tommy's Tales) 2) Island of Dry Bones, and 3) Nether World of Captain Nephren. All in search of the Red, Green and Blue Orbs that will restore Onibeus and bring an end to Captain Herod and Captain Nephren's reign of terror.

ABOUT THE AUTHOR

Gerald Sharpe was born in New Jersey, but now lives in South Florida. Growing up in a dysfunctional family gave him the opportunity to be creative as a child. In fact, the seven characters of the What Lies Beneath The Bed – Series are the seven personalities that he created to keep him company while he was a young boy.

School was always a struggle for him and he was never really a reader. He graduated from the University of Central Florida with a Marketing degree and prior to this series, never read a complete book. Today, that is different!

He feels truly blessed and fortunate to write this series of books. With the support of his loving family, Gerald has made great strides in mastering his storytelling. He hopes these books will encourage children and adults, alike, to chase a dream or bring to reality what seems impossible.

What Lies Beneath The Bed

The Series

Tommy's Tales – Book 1 – June 2006

Parade of Lights – Book 2 – August 2007

Pirates of The Sea – Book 3 – August 2008

? – Book 4 – TBD

? – Book 5 – TBD

? – Book 6 – TBD

? – Book 7 – TBD

Dear Reader,

Thank you for reading, **What Lies Beneath The Bed – Parade of Lights**. We suggest that you read **Tommy's Tales** (book 1), if you haven't done so already, and read the rest of the **What Lies Beneath The Bed – Series**.... And please tell you friends!

Sincerely,

Matilda and Omit

Ps The movies will be even better than the books!

Pss www.whatliesbeneaththebed.com